The Souls Harvest

by

Ade L. Sardo

ISBN: 978-1-0369-6516-7

For those who observe the world through the cracks in their soul.

For those who are afraid of their colours.

Never be ashamed of believing in flying frogs.

Always choose yourself.

Now, turn the page and let's make a deal.

Populations

Harvesters (singular: Harvester): individuals with the ability to extract, handle and manipulate souls. They live on the island of Libera.

Herionos (singular: Herionos; pronounced: her-'ayo-noʐ): a group of Horigeans who rebelled against the Harvesters during the Great Famine and forced them into exile in Libera.

Horigeans (singular: origeans; pronounced: ho-'rɪ-dgɛ-an{ʐ}): individuals with no powers. They live in Horigos.

Nistarei (singular: Nistares; pronounced: 'nɪ-sta-rey/'nɪ-sta-rɛʐ): Horigeans who have bargained half of their soul in exchange for riches, a longer life or other goods.

Rogues (singular: Rogue): Harvesters, born in Horigos, whose powers were not trained in time. They roam Horigos in search of souls to devour.

***Reds:** Corrupted souls mentioned in old books. We don't have tangible traces of them. Most believe they were invented to scare Horigeans' children.

Index of Places - Libera

Grace Wards: an invisible barrier, created by Roden Breith, that protects and hides Libera from Horigos.

Libera (pronounced: 'lɪ-bɛ-ra): the island where the Harvesters live and train. Protected by an invisible barrier, tethered to Roden Breith.

Sagetia (pronounced: sa-'jɛtsia): Libera's Academic quarter. Harvesters who decided to work directly for Roden Breith live here.

Anagessys (pronounced: Ana-'ghes-sis): one of the two largest villages in Libera. It is set in the southernmost part of the island.

Evemerys (pronounced: Ev-'ɛ-meriz): Anagessys' twin village.

Index of Places - Horigos

Brenath (pronounced: 'brɛ-nath): the largest village in the southernmost part of Horigos. The final massacre before the exile of the Harvesters was consumed on its sandy beaches.

Cleryce (pronounced: 'klɛ-rɪs): the most populated and modern city in Horigos.

Corlea (pronounced: kor-'lɛ-a): a small, abandoned islet, connected to The Mother's territory by a man-made stone bridge.

The Mother: a mountain range in the northernmost part of Horigos.

Fields: a territory in Horigos where Harvesters collect and monitor Nistarei's soulless bodies.

X's: records of these provinces were lost after the battle of Brenath.

Harvesters Divisions

Reapers: Trained to harvest what's left of Horigean souls, once their time to pay back Roden is up.

Deleteri (singular no gender Deleterio; pronounced: Dɛ-lɛ-'tɛ-rɪ / dɛ-lɛ-'tɛ-rio): Trained to guide empty Horigean bodies to the Fields, and to scrape the last of their humanity off their minds.

Writers: Trained to reshape residual, positive memories of those souls selected to be reassigned to a newborn Horigean, after they've been cleansed.

Donatori (singular no gender Donatore; pronounced: do-na-'to-rɪ / do-na'to-rɛ): Trained to select and match cleansed souls with their new bodies.

**The notion of cleansing and reassignment has never been confirmed or denied by the Harvesters. Horigeans who paid what Roden was owed for his services are bound to secrecy.*

HORIGOS
THE MOTHER
CORLEA
THE FIELDS
SECTOR 43
CLERYCE
BRENATH

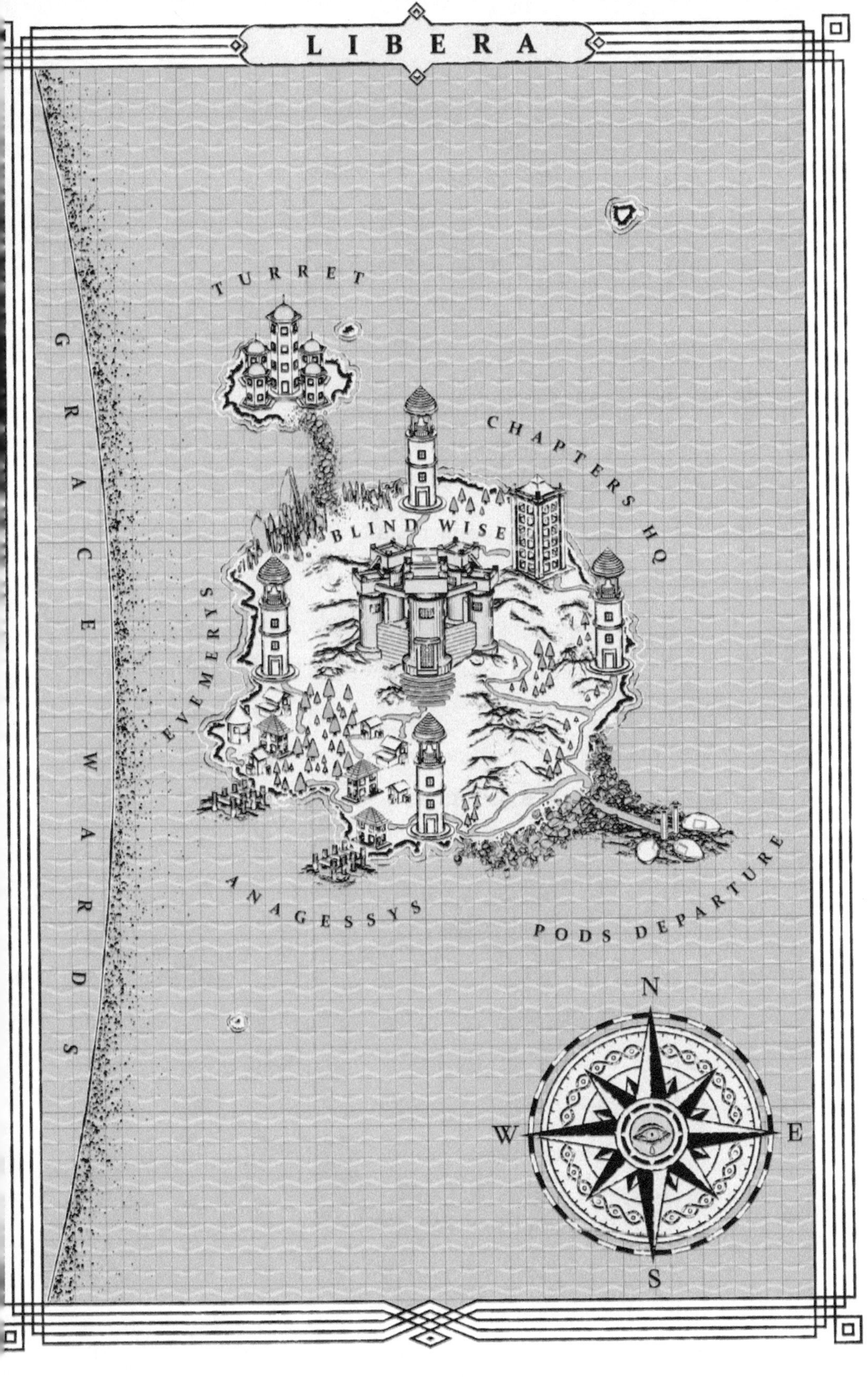

LIBERA
GRACE WARDS
TURRET
CHAPTERS HQ
BLIND WISE
EVEMERYS
ANAGESSYS
PODS DEPARTURE
N
W
E
S

Chapter 1- Kernels
July

It ends with a kernel.

Sometimes they burn so hot it's hard to remember they can't hurt me. They can be as light as a feather, but those assigned to me often reek of decay, even if only minutes have passed since they last floated inside their owners' warm chests.

I run a finger over my roll-up bag, splayed across a discarded table, admiring the superb craftsmanship of the vials, all tidily arranged in the leather loops.

A light purple puff of air escapes my lips when I lower my mask to speak. "I bet your soul smells like poison. Acrid and nasty, like the sweets you sell to your clients," I hiss at the woman curled against the metal back door of her confectionery shop.

She studies me, nostrils flaring, brows twitching. "That wasn't part of the deal. Roden never mentioned there were right and wrong ways to repay him. And what are the lives of a few greedy gutter rats to you Harvesters anyway?" She spits the words as if they could hurt me.

My glass vials are almost frozen as I caress them one by one, carefully deciding which will better suit the size of the woman's soul. Some are already glowing purple, filled with the Nistarei's souls I harvested tonight.

I stop my ritual, feeling the anger in the Nistares' eyes. "You know, I wanted to offer you special treatment because you're my last one today, but you've just ruined it. If only you had picked your words more carefully…but you don't sound sorry at all," I shrug, as I slide out a snake-shaped vial from one of the loops, without taking my eyes off of her.

I doubt she has enough energy left to run away. She reminds me of a frightened beast, curled upon the steps of her shop, under a flickering exit sign that turns her soaked hair green, like the poison she's been selling to her clients. But she could fuck up my mission with a knife to her heart—or worse.

Finding a kernel inside a mangled heart is hard, not impossible. But the aftermath of a bullet is… I shiver at the thought.

I huff a laugh.

My footsteps are barely audible over the pouring rain as I approach her.

"How old are you?" I ask, resting my right boot on the first step and bracing my arm on my knee. She is so close; I cannot ignore her hollow eyes and the dark circles, which match the shade of her lipstick.

"Shouldn't you know?" She bites back, recoiling against the door as if it could swallow her and transport her to somewhere safe, away from me. "Didn't Roden fill you in with all the details before unleashing you on Horigos like a ravenous wolf?"

I chuckle, turning the vial between my fingers as a raindrop slithers down its surface before falling into the gap between my fingerless glove and my black sleeve. The icy cold water against my skin is exciting, compared to the heat that rises through my body every time I'm in the presence of a Nistares.

"I've been called worse. Fine, if you don't fancy a little chat before the grand finale..." I narrow my eyes, pressing my fingertip against the sharp point of my vial.

The emerald jumper dress she wears must have been beautiful before mud and water turned it into a shapeless mass of wool that rolls up, revealing her thin legs when she shifts her position to look straight at me.

"Slap that condescending look off your face, and stop playing with me, pup. Do what you've been ordered to, and fuck off. I'm ready." She laughs somberly, a sound that soon turns into a cough.

I sigh—the party's over.

One quick move and I'm crouched in front of her, my left hand pressing over her mouth, my right holding the vial to her heart. "It's funny how someone with hundreds of innocent deaths on her shoulders can so easily judge me for simply doing my job," I chide her.

The terror in her eyes excites me. I run the tip of my tongue over my upper lip, savouring the taste of terror and disgust exuding from her pores, both for myself and what I represent to her and the rest of the Horigeans.

The storm has died down to a shy rain. The sound of invisible vehicles in the distance, Horigeans starting their day, and distant voices remind me that an undesired audience may soon join me. I quickly look up, ensuring nobody is enjoying the violet sunrise from one of the windows above us.

"Right, time's up. See? I've been gentle despite your stinky attitude." I gingerly lift my left hand, freeing her mouth.

She gasps, eyes wide with realisation.

An acrid smell tickles my nostrils when the tip of the vial punctures the middle of her chest, searing the fabric of her dress.

A satisfied smirk stretches on my lips...

"Nineteen."

I yank down my hood, blinking away ice-cold raindrops and confusion.

"I'm nineteen," the woman repeats, short of breath, staring at me with a different light in her eyes. "And if I could go back..." She struggles to sit upright on the hard, wet floor.

It can't be. She's too young to bargain her soul. Roden wouldn't have...

I hastily withdraw the vial and leap away from her, shaking my hair free. It lashes behind me in the wind, leaving my face perfectly visible in the yellow light of the street lamps.

I hate the expression of pleasure on her face caused by my uncontrolled reaction.

A feral grin grows on her lips. "I'll do it again. Every. Single. Fucking. Time."

A window screeches above us, and I jerk my head up. Unsteady fingertips push it open, followed by a head of brown curls.

"Shit!" I snap, pulling my hood back up and bending over the woman to grab her by her arms.

I find it easy to pull her up and turn her to face the wall, but a hiss of discomfort escapes my lips at the view of her bare back, her vertebrae sticking out white under her bruised skin.

Nineteen...

No distractions. Surely Roden won't discuss it later, but Galen may have the answer I need.

I press my body against hers, sliding a hand over her mouth again. "Don't try anything reckless. You're the last soul I'm harvesting today, and I'm not planning casualties because of you." I whisper in her ear. The aroma of vanilla, sugar, and lemon she's used to mask the real taste of her delicacies lingers in her hair.

I slowly turn around and move towards the metal door, ignoring her humid laugh against the palm of my hand that muffled her words. "Is this how Harvesters deal with unwanted accidents? You convince yourself that if someone else gets killed during your hunting, it is also our fault, so you can walk away like the perfect beings you think you are?"

"Shut up. You don't know anything about me." My voice doesn't come out as controlled as I would like it.

"Mummy, come look at the sky! It's *prurpel.* Nana says that's when the happy souls come back." Despite being high above, the child's voice sounds too close. Dangerously close.

I halt, holding my breath, but the young woman scoffs beneath my hand. "Happy. What about stolen?"

The vial I concealed beneath my right glove vibrates as if responding to my increasing worry, urging me to stop hesitating.

Another voice comes from above. "Ludo, I've told you not to lean out of the window if I'm not around. Come on, breakfast's ready…"

The window shuts, to my relief.

I've already risked too much. I push the woman down the steps and through the dead-end alley before us, where no curious eyes can witness my harvesting ritual.

Nineteen…

She's only a few years younger than me.

I set her against a brick wall, watching her struggle to remain upright. The green dress, ripped and scorched above her chest, hangs too large on her frame. There are shadows under her cheekbones, and her lips are cracked, as if she hasn't touched water in days.

"Is this part of your job as well? Staring at your crop with disgust before you kill *it*?" The angry energy in her voice shouldn't belong to a body so emaciated. "Does it make you feel better?"

"You talk too much."

"I've got nothing to lose." A smirk flashes on her face before she starts coughing again.

"You don't know that," I blurt out when it's already too late. I'm not supposed to talk to them. This is why I chose to be a Reaper rather than a Donatore. I cut ties. I don't want memories.

I curl my fingers around the glass vial. The rain has started to fall again, and every drop that touches its tip sizzles into a whiff of smoke.

My hair has become a dark mass plastered to my back, face and neck, prickling at my skin as if charged with the electricity carried by distant thunder.

She glares at me. "Shut up. You don't know anything about me," she says mockingly. But her eyes are starting to grow tired, her lids heavy. "Let's end it here. Just take what's not yours and go back to living your superior life." She tilts her head back against the wall, fidgeting with the burnt dress, ripping the fabric enough to reveal the pale skin beneath.

Her decay started when she accepted Roden's deal. He promised her money, fame, or perhaps just a nicer house, and like many before her, I'm sure she thought she could pay him back in full while he was safely protecting her most precious bargaining chip—all the kernels of her soul, but one.

I look away, telling myself I'm just checking that nobody is coming. "You could have used the time we gave you to repay your debt without destroying your morals. You could've bargained for more time—" The weight of the lies on my tongue chokes me.

The fabric rips a bit more as she barks a laugh, "If your beloved Roden Breith is so powerful and wealthy enough to respond to all our desperate requests, why doesn't he just fucking help us—" A wet and violent cough shakes her fragile body, and she holds up a hand to keep me away. She raises her red-rimmed eyes at me, fire burning behind them as she says through clenched teeth, "I bet he loves pleasuring himself with all those souls. At night. When his dear Harvesters are not watching."

I snap my head up to her bare, bony chest, where a tiny burn has appeared, to her hair pooling around her like a dark hole ready to swallow her, to her curved posture as if the weight of the lives she's taken is crushing her down.

"I promise it won't hurt—" I dash, holding the vial over my head like a knife.

The last thing I register is her mouth open in a silent scream, her eyes wide with a mixture of fear and relief. I hug her with my left arm while I push the tip of the vial between her breasts, sliding it in as it turns warm in my hand. Whatever is left of her soul resists my call, and I push the vial further in, until her last kernel slowly wraps around my fingers. Elation runs through my body as my thirsty vial drinks the soul's shimmering tendrils.

In a matter of seconds, the woman will begin to shake. They all do. It's their souls desperately clinging to life.

"We do what we must. We all do," I whisper in her ear, even if she can no longer hear me.

To the eyes of a stranger, I'm sure we look like lovers stealing a forbidden embrace in the shy light of the new morning. A last shiver of the folly of two souls whose only desire is to feel more.

I wait for the tremor, but it never comes. She lets out a deep sigh, followed by a shorter one, before folding heavily in my arms. Her chest stops moving as the vial vibrates and hums to me.

"Three. Two…"

As always happens, the lungs slowly start pumping air in and out with an unnatural, steady rhythm.

What about stolen?

I swat her words away and gently lower her onto the rain-wet pavement, resting her back against the wall. She will wake up soon and will not remember any of her surroundings. Not the narrow street stretching towards the market square, not the buildings slowly waking up for the day. Her skin will no longer feel the wind or the sun. I could cut her arm, and she wouldn't flinch.

But her eyes…Her eyes will turn milky-blue, and she will see the shimmer of every soul walking too close to her. Craving a new soul, her body will roam Horigos, leaving behind only death and half-consumed bodies until her muscles will atrophy.

The purple kernel in my vial beats fast, trying to break the glass and return to its owner.

I stare at it as it quickly forgets where it belonged and turns into the weak, flickering memory of a soul.

"You had an entire life in front of you," I whisper to the life-size doll at my feet. My words are trapped by the wind and fly away.

The sky behind the buildings of Cleryce's market square is quickly turning brighter, but the temperature is still that of a stormy night.

With the vial safe in the pocket of my trousers, I take off my jacket and gently place it on the woman's back.

"You're getting soft."

I glance over my shoulder as Galen approaches between two rows of market stalls to my left. As he strides between them, the symmetrical lines of street lamps die one by one. A tall walking shadow in all black chased by the first rays of sunshine.

"You know they can't tell the difference between hot and cold. I doubt she will complain to the other Nistarei in the Fields."

As the adrenaline leaves my body, the icy morning breeze smacks me, and I shiver a little.

"She may have lost her soul, but nobody ever told us to deny their last strands of dignity. What's left of her dress doesn't leave much to the imagination." I say before pulling off my gloves with my mouth.

With both gloves between my teeth, I give Galen a side look and twist my hair up into a messy braid to stop it from dripping inside the collar of my already-soaked top.

"Dignity?" His laugh is low and sad. "She should've thought about that when she accepted—"

I snap the gloves out of my mouth, glaring at him, "She was just nineteen, for fuck's sake. Did you know that?"

I look away, biting my tongue before I can say anything worse. He's still my leader, even if we've been friends since he was seven and I was five.

Something rustles onto my right.

"Here." Galen steps behind me, covering my shoulders with his thick leather jacket. "You don't think straight when you're uncomfortable, cold and hungry."

We're not allowed to consume solid food twenty-four hours before a mission. They say it dulls our senses and makes it difficult to sense a Nistares. We may accidentally harvest the wrong soul or let the right one go without even noticing.

The jacket is three sizes bigger than mine, but Galen's body heat still lingers inside.

"I'm sorry. It's just…Roden didn't tell me she was so young. I didn't think it was possible. It's easier when they're…"

"Older?"

"Hopeless."

Galen steps closer, and his left arm brushes my shoulder. "Who told you she wasn't?"

Our shadows stretch before us. Galen's, longer than mine, reaches the spot on the kerb where the Nistares sits, shading her completely. As if sensing his presence and what it entails, her body twitches slightly.

"She had a light in her eyes. She was not afraid. And she despised me."

"They all do, Sof. Nobody likes a Reaper. If you wish to be loved and needed by them, you should have listened to Popplewish and become a Donatore." He nudges me gently.

I wrap his jacket tighter around me, staring at the woman, her head lolling over her chest.

"And miss the fun of working with you?" I offer an uncertain smile. "Never. But don't call me that again. You know I don't like that name."

The sun, creeping onto the horizon, ignites Galen's curls with a rich tinge of chocolate while the ends naturally fade to a dark caramel shade.

I step into his shade to avoid being blinded by the light and study his face. "How long have you been spying on me?" I ask, sizing him up.

"What…How?" I enjoy the defeat in his voice as he opens his arms, only to let them fall right after.

I wave a hand in his face, tilting my head back to look him straight in the eyes. "Your hair is soaking wet," I quickly point at his boots, "And there's fresh mud on your shoes. There is no way you've just landed. You were taking a stroll, waiting for me to be done here, or…"

Galen stares at me for a moment, trying to keep a straight face, but a smirk flashes on his lips.

"Or… I was admiring your talent and how great I am at being your mentor, *July*." His voice drags over the version of my name he knows I prefer.

"You were," I retort, elbowing his side. "Remember, I graduated one year after you. We're equal; you only have the privilege of calling yourself senior and having a bigger accommodation. And…" I poke him in the chest, "A bigger ego."

Initially, he seems puzzled, but then bursts into a roaring, contagious laugh. "If Popplewish could hear you now, she would send you back to training without a second thought."

For a moment, I set aside who we are and what I've just done and laugh with Galen, but my mind soon travels back to the woman sitting on the cold stones of the alley.

The building where she opened her shop wasn't there until a year ago. None of the surrounding buildings were. Hundreds of years ago, Cleryce was home to small townhouses with square open roofs, crowded with miniature lemon trees and oleanders, a few shops, and a little market used mainly by the nearby villages.

Nobody wanted to live on The Fields' outskirts. But recently, the north-western province of Horigos has seemed to attract myriads of desperate Nistarei.

"I'd better go," I blurt out. I need to go back to Libera and for Galen to take this body away from me before more questions start to tickle my brain.

I make to give him back his jacket, but he adjusts it on my shoulders. "You know you could have more than this. Be more than a Reaper…" His unsaid thoughts linger between us.

We've had this conversation many times, but my answer is always the same. "I don't need to see what happens to them after I've done my job. Knowing the theory is already too much."

I shrug his jacket off before he can say anything else, but he stops me. "I'll bring yours back to Libera. Keep mine and go home without catching a cold. You know how Popplewish loves a report straight after a mission before the Deleteri clean your mind of *upsetting* details." He tilts his head to one side, his hands lingering on my shoulders.

Tiny droplets hang from the locks of hair plastered on his

forehead until one finally decides to slide over the bridge of his straight nose.

He follows its path, crossing his eyes until I give up and huff a laugh. "You're such a child."

It takes only a blink of my eyes for his expression to change. His eyes, the left one brown specked with silver, and the right one pale blue, narrow, muting all the light reflected in them, turning almost charcoal as Galen pulls me against his chest and slowly leans forward, nuzzling the curve of my neck.

"You know very well I'm not." His lips graze my ear. His words are only for me, even if we're the only people in the street.

I lift my hands to his shoulders and gently push him away, staring at the tips of my boots. As I mumble something nonsensical, I eventually look up with a forced serious expression, and find him biting at his lower lip, one eyebrow arched.

A long second stretches between us.

We both shake our heads at the same time. Galen scratches his head, clearing his throat, and I step away, catching my breath.

Many Reapers like me, and Deleteri like Galen, find relief from the rush of adrenaline by sharing a bed for a night or two after a mission. No promises. No bonds. Galen and I fell into that deep of easy release and pleasure once, but there is something binding our wills that stops us from exploring the *after*.

When the moment has passed, I turn my face to check on the empty body I left behind, but his voice gently pulls me out of my reverie.

"Did something happen?" His hand is comforting on my shoulder.

"She wasn't like the others. She didn't cry, didn't try to run away." I take a deep breath to steady my hammering heart. "Her eyes were on me the entire time as if she didn't want to miss any detail of her last moments…"

"Sof—July…I…" Galen steps back, searching my face for the right words to say.

I run my hands over my face and through my hair, letting it come undone again. My eyes find Galen's. "She told me she would have done it again."

Instinctively, I touch the pocket where I tucked the glass vial. "I need to recover my bag before someone finds it and gets too curious about all the weird glowing shit in there."

Galen stretches out a hand, but I put more space between us as he asks, "Would you like me to go with you?"

Yes. "No, I'm okay. I…need to reset."

Reset—this is what they do to us after every harvest. They wipe our memory clean of any unpleasant details. Tomorrow, the young woman who didn't look away will only be a Nistares in a pretty emerald dress.

Galen breathes a half-smile, "I'll see you back in Libera, I guess." His voice is heavy with unasked questions.

I nod and turn to be on my way, but before we're too far from each other, I glance over my shoulder. "She referred to Nistarei's souls as stolen."

There are ways to bend the rules and remember what we want after a mission. Galen and I have a secret code to tell each other, 'This is what I want to keep.' We always have a way to mark our very last words, a final message that must be kept safe because it has a special meaning.

I see him ready to follow me in the corner of my eye, but I hold a hand up, behind me, to silence him. *Make me remember.*

When I turn the corner, I'm glad nobody is in the alley, rummaging on the table and in my bag, so I'm free to collect my harvesting tools and disappear. The back door of the woman's shop is still shut, but the exit signal has stopped flickering.

I pull Galen's hood up, fish the vial out of my pocket, and nearly drop it.

The soul inside glows red like a flame, not purple like the others I collected last night.

And by this time tomorrow, this detail will have been wiped out of my mind.

Chapter 2- Harvester's Eyes
July

"Sofia July Crimson, your report should have been on my desk two hours ago. Have I gone blind? Have you started to use invisible paper? Please, explain."

Standing tall behind her desk, Miss Popplewish fights to keep her annoyance under control and her tone flat, but her fingers, drumming on the mahogany desk, betray her fast-racing thoughts.

Miss Evelyn Popplewish. Lovely, gentle and ferociously keen to change my mind and turn me into a Donatore because that will make me softer and less lonely.

No, thank you. I'm perfectly fine on my own.

Trying to prove my point, again, won't take us anywhere. So, I pick a more neutral start. "I'm sorry," I pant by the threshold, a bottle of water in one hand and a mess of wrinkled papers in the other. "I hav… I have it, Miss P."

She dropped the case against the too-friendly version of her name only weeks after I'd pioneered it—the night she caught me and Galen downing a bottle of red in the orchard. She reprimanded us, and we promised we would never force the cellar open again.

Galen and I threw up all our past and future sins that night, but it was the best birthday I'd ever had.

"Please don't tell me this is your first draft, Sofia—" Her lips disappear into a thin line as if trying to take back the version of my name she knows I hate. I move one foot over the threshold, clutching the report to my chest, pretending I didn't hear it.

"What's a draft anyway?" I sigh, marching inside her classroom, hoping my attitude would mask my terrible attempt at an excuse. "Does it even have a universal meaning?"

As I lay my work on Popplewish's desk, she looks at me from behind her narrow glasses. "Playing with words won't save you forever… July."

The amount of knowledge required to be excellent, like Popplewish, would take its toll on anyone's body and mind. Her face is a portrait of ancient wisdom and infinite patience. I can see it streaming like a river in the lines on her forehead when she tries to remember that she was once young and hungry for life, like I am.

But her eyes have never changed. No rims, small black irises, and soft nuances of indigo, turquoise and blue twirling in the space where the white sclera is supposed to be. Miniature galaxies behind fair lashes.

Our Harvester's eyes and our breath - light purple, unless we're in distress or excited - are the physical attributes that distinguish us from the Horigeans. The purer the Harvester line running within our families, the more peculiar the eyes. Mine are not that mesmerising like hers or Galen's. My right is *just* green, like leaves in spring and wet frogs; my left is pomegranate-red with tiny yellow freckles and a slit pupil. Something that Horigean people recoil from, and which I prefer to keep concealed when I'm on a mission.

She sighs, ironing my papers with her hands; her eyes linger on me as I shrink, torturing the skin around my nails with my hands behind my back.

Despite my long black hair and cherry-black smirk, to her, I am still that unaware little girl that she brought to Libera when my talent manifested and freaked out my parents.

I can sense souls close to their end—or so I thought until I learned that all I experience is their final, atrocious plea for mercy as they approach the deadline Roden gave them once they've shaken hands, when they turned from Horigeans into Nistarei. Doomed half-souls, destined to become Roden's precious possessions because the deals they strike are never fair.

This *feeling* works the same for all Reapers, but they must be told where to go and whom to look for; *I* only need to know where the Nistares lives. Not a skill a mother would be happy to share at her weekly gatherings of the *I Found the Best Freaking Yeast for Cakes* group.

I, too, once believed it abnormal and mostly unfair, as it only worked with strangers and when it wanted to. But despite my parents' worries and long nights spent on their knees praying for my soul, I thought it was also fabulous because it made me—*me*.

I never feared the feeling of my mouth going dry, of my heart beating so fast it felt like catching fire, or the shade of my breath turning dark purple, almost black in the presence of a Nistares. All I knew was the uncontrollable need to be with them in their final hours.

Until Popplewish suggested that I could collect those souls like cherries, and that I had the gift to offer some of them another chance at life.

The familiar scent of paper brings me back from my memories when Miss P. waves the report under my nose. "July? Are you even listening? You need to work on your tidiness. Remember what I said when you returned from your first mission?" Her face softens.

"Truth tastes sweeter if spoken well," I recite.

"Your reports are always excellent. Straight to the point, no fancy descriptions of your crop, their desperate pleas, or attempts to escape. As if they willingly deliver their last kernel to you, without asking for more time to pay Roden back…"

More time. Something itches at the base of my skull.

Miss P. doesn't seem to notice as she continues, "Neat and clean like the marks you leave on their chests when you harvest their souls." She releases a big breath, lowering the paper onto her desk.

I chew on my lip, lost for words, as the silence grows thick between us, disturbed only by the sound of my right foot tapping uncomfortably on the shiny marble floor.

The more I hesitate, the more her glasses slide down her nose like sand in an hourglass.

"It looks like you don't want to process the outcome of your actions and can't wait to throw them behind you. You could be——"

"The greatest Donatore in centuries," I interrupt her, throwing my hands up before spinning on my heel, rushing to one of the chairs behind me to hide my blushing face. I sit down, finding the floor pattern incredibly interesting as I study the dark veins of its tiles.

"What else is there to learn?" I shrug, still not making eye contact. "I've been doing this job for years, I know its routine by heart. Roden finds out someone cannot hold up their end of the deal. And," - the image of the woman in green flashes behind my eyes - "that they opted for easier ways out, like using their newfound wealth to become a name in the dark market, or to work as Rogues' hunters. I literally *burn* my way into their heart and wake up the day after like nothing happened…"

I take a breath. "I honestly still don't understand why we're not going after whoever is helping the Nistarei steal Rogues' souls instead of punishing them—I mean, how did they even find out about the existence of Rogues?"

I brace my forearms on my knees, balancing the bottle on my left palm, hoping to find answers in the sloshing water.

"Punishing? July, *they* come looking for us. We don't force them." Her voice rises, and I sink deeper in my chair. "They decided, long ago, that bargaining their souls for instant riches was better than working hard."

My face quickly turns hot and red. If I can feel it, Popplewish can surely see it and understand the reason behind it.

I slap a hand on my thigh. "Working hard? When was the last time you visited Horigos? Not the Fields for a routine check on empty vessels, not for an official meeting with Horigean leaders—I'm talking about its suburbs, where people cannot work harder because they've already broken their spines over…" I swallow tears and gulp air, feeling my eyes sting. "There's nothing left to work hard for…And the Rogues—"

I jump at the sudden noise of my report slamming on Popplewish's desk. I went too far.

I close my eyes, breathe, and slowly reopen them to assess her stance, expecting whatever sanction I called upon myself.

But all she offers is a loud sigh as if to reassure me she won't write my name on the insubordination list. "That business is just a theory. We don't have proof of any Rogues being captured—or worse, harvested by Horigeans. You, better than anyone else, should know."

I hold her stare, not because I've stopped feeling small in her presence, but because my opinion will never sound strong if I can't hold my head up.

I shake my head, unsure, toying with the bottle lid. "What if there *is* someone else like me? Not just a Reaper, but someone who can harvest the souls of the gifted ones, of the Harvesters that Roden never had a chance to find and train?" I set down the bottle and press my hands between my knees to stop myself from fidgeting.

A loud screech of Popplewish's chair tells me I won't like her answer. "You know that's impossible. And even thinking that Roden somehow didn't realise someone like you exists is madness. I'd say arrogant enough to deserve temporary isolation."

"Right, because Roden has never lost a Harvester before—" I blurt out, accidentally kicking the bottle away from me. I snap my head up so quickly my hair comes undone, cascading like dark curtains on my shoulder—the perfect image of a perfect arrogant fool.

"Enough," Popplewish whispers a warning, eyeing the door before walking towards me, her fingers interlaced on her front. "Roden loves his people, and he is the reason why you're still alive."

But my brain is in motion and impossible to control. "Love? I'm alive because *he* gave up on Rogues, and I'm the only one who can hunt them down." I instantly cover my mouth, regretting my audacity, surely shining behind my wide eyes. My heart gallops in my ribcage.

Miss P. drops her head, looking at her hands as if her answer to my sudden folly is carved along her long fingers.

Every step resonates in my ears like the ticking of a clock counting down the seconds separating me from my punishment.

When she's close enough, I can see the colours in her eyes twirling and darkening. She says somberly, "You know it's not that simple. You're not just a tool, but you are the only one who can gift those Rogues with the peace they deserve. It is not lack of love that forces Roden's hand to find them, but his need for atonement."

"He wakes up every day with the constant reminder that he

saved us, his people, but that there are still many out there, he couldn't sense in time, damned to live with a gift they will never understand. A talent that would have driven you to madness had he failed to find you."

I contemplate her words. Wise, righteous, but still not fully sitting well with me. "But he is not the one who has to live with the voices of Rogues begging for one more day. Harvesting their souls is not like plucking Nistarei's souls. It hurts *me*—every single time. It's like dismembering my own heart..." I realise I'm crying only when a tear drops onto the back of my hand.

Popplewish's tall, slender figure, wrapped in a mustard shawl, crisp white blouse and wide light blue trousers, blurs behind the veil of my tears, like a mirage in the desert. But her hand is warm and solid on my knee when she crouches before me.

"You know you could stop if you wish," she reminds me.

I shift in the chair, blinking her hand into focus, registering the freckles on her skin and the marks of black ink on her fingers.

I shrug, offering a crooked smile. "It's too late for that. If I stop, there will still be Rogues out there losing their minds because their untrained gift slowly eats them alive. I could never live with the idea of innocent people abandoned to their destiny because I was too weak to accept mine."

And yet, Roden seems to live well even if he loses hundreds of them every year because he fails to find them before their fifth birthday. But I keep that to myself. Today, I've already walked too close to the edge.

A newfound peace lingers between us, until Popplewish

straightens back up, flattens the creases of her trousers, and walks opposite the classroom door, where the bottle has rolled, to pick it up.

She doesn't need words. When she turns back to me, it's all in her eyes—the gleam of understanding that speaks more than a thousand words.

The plastic bottle screeches in her hand, the annoying sound sending shivers down my spine.

"As you wish, July. My door's always open should you change your mind…" The smile she dispenses hurts me more than the discouragement in her voice. The heels of her shoes don't make a sound when she turns her back, a silent dismissal.

No matter her age, she still deserves the nickname she was famous for as a young Reaper—*Silent End*.

"You'll have my comments on your report before the end of the week. Off you go," she adds, standing by one of the bay windows.

I'm already at the door when I hear the whoosh of her linen trousers caressing the floor as she walks back to her desk. I can't help but throw her a last look over my shoulder.

Sat behind her desk, she reminds me of a normal sixty-something-year-old teacher. Respectable, with fewer doctrines than her first day in class and a collection of books to flip through, like photo albums of her knowledge—except for the fact that she celebrated her sixtieth birthday over forty years ago.

We don't age like Horigeans. Our souls, blood, veins, and tissue are born different. But only Roden and a few senior Harvesters, like

Evelyn Popplewish, treasure the secret behind it until their time approaches, and they are finally allowed to select someone in Libera they trust enough to carry their knowledge.

"I'm sorry..." I breathe against the door. My forehead pressed against the rough wood.

Evelyn Popplewish is already mentioned in our history books, and I've just refused her wisdom and help.

Chapter 3 - What a Way to Start a Day
Galen

The comments that always follow me every time I enter July's apartment early in the morning subside as I close her door behind me.

The corridor of her floor seems never to be empty, no matter the time of day. The faces are usually the same, but they always treat my presence as if they've never seen me before. But today, I must have given them a majestic spectacle by rushing up the stairs and barging inside her apartment like Libera's on fire.

Panting in the least disgraceful way possible, I cross the small living space, with its pale blue wooden kitchenette, past the sofa bed I sleep on at least once a week, and slowly open the door to her bedroom.

"Sof, you up?" I whisper in the crack between the door and its frame, hoping she is because last night I promised I'd wake her up for her appointment with Popplewish.

When not even an upset groan comes as a response, I walk inside, finding the room empty and the bed a tangle of sheets.

"July, are you in the shower?" I yell this time, but the door to her en-suite is wide open with no sign of steam or running water.

Odd. I sit on the edge of her bed, resting my right shoulder against the dark grey headboard to take in the mess we made last night when we decided it'd be tomorrow's problem.

A couple of cardboard boxes lay abandoned on the floor, revealing the little food Sof didn't manage to devour after her mission in Cleryce. A surprisingly tall pyramid of plastic cups towers over a pile of clothes scattered on the floor, right next to several empty bottles of wine, more than two people should be allowed to drink in one sitting.

I run a hand over my face. "At least there is no bucket by the bed," I mutter, closing my eyes and making myself comfortable, resting my head against the headboard.

I breathe in the sour smell of the leftovers and the lingering trace of Sof. The scent of her damp hair from last night's rain, the orange pillow spray she swears does miracles against hangovers, and the aroma of the coffee she must have had this morning.

If my head is still spinning after the amount of wine we had, I bet hers is not feeling any less rough.

The room begins to blur and fade behind my heavy eyelids, and I would quickly fall asleep if it weren't for the sudden, angry buzzing of a phone hammering at my brain.

In time, I crack an eye open to see it vibrating too close to the edge of Sof's bedside table. My phone!

"That's why you didn't tell me you were heading out early," I exclaim, leaping out of the bed and catching the phone before it hits the floor.

The phone starts aggressively vibrating again in my hand.

She's just left my classroom. We need to talk. Plans have slightly changed.

As if that's never happened before.

I check my reflection in the mirror above July's desk. There are fresh scratches on my neck and one on my left cheek, a gentle reminder of how strong young Nistarei can be after they wake up without a soul. I touch the one on my face and wince. It won't scar, but it does hurt.

And July's last crop from yesterday was a particularly angry one.

She referred to Nistarei's souls as stolen. I wonder when her mind will click and when she'll come running, asking if she left me any last words.

I put the phone back on the desk, gripping its edge with both hands and let my head hang between my shoulders to stretch the muscles in my neck.

I study the chaotic array of random objects. "This desk is a mess," I murmur, moving my gaze from a stack of papers to various books to a banana peel, and a half-empty glass of water nursing a dead leaf.

I lift my head to find my reflection staring at me. My hair is tousled and long enough for the echo of July's voice to whisper in my head: *I'll chop it myself if you don't.*

I grin in the mirror as if she's right before me. "Do I rearrange your desk and drive you mad when you find out I destroyed your perfect chaos?"

Another buzz interrupts my one-way dialogue.

Would you mind taking the time to reply to my messages?

P.

"Would you stop signing your messages when you are the one sending them from your freaking number?" I scoff.

I guess I can let P. wait a little longer, take my time to neatly reposition July's books in alphabetical order, and throw away the banana skin.

"And what do we have here?" I ask of the corner of a large, thick envelope peeking out from under the stack of books. "Wait a minute…"

I know the stamp on the bottom corner. A cool breeze blows in from the window July left open.

My phone screen lights up again.

"For fuck's sake, P." I snap, snatching my phone and a hoodie, which I must have left on July's chair days ago.

I'm out of July's place so fast that the door slams, making more than one head turn. An entire corridor of Harvesters heading out for their day stares at me as I storm away, pretending the piece of clothing fits me perfectly.

Not my hoodie.

Chapter 4 - Changes
July

Miss Popplewish's quarters occupy the top floor of one of the enormous buildings forming the Academy District. *Sagetia—* a citadel built on Libera's northernmost side to accommodate all senior Harvesters, professors and trainees.

Non-residents have access to the district only during specific times of day. Its gates shut as soon as the sun goes down, and its tall walls offer an extra layer of protection. Besides, the stairs to the gates are so steep that nobody would dare climb them at night.

Those who decide to join the ranks of the Donatori, Reapers, Deleteri, and Writers move to Sagetia from the surrounding small villages to start their studies and training when they turn fifteen.

If they were born on the island, that is.

I was born in Horigos and didn't have the opportunity to choose my path. When I was told I was a special kind of Reaper, I clung to that statement tooth and nail; I made it my entire new identity.

I pull Miss P.'s door shut behind me and shield my eyes from the bright light pouring in from the large windows, which overlook the orchard ten floors down; a colourful sequence of cherry, peach and orange trees that don't seem to suffer the change of seasons.

The silence up here is pure. Not even the birds dare to chirp when flying by the windows.

My eyes are still adjusting to the light when a whistle - one I could always give a face to even in the deepest of darkness - makes its way to my ear, breaking the quiet of the corridor.

"On a scale from one to I-got-lucky-again, where do you stand?" Galen asks, jumping the last two steps at once, blowing away an unruly, curly lock from his eyes.

"You don't get to look at me like that. If it weren't for the million alarms I set last night, I'd still be sleeping while Popplewish picks the most painful way to strip me of my Reaper badge." I complain from the opposite end of the corridor, crossing my arms. "You were supposed to knock the hell out of my door and wake me up."

"Come on, Sof, I don't see papers in your hand. That means Popplewish accepted your report. Don't be so dramatic. I mean, I should be the one complaining after half of Sagetia saw me like this…" He looks down at the red piece of cloth that is desperately trying to stretch over his broad chest, exposing his belly button.

I press my lips together, fighting the urge to laugh at the sight of this tall, young man, feared and respected by so many younger Harvesters, tugging at the sleeves of my hoodie, hoping to make them the right size for his muscly forearms.

I try keeping a straight face while sauntering towards him. "Fine, you're having a worse day than I am. And…yeah, yeah, she's accepted my report." I poke him in the chest twice.

Since I've known him, Galen has grown a bit taller every year. Even when it was time for him to stop, and I'd already reached my maximum extension, which was not that much of a difference from when I was fifteen, as he likes to remind me whenever he can.

When he doesn't move from the edge of the stairs, taking up the entire space like a living wall between me and the floors below, I poke him again. Harder.

"Don't you think you owe me an apology?" he suggests.

I tilt my head, interlacing my fingers behind my back. "Not until you change into something more respectable," I click my tongue twice with disappointment.

"Glad to see your sarcasm doesn't know the meaning of hangover and…I've already had my dose of judgemental looks, thank you very much. Please don't push the knife deeper." He sighs theatrically, leaning against the wall to his left.

I give him a condescending look before opening my shoulder bag.

"Here," I mumble, diving inside my bag. "Put this on before someone else sees you…" I shove the grey jumper I was supposed to give back to him ages ago into his chest.

My jaw drops. He's already wiggling out of my hoodie, pulling up the thin cotton shirt he wears underneath. A fluffy cloud travelling by a window suddenly becomes very interesting. I've seen him bare-chested before, but not in an official public place, with a high chance of being caught staring at my friend's muscles by Miss

P.

"It's not something you haven't seen—or touched—before." The t-shirt muffles his voice before his head pops out again, his chestnut curls even messier than before.

"Galen…"

"I know…" He folds my hoodie neatly and offers it to me with a smile. "You don't want to talk about it." We've been friends and working together for so long that it's hard to define what we are sometimes. Every time we grow too close, in a less friendly way, something pulls me back, something I can't control. The last time it happened, I promised myself I no longer want to be the cause of the hurtful look of longing in Galen's eyes.

I chew on the inside of my cheek, staring at his face. It's something that calms me down and grounds me.

He seems to know that, and for as long as I need, I know he will never avert his eyes.

My heart begins to speed up.

Shit. What was that?

I shake my head and put the hoodie back in my bag. "It's not that…They found another Rogue. I'm crossing again in a couple of weeks." I exhale, pressing a hand to my chest as if out of breath. "Why are you here anyway? I didn't know you had an appointment with Miss P." Perhaps the question will distract him from what I've just revealed.

He pushes away from the wall and clutches my shoulder, towering above me. "That's insane. Who approved this? You've just come back…"

Distracted, not even a little.

I blink quickly. "Hey, who's being over-dramatic now? You know I don't have a say when Roden senses a Rogue. I'm not privileged like the rest of you—" I bite my lip, but it's too late to take it back.

His expression veers towards worry rather than disappointment.

His fingers cling to my shoulder like I'm about to run away. "They can't send you out so soon; it's not safe. Is this why you kept the details of your next mission hidden from me?" And now it's his time to regret words spoken too soon.

My eyes narrow. "And how do you know that?" I straighten, my arms akimbo, hoping to look a couple of inches taller.

I understand where he comes from, his sudden fear. Whenever we complete a mission, we need to spend enough time in Libera to make sure our Writers reset the memory of those who accidentally saw us, mostly relatives and friends of our crops.

Galen picks at his days-old stubble, retreating and giving me space. "What happens if you get caught?"

Here we are… I open my mouth, but he cuts me off.

"What if anyone saw us before I transported the body of that woman to the Fields?" His eyes roam furiously over my face, the silver specks in the left one catching the light from the window and turning into miniature stars.

I take a big breath and blow it out when he stops me again.

"You know you could be captured and locked in their jails if you end up in an unfriendly province. Roden won't be able to let you out for at least a couple of years. Not even dear Galen could save you." His voice climbs to a dangerous level.

Alarmed by his reaction, I cast a look over my shoulder to make sure Popplewish hadn't come out.

"Are you done?" I eventually ask.

He nods, lips pursed, and gestures to the stairs behind him, moving aside to let me pass.

I stretch one hand, picking at the hem of his right sleeve. "I know crossing only days before our birthday is not ideal. But orders are orders." I give him a side look and pucker my lips.

In response, he brings the collar of his jumper to his lips and starts nipping at it.

I let go of his sleeve, rolling my eyes. "Don't be so dramatic and stop doing that. It's gross. Besides, we don't know if I'm returning to Cleryce. It could be anywhere. Unless some random Herionos pops up from a manhole while I'm distracted, I should come back unseen and in one piece."

"Don't even mention them..." he sounds truly worried.

"Come on, Galen. You're too smart to believe they're still around, waiting to make our lives miserable. When was the last time you saw one of them? And I'm not talking about pictures in some history book."

My words trail behind me as I start walking down the stairs, waving my hand to swat off whatever horrible image he may be picturing of me dead in a dark alley of Horigos. Or worse, behind bars.

I give him time to think, knowing the answer already, but he remains quiet even when I'm halfway down the stairs.

I pause, flashing him a grin over my shoulder before answering my own question. "Correct! Never. Also, I've never called you dear…" I mock him from the square landing between two floors. "And get a haircut, or I'll give you one," I shout, cupping my hands over my mouth.

I wait a second for him to run down chasing me, like when we were kids, but he remains where I've left him, hands in the pockets of his black trousers.

"You go ahead. I need to speak with Popplewish anyway," he dismisses me. Deep down, I'm glad we don't have to discuss my mission—for now.

Harvesters our age can refuse a mission if they don't feel ready; some of us still don't know how to cut the flimsy thread of affection that sometimes blooms between them and their Nistarei. Some of us take months before feeling ready to dive into a new mission.

But Galen knows I don't fit into either of those groups, and he *will* pester me to find out why I didn't back down from the offer sooner or later.

Chapter 5 - Circles
July

Walking down the stairs should be easier than climbing. Gravity and bullshit like that. Well, it is not. Try rushing down ten floors, with a side of sleep deprivation and the guilt of keeping secrets from the person that matters the most to you—plus the prickling feeling that that person is probably doing the same with you.

Galen didn't mention he had a meeting with Miss P. today… The thought accompanies me until I lean against the sturdy portal of the building, inhaling with my eyes closed.

Spring is sailing towards Libera's shores, carrying the smell of blooming almond trees and the excited voices of young Harvesters fantasising about their first crossing to Horigos with a senior Reaper.

The Harvesters became my family when I turned five. Still, I swear I notice kids not older than three running around the corridors, pretending to perform the soul-picking ritual on one another, still unaware of the invisible scars the actual event would leave inside their minds.

Some of us were born and raised here, like Galen. However, a thin strain of our nature still hides in some parts of Horigos, in the veins of mixed-blood beings, children of the forbidden unions between Horigeans and Harvesters that Roden declared illegal at the peak of the Great Famine.

Roden has only a small window of time to find those Harvesters and bring them to Libera before their blood - the very core of our talent that Horigeans hate and desire in equal measure - turns wild and destroys their minds and souls from within.

I'm the living proof, and for some fucking stupid coincidence, I'm the only one who can rip their chest apart and pick their soul before their untrained gift turns them into monsters capable of devouring innocent Horigeans' souls *and* Harvesters'. It's not a surprise that someone is trying to get to the Rogues before Roden.

I don't have crisp memories of my life before. Parents, yes, I had two of those, but their faces are a blurry mush of faded pictures. All I can remember is their relief—and mine—when Roden sent Popplewish to collect me a few weeks after my talent manifested. I hope our Writers gave them better memories than the ones they had with me.

"July… Come, join us for a quick debrief." I forgot that Spring also means that Mr. Tydell takes his post-op talks out in Sagetia's largest park… *Damn it, Galen, it's all your fault.* I was too busy guessing why he kept his meeting a secret to notice I walked right into the circle of Mr. Tydell's opinion-sharing group.

"Another time, Mr. Tydell," I say with a stupid smile plastered on my face, pretending I'm searching for someone far away.

"Only for a few minutes. I'm aware you've just come back from Cleryce. Our junior students would certainly benefit from your fresh memories."

I shoot him a quick glare before running my eyes over the faces of the six young Harvesters who sat cross-legged in a circle. I was one of them years ago, losing myself in Popplewish's words.

"Another time." I quickly dismiss Alphonse Tydell's hopeful expression with a shrug, scratching my neck as I slowly retreat.

In the distance, the castle towering over the island like a silent guardian made of stone becomes smaller with every step I take away from Tydell. Legend says Roden relocated it in one night from Horigos to Libera; the impossibility of such an event makes it an excellent subject for wowing junior students.

I continue walking backwards, keeping my eyes trained on the peaceful image of the castle, when chaos strikes me with the sound of an unexpected question, from a too-well-known and not very welcome voice. "Did you ask him?"

"I'm sorry, what? Who…?" I spin around.

Burnt-orange eyes, long lashes and pink cheeks make me recoil as if facing a hungry badger. "Oh, Lucretia… I didn't hear you coming…" I wish I had. Or, at least, possess the power to disappear in the blink of an eye to avoid wasting time with her.

A well-rehearsed flick of her hair. "Well, of course not. I'm mastering the art of soft walking. You know I'm in line to be the next Silent End?"

"Yeah, that's not really a title…" I don't have time to argue with a child. "What do you want, Lue?" I ask, pretending I don't know what she's alluding to. Perhaps she will go away if treated like an annoying fly.

But she curls her fingers under her chin, giving me dreadful puppy eyes. A lion's cub ready to strike, that's all I can see. "What did he say? Please don't leave me hanging, July. My final co-crossing is in a few days, and there's no better Harvester I can think of to go with me."

You sneaky little viper. "Oh, that… I didn't have time to ask Galen, sorry." A shrug and a fake smile, I'm not giving her more. Galen and I have been granted the chance to accompany junior Reapers and Deleteri before they start solo missions, and Lucretia picked Galen as her designated victim.

She pouts, taking my hand in hers, patting its back. "I hope you're not procrastinating because you think, well…You know what they say about Harvesters co-crossing—"

"I don't."

I do, but I don't have time to explain that even if they cross the Grace Wards together, they will not fall in love because nothing romantic or magical happens during crossings, just skin and bones stretching and adjusting to the change of dimensions like a mass of dough being reshaped by invisible hands.

However, I do have time to shatter her perfectly curated, inflated ego. I cover her hand with mine, patting it like her with mine, and croon, "I'm truly sorry, Lue, but I believe you're strong enough to understand that - maybe - a Deleteri leader just doesn't want to co-cross because he has more urgent matters to care about. I'm sure you can pick someone less…Just someone less." I step back to enjoy the friendly mask dropping from her face.

She starts sobbing. *Oh, she is good.* If I don't say something now, she won't let me go, especially when we both spot a small group of girls walking towards us.

No. I can't deal with her court of geese.

I grab her shoulders, ignoring the sickening whiff of honey and strawberry wafting from her entire body. "Hey, I'm not saying he refused. But he could. So, just be prepared." My lips drop into a lopsided smile.

Galen has already declined, but Lucretia is known to be extremely moody.

When she opens her mouth to argue, I let her go and retreat as fast as possible. "I'll talk to him. Again. Tonight. Promise." I mark each word with a step away from her narcissistic aura.

"One day, I could be the one deciding your next mission!" she yells at me. Amazing how quickly she's recovered her stone-cold expression to hide her defeated look from her friends.

I zip up my leather jacket to my chin and pull the hood over my head. I don't need to be stopped by whoever needs second-hand books or just wants to be seen talking to a senior Reaper. Something rattles in my jacket as I speed up. I distractedly touch my fingers to the object inside my left pocket, hardly suppressing a laugh—hideous heart-shaped sunglasses. Somehow, Galen must have sneaked them in there. They are atrocious, but they will do the trick and disguise my face.

It's almost lunchtime when I rest my back against my bedroom door.

I close my eyes and send the glasses flying over what I hope is the bed. I need a moment before facing the mess Galen and I made last night, which is - no doubt - still waiting for me like a loyal cat with scabs—you have to take care of its stinky fur because that is probably your fault.

I wait for the sour stench of rancid leftovers and wine to kick me in the nose…

"You didn't…" I mouth as I open my right eye first before pushing away from the door in disbelief. There are no books or empty bottles on the floor, and the clothes I threw on a chair last night are now neatly folded on top of my chest of drawers.

"I didn't even know I had fresh bed sheets!" I exclaim, inhaling the fresh scent of cotton in my room.

A good chunk of Libera's population would fall at Galen's feet like overripe plums. I've heard so many people praising the tiny silver accents in his left eye, his shiny curls, and perfect skin, as well as his gentle hands and hypnotising voice. But if only they knew him the way I do—he is so much more than that.

I rub a hand across my face, trying to banish the earlier image of

Galen stripping in Popplewish's corridor. I see why people around us think he's untouchable. How can they understand who we are when we're the first ones not knowing what's between us?

It'd be so easy if I could give it a name.

Shit! Overwhelmed by Galen's way of saying sorry, I completely forgot I had left the envelope with my next assignment on my desk. *Please, please be there…*

I hurl myself across the room. My desk looks exactly the same as it did this morning, but with all the objects rearranged tidily. An empty candle jar filled with potpourri, my laptop, pens, and a pile of books, which I thought was wise to start reading simultaneously.

"I swear there was a banana peel here…" I look around, tapping a finger on my bottom lip.

I shrug, giving up the search, and sit down as exhausted as if I've just finished a marathon. The corner of an envelope pops out from under a book about Horigeans' habits and how to look and live like them.

The surprise and worry on Galen's face earlier this morning were genuine; he didn't see the assignment, but better safe than sorry. Besides, I don't even know where Roden is sending me this time. Before rushing to Miss P., I only had time to look at the date of my next jump, thirteen days before *our* birthday.

At this point, I genuinely hope they've picked a nice place. We can't choose where to go, and all our targets are selected based on our personal experience, age, skills and personalities. When I'm not dealing with Rogues, I turn my attention to those Nistarei whose time to repay Roden has expired. The image of the young woman with the green dress comes knocking at my brain's door and runs away before I can understand why.

Popplewish says that every soul can be helpful and has something to give. And I repeat this to myself when I reap a soul and leave behind a walking puppet ready for the Fields. Their souls can still be *recycled,* even if this is not the correct term or a word I'd use in front of anyone.

I slide my finger under the sticky top of the envelope, and my heart speeds up. I requested, for once, to be assigned to someone who at least tried to use what Roden gave them in the best way possible. I do not want to share my experience during Tydell's circles, but I need to understand why other Reapers find it so exciting to harvest an almost sinless soul. Where does their need to mourn afterwards come from? Why, even the Deleteri, who don't see or touch those souls but only guide the empty vessels towards the Fields, prefer to be left alone for some time after a mission?

There have been days when Galen disappeared to deal with his personal demons.

But if I ask him to help me forget all those burnt chests and empty eyes, he will always set aside whatever pain he's feeling to hold me in his arms for as many nights as I need.

Chapter 6 - Masks
Galen

The doorknob threatens to come off when I barge into Evelyn's classroom. "Plans have *slightly* changed?" I fight to keep my tone flat, but my voice doesn't obey.

Popplewish steps away from the window, holding a mug. The steam fogs her glasses when she takes a sip. "Keep your voice down, please."

I take a deep breath. "She's gone, don't worry." I close the door, lock it and lean my back against it. "I take it the sudden decision to change her next crossing wasn't your idea."

Her unique trait will never cease to amaze me. Despite the years of missions together, how she walks without making a sound is still a mystery to me.

However, the grace with which she crosses the distance between us enhances the torment on her face: her frown, her tight lips, and her hand slightly shaking when she brings the mug to her lips.

"Tabitha managed to send a message. Numerous red souls are travelling from The Mother heading south, towards Brenath; we may have overestimated the time on our side." She points me to the lines of empty chairs, but I reject the silent offer to sit down. To stay still. To think before reacting.

I push away from the door. "Cryptic doesn't work with me. You *must* have a fucking good reason to throw the Reds in a conversation about July." I don't need to play the part of the student here.

Her shoulders slump. "Roden decided to let some Reds free of roaming Horigos… and found *him* again. Earlier than expected, I know—" she sighs.

"What? That's not possible. How…No, you know what? That must be a mistake. Maybe the Reds only sensed a Rogue that *vibrates* like him…" I march to the window where the heavy curtains are wide open, letting the sun in.

Popplewish flinches, but doesn't move. "Galen, I understand your worries. But we knew this moment would come. And we've delayed for too long… Denial won't change anything."

I slam a fist on the windowsill, and my hand starts throbbing almost instantly. My head feels heavy. The tension between my shoulder blades makes my arms shake when I grab the cold marble to keep my hands busy instead of tearing the curtains down. Or worse.

"That was the plan *when* she was ready to execute it without risking her life. Or *his*. The kernels she's taken so far could be anywhere!" I can barely hear myself. My breath is so loud and fast that my vision blurs.

"Do you know the last soul she harvested was red?"

I startle. *Fucking Silent End.* I realise she's behind me only when her hand lightly touches my back.

I answer with a sharp nod. "We didn't have time to discuss details…"

"Do you know what that means?"

My shoulders drop. "Roden would never risk her life in such a stupid way. *He* needs her alive. If *she* goes, his plan dies with her…"

The reflection of Evelyn's face in the window tells me she's carefully choosing her words.

But I anticipate her. "What the fuck is *he* doing so close to Brenath anyways?" I turn to face her, refusal building up behind her eyes. "And don't even try to—If *he*'s hiding in that area, you're sending July straight into the lion's cage. Who knows how many red souls are marching towards him right as we speak? Have the others agreed to this suicidal mission? I'm going with her. End of."

She shakes her head dismissively. "You know this is not allowed. We need you here. Besides, we have great resources in Horigos, who'll keep an eye on Sof, especially now."

I'm trapped. Popplewish is so close I can see her eyes darting side to side, studying my face.

"Her name, to you, is July." I croak.

"I knew this would happen." She says, setting the mug down and stepping closer. Her attention is on the people coming and going in the garden below her window, but her profile hardly hides her sorrow.

I should be infuriated, but I laugh with a cold tone that doesn't belong to me and chills me down to my core. "Oh no…You don't get to treat me like one of your recruits. Do not play the sentimental card with me to justify your orders and belittle my role." I point a finger at the empty chairs, at invisible students.

The colours in her eyes swirl as she casts me a sideways glance, breathing out a sigh.

Tucking a strand of hair back into her crown braid, she strikes. Lethal and practical. "I understand your internal conflict. You're not the first one forced into this role. And maybe it was my fault. I should have noticed the signs years ago."

I drop my chin, laughing again; the only way to let the bitterness out of my system before I lose control. "You are something else, Evelyn, I admit that. After all these years, I still struggle to appreciate your best skill. That I-don't-give-a-fuck aura."

She gasps. When I look up, her eyes are wide and have almost lost all their bright colours.

"I give it to you; I wish I could put on half of the masks you mastered so well in your years fighting for *the* cause. But if the price to pay is to chew up and spit out everyone around you, I'd rather—" I take a deep breath.

What? Abandon Libera? Abandon—her?

"Galen," she reaches her hand to mine, but I draw back.

"Drop the motherly façade. You may have the experience on your side, but you left your humanity on the shore of Brenath." I sound weary, deflated.

A sigh. When I lift my head, she's already by the door, unlocking it. The air inside the room is no longer pleasantly warm. It clogs my lungs, turning my clothes heavy with unspoken words. *I need out. Now.*

She cracks the door open as if reading my thoughts and moves back to her desk. Just sitting there with neat piles of papers to review, waiting for her, she looks like a typical, standard teacher. But I know too well the sharp, silent, killing blade she can be.

I stop at her desk, flattening my hand on the shiny surface. "Am I allowed to know where exactly you're sending her?"

"You know the rules."

As if they ever worked. "Understood."

"Don't make it more difficult than it already is. Don't ask her, please. Don't force Roden to do that to your mind."

I scoff, "If you're done with your do-not list, is there anything I can fucking do?"

"Remember who she is."

I nod, drumming my fingers on the desk, "Right, the cause first and foremost."

"You'll receive orders soon."

There she is. The unbreakable commander. The face behind those hundreds of masks.

I'm at the door when she speaks again, "Feelings can be dangerous. Love—"

"Don't try to explain things you don't know." I don't look back, and I slam the door behind me.

Chapter 7 - Goldfish Pond
Evelyn

As I keep staring at it, the familiar pattern of my classroom door blurs. I blink it into focus before pushing back my chair to stand and walk back to the window, where my tea has gone cold.

I stretch my neck, rigid with the tension accumulated in the last two hours, allowing my eyes to rest on the placid blue sky divided into four perfect squares by my window frame.

For years, I observed students and teachers wearing out the path that rolls down from the castle, the Blind Wise, and through the gates and the broad stone staircase beyond them, before disappearing into the sandy shore.

I witnessed seasons chase one another, stripping the trees of their leaves and feeding their new blossoms. The change in our people, our dreams, our drive, the will to answer the Horigeans' cry for help after the Great Famine. Even though they forced us to abandon the land that we had shared in peace for so long.

"Oh my, I hate this thing," I gasp when the phone vibrates in my pocket with no shame. "Popplewish speaking."

"That, or I had your number wrong for years, Evelyn."

I take a deep breath. "Amelia, how can I help?"

"You could start by making sure my efforts are not wasted." Her voice travels like a needle between our phones.

"Everything is under control," I reply, massaging my temple, picturing my patience as a pond with little goldfish. One fish materialises midair and falls into the water, expanding my pond and tolerance.

Amelia clears her throat on the other end, louder than necessary, "Evelyn, my dear, are you there?"

"Yes—"

"Oh, good, because I'm very busy. I've heard Sofia and Galen were with you just moments ago. And left both looking...*flustered*. Hope everything is proceeding as agreed. We surely don't want to review the whole plan for a silly mistake."

This woman is killing all my goldfish. "It will be better if we all focus on our tasks rather than using our time to micromanage other people's roles. I believe this is what you're trying to say?"

She sighs, "Sure, I would never. I'm happy to hear everything is fine."

"Goodbye, Amelia." I hang up. I could always blame it on weak reception.

The phone feels heavy in my hand. I should put it back in my pocket and go, but my fingers don't belong to the adult Evelyn, who follows orders for everyone's sake, the Evelyn who's forgotten about her ideals. These fingers belong to Eve, not yet the Silent

End. A young Reaper who still believes her gift is not a curse but a misunderstood blessing.

My fingers tremble when I type:

Something is not right. We're moving tonight. You only have a few more hours, and then you'll be on your own. Use your time wisely.

I reread the message to make sure the information is clear.

Sent.

Received. I nod to myself when the ticks appear next to my text.

Deleted, because phones are fickle little things, easy to misplace.

Chapter 8 - Red Soul
July

I've been calling Galen for hours.

"Where the hell are you?" Grunting, I toss my phone, which lands just mere inches from the edge of my bed.

Having to go back to Horigos in such a short time without being able to share the details with him is killing me. But if I tell Galen that the Rogue Roden found, happens to live somewhere between Cleryce and Brenath, he surely will put up a fight and perhaps use the authority that comes with his role to drag me out of it.

I sigh aloud, spinning on my chair with my hands behind my head while rehearsing a dozen speeches to support the righteousness of my stance.

The door bursts open when I'm in the middle of another, very reasonable and very apologetic, mental dialogue with an invisible, very upset Galen.

"What the hell!" I almost fall off the spinning chair, dashing for my desk to hide the assignment, resting there in plain sight.

"You weren't joking about your next mission. It wasn't just a stupid revenge because you were mad at me. Evelyn confirmed—"

The very upset Galen materialises in my bedroom, a hand splayed against the door, the other curled in a fist at his side.

I quickly compose myself, turning away from my desk and sitting on its edge, arms crossed, pressing the assignment against my chest. "And why exactly did you ask her? Hang on a minute...When did she become Evelyn to you? And she simply told you? Since when...ah, never mind. You should know better than anyone else that Rogues' harvesting is strictly confidential. Even to leaders. Including you."

How could a few sheets of paper feel so heavy? Or is that just Galen's judgemental look weighing on my conscience?

"Do you want to tell me where they're sending you, or should I rip those stupid papers out of your hands?" he demands, slamming the door shut with such violence I fear it will fall off its hinges.

I stare at him as he paces up and down the room, waiting for his temper to cool down.

My bed complains when he plops on the mattress, bracing his arms on his knees and interlacing his fingers as if to contain his thoughts.

We both know this should remain between Roden and me, and I'm not supposed to tell anyone, but...

"Sector 43. IDon'tKnowWhereExactly!" I blurt out.

Sector 43 has recently become well known to Harvesters because Roden believes that's the spot where hotbeds of rebels, who want us and our business gone forever, hide. It is a stretch of nobody's land, dotted with abandoned buildings destroyed during the Famine and solitary settlements of farmers and veterans who fought in the war that saw our people exiled.

Galen tilts his head up, trying to focus on the ceiling rather than my face, and runs his fingers through his hair with a harsh intake of breath.

I sit back on my chair, roll it closer to him and lean forward, resting a hand on his knee. "I'll be fine. I won't get near Brenath…Miss P. says they'll send a team right behind me for cover. She reassured me they would call me back if they noticed any suspicious movement. She— "

"Popplewish knows what Roden wants her to know," he snorts, falling on his back with his hands behind his head.

I jump off my chair. "Galen, do you hear yourself? I hope this is just your disappointment talking because I surely don't want to be part of this sudden need for rebellion. Popplewish revealing details of my mission to you is already on the verge of insubordination. But *you*…talking shit about Roden…"

"Sof…" He is the only one who can call me that. Besides, an argument over my name is the last thing we need. "You're missing the point…" His voice trails off as if there's more he'd like to say.

The ceiling and the naked walls of my room must have lost their charm. I startle when Galen bolts up to look at me with an expression that makes my heart shrink and ache. I can read his mind as if mine.

"Is this about the red soul? Has Popplewish told you about that as well?" I sit on the bed, next to him, folding my hands on my lap.

Galen's shoulder lightly brushes mine, his muscles rigid against mine. "You're cutting me off…"

That was unexpected. He uses this voice only with his junior Deleteri, never with me, because it only carries orders and barriers.

"Why…What do you mean?"

"You shouldn't remember that." He stands up, crossing the small space between my bed and the window behind my desk. Resting his back against the wall, he crosses his arms, giving me a deadpan look.

My eyes widen. That's all on me. "I—you were gone when I realised, and I knew they would have taken that memory because…It pulsed bright red. It wasn't like the others. I can't explain it, but I felt as if it was still *sentient.*"

He pushes away from the wall. "How did you remember?"

"I wrote it down before they picked me up," I shrug.

"You what?" He pounces, his arms stretched out as if shielding me from sudden, unexpected danger.

In just a few steps, he's once again close to me, crouching at my feet, covering my hands with his. "Please tell me that piece of paper is gone. Burnt. Destroyed."

My heart shrinks at his reaction. "I'm still here making you worry, so…" I try a smile, but his gaze only darkens. His chest rises as he tries to calm whatever turmoil of thoughts is going on in his head.

I give him time, searching his face for any clue I'm safe to speak again.

Until he stands up, pulling me up with him and in his arms.

"You are so fucking reckless; I swear you'll be the death of me." My hair muffles his last words as he kisses my head, tightening his hold around me.

I rest my ear against his chest and listen to his heart beating fast, stealing one more second to enjoy his warmth and the smell of fresh cotton from his white shirt before wiggling out to look him in the eyes.

"There is nothing I'd like more than to take you with me to find this Rogue. But risking the protocol and Roden's fury will be a greater risk than me having to cross so close to Brenath. Besides, Popplewish says there's a new team stationed just over the border, should I need cover and help."

I cock my head to one side, performing the most innocent smile ever.

"Did she tell you exactly where and how to reach them? Do you have names?" Galen gently pushes me away but keeps his hands around my waist.

"Is the Deleteri leader asking, or...?"

"This is not an interrogation." He steps away, his hands falling, breaking that contact, I know I will miss in the next few days.

I'm still holding my next assignment. My eyes travel from the paper to his face—expressionless to anyone else—but I can see beyond those curtains of dark lashes.

"Tonight. Dinner's on me. Here's not safe..." I say, nodding at my bedroom door securely shut.

His eyes widen in surprise, "Are you sure?"

I puff my cheeks, "You've been acting all dramatic until a minute ago, and now you're concerned about safety? Just promise me you won't find a way to follow me. This is just another Rogue…"

A smile on those serious lips, at last. He consumes the tiny space between us, taking the papers out of my hands and letting them fall on the carpeted floor.

His eyes shine with the reflection of the young boy I met during my first week on the island—eyes I struggled to read for a long time. And there they are now, questioning, curious, caring, and mischievous as he runs a hand through his dark curls.

"I'll miss you," he whispers, closing his eyes in time to miss a sudden rush of blood beneath my skin.

What the…

I find a way out between him and the bed and use it to move us both around as if dancing to no music, averting my gaze from his.

"I need to stay focused," I blurt out.

"I know you can do that just fine…" he takes my right hand, turns it palm up and kisses it with such attention I'm jealous of my skin.

"Galen…we've been there…" I rasp.

He slowly runs his lips from my palm to the thin spot of skin on my wrist, and as if he could feel my pulse quickening under his touch, he smirks, switching from the friend I've known nearly my entire life to someone able to fire up every inch of my body.

But as much as we both may want this, I bite my lips, chastising my will.

"You should go," I say, stretching a hand to caress his cheek. My voice is not even close to being as strong as I'd like.

He stops, but the warm breath escaping his mouth keeps tickling my skin, full of promises I'm too scared to listen to.

"I'll miss all of you," he mutters against my bare arm before stepping away.

"Out!" I force some authority out of me to sound convincing. And for my sanity.

"Getoutofhere…" I push him down to the corridor and the door, opening it for him. The students sharing my floor are used to Galen and me bickering any other day; it'll sound like another silly argument to them.

He lingers by the threshold, his face still flushed a soft pink. "There is something I wanted to tell you for a while now…"

"And you will when the right time comes," I answer before he can say anything else. The last thing I need now is some personal confession that will only make the day I have to leave a bit more painful.

He throws his arms up, "But you didn't even let me finish."

I shake my head, rushing him out into the corridor outside my room, keeping my head down like a small bull. "Tonight, okay?"

Seeing him drop his head in defeat and turn away from me hurts a little. But I can hear him chortling as he goes, "I'll be downstairs at eight sharp. Don't be late...for once." His laugh echoes across the corridor, audible even when I shut the door.

Best sound ever.

Chapter 9 - Shrimp and Ranks
July

I sometimes ask myself what my life would have been like if Roden had never found me.

My name would probably be carved amongst those on the tall, white stones surrounding the very edges of Libera, like pale fingers stretched in a final cry for mercy. One of those children Roden failed to sense in time, who developed the gift too late and were damned to lose their minds because there was nobody there to train them.

Roden keeps saying there will come a day when we will save those souls, even if their ravenous talent has consumed their minds. But, for now, I can only harvest their souls and deliver them to him for a painless end.

Not quite the same end the Nistarei receive instead. They are turned into empty vessels piled in controlled areas, where our Writers try to find a way to reuse their bodies and lingering memories.

I realise I've been staring at the square outside my window for too long when my forehead becomes numb.

Primrose Square is quiet this evening. A young couple holds hands under the marble arches leading to the beach. Beyond the couple, the slim shadows of the torches dotting the shore of Libera stretch on the sand before disappearing into the water.

This is where I spend almost half of my monthly wage—a place with an ocean view and a perfect hiding spot to spy on other people's everyday lives.

Libera's selection of restaurants is quite limited; students prefer not to spend money when the Academy kitchen is open twenty-four-seven and affordable. But I promised Galen I would treat him tonight. Besides, expensive food and service mean fewer ears eager to listen to your every word.

Our chefs try hard to keep up with Horigean cuisine. Still, the list of local producers is very short because we need to ensure that only a few trusted people know how to find Libera so as not to risk the secrecy of our location.

Sipping by a window at my now lukewarm drink, I spot Galen strolling down the road with his nose up in the air, listening to music. His favourite way to cool down and find the right way to be civil with a friend he's just argued with. I don't see him dressed up so often, but when he does, I know he means business. And I am his business tonight.

When I lift my highball glass, it catches the reflection of a bike flashing in and out of the street lights opposite the restaurant.

Why is Lucretia cycling so fast alone at this time? She's not famous for being spotted on her own. I try to hide behind the thin slice of cucumber drowning in my drink, and I re-emerge from my pathetic hideout only when I'm sure she hasn't detected my presence and is not coming back to ask me about Galen again.

The bell dangling above the door frame announces the arrival of a new guest. With his charming smile and refined appearance, his hair pulled back, and his strategically unshaven but still perfectly groomed stubble, he looks so in control and the perfect fit for whatever situation he finds himself in.

"I think someone's waiting for me…" I hear Galen saying to a young man behind the reception desk.

"Forgive me if I don't pull out your chair," I tease him after the host walks him to our table.

"Never mind, you're already paying for the bottle of the most expensive wine on the list that I've just ordered for us," he winks.

He sits, fingers interlaced over the table like a businessman ready to talk profit and loss. "So… I'm all ears." He props an elbow on the table, casually resting his right cheek in his hand. But he's studying me like a cat does with food before eating it.

I knew he would not waste a minute.

I grab both sides of the table and take a deep breath. He's wearing contacts tonight, but I prefer him with glasses. At least there's always a thin barrier between me and his piercing eyes, and I can always check how my face reacts to his words in their reflection.

I lean forward, and he copies me as if we're teens about to share a secret.

I push it all out, no time to ponder, "What were my last words to you the other night? I know I told you something before I discovered the odd shade of that woman's soul, or else, I wouldn't need to write it down. Does this have anything to do with the recycling squads? You're always itching to repeat any words I gave you after a mission as soon as you can…But you haven't yet…" Right to the point before we can even order starters.

I only blink once, and the amusement on Galen's face disappears. I retreat like a turtle back into its shell.

His eyes shoot left and right, making sure nobody is close enough to us when he whispers, "What the hell? I thought we were here to discuss your next mission. What's with the rec…" He leans in closer, beckoning me to do the same. "The squads? Seriously? First, the mission near Brenath. Now—this? What's with you and risky situations lately, eh?"

I can see through Galen as though he's the translucent slice of cucumber in my drink. And I've never seen him in such distress.

I shrug, sinking back in my chair, and flip through the menu to avoid eye contact, "Why are you freaking out? I was just making conversation. You know as well as I that a red soul is not…*expected*." I can see his eyes getting wider and his eyebrows nearly disappearing under some loose curls.

"Besides, every single student speculates at least once a week on what happens to the Nistarei's souls we retrieve by the hundreds any other day. And I'm not talking about the good ones…Oh, the sea bass sounds delicious…" I add impassible.

"July stop."

"Stop what? Expressing a simple opinion about a subject that's supposed to be part of our job? I - seriously - I don't know why everybody is so touchy when it comes to learning."

The skin on his knuckles stretches, revealing the bones flexing beneath. "This is not about learning. Souls are fickle, and you were handling that of a not-very-reputable Horigean. That could have been anything, but you had to opt for the most dangerous and absurd theory?" he hisses.

Now it's my time to make my point. "A theory? Then, please explain how centuries of rotten souls can be contained in the Fields. If the Writers can only plant back souls if they were nearly pure when harvested, and we know there aren't that many, where do we find the space to store millions of corrupted souls? The maps count a few dozen active fields. Not a lot for the amount of souls I alone collect in six months' worth of work."

I knock back what's left of my drink, then put the glass down on the table as slowly as possible, hoping for an answer, but all I find is Galen's face drained of all its blood.

I sigh, "If you don't feel like sharing, at least tell me—what did I say to you that night?"

He remains immobile, but his mouth moves, "How long have

you been looking into this?"

I shake my head, "My last words first—please."

My knife and fork clink loudly, and my glass dangerously tilts over when Galen pulls at the white tablecloth. He not only leans towards me, but navigates the space between us, dragging his chair next to mine.

"This may be fun for you, and I know how much you like a great discovery. Especially if you're the one with the credit. But you know how a well-told rumour can turn into propaganda. And you know that part of our history has been banned from being told. Even speculating about the fate of rotten souls can be seen as insubordination," he whispers in my ear, cocking his head towards mine, giving the impression of two lovers about to be cheesy in public.

"Fine then…" I flap my napkin in the air, unfolding it and flattening it on my legs. My chin is so high when I speak that the muscles in my neck hurt. "Let's forget I even mentioned it. Shall we order?" I respect Galen and his rank, but his affection for official or unspoken rules sometimes gets on my nerves.

"Sof," he places a hand on my shoulder and takes the menu away from me with the other. "Don't give me that look. When you said you wanted to talk tonight, I thought it would have been about the Rogue and your desire to dive back into it so soon. Not your sudden need to test Popplewish's patience."

I give him a side-eye because if I open my mouth, we will probably end up fighting and get kicked out of the restaurant.

His chair complains when he moves back to his side of the table, offering me space to think and breathe. "Fine, I'll do the talk first," he declares when I lift a finger to call the waiter over.

I point at random dishes on the menu, hoping I don't pick anything like liver or kidneys.

"And for you, sir?"

"I'll have the same," Galen answers in such a rush he doesn't even look at the waiter, who leaves the table after glaring at us with disdain.

"Your words for me that night," Galen continues. "You said something about stolen souls."

"Is that it? No context, no reason why I said that?" I narrow my eyes.

When I leave a message for *my future self*, I use as many details as possible.

Galen interlaces his fingers under his chin, looking as innocent as a lion cub. "That's it." He echoes me.

"Now," he smiles at the waiter who's back with our orders and politely thanks him. "Please feed my curiosity and tell me when you decided to entertain your beautiful brain with the *RS*."

I hold a fork loaded with a giant shrimp dipped in sweet chilli sauce in front of my mouth, "You mean the rec—"

"Yes, July," he pinches his nose, looking at me with half-lidded eyes, "those."

I smirk and stare at him over the pale pink shrimp. "Apparently, the higher your rank, the smaller the chance the students will open up to you. I think I know something you don't know."

Chapter 10 - The Scream
July

Many libraries in Libera are built to preserve the history and knowledge of our people. But my favourite is the Turret.

Erected on one of the smaller islets rising to the west, it can only be visited by boat and only for a few hours. At sundown, the sea completely submerges it, turning it into a floating building, surrounded by four dome-shaped structures connected to the Turret by glass corridors.

It hosts a small cafeteria that used to be a deposit for old desks, chairs, and vintage uniforms. That was until one day, someone decided to revamp it and use it as a base for student groups—a very long time ago. I believe the founders are no longer around, but the Turret still holds a special aura of free speech and independence, with its old students' mottoes painted on its walls: "A Soul for a Soul" and "Souls Don't Belong."

A place of knowledge and quiet. Until a few days ago, when a swarm of wannabe(es) queens crushed my inner peace under their ankle-killer heels and judgemental looks, bursting inside the cafeteria and unrolling a red carpet of vanity and shallowness for the real Queen—Lucretia Accolti.

"Galen, I swear," I run a hand through my hair with annoyance after he's asked me for the third time if I was sure it was Lue I saw in the Turret.

I proceed with my story before he can stop me again, "And that's not even the oddest part. Also, you promised no more interruptions."

I point a judging finger at his face, and he sighs, leaning back on his chair and sipping his wine. "Go on, then."

"She was there with two older girls, judging by that ridiculous senior patch the Academy wants us to wear when out and about with newcomers. They noticed me and quickly hid behind one of the bookshelves. But because I had my earphones on, they believed they could talk freely—ah! Idiots. They didn't even consider that I could brush my hand against one ear and switch the music off."

I close my mouth just long enough to appreciate Galen's proud face - *that's my clever July!* - but he waits for more, distractedly drumming his fingers on the table, keeping his promise not to interrupt me until I'm done talking.

When the waiter comes to clear our table, I use the time to gather the memories of that day in the most concise and best way. "Thanks…" we say in unison with that rigid smile we all smack on our faces while waiting for our table to be crockery-free.

"Where was I? Oh, yes. So, I heard them talking about a new shipment of fabric from Horigos. They went on for something like twenty tedious minutes. But I knew something else was brewing because they were just not in the right place."

I fiddle with my fork as I fish the details of that day from the back of my mind. Galen nods and scratches his chin. He's hooked so much that the intensity of his gaze almost makes me feel…Uncomfortable? Odd.

I set the fork down. "You look like you're trying to dig a hole in my head and get the rest of the story right out. Anyways," I look around and behind me, just as a precaution, then lean forward. "They changed the subject once they were sure nobody was around. I saw Lucretia, through the space between bookshelves, exchanging looks with the other girls, nodding and taking her phone out of her bag."

"Nudes?" Galen remains unfazed while mocking me, swirling his glass of red, with one hand bracing over the back of his chair.

"Oh, shut up. This is serious." I stretch over the table and lower my voice, "It was a video. The sound was muffled. But—oh, you should have seen their eyes…"

The waiter returns with our mains and gives me a weird look as we cross our eyes.

"Low blood pressure," Galen lies to justify my concerned face.

"Sugared water may help. Would you like a glass, Miss?"

"Yes, please…" I reply quickly to send him away. I'll say sorry later with a good tip.

"I don't know what they saw, but I heard a scream…." I blurt out with one breath, then take a new one so deep my shoulders rise and nearly swallow my neck. "I didn't move because I didn't want them to know I'd heard. Even when one of them peeped from behind the shelf to check nobody was coming, I started to bob my head pretending I was listening to music."

"The waiter's coming back…" Galen gestures quickly, and I pause my story.

"There you go, Miss, water with sugar and the sides to your mains. Enjoy." The young man lingers longer than he should and only turns around when I grab the sugary drink and gulp half of it. I bet he wants to be sure I don't faint halfway through our meal before the bill is on the table.

Galen chuckles as I wrinkle my nose, "That's enough sugar for the next five months. Anyways…that scream. It was not *human*. I don't know how else I can explain it. High-pitched, if it was male or female... I couldn't say. Lucretia didn't dare play it again."

"What about the other people in the Turret? Surely something like that wouldn't stay a secret for long," Galen asks, as though my mention of a terrifying scream was just a garnish to my story. But, if I know him well, he's probably making a mental list of all the possible reasons behind that scream.

I shake my head. "It was early morning, and nobody was there except us. Besides, Lucretia is not the type of girl who finds it amusing to share scary videos. As she would say, '*uncoolness* is not my vibe'." The vegetables on my plate have gone cold, but I take a few bites.

"So? What did they say?" Galen presses me. At least one of us has enjoyed his food. His plate is empty, and he's taking the liberty of nibbling at my potatoes.

I move my chair so that I can face the window, and nobody else in the room but Galen can see my face or read my lips, "Not much, but one of Lue's friends asked who sent her the video and snatched the phone to stare at the silent screen. I think that girl saw that video before."

"And?" he asks, attacking my last burnt-fried potato with his fork.

My mouth is dry as if I've been talking for hours.

I take a sip of water. "Well, Lucretia refused to reveal her source but said something even more unsettling... She asked her friend if that is what rec... *recycling squads* are trained for," I let my words glide and sink.

I'm sure Galen is about to hurry me to pay and leave before Roden pops out of nowhere, raids the restaurant, and takes us away handcuffed because I said the forbidden words.

I give him a minute.

Fine. Maybe two minutes...and a half? Not a word. I'm sure he hasn't blinked, either. Instead, he's staring at me, holding up that last burnt potato stabbed on his fork.

"Hey, did you hear—?" I try my best to sound relaxed, waving a hand in his face.

"Is this why you want to go back out there so soon?" He surprises me. I was ready for him to freak out. Again.

"Among other reasons, yes..." I admit.

"Is there more?" He puts the fork down and waves away the

waiter who's coming back to take our empty plates. Very odd, coming from the most polite person I've ever met.

"I just," searching for the right words, I hear my stomach gurgling. I wasn't ready for this. "I asked Popplewish to send me out again before all this happened. I wanted to experience something different, to come back with more than a bitter taste for a lost life. You always seem to hold special memories of your Nistarei, and I haven't had that in—well, never had that really… Never wanted it."

He nods and mumbles something, toying with the bread crumbs on the tablecloth as if he could find the answer there, and rolling between two fingers a slim silver chain at his neck I've never seen before, half hidden under his jumper. But when he looks back at me, he frowns, "Sof, you okay? Your forehead is sweaty."

I touch my head, and my fingertips come back shiny with sweat. "I skipped lunch, maybe that's all. Wine on an empty stomach is never a great combination." I try a smile, but my stomach lurches, and I press both hands on my belly to muffle the awkward sound.

Galen stands up so quickly that his chair balances on its back legs before tumbling to the floor. "We'd better go…"

My eyes must be watery because Galen's face wobbles like seaweed in choppy waters. I tried to articulate some words: *it's all fine, I'm fine, no need to go…* But they stay in my head, and I hear him calling the waiter over with our bill.

As he drops some cash on the table and helps me to my feet, he whispers close to my ear, "Can you stand?"

My shaky knees answer for me.

"Unfortunately, my friend is not feeling well still… That should cover for your tip as well," Galen explains calmly, but I can't ignore the nervous edge in his voice.

"Galen…" I can barely hear my voice.

He shushes me while wrapping an arm around my waist, flipping my right arm over his shoulder. "Just breathe. In and out."

We're not far from the entrance, but it feels like an endless path to me. A bell rings in the back of my mind, and a door slams shut.

"Sorry…" It's the last thing I manage to say before collapsing on the street outside the restaurant.

What comes after is all a smelly blur, a burning throat and sharp pieces of tarmac pressing against the palms of my hands and knees. Galen is talking, crouched next to me, and I try to follow the sound of his voice as he gently lifts me, rubbing my back.

"Sof, listen to me…" I don't like the hurry in his voice. I'm only drunk, not in danger. "July? Keep your eyes open."

Is it my mind playing with my senses, or is he trying to move us away from this place as if wolves are chasing us?

I roll my tongue inside my mouth, and the taste makes me retch. "I think… I'm going to…" I try to push him away, at least to save his nice outfit. Still, Galen doesn't let go and holds me tight while dragging me to the other side of the road, towards the wood dividing the urbanised side of the island from the seashore and creating a natural border between the villages of Evemerys and Anagessys.

Galen's breath is heavy and fast, and when I look up, he's scanning the area as if waiting for someone to come. His jaw tenses. "Who else did you tell about what happened in the Turret?"

Odd question, given that I'm probably suffering the effects of some sort of food poisoning. I only have the energy to answer with monosyllables: "Just…you…" I dig my nails into his jumper desperately, trying to stay upright.

At the same moment, his phone rings, and he snatches it out of his pocket as if it were on fire, answering with a chaotic stream of words. "Good timing, I need help. Now. The woods…" he pauses to scan the line of trees before us, "I can make it in fifteen minutes. Ten. If she doesn't pass out."

Pass out. There have been times when Galen had described me using that verb, like the morning after a too-happy night out. But he'd done it laughing and pointing at me while munching on a box of doughnuts. Now, it's not the same. He's afraid and worried. His voice trembles when he says my name.

I hear a click, and the call ends. "You'll be fine, Sof… stay with me."

I'm sorry. I only manage to picture the words in my mind. I shape them big and bold, thick and flashing. Maybe he will read them behind my eyes. I hope he will quickly because I'm too tired, and my eyelids are giving up.

Chapter 11 - Tearless Silent End
Evelyn

Something is off. "Just pick up the phone…" The echo of my steps is the only sound breaking the tedious sequence of unanswered rings on the other end of the line.

"Come on, pick—"

"Good timing, I need help…"

"Galen, hang on, I can't hear you. Let me go outside."

I should've known. As my left hand struggles to turn the key of my balcony's door, my brain can't stop thinking it's my fault. I should have been more cautious.

My fingers slip off the door handle a couple of times, but the lock eventually clicks open, and I step into the refreshing night breeze. "Tell me where you are."

"The woods…"

I scan the dark silhouette of Libera's horizon, fooling myself that if I stare long enough, I will spot Galen walking safely towards me. But the disembodied panting and harsh intakes of breath coming from his end kick me out of my reverie. "I'll be there soon. You keep her awake."

I run out of my office and down the stairs so quickly I realise I'm in my car only when the small, yellow tree, dangling from the rear-view mirror, sends lemon scent up my nostrils.

I throw my phone on the passenger seat before I start the engine, but it rings again. I pick it up without looking at the screen and activate the speaker before tossing it away again. "Galen, I'm nearly there. Just left my place—"

"Ah, so Amelia was right. And here I was, thinking she was just eager to climb to the top of my esteem."

When Roden's voice floods the car, I nearly lose control of the steering wheel, letting it go for a second, as if covered in thorns. "Roden, sir, I…Amelia should have asked before passing on the wrong details." I manage a lie. One *I* don't believe. For a long moment, the phone stays silent. I must remember I've been doing this for longer than that silly woman.

Then, "Yes, my dear, I knew there was more to the story. Someone like you would never betray our cause. Not after so many years of trials and *errors*."

"Souls. I still like to call them by their real nature, if you don't mind." I've regained at least some of the confidence that comes with my role.

"Of course. Of course, my dear, but if I remember well, you're the Silent End, not only thanks to your soft steps. You are the apotheosis of emotional detachment. I told Amelia this when she tried to convince me you were working with that rebel, a disgrace to all Harvesters. What's her name again? Tabitha-something…"

I hope he can't hear my worst fears get stuck in my throat as I push them down, back into my stomach. One breath in, one goldfish out. A breath out, and the fish is safe in the pond. I quickly look at my phone, laughing, as though I could make my reaction more credible. "That's ridiculous. I was about to tell Amelia the beauty of something called damage control, but she didn't give me the time. Why would I risk my position by associating with rebels—"

"Exactly, my dear, why would you?"

Come on, Roden, enough with this game.

"Anyway, someone once taught me that a great leader always recognises his disciples' mistakes and sets them straight before having to employ extreme punishments. You know how I hate the sight of wounds and blood." His voice trails off with a cold laugh.

I shiver, even though the windows are all up. "I'm sure Amelia doesn't deserve—"

"Oh no, dear. Not Amelia. Now, you drive safely and make sure you deliver July to HQ while she's still breathing. And let's try to keep young Galen out of this. For everybody's sake. We will think about something to make him right later."

And just like that, the call's over.

I let the phone beep for as long as possible to make sure I'm alone again. His presence lingers in my car like the memory of a nightmare in the minutes after waking.

The sight of the wood shakes something inside me, and I draw back my tears before they roll down.

The Silent End does not cry.

81

Chapter 12 - Voices in the Woods
July

Riding the end of Winter's tail, the sea breeze blows humid and sticky on my face.

Galen must have picked me up at some point and carried me through the woods. My senses switch on and off, but I'm sure I've only seen trees for the past hour. Or was it longer?

The steady sound of leaves, the voices of nocturnal animals, and the image of the trees chasing one another, as if on a conveyor belt, threaten to lull me to sleep.

But Galen's voice keeps me awake as he repeats the same words I've heard since this weird dream started, "We're almost there...she can help you...stay with me…"

I've been in the woods before. Every student old enough to understand the hedonistic meaning of a romantic night walk amongst the trees has spent at least a couple of *enjoyable* hours hidden in the thicket of this place. Tonight, however, there are only shadows and disembodied voices lurking amongst the branches and tall grass.

My fingers search for a piece of Galen to grab and cling onto.

"Don't leave me…" I implore, weakly.

"I'm not going anywhere, July." The moonlight cannot filter through the intricate pattern of foliage, and it isn't easy to read his expression. But it hits me as he whispers my name.

I'm not going anywhere, July. Two voices telling me the same phrase mix inside my mind. This is more than the awful aftermath of wine on an empty stomach.

I bite my lips, and the pain grants me an extra second of lucidity before whatever substance did this to me knocks me down again. "Poison…"

I'm not sure if Galen can see my face in the darkness. I know he's listening, but all I can hear in response is his laboured breath and his heart pounding against my ear.

My head bounces against his shoulder as I taste my tears before they roll down my chin. Maybe this is what the Nistarei experience in their last moments: lightness and abandonment.

I close my eyes like I saw some of them doing when I touch my vials to their chests, demanding access to their naked souls. They don't want my face to be the last thing they see.

I'm still alive. Though—not yet fully awake. The absence of words from Galen doesn't help my foggy brain. All I can do to stay alert is to focus on my thoughts. Conjectures. Questions that, if presented to Popplewish, would only get preset answers—safe answers.

What difference does having a good soul make if we harvest them when their deadline expires instead of granting more time? Are empty vessels abandoned in the Fields really just that—empty bodies?

They teach us that good Horigeans' souls are stripped of all their memories and sent back to Horigos, cocooned inside newborns. A few chosen ones every week.

But who gives us the right to pick and choose which soul is worthy of a new chance at life?

Galen's steady walk cradles me in and out of a haze, but I gather my last energies to mumble, my lips dry and sticky at once, "Our gift... Does this make us better than the Herionos? What about the red souls? What about *my* Rogues?" I'm not sure if Galen has replied, but I'm sure he's stopped for a moment.

Is this the sea lapping on the shore? When did we get out of the woods?

"Your suspicions were right then." A muffled female voice breaks the silence.

Darkness is everywhere, but Galen shields me from the shadows dancing above me. He adjusts my half-unconscious body against his and replies to the woman, "Partially. She only has fragments of proof, but she's smart, and it won't take her long to figure out the rest."

"Do you think she remembered anything else? Did you ask her?"

"Well, Evelyn, you and the rest of the Chapter should have raised the issue *before* granting her permission with such short notice, but to answer your question…No, she did it because of her need to understand people's nature and hers. I think there's nothing else *he* needs to worry about. For now. As for you—prepare yourself for a bigger concern…"

Galen gently places his hand on my shoulder, smoothing out the wrinkles in my shirt. If only I had the strength to lift my head and say something. Has he lowered his voice, or am I just fading away?

The noise of an electric car window opening catches my attention, and I try to squint my eyes, focusing on the woman's voice when she asks from inside the car, "What do you mean?"

Popplewish? It can't be…

Galen bends forward a little, his arms holding me tighter, "Someone's leaked the video of a soul turning Red—"

"Nonsense," Popplewish interrupts him.

"You'd better put together your best team, Eve, because the video has already been shared among junior and senior students. July caught Lucretia watching it. That put a massive target on Lucretia's back, making her *our* problem now. You know Roden has eyes everywhere."

"And ears! Have you gone mad? It's not safe here…" Popplewish hisses.

My body shifts position as Galen tugs me closer to his face, his breath warm on my cheek. His fingers stretch across my face, reaching for his neck. "Relax." I hear him saying, before something jingles next to my ear.

"That thing can be dangerous in the wrong hands; take it back…

How long ago?" Popplewish mutters, and a thud tells me she's hit something, perhaps the steering wheel, in frustration.

"About a week ago." Galen grabs me tighter and pulls back slightly. "What are you going to do with her?"

A long sigh. "Don't be silly. Just put her in the back seat." Nothing happens, nothing moves. But then, "I said, leave her with me. I can take it from here." Exasperation is something I never thought Miss Popplewish would be familiar with.

The car door opens. Galen steps back a little more, and my stomach turns.

"I'm coming with you, and I will keep an eye on her. Don't worry. She'll sleep for hours—"

"You don't need to explain why... I can smell the reason..." Popplewish replies, igniting the engines. "Did you use extra?" she adds, louder over the noise of her car. I would never imagine Miss P. driving such a powerful thing—it roars like a beast.

Galen's body tenses. Something is rumbling in his chest, like an animal growling before the attack. "Do you think *I* drugged her? Are you out of your mind?"

Another sigh. No. A gasp.

"Fuck. We need to go now—"

Crouching on the back seat, Galen's attentive hands adjust my floppy body. From behind my half-closed eyelids, I can't make out the expression on his face, and when he slides something soft under my head to make me comfortable, a knot stops in my throat. As far as I understood, we're in a hurry, but he takes the time to ensure I'm comfortable.

Something light, like a butterfly's wings, grazes my lips. For a second, I swear, our eyes lock when he quickly kisses me.

When he speaks again, as he sits next to me, adjusting my legs over his, there is gravity in his voice. "How did they get there before me? How did they know?"

He shifts on the seat. His hand brushes my leg as he searches for something in his pocket, the brief touch confirming that I'm still alive, awake, and not dreaming.

"Here, you can have it back. I would never use it on her anyway. Besides, since when does the Chapter become so comfortable using drugs on students?"

What?

The back seat shakes under his weight when he leans forward. My right arm is dangling lifeless on the side of the leather seat, and Galen gingerly folds it back over my chest.

The hissing sound of a seat belt being slid across my body precedes Galen's voice. "You're safe. I'm here…" he repeats a couple of times.

A safe and comfortable hostage?

His voice almost lulls me to sleep. Until he stops and the leather seat screeches under his angry grip. "You didn't answer my question." This rage doesn't belong to him.

What's happening? I don't want to associate this voice with his face…

"Because I don't have to." The engines roar, but Popplewish's voice reaches the back of the car as if she's sitting next to me. "All you need to know is that July will recover soon. Remind me, please, how long have you been part of the Chapter?"

"Long enough to regret the day I said yes."

"Not enough time to remember that we walk on a thin, weak edge ready to crack at any point." Popplewish has lowered her voice, but Galen's body twitches against mine. "Don't forget why you were allowed in the Chapter and how quickly *we* can revoke your role."

He leans closer to the driver's seat, holding my legs on his so I don't fall over. "I can't keep doing my job without at least some explanations. July will wake up completely oblivious tomorrow morning, but I am the one who will need to deal with her nightmares and flashbacks—again. I believe the Chapter owes me this. Unless they're willing to gamble also with *my* ignorance and the mistakes it could cause—"

Nothing of what they're talking about makes sense to me, but I'm the one who's been served shrimp with a side of freaking drugs.

"Enough." Popplewish sounds final, ominous. But then, "Roden wants to speak with her in person. I fear he's decided to act *differently* this time. He knows time is running out."

"Bullshit!" Galen slaps the seat. A puff of leathery smell and dust twists my stomach, but I'm still too weak even to gag. "At least admit you knew about the drug. How long have you been planning this and haven't told me? To send her back to *him* so soon, when it's not even been a couple of years since the last accident?"

Him? What—who are they talking about?

"Two years is a long time for some. And *we* don't have the means to delay Roden's decision. Roden knows *he* only has a small kernel left. She *is* our only hope now…"

"Oh, stop the farce! I was an idiot thinking you looked shocked when you met us in the woods—"

"I did not know Roden had opted for something so drastic. And even if so, what do you suggest I should have done? Stop him? Don't you think that would have put me—us—in a dangerous position? This is not the first time for her, or you. For any of us. So tell me, what's changed?"

Popplewish's question lingers above us, heavy with pressure. "Or should I ask, what's changed with you?"

Galen's hand finds mine, and our fingers interlace. "Do not go there again—"

"Or what?" No answer follows from Galen. "That's what I thought. You can stay, but I don't want to hear any more stupid theories. Or you can leave the car now."

The engines roar again, this time ready to sprint.

Galen remains quiet for a moment, gently squeezing my hand. A hesitation louder than hundreds of screams before he finds his voice again, "The waiter…You allowed a stranger to administer a dose to an innocent person? To… her …" he mumbles.

Popplewish clucks her tongue, "And that's why you're not ready. You're too passionate and fail to keep focus when people you love are involved. The dosage was very low, but I had to administer her *something*, or we wouldn't be here talking so openly otherwise…"

"I should have left her in Cleryce when I had the chance. Ask Mack to create another one of these…" That metallic sound again.

The car jolts forward, and the pressure flattens me against the seat.

Popplewish's voice travels impatiently through the wind that blows inside the vehicle from the open window. "I don't intend to discuss this matter in a speeding car. I'm taking you back to your place before heading to HQ. As far as Roden knows, you headed home after I took July into my care. End of story."

"The headquarters? Fuck, Eve, to the Deleteri? Seriously? What is he planning to lie on this time that may need their intervention?"

I swear, the car is roaring louder as if echoing Popplewish's unconventional reaction. I want to scream, run away. Despite having Galen so close to me, holding me tight so I don't fall from the car seat, I can't shake off the thought that he knows what is happening to me. And what is happening to me sounds dangerous.

What the hell is going on? My brain is fighting against the idea that this could even be real. *Why does the Chapter want to meet me? What's a Chapter…* I must be having a dream; I don't remember. My head hurts.

Galen slams back against the seat, letting out a loud breath, "Will she still remember me once they're done?"

"She will remember some."

"This ride? I mean, she's unconscious. Is this really necessary?"

"Her body is, perhaps. But we don't know how much her mind will retain."

Nothing. I promise. I will retain nothing. If I could only voice that…

The last part of their conversation fades quickly. Too quickly. And, perhaps, I didn't even catch their exact words. Forgetting Galen?

How can I forget someone I care for so much?

Chapter 13 - HQ
Galen

The car runs faster than my thoughts, and everything outside is just blurry smears of black and green shooting past out of the corner of my eye. July's breath is slow but regular. I hope she's asleep to make the Deleteri's job quicker and painless.

"They'll know what to do," Evelyn states as if having read my mind.

"They'll delete what they are told to. It is not a matter of experience. They shouldn't have been involved at all," I snap.

Evelyn doesn't need to voice her feelings. The reflection of her eyes in the rear-view mirror bears a silent prayer for trust while her hands grip the wheel with such worry that her knuckles turn white under the freckled skin.

"What's changed?" I ask, trying to control my voice this time. "Why the Deleteri and not the Writers?"

She takes a deep breath as if to keep our conversation as civil as possible. "She's seen too much, heard too much. Roden thinks their work won't be enough this time, and flashes of the past may come back to her—not only in her sleep."

I glance at July. Her face has relaxed completely as if she's just peacefully asleep in the backseat of a friend's car.

I intercept Eve's eyes in the mirror a second time. "How's she doing?" she asks.

"Drugged and betrayed." I hold her gaze—fuck the hierarchy, she can take my judgemental look.

"Being so resentful and bitter won't change anything. It will only wear out your mind."

Evelyn slows the car down. Another vehicle drives past ours in the opposite direction, and I follow its journey until it disappears in the darkness of the otherwise deserted road.

"Roden managed to sense *him*," Evelyn throws me a quick look from the front seat. "We don't know if the Wards were done or simply too many Reds moved towards him, but Mack is looking into it. I had to act fast. Delaying July's crossing would have raised suspicions," she mumbles as a way for a pathetic excuse, which I decide to accept to avoid further confrontation.

"Do you think *Kristyon* wandered out too far from the perimeter, without supervision? I swear if he did—" The name slips from my lips, and I freeze.

"For souls' sake, Galen!" I capture Evelyn's concerned gaze as she glares at me from the mirror before she shoots a glance over her shoulder to July, sighing, "You'll do what exactly?"

July moans in her sleep and rolls onto her side, folding her hands under her cheeks.

"Is she awake?"

"Just keep driving. I need to think."

The headquarters is an anonymous, grey structure built on the most northeastern point of Libera, with no easy access by car unless you know where to look. From the outside, it looks like a huge, boring warehouse used to store old furniture, with tall windows covered in dust and masked from the inside to avoid curious looks.

"I still wonder how, in all these years, nobody has ever tried to squat in this place." Mine is just an observation, but it captures Eve's attention as she parks at the back of the building.

She turns in her seat, bracing one arm on the headrest, her glasses sliding down her nose as she jerks her chin at July's sleeping body. "That's what happens when someone asks too many questions about the wrong place and the wrong people. Do you still want me to answer you? Remember, July's brain is still active and could store information that should stay hidden."

"Don't act witty with me, Eve. You shut me out—"

"I told you, it was an emergency fix," she sighs.

"The benefit of the doubt. This is all I can offer you for now, but I will consider you personally responsible should they—*Roden*—even as much as think about hurting her," I hiss, realising I've just threatened the only person who could end my career and probably my fucking life.

"You know he won't."

"Of course, because who would destroy such a precious weapon?" I bite my tongue and recoil against my seat, watching Evelyn as she unbuckles her seat belt, gets out of the car, and opens my door, resting one arm on the metal frame.

"Do you need help carrying her?" she offers.

"No need, I can manage." I ignore her mortified look and slowly abandon my seat to get out and walk to the other side of the car.

I grab July's shoulders as if she's made of crystal, and I hear her mumbling something in her sleep about carrot cake. Some locks of hair are plastered to her face with sweat and dust from our time in the woods.

"Watch her head..." Eve materialises behind me and promptly stretches out one hand to support July's neck.

"Thanks," I murmur.

"Never think I stopped caring. Everything I do is for hers and your own good," Eve whispers, pressing her free hand on my shoulder.

I nod, and together, we walk around the building, where the main door is already ajar as if waiting for our arrival.

Chapter 14 - Wounds Will Heal
Evelyn

"I need you to leave as soon as possible," I beg Galen. "Don't you think we've been spotted already? Roden is probably looking at us right now," Galen huffs a laugh.

"Sarcasm won't help us. And put that hand down. Sometimes you look more like…Never mind…" I say, glancing over my shoulder as I pace in front of him, massaging my right temple.

"I'm just waving a virtual white flag. Are we all not on the same side?" He shrugs quickly, still holding July in his arms.

It hurts to see him this protective, as if July may turn to dust if anyone else but him touches her.

But I know he is right. Surely Roden is checking our every move, and I can't start an argument over who should carry July, risking the impression that I'm too involved.

"Fine. I'll make something up but don't linger around here too long. Just get changed and go. You know how to move around HQ," I concede.

I should've noticed the signs years ago, but trying to break their bond now is impossible, if not dangerous.

The way he studies July's face, checking the rhythm of her breath. The way his thumb gently strikes her temple while his hand cradles her head…

"Please, lead on," Galen snaps when he notices I'm staring.

The entrance hall greets us with its usual scent of nothingness. Despite having walked on its marble floors hundreds of times, I still admire its perfection, so different from the building's decaying façade.

This place is so quiet and silent, I should be able to hear myself and Galen breathing, maybe even our heartbeats. Yet, I don't even notice Galen approaching from my right, his footsteps so light despite carrying his and July's weight.

"Are you sure?" His voice should echo from one end of the hall to the other, but the rules of sound don't apply here.

"Certain. I'll go meet the Chapter and take care of this matter." I stretch my arms towards him despite the look of doubt on his young face.

"Where will you take her?" He gingerly lowers July's body, letting her tiptoes touch the floor, her knees bending like those of a puppet with loose strings.

"He wants to see her in the screens room." I realise my mistake when it's already too late to take it back.

"Why?" Galen cocks his head and moves a step back, taking July with him.

"I don't know, I swear. I guess Roden is reassessing the situation." I scan the room, leaning forward and whispering, "We all are…"

Galen studies my face, sighs and eventually offers me July as if giving me a rare and fragile piece of porcelain. "That can only mean Roden will tell her the truth this time." Not a question.

"He didn't confirm, but it may be inevitable. He knows this is his last chance." I take July in my arms, nodding a wordless *thank you*. "Now, go. I'll meet you back in my office when it's all done."

He nods, extending one hand and hovering it over July's face before he turns his back and silently walks away with his head bowed, speaking volumes of pain and worry.

But wounds will heal somehow if we play this right.

The lift to the screens room is strategically hidden behind a tall portrait on the left side of the hall. It depicts an idyllic scene of Libera with students playing in its gardens, surrounded by flowers that have never really grown on the island.

When I touch my fingertips to the frame, it slides to one side, as if responding to my unspoken request, revealing the creation of a genius mind. A lift, that is, seamlessly built into the wall, making it impossible to notice when closed. Like the frame, it also seems to listen to my prayer, *Let me in and be done with this*, as it opens under my touch.

July is no longer the little girl I brought to Libera; her trained muscles twitch and quiver in my hold. As much as I would like, I can't hold her up any longer. Once in the lift, I gently prop her against one side and help her body slowly slide down, like an abandoned doll, in the corner of the lift.

I'm not a stupid piece of stuffed rag, her voice complains in my head.

The lift begins descending almost immediately. Although there's no apparent source of artificial light inside, it remains bright, as if some of the illumination from the hall is trapped in here with us.

"Welcome, Evelyn Popplewish," a metallic voice greets me. I don't react; I've heard that voice so many times before. "Which level?"

"To the screens," I quickly answer.

"Access granted."

The descent is smooth, as if the lift is gliding through oil. It's a pity that great minds like the one behind this structure can no longer set foot in Libera.

When greatness destroys greatness, someone said once, but my time for reminiscing ends as the lift comes to a soft halt as if it's landed on a pile of pillows, and its door opens at the most eerie and dreadful room of the entire island.

I pick July up, relieved to hear her breathing regularly when I help her out of the lift.

Today, the room feels different. Not that I enjoy spending any time down here, but the comforting melody of a piano masterfully played warms up the space and softens the dull grey of the walls.

Until Roden's voice clashes with the notes, "I decided to make it more *homey.* Isn't this what the students like to say?" Sitting at the piano with his back to me, he sways left to right, running his hands over the black and white keys.

I adjust July's body when one of her arms slides down mine, and her head, partially covered by her hair, rests against my shoulder.

"Whatever pleases you," I reply from the opposite side of the room.

Roden continues to play and asks, "Do you know this piece? It was composed ages ago by a Horigean musician, a visionary, I'd rather say. It's about white clouds. Inspiring, isn't it?"

The notes dim and fade until they are nothing but indistinct sounds among the many disembodied voices that constantly fill the room.

"It is certainly beautiful," I say as I move in his direction, trying to sound relaxed. I have a feeling he can see me despite his position. Besides, not even the Silent End moves undetected in his presence, and his senses can always tell if someone is walking towards him as a humble ally or hiding a knife behind their back, to use at the right moment against him.

"I believe you have *something* for me, my child?" Without notice, he stands tall, his spine straight as if age got bored of him in his thirties and forgot he was meant to grow old.

"*Someone*—yes. She is still unconscious, I'm afraid—" I chew the inside of my cheek to silence any possible bitter remark.

"I can take it from here, my sweet Evelyn. You're free to go." There is nothing paternal in his voice.

"But—" I try to buy some time.

He ignores me and turns around to grab his walking cane, left by one side of the piano, and to lower the lid over the keys. His long fingers let go; the lid slams with a thundery sound that fills the room for a long second. "You've done what was asked. Now get ready for the meeting. Unless you have other plans?" Roden spins on his shiny black shoes.

His smile freezes the blood in my veins. I clench my teeth but hold my chin up. "She should wake up in less than an hour and may need food and water before anything else."

Every time his cane touches the ground, my nerves react as if an invisible hand is sticking needles in my limbs. He gets closer and closer and only stops when there are barely a few steps between us. I can only stare at the cane's tip as he extends it towards my face.

"I've always allowed my children too much freedom, and you are making me regret it." His pale grey eyes narrow to hard ice chips, the lack of pupils making his gaze impossible to hold for too long.

I don't have time to react; he's too fast, and I realise he's hit my hand with the walking stick only when burning pain spreads up to my wrist. My jaw is so tense that I fear my teeth will shatter, but it's the only way to maintain the undignified, submissive façade required in our creator's presence. To reassure him that I'm still subject to his self-glorified patriarchal figure.

"Apologies, Roden, but we won't get much out of her if she doesn't even have the strength to stand or talk," I bow my head slightly. "But, of course, you know better." I reluctantly ease my grip around July's waist and slide her arm off my shoulder.

"Indeed, I do," he chirps, opening his arms to welcome July's body, which nestles into Roden's hug as if responding to a call to safety I can't hear.

"If looks could kill," Roden whispers, looking straight into my eyes before gesturing to the wall behind me, where the lift awaits me.

I stare at him for a long minute for a glimpse of the fatherly figure he still represents to some of us. The first of our kind who stopped hiding his ability to handle souls as if they were pieces of clay and instead began trading them, taking advantage of those left poor and hopeless by the Great Famine, selling the souls of the Horigeans who didn't pay him back in time to the highest bidder.

But all I can see when he huffs a cold laugh in my face, tightening his arms around July's body, is the man who turned us into Harvesters, as Horigeans started to call us after realising that the souls of those who couldn't hold up their end of the bargain would never return where they belonged. The man who eventually forced us to abandon Horigos to seek safety in Libera when the Horigeans rose against us.

As if reading my thoughts, Roden leans forward and gently kisses my cheek. "You've always been my favourite. The rebel daughter who came back; the smartest. Too intelligent, perhaps."

I shiver the moment he steps away, and my eyes fall on July, so defenceless in his hold. I know he will keep her safe, but my heart skips a beat.

Safe doesn't mean unharmed.

Chapter 15 - Roden's Eyes
July

It was not a nightmare, that much I know. And that my back hurts like hell from having spent too much time—hours?—on a hard, cold surface.

Is it still nighttime?

No, wait… *Shit!*

I'm blindfolded. My fingers throb painfully, to the point I fear my skin will soon burst open because something is constricting my blood from flowing as it should. At least, whoever's dumped me here didn't think I could cause much trouble with just my voice, and they left my mouth uncovered.

"Hello? Anybody there? Where am I? Galen?!" I didn't know I could reach such a high pitch of desperation.

Let's focus, let's take a metaphorical step back. Dinner—Galen and I were having dinner, and I got… *Drunk?* I don't remember having more than one or two glasses.

"Oh, shit, did I throw up on Galen's expensive shoes…" My voice rolls out of my mouth and lingers somewhere in front of me before fading away.

My brain's a ball of fog where memories stretch like hot cheese, pulled between my need for reassurance that I'm not about to die alone, in some stranger's basement, and the uncomfortable feeling that I'm right where I should be.

"What the fuck is going on?" I shout, but yelling into an (*empty?*) room doesn't improve my current situation, as nobody replies.

Fine. Let's try a more direct approach.

"You…kidnapped the wrong person." *Oh, please, don't say I'm the right person.*

Still no answer. I sway my legs left and right to test the space surrounding me and to see if my kidnapper decides to make themselves known by stopping my pathetic attempt to break free. But all I can hear is a low, constant humming of electricity and crackling sounds, suppressing indistinct voices, words that don't make sense, like a TV screen with a bad signal.

Exhausted and achy, I lean back until my head finds a wall. *Shit—if I were at least able to free my hands.*

I touch my fingers to the hard surface behind me, scouting for a rough patch, a nail, or anything I could use to cut whatever is around my wrists, but it all feels like a solid, perfectly smooth piece of stone.

Back to square one, then.

"Hey, is this your big plan? To keep me in a room and watch me slowly rot away? That's some disgusting kink you have." I expel all the air in my lungs. Well, if this wasn't the plan before, I may have just fucked up grandly by proving I'm not the smartest bargaining chip but a very deafening, disposable one.

I drop my head, focusing on the steady sound of my breath, and bend my right knee in an attempt to get up, using the wall for support—but my legs are heavy as trunks and pull me back down.

Reset.

Why am I here? "If I could only use this wall to pull me up…"

Reset.

Galen always says that when in doubt, I just need to breathe and let go.

*Breathe…let go…*Nope!

Someone's watching me. It's like an invisible finger tracing a line along my forehead and down the side of my face, making the little hairs on my neck stand up.

I shake my head and wiggle my fingers, eager to find a clearer perspective of what's happening to me. A flashback of Galen and me sitting at the restaurant fires in my head, along with a single word—*squads.*

I know what I have to do.

I have to provoke whoever is enjoying my display of confusion. "Do you like watching your victims while they go crazy, eh? Nice touch, very *villanesque* of you. I see, I see—you like to remain secretive… "

Squads.

"Hang on, am I here because I mentioned to Galen about the recycling squ— "

What was I about to say? It was just one word, but it got stuck between my throat and lips, and I can no longer remember it.

Galen's face floats behind my eyes. He's not with me; had he been here, he would have said something already. If only a joke to cheer me up, no matter the danger of our position.

I drop my chin, my head heavy with the need to speak words I no longer seem to know. Frustration finally gets the upper hand. "Please," I whisper on the verge of tears. I don't believe that showing your weak side makes you stronger, but I haven't felt this vulnerable in a very long time.

I jolt awake to the sound of—no, it's not a voice, but a noise I can only describe as the gears of some machinery, rotating and marrying their dents and hollows in a perpetual movement. I turn my head left and right to follow the screeching notes bouncing off the walls, chasing each other, stretching to a distance that makes me picture my prison very empty and very wide.

Until the noise subsides to a low hum and stops, making space for the sound of steps slowly approaching me.

"How's your head?" A stream of energy speaks to me, flowing directly into my core, and wipes all the confusion from my mind by reigniting inside my head the past few hours of my life like a slap in the face.

All my words come back to me in a rush. "I feel like a giant hammer has beaten me. Thanks for your concern. What's next? A tea party before you send ransom letters to…whoever you think may care enough about me? I hope you don't expect me to ask how *your* day is going."

I'm not really sure what my value is, but if they've kept me alive until now, I'm entitled to ask questions, loads of them. But for some reason, they're all bottled up and struggle to come out one at a time. When one surfaces, another one immediately follows. They chase each other in a race to reach my tongue first, but end up colliding and popping like soap bubbles.

I tilt my head, searching for the disembodied steps, but whoever is in the room with me has stopped walking. Perhaps to enjoy the miserable show I put on for them.

I take a big breath, ready to blow out my defence once more, but the invisible walker starts moving again, each step accompanied by a clicking sound.

I snap my head back up, but something seals my mind and lips. *I must listen...*

No. No. I need to ask questions.

"Miss Crimson." The voice belongs to a man who has been speaking for years. Centuries. It's controlled, with no inflexion whatsoever, and is so soothing I could listen to it all day long.

"Have we met before? I don't remember your voice... And judging by how you treat your guests, I don't think you're the type of person I'd like to deal with. Ever." I blurt out my words because I fear I only have a few seconds of autonomy.

I'm panting, like I've run for miles and just stopped. "Where's my friend? What did you do to him?" *Please don't say Galen's been next to me all this time, but he's no longer moving or able to talk. Please don't even say his name…*

The stranger stops and chuckles with amusement. He sounds very close, as if we are at eye level. I can smell amber and musk cologne when he purrs, "Galen is fine."

My heart sinks. He is fine—and he is *now* part of this terrible picture.

I'm not here by accident; this man knows our names. My brain begins to sketch a question, but the words I need to voice haven't yet been invented.

The wall behind me pulls some of my hair when I press my head against it, trying to move away from the stranger. "Who are you?" I bite my lips until I taste blood, until my voice breaks. Tears wet the fabric tied around my eyes, and my lids sting, but the discomfort is nothing compared to what I experience when the man unties the cloth and reveals his face, which appears hazy behind my veil of tears—but too fucking familiar.

I blink the blur away, and my jaw drops when I recognise those chips of grey ice.

Roden's eyes.

"Sir, I…Why didn't I recognise your voice? How—" I stare at him, bewildered, when a sudden rattling, static sound explodes from the wall behind him.

I jerk my head to one side, looking over his shoulder. "What are all these screens for?" I blink fast to clear my view, finally recognising the source of the humming noise I heard when I regained my senses.

"Those, my child, are *my* windows to Horigos," Roden replies, standing up and turning his back to me.

I know there is something I mean to ask him, an urgent question, something I probably did ask a moment ago and forgot the answer for some odd reason.

He's tall, and not even this vast room, empty save for a shiny white piano and the screens, can diminish his stature. This man can tower over any person and take up space, making himself bigger if needed. This man both scares me and makes me feel safe.

Perhaps this is why, instead of trying to get up and leave, I remain with my back against the wall, waiting for him to speak again.

Are you crazy? Get up; this is not right. Remember the—

I must have hit my head. I hate this sense of forgotten thoughts.

"Aren't they majestic?" Roden opens his arm as if embracing the screens that cover the walls, from floor to a never-ending ceiling.

"This is where I decide which Horigean truly needs *me*. Every screen is a cry for help, my dear," he explains, cocking his head left and right.

One of the lower screens is projecting the video of a man, wearing faded newspapers as if they were a three-piece suit, pushing a shopping trolley filled to the brim with rubbish. While on the screen to the left, a girl runs by a river, as thin as the birch trees she passes by.

The scene rolls down and off the screen, only to reappear five positions below. The girl is no longer running, but drifting on the water, her hair floating like golden seaweed.

"What's just happened?" I can hardly tear my attention off the girl and focus on Roden.

He stands still momentarily, then eventually looks at me from over his shoulder, elegantly spinning his walking stick like an old-fashioned dancer—a friendly smile on his face as if amused by my interest in the fate of a stranger.

"The lower they go, the more desperate they are. And—ready to make a deal." Simple as that.

He puts both hands on the pommel of his cane and taps the point of his shiny white shoe to the rhythm of music I can't hear. Behind him, the river scene has slid to the very bottom of the wall. My eyes widen as the top of the girl's screen begins to turn black like a curtain slowly falling on a stage.

"What if they don't want to make a deal?" I mutter.

Roden's eyes narrow on me, but he doesn't move an inch.

I've seen his face many times, but it still shocks me how young he looks, despite his actual age, which is a detail - I imagine - he only shares with a chosen few, like Popplewish.

His face is one tone away from a wax mask, but not as fake—full lips and dark eyebrows, nearly as black as his hair. Everything about him is intense, powerful, and colourful, as though more life flows into him, extra blood in his veins, and more air than usual fills his lungs.

I wait for his answer, but something whispers in the back of my mind, disturbing my meeting with the Creator...*We're on the floor. Why am I on the floor—*

Roden hits the marble with his cane twice, and I blink as if someone has shone a bright light in my eyes.

"What if they like their life as it is?" I vomit the question as if I've been punched in my guts.

The corners of Roden's mouth lift in a wicked smile. "We show them what a waste of a good soul their choice would be."

"But that's *their* soul—"

His cane bites the floor again, but this time, a shooting pain behind my eyes silences me.

One second passes and the pain is gone.

"What was I saying?" I mumble. My tongue is like a fat piece of meat that doesn't belong to me.

Still smiling at me, Roden pulls a small remote control from the pocket of his perfectly ironed dark blue trousers and switches off all the screens.

I follow his every move in a daze, feeling like I'm not really here and he's just a projection.

Until he stands inches away from me, kneeling to meet my eyes. "Full of questions, are we? And I do like curiosity. In the right measure." The lower he gets, the more his voice changes, turning every word into shards of ice that scratch my mind.

And yet, his hand is warm and soft against my cheek when he says, "How about I show you the truth?"

Chapter 16 - Talking Mist
July

When the wall behind me begins to rumble and shake, I do not pay it much attention because my mind is filled with memories of the day I met Roden for the first time. That lucky day, he sensed me—one of his many children—and brought me to Libera.

Nearly twenty-two years have passed, and his face remains unchanged. The shade of his eyes is still that of a blue sky, sometimes darkened by passing clouds. I cannot forget that he is the saviour who sacrificed his very soul to create the beating essence of Libera, a realm of freedom for his people. A confined kingdom where he can keep an eye on all of us. *His* kingdom and his prison—because he and Libera are tethered to each other.

"My child, if you don't step aside, I'm afraid we'll reach an impasse," Roden states, with the same simplicity he's explained to me the meaning of the dozens of screens flickering in front of me.

He gently pulls me to my feet, spins me around and frees my wrists. My mind floats empty and light under his touch. A heavy piece of black rope falls to the floor with a thump like a dead, beautiful butterfly.

But my knees shake as if my body is trying to reject that connection.

"Have I done something wrong? Why am I *here*?" A thought is nagging in my mind, but it keeps slipping away whenever Roden speaks, blinks, or taps his cane on the floor.

But this is real. The pain in my wrists is real. The pounding in my head. The bitter tang in my mouth mixed with blood.

Roden clucks his tongue. "The punishment for a wrong action would mean stripping you of your precious talent and chucking you amongst the Rogues as if you were never trained to be a Harvester." He cocks his head, sliding his icy glare from one side of my face to the other.

I hold my breath and, even if my lungs begin to burn, I don't seem to remember how to exhale.

"But then I would need to quickly find someone else as skilled as you to separate your body from your useless, rotting soul. *And*—destroy it forever." He sighs as if talking about a domestic, annoying chore.

I swallow a lump of dread as he caresses my cheek with the back of his hand, brushing a lock of hair off my face, incapable of deciding if it's fear making me shake or if the floor is vibrating under my feet.

Roden's breath is like a wintry gust against my ear when he whispers, "Tell me, child, have you done anything to deserve such a treatment?"

Did I? I open my mouth, hoping the correct answer is waiting on my tongue, ready to come out, when the shaking halts.

Roden clutches my shoulder and gently - my body doesn't feel like resisting anyway - pulls me away from the wall. "Ah," he looks up at the ceiling. "The Chapter is here, and they're waiting for you."

I have met Roden many times, and each time, it was just to receive an assignment, and only if that concerned a Rogue, never a simple Nistares. He briefs me on where to find the Rogue, and I empty their bodies as quickly as possible so that Galen and his team can collect the vessels while I return to Libera with a vial full of black powder. Nothing like the purple glow of the Nistarei's souls, who keep fighting for freedom, even hours after my passage, flapping against the glass like trapped fireflies.

Stolen…

…glowing red…

An invisible, electric thread runs from my left temple to the right. "A wandering mind killed the cat. Not curiosity, I say." The tip of Roden's finger is like a needle slowly drilling into my head.

"I don't…" *Is this even my voice I hear?*

His hold on my shoulders tightens to the point I fear for my bones. "Now, now. We don't want to make them wait. Some of them can be very *unpleasant* to deal with if the person they want to see is late. Especially if they had to wake up on short notice at dawn."

As if activated by Roden's voice, the whole building rumbles beneath me, and a thin line appears on the wall opposite me, splitting into giant sliding doors.

When Roden slides his hands off me and extends them towards a lift that wasn't there until a moment ago, my world starts rotating again.

"After you." An order—not an invitation.

The light inside the huge lift is warm but unnatural because it comes from…

I step inside it, mesmerised by its golden glow. "Nowhere," I mutter.

"Marvellous, isn't it?" Roden comments, sauntering behind me. "The creation of a great mind."

I slowly turn and stare at Roden, agape, as he fills the entire space of the entrance. I'm probably too weak and tired to judge reality, but he seems to have grown taller within the few seconds I walked in front of him. His shoulders are larger and imposing.

A line forms between his eyebrows as he admires the inside of the lift, nodding his head. "Such a young, talented mind." His cane hits the metal floor so hard I jump back. "Why, what a pity it was, having to turn it off. He didn't bend, didn't break. Not even in front of his weeping, annoying children…"

My heart gasps.

For a split second, Roden forgets about me, and he stands alone inside the lift while I'm just like a ghost watching him, agape, with teary eyes.

Something starts bubbling inside me, and all the thoughts, so far pushed underwater by an invisible force, begin to fight their way to the surface.

But just when I'm about to lift my head above the water, something pushes me back.

Tap. Tap. Tap.

Wait, what was I thinking…?

Roden is staring at me like a statue framed by the warm light of the lift. He is immobile except for his right wrist, which flicks his walking stick against the metal wall.

I exhale, my entire body deflates, and every word in my head loses importance.

"What's happening to me?"

"It's just your soul, child. It's resounding with mine." He explains as if I'm supposed to understand. And oddly—I feel *safe*.

But you kept me here like a pris—

He flashes a cold smile at me, and my chaotic thoughts go silent again.

But this time, some sort of recognition lingers; even if I'm drowning, Roden will always allow me one big breath before I get too dangerously close to death.

We sigh simultaneously.

Our chests rise and fall in unison.

"I think you are ready now." He turns and touches his fingers to the side wall. "To the Chapter, please".

"Roden?"

He hums in response and taps the floor twice with the end of his golden-crowned cane. The doors slide shut without a sound, and the lift starts upwards.

"Yes, July?"

Not 'his child' anymore?

I hesitate, studying the tip of my shoes as though I've just discovered I have feet. "Will I remember these last few hours after the Chapter has finished with me?" I wait for that familiar and dreadful sense of forgetfulness to embrace me again. But it doesn't come.

When I look up, Roden is studying me the way adults do when children ask, *Why doesn't the sun fall,* and *can frogs fly?*

"That depends on you, of course."

The lift seems to ascend endlessly until it abruptly halts, its doors open, and white light envelops me with wisps of smoke that curl around my legs and waist. Within its milky mist, I hear voices - talking, singing, crying - but their words are unintelligible.

"Earlier, you saw their faces. This is how I listen to them." Roden's voice is smooth and calm.

"Nistarei." My lips barely move, and I can't stop staring at the light.

Within the compact misty mass are minuscule floating dots of brighter light, so shiny and inviting that I can't stop myself from stretching a hand towards them. But all I experience is a sharp pain when Roden hits my fingers with his cane.

"Curiosity is not just the cat's enemy, Miss Crimson. We are not there yet. Be patient because *up-up-up we go again,*" he croons, and his voice trails while he repeats that line a few more times.

Once more, the thoughts in my head turn light and thin because *they do not matter.*

I don't matter unless Roden allows it.

Chapter 17 - The Chapter
July

We restart our journey inside the lift, whose doors are so shiny I can see Roden's reflection in them, watching my every move while he taps a finger on the head of his walking stick—a knot of silver and golden, intertwined threads, protecting a purple stone.

I notice we've come to a halt only when the doors open, revealing an oval hall made entirely of marble, with sleek walls lined by darkened windows. A space that smells like…

Emptiness.

"Ah, perfect timing." Roden clicks his tongue and smiles at a petite young woman, dressed like she has to attend a ball, who appears on our left, carrying a bundle of papers too thick for her delicate arms.

"Mr Breith, they're ready for you in room thirty-nine," she chimes, with the voice of a bird.

"Many thanks, Theresa. How many years has it been since I offered you this role? You can call me Roden," he purrs.

I shiver as if shaking off maggots crawling up my back.

We don't wait for Theresa to bow, giggle, or do whatever suits her character. "Let's go meet the Chapter then." Roden rushes me off the lift, flattening a hand against my back before stepping in front of me.

"The Chapter?" I echo, tasting the start of a thought at the back of my mind. But the thought is gone as soon as my focus seems to have broken free from its cage. When no answer comes, I waddle behind him like a loyal puppy.

Our steps have no sound, no matter my heels or Roden's expensive shoes. I'm still in the outfit I chose for my dinner with Galen - a mid-length, deep-red, pleated skirt, a black sleeveless top, and leather ankle boots. I must have lost my jacket somewhere between the restaurant and—

I was in a car...

Tap. Tap.

A thick curtain shadows my memories with comforting warmth.

I should be shivering, or at least feeling uncomfortable, surrounded by all this cold marble and with nothing covering my naked arms. Instead, the hall is just the right temperature, even though the glass of the windows is so dark I bet not even the brightest light could filter through.

I stare at Roden's back. He has fallen silent and is cocking his head side to side as if tuning in to a melody I can't hear.

As soon as we stepped out of the lift, I perceived the hall as a small space with a single door at the opposite end.

However, as we walk further, I realise that the architect must have used a mind-blowing optical illusion, because the oval-shaped hall stretches into a corridor, and our walk to the door appears to be longer than I thought it would be.

I doubt Roden will explain the trick, but this gives me time to look around—and up. There are no chandeliers or light bulbs, yet the room is filled with light.

Where has Theresa disappeared to? I look over my shoulder and struggle even to see the lift entrance or the other thirty-something rooms that should precede the one we're heading to.

"Don't worry, a bit of dizziness is normal. This hall is something else. Consider yourself lucky, my dear. Few people can say they've had the honour to appreciate this marvellous construction. Ah, such a great mind and such a pity…" Roden's voice is warm and comforting as he steps to one side, gesturing for me to go ahead.

Well, no. I don't know half of it, dear Roden; I'd like to stop and comment.

Instead, I nod like a marionette, follow his demand - once again - and almost bump my nose against door-thirty-freaking-nine, which had decided to cut the distance between us and materialise right in front of me when I thought we still had miles to go.

I blink, perplexed, searching over my shoulder for an explanation on Roden's face as he gently pushes me out of the way, huffing an amused laugh.

One swift rotation of the doorknob, under his hand's light touch, and the silence that has accompanied us until now leaves the stage, replaced by a concert of shrieking chairs, hectic voices and the clanging of glasses.

"If he decides to make an appearance…"

"Roden…"

"*Sir*, I believe that is what you meant to say…"

"Shush. Amelia."

"Oh, here we go, now she's going to go full on *how-dare-you-shush-me*…"

"Silence! They're here."

"Sir, welcome…"

The threshold is narrow, and I have to wait behind Roden, but all the voices carry the same tone—taken aback and reverential.

The people in the room stop talking and turn in our direction, like trained soldiers, as Roden saunters inside, just far enough for me to squeeze in.

"Friends, please, take a seat." Roden's hand flutters over the room, virtually patting every head. "Or am I to think you were about to leave? I like to believe my invitation, although with short notice, found you all in good health. You have been chosen to be part of my Chapter; therefore, should you be summoned in the middle of the night, you are expected to be ready."

I follow his movements as he scans the room from left to right before adding, "Always." At the sudden switch in his voice from a welcoming tone to that of a born and bred leader, all members of the Chapter nod at once, and some of them finally place their *chosen* butts on the chairs.

What is this farce?

Roden turns to me and my mind shuts down. All that matters is that I listen to *him*.

"Don't be afraid, July," he addresses me. "After all, we are here for you today."

For or because of?

The room quickly fills with the sounds of complaining. Some are only muttered through yawns. Some—intentionally louder.

Ignoring their reactions, Roden marches towards nobody in particular, but instead to a display of coffee and fruit, beautifully arranged on a table by the wall opposite the door.

I linger by the entrance for a little longer, studying sleepy, all familiar faces and hands holding steaming mugs of coffee.

Alphonse Tydell is staring at me, sitting at the very end of a long table in the middle of the room. He is wearing what appears to be expensive mustard silk pyjamas, with his hair wet but elegantly combed back. His lips close and open, like those of a fish out of breath, as he squints and massages his eyes, seemingly shocked to see *me* here instead of any other student.

My chest shrinks a little at his baffled and disappointed expression, even though I'm unsure what I should feel guilty for.

Standing by Mr. Tydell's right, Amelia Kram glares at me from over a pair of shades large enough to cover her smooth-skinned face. She's one of the youngest teachers, an expert in Horigos regional idioms. Her classes are optional, and I've never found learning Vinenzia's long-lost dialect useful other than to sound annoyingly pompous. Removing her glasses and pulling out a chair with manicured fingers - a gold ring shining on each one - she sits without taking her lilac eyes off me. Her brows arch slightly, as she stares at me like I'm an insignificant insect that has sneaked inside the room without invitation.

The other Chapter members have gathered around the little banquet table to refill their cups and exchange some words with Roden, but his mouth seems to move only to drink coffee and nibble on a strawberry.

Ignored by the person they unquestionably adore more than their own lives, Nikrah Skell - expert in Horigos' history - and Master Donatori, Proja Dryb'He, stalk back to their chairs in silence.

"I don't know if I should be congratulating you or be upset." A voice sparks over my shoulders, pushing me further inside the room like a gust of wind.

I instinctively turn around, forgetting the other people in the room, and stare at Evelyn Popplewish, clapping as if marking the end of an outstanding performance.

From the moment I woke up in the room full of screens to my meeting with Roden, to later when we stepped inside the lift, nothing made much sense to me; like the pages of a book full of pictures being flipped too fast before my eyes.

But, now, all I can remember of that book is its last page—Evelyn Popplewish's face. Well, one of her faces. One which I've never seen before. Heavy, concerned, but also veiled by an inexplicable hint of pride.

She drove me here.

No. That is not a proper thought. Better forget about it and shove it under the rug of things I'm not supposed to know.

"Why am I here?" I mumble instead. My gaze rests on her face and tight lips, pressed together as if keeping her words at bay. "Miss Popplewish, have I done something wrong?"

When she holds her hands up and lets them fall to her side with a sigh, confusion and a touch of worry rush through me.

"Roden, is she still *oblivious*?" A pressing edge marks her tone.

In response, a high-pitched, little cry comes from behind me, and I cast a curious look in its direction, only to witness Tydell looking down at the table and shrinking in his chair.

Clearing his throat, Nikrah cuts short his exchange of words with Amelia, brushing biscuit crumbs from his black shirt. "She wouldn't be if *someone* had arrived on time—like the rest of us." He leans over the table, resting his chin in his hands, shooting a rigid smirk at Popplewish.

"At least some of us had the decency to make it on time *and* look presentable." A petite silhouette steps out of a dark corner. Like shards of broken crystal in a sea of black sclera, her eyes cut through me with such an intensity that I couldn't look anywhere else, even if I wanted to.

I fully turn towards her, my jaw drops a little as Lily Drestall, the very first female Master Writer in our history, flashes a smile at me before moving her attention to Professor Skell.

"Have you forgotten to shower after your gym session, Nikrah?"

She looks him up, and wrinkles her nose in disgust and, tucking behind her ear a curly lock of shiny, black hair that's escaped from her immaculate bun, she aims for a chair as far from him as possible.

Proja Dryb'He, the Donatore, famous for his impeccable art of allocating new souls to their new bodies whilst leaving no memories of their past lives, runs a hand through his dark hair, slumping back in his chair. His purple pupils shrink, almost swallowed by the total black of his eyes, when he comments, annoyed, "Can you two take your former not-so-former lovers' arguments somewhere else? Don't forget there's a young mind in the room—"

"Debatable. When did you become such a prude, Projjy?" Nikrah stands up, squares his large shoulders and broad chest, picks up his chair, and moves to sit between Amelia and Tydell, whose face shows all his unspoken discomfort when Nikrah pushes him aside to make space.

Nikrah offers Tydell a smirk, then continues, "Besides, Evelyn said it—Miss Crimson's mind is still sleeping in whatever lavender field Roden sent her to. And," he inflates his chest, tapping a finger on his right bicep, "Don't act annoyed when you, and lovely Amelia here, would have also loved to share a piece of this."

"Pompous buffoons," I hear Amelia muttering while lifting a cup of coffee to her overly plumped lips.

This is not normal… These are my teachers… this… "Wait.." I voice my train of thought without realising it, surprised when I'm finally allowed to grasp my own words and memories—myself.

But Roden has other plans. "Enough," he hits the floor twice with the end of his walking stick.

I jump, and so does Alphonse Tydell, as his pink eyes widen and fall on me while the other teachers only clear their throats or hum in agreement.

"Thank you," Roden continues with a quick bow. "Evelyn, please, an open heart is all I ask. July needed a bit more time; her mind was too agitated when I met her."

"But we don't have time—" Popplewish replies from behind me.

"Well, we'll have to make it then… After all, you only brought her here last night. A sudden change of plans requires quick thinking."

"What about safety?" Popplewish disputes.

"Do you think it would've been better to let her snoop around and ask questions of the wrong people? What I asked you to do was probably the only thing that saved the Chapter and July. Let's not forget about your pretty protégé…"

Popplewish lets out a loud sigh of exasperation. "And I'm starting to regret it, Roden. She seems to fight harder every time her memory gets reset."

I can't ignore her fists clenching when she walks past me. Her dark blue velvet nightgown sweeps the floor, but everything around her remains silent, unmovable, as if her feet don't even touch the ground.

Would she remember me?

My head spins slightly, but I know I must stay alert. I listen to their dialogue as if watching from behind a glass wall.

Roden observes Popplewish from behind his steaming cup of coffee, his icy, grey eyes narrow on her back as if searching for something she left unspoken. Then he takes a quick sip and says, "We can't let *him* escape again, and July is our only weapon at the moment. What would you like to do? Waiting, who knows for how many years, hoping we find someone else with her power? Unless you want me to—"

"As you wish," Popplewish snaps at him, spinning towards me.

I've never seen her drop her guard like this. Defeated, she stares at me, the need to tell me something flashing behind her pastel eyes. But I'm soon left staring at her back again as she walks to the table and sits next to Lily Drestall, acknowledging her with a nod and half a smile.

Roden summons the attention he *deserves* by tapping the top of his cane against the wooden edge of the table. "Good, now we can all sit comfortably, and—" he stops, focusing on the door, still open, behind me.

Theresa sways in, like a feather across the floor, as she glides up to me, holding an extra chair. When she puts the chair down, Roden snaps his fingers—and I collapse on it like a rag doll.

The flimsy veil that has covered my true sight up until now shreds, and I begin to connect each face in the room to a specific memory. Nikrah Skell's intense blue eyes, with a little sunshine explosion in the centre, his lists of dates, and comparison of the various ages of Horigos to a giant pile of pancakes. Proja Dryb'He and his lessons on handling a still-pumping soul and placing it back in its new vessel without damaging it.

When I look at Popplewish, the image flashing in my mind almost stops my heart. For a split second, I'm in the back of her car, fearing for my life and doubting Galen—my best friend.

Would she remember… me

… some.

"No!" I take my head in my hands, terrified all my memories will fall through the cracks again. "I want to remember it all."

Roden, unfazed as if I didn't just shout in front of everyone, walks towards me, holding one hand up, "Breathe, July—"

I push my chair back, shaking my head, "Don't come near me… Where is Galen?" I search around the room, hoping to see his face.

I stand up too abruptly, and my legs don't respond when I try to run away. My eyes dart from face to face so quickly it hurts. I shut them tight, feeling a hand hovering over my shoulder like static electricity.

"July, calm down…" Popplewish's voice is like a wake-up call from a nightmare.

I press my fists onto my eyes, and my ribcage inflates nearly to its breaking point. When I exhale, a needle pricks the bubble of emotions stuck in my belly and memories begin to bleed out.

Immaterial, hot blades slice through my chest when all the memories climb back out, digging their claws into my mind. Of me throwing up outside a restaurant and a car taking me somewhere while I'm half-conscious. The screens, the voices—the light. It has to be real; I'm not imagining it because what I taste on my tongue is blood, not just the bitter flavour of lies.

"Quick, give her a tissue…" A quivering voice speaks from someplace far.

"She's bleeding," another voice adds, worried.

"It's just a scratch, leave her alone…" Popplewish—Evelyn Popplewish. She's trapped me in this never-ending nightmare.

"Galen…" I find my voice again.

I open my eyes in shock, panting. My hands are sweaty, and something warm is trickling down from the corner of my mouth. I double over, spitting blood on the marble floor.

With my head between my hands, I pray for my brain to stop igniting memories like fireworks—the lift, the infinite hall, Roden tapping that damn walking stick. Memories play behind my eyes, like the scenes from Nistarei's everyday life I witnessed on the screens.

Witnessed to their end.

All those faces. Who are we to decide?

Someone puts a hand on my back while I whisper *Galen* repeatedly—my anchor. When I finally look up, I don't see Galen's eyes, but the swirling galaxies in Miss P's irises. And for a moment, she's again the sweet, wise creature I have loved and respected my whole life.

"It's all right. The reset process can be confusing if done too many times, but you'll be okay." Popplewish brushes the top of my head, and as much as I want to forget about everything and leave it all behind, a terrible presentiment weighs me down, gurgling from my guts now that she stands so close to me.

I wriggle free of her touch and put some space between us. My feet are unsteady, and my knees shake, but I can't stand her presence. My stomach churns.

I need to open my mouth, whether to throw up or to spit accusations, and I don't care who is watching me, about their role, or if they can harm me—too late for that anyway. "Too many times?" I blurt out. "How many times did you fuck with my brain?"

Fuck! I clench my stomach and jerk my head back up to look Evelyn straight in the eyes, digging my teeth in where my cheek split to stay alert and focused, "You are the recycling squad."

Chapter 18 - Facing Wars
July

I speak again before anyone can stop me, "All these years, pretending it was all a myth and forbidding students to talk about it and research it. This is why. *This* is the reason. You were hiding in plain sight."

I'm addressing every person in the room, studying their reaction, and taking a mental note of each face. A sudden need to laugh roars inside me, and my focus stops on Roden. His aura of authority quickly melts before my eyes.

"If you've dragged me here to end this—explain one thing to me. What do you really do with the souls *I* bring back to you? Those poor Rogues, *you* didn't have time to save… What terrible power do the squads have that makes people scream in agony?" I clamp my mouth shut, but it's too late.

"Careful with the accusations," Nikrah Skell mutters without looking at me, distractedly observing his nails.

"What a bunch of nonsensical blabbering," Amelia chimes in, starting to get up, her lilac eyes slicing over me.

But Nikrah places a hand over Amelia's, his eyes fixed on me,

"Stay, you'll thank me later. I can't wait to hear what else Miss Crimson thinks we do." He interlaces his fingers behind his neck, leaning back in his chair as if watching a show. "Go ahead, July, tell us more."

I ignore his arrogant comments. If I have to go, I may as well do it knowing what I'm risking my life for. I return my attention to Roden, "At least, swear you didn't hurt Galen. He has no part in this; it was all my fault. I wanted to know—"

Before I can blurt out more details I'm not even sure they're aware of, Nikrah sighs dramatically, "Galen, Galen, Galen. I thought you had this under control, Eve. But it sounds to me like you've completely let them loose this time. Great job." He claps twice, patronisingly.

Popplewish glares at him. "Remember how and why you were allowed into the Chapter."

Her words strike home, and Nikrah shrinks in his chair.

Ignoring more whispered comments in the background, Popplewish moves a few steps towards me, but I stretch an arm out to keep her away.

She sighs, "Oh, please, just stop being silly and listen, young lady." She pinches the bridge of her nose.

My mouth opens, but Roden is quicker. "Not one curly hair on his head has been pulled. That much I can promise you." He smiles, opening his arms as if to prove himself harmless. "Why don't we start from what you think you know? I've heard you've been busy, scavenging for clues here and there, and I would like you to tell me about this video my friends here are so afraid of."

In the background, Tydell squeals, causing Amelia to grin and Lily to grunt in exasperation. "Control yourself, Tydell. You sound like a pig ready for the butcher," the latter hisses, giving him a sideways glare.

I stall, "How do you know about the video?"

"Ah, so there is one," Roden clicks his tongue with satisfaction, and I silently curse my loose tongue.

"I don't know very much," I begin, keeping my voice steady, causing more whispering and mumbling from the Chapter.

Amelia snaps her head at Proja, her auburn bob slapping her right cheek, her lips forming a soundless word I can't understand. But when Proja shakes his head slowly, Amelia drops the subject and returns to looking at me.

Popplewish runs a hand over the smooth side of the table, as if hoping to find the right thing to say carved on the polished wooden surface. "You can speak freely. Nobody is here to judge or harm you but to understand and rectify mistakes."

"Hold on a second. This wasn't agreed—" Nikrah starts, but it's his turn to be shushed.

"With all due respect, Nik, shove your not-agreed thoughts back in your mouth and shut up for once. Not everybody loves the sound of your voice as much as you do." A remarkably composed and controlled Lily Drestall slams her delicate hand on the table, making Nikrah flinch and scowl, but ultimately leaving him speechless.

The short argument only distracts me for a second, and images of the night before spark in my mind when my eyes meet Popplewish's again. I give her and Roden a polite smile, anchoring myself with the deepest breath I can take. My chest expands and my shoulders rise. I hold it for as long as I can before I open my mouth to let it all out.

The room falls silent as I describe that day in the cafeteria: my encounter with some students looking at a video, the skin-crawling sound of a suffering beast. I don't hold back on any details except for Lucretia's name. She's not my friend, but I'm not ready to throw her under the Chapter-bus.

When I'm done talking, Roden starts walking towards me. I shake the stiffness off my shoulders and wait for his verdict.

With one hand behind his back and the other on his cane, a golden ring with his initials engraved, twinkling on his left ring finger, he saunters towards me, tilting his head to one side like I'm just a cute puppy.

"I can't deny this is an embarrassing incident, but it is not irrevocable. Thank you for your honesty, Miss Crimson."

He doesn't only take me by surprise, but I can hear some of the people present sucking in disappointment and tons of questions, which Roden ignores, as if they were but a choir of fruit flies. "My fellow friends, we are here today, not to judge." He stops behind me, and for a split second, I worry he will play his freaky trick on me again and take all my memories. But he pats my head and giggles, "No need to fear. I want your mind to be as clear and awake as possible."

His touch is light on my hair, like the nerve-soothing warmth of a hot shower after hours spent training outdoors in winter. But I fear it will burn me to ashes if I say the wrong thing.

Roden gently leads me towards the empty seat, and I let him.

"Miss Crimson, I – *we* – are very sorry you had to live with such a sword dangling over your head."

My chair is made of hardwood, but it is a more comfortable seat after the hard floor I woke up on earlier. From this new perspective, Roden looks taller and grander, but I set his aura of authority aside and say - "It'd be great if I knew what this sword is made of—" - causing a new wave of whispers and comments. I will make them talk, even if they're unwilling to give me answers.

Amelia drums her fingers on the table, singsonging to herself, but loud enough so everyone can hear, "Careful what you wish for—"

"Amelia!" Popplewish cuts her off and sits next to me. Her hand slides over mine, but I retract it like one of those anemones I love watching on Horigos zoos when I have time to kill. Except I'm not the one with the poisonous touch in the room.

As if sensing the growing tension, Roden cocks his head, giving me another of his fatherly looks. "Do not doubt, not even for a second, that we don't appreciate that you've kept your fears a secret all this time. Well, we know you talked to lovely Galen, but that's also *fixable*," he smiles.

I shiver and grip the bottom of my chair, bracing myself for what's coming.

"What will you do to my soul?" Once again, my mouth is faster than my judgement, and I am not the only one startled by my stupid question. Alphonse Tydell gasps, and Proja stands up in such a rush that his chair topples back.

"Am I the only one thinking Miss Crimson kept the juicy part of her story from us?" Amelia echoes Proja's reaction with more elegance, her white gold bracelets jingling melodiously, like her voice, when she interlaces her fingers under her chin. "She seems to know more than we thought. Why waste our time? In the past, cases like this were archived in the blink of an eye—"

Nikrah finishes her sentence with a smirk on his face, "Ah, the straightforward old days."

For once, Miss P. keeps her opinion to herself. She has to have one; she clearly does, but the pain in her eyes when I look at her suggests that I may have crossed the line.

"Roden, if I may," Popplewish presses both hands on the table and straightens her spine as if uncoiling one word at a time, "We are misplacing the attention of this meeting. July has already been through a rough night - not that she didn't deserve it - but I'd suggest, for the sake of the Chapter and our sleep-deprived minds, to get straight to the point."

For the first time in hours, we are on the same page, but I quickly look away to a random point on the wall instead of giving her the satisfaction of seeing agreement in my eyes.

I know she's moved her gaze onto me. It tickles me with the

same electricity that made the hair on my neck stand up when younger Galen and I were busy in some illegal business, and Miss P. would take her time to observe us before making an appearance.

In the corner of my eye, I catch Roden nodding at her with approval before she bows her head and continues. "Do you know, July, what happens when the truth is bent a million times?"

"It turns into a lie?" I echo her questioning tone.

"Correct."

Finally, some common ground. I'm all in as I blurt out, "Like making us believe that some souls are so rotten they cannot be saved? Or represent a threat to our people, like the Rogues? Sometimes, I do believe, we throw them an infected hook, coated in gold and sugar, that makes them decay the moment they accept Roden's deal..."

Someone scoffs. Nikrah, most likely, but nobody acknowledges him.

Unexpectedly, Popplewish smiles. She was waiting for me to run the race and meet her at this exact point. "Do you know the natural evolution of a well-constructed but terrible lie?"

"Argument? Questions? Mistrust?" I shrug.

"War."

I open my mouth and close it, finding myself wordless.

How did we get from a video shared among students to war?

I can't take my eyes off Popplewish, as if no one else is in here with us.

She reciprocates my questioning look before pushing against the table to stand up and heading to the other end of the room. Her movements are fluid, almost staged. The way she meets the eyes of the other professors, the brief pause she takes to look back at me before sliding her fingers up the wall. "I'd like to show you something. Sometimes images are better than words."

I hear the click of a switch, and the light begins to drip off the ceiling, like wax down a candle, before being sucked in by the floor.

When my eyes adjust, and the darkness makes space for a more subtle luminescence, I hear a rolling sound as a white screen unfolds behind Popplewish.

She folds her hands over her lap. "There is someone I'd like you to meet."

Chapter 19 - Fair Exchange
July

February 12th - Sector 43 - 6.30 AM

§ Subject 0-Version 25 §

While the meaningless words flash on the screen, chairs move to face the white panel, accompanied by muffled comments that quickly fade into utter silence.

Pictures start rolling on the white fabric sheet, showing a woman giving birth with a man kneeling at her bedside. When I blink, the scene is gone, replaced by a reverse countdown from zero to five. The chubby face of a young boy pops up after the number five has flashed twice; tears mark his cheeks.

I look down, following the child's gaze to the cause of his pain—the broken toy resting in his little hands.

The scene starts shrinking into a black dot until it completely covers the sad face, and the number six appears in the middle.

A couple. Their pale features, like treetops in the mist, stare at the boy while he stands under a kitchen door frame. It's hard to tell if his shoulders are shaking or if we are disturbing the fabric panel with our breath.

Is he scared?

Eight. This is not a countdown, but the boy's age.

There's an envelope on the kitchen table, and the woman from the previous picture is holding a cheque—big money, judging by the glass falling from her open hand towards the floor, already splattered with milk.

The woman's eyes are wide, but what calls to me are her lips, tight, stretched against her teeth, trying to hold back a smile.

Then something else distracts me. Dark red letters are watermarked on the back of the cheque, the same as on Roden's ring—RB.

I blink faster, hoping to speed up to the end because I can't bear the pain slithering through those pictures. I don't even know the child's name, but he makes me feel uncomfortable, as if his pain projects off the pictures onto me.

The screen twitches, and the picture turns into a video of a room with walls covered in posters of galaxies and winged creatures. The little boy is asleep, one arm resting over his head. Whoever is recording him zooms in, and I press my back against my chair as if preparing for the drop of a roller coaster.

He moves in his sleep and turns over.

I reckon he is now a teenager. I squint and lean over to look closer at his face, the shape of his jaw shadowed by a young beard. His light brown hair is ruffled against the pillow. Underneath the lids, his eyes are moving fast, left and right. They're not entirely shut, and a hint of light green, between the double line of dark lashes, captures my attention.

"He's having a nightmare," I say between my teeth, but nobody seems to be paying attention to me. I clench my fingers into fists when a slight wince flashes across his face. We both hold our breaths momentarily, separated by many miles and years.

"Not again, please." The boy jolts upright and screams; his face is pale and covered in sweat. As pale as I fear mine has suddenly become, the moment his eyes pierce the screen and meet mine. The hair on my arms stands up...

I shake my head... *I must have imagined it.* The echo of his pain lingers in the room, but nobody seems to care except for me. I quickly look around, and every face I meet is relaxed as if they've all watched this before.

The young man and his room fade to a black flashing dot on the screen, and light begins to spread all around me, forcing me to face the Chapter and its lies once again.

"What you've just witnessed is a *glitch*, July. An experiment, some may call it. But we prefer—a rebel soul." Popplewish's voice rolls across the table.

I was never so bold as to hold Miss P.'s gaze for longer than a few seconds, but how she's just spoken of that poor, scared child makes my blood boil. "A glitch? That's a living being, for fuck's sake—"

"That language is not—" Lily Drestall starts.

I push back in my chair, which skitters across the floor and stops inches from hitting the wall behind me. I'm too aware of my face getting red and warm with rage as I snap at Lily with disgust, throwing my hands up, "What? Appropriate? Accepted? Was it appropriate to pay a mother to give away her son? Because that's what the cheque was for, wasn't it? You bought *him*." I scan the room, which is lined with emotionless faces, like dusty portraits from centuries ago.

Lily distractedly spins a thin gold ring around her finger, but her voice is sharp when she says, "What a ridiculous assumption. Have you ever considered observing what *you* think is the truth from another perspective? *Before* voicing your opinions, perhaps?"

I root my feet into the floor. "A bad apple tastes rotten from whatever side you bite it." I can hardly hear myself speaking over the throbbing sound in my head.

Roden, who has enjoyed my outburst from his spot next to the screen, pulls out a purple handkerchief from his pocket and starts polishing the jewelled top of his cane. "I'd rather say it was a fair exchange of *goods*, Miss Crimson," he says, slightly arching his eyebrows without looking at me.

At the same time, Miss Popplewish activates the switch on the wall to roll the screen back up. "July," she calls for my attention, "We didn't experiment on him. We just took him back. Those people took care of him, but they also had to use their own savings to provide him with a roof, warm clothes, and a normal life. They brought him up as if he were their biological son." She pauses, searches for Roden's eyes, then sighs loudly. "He's a Rogue of a kind you've never met before."

I bite the inside of my cheek, which still hurts and tastes of blood.

Amelia intervenes, yawning dramatically, "This romantic, poetic reveal is killing me, Eve. Just give her the whole story so we can return to our lives." Her hair frames one side of her face when she rests her head on her left hand.

I look around to study everyone's reaction, but I freeze when I meet Roden's eyes, glaring at me with a new, daunting light. "Absolutely." His hands tighten on the walking cane pommel as he leans forward with a satisfied smirk. "Miss Crimson can have whatever she needs— If we reach a *deal...*"

I don't know where I found the energy to react, but my hands slam on the table, causing a brief commotion. "A deal? *You* drugged me, kidnapped me, hurt me," I hold up my wrists, still carrying the marks left by the ties, "And all you have to offer is a freaking deal? Is this your way to make me believe I still have a choice?"

Nikrah laughs nervously while Amelia leaves her seat to grab a fresh cup of coffee. "We're never going to leave this room," I hear her muttering.

Roden's serene face twitches with surprise. He scans me, head to toe and his nose wrinkles as if I smell like a perfect-plan breaker.

I swallow a knot of fear but continue, "Since I can remember, I've been following orders. Your orders—and never, not once, questioned my actions..."

Tydell shifts in his chair as if on fire, while Proja coughs, covering his mouth. "Egocentric little—"

"Not now, Proja." Lily snaps, making my attention fall briefly on the Master Donatori's tanned face.

I ride the wave of adrenaline currently keeping me awake. "Let's pretend I'm an egocentric little prick. You're a Master Donatori. You surely know what happens to the decaying souls I bring back from Horigos. Not the nice ones who've tried their best to pay Roden back but didn't succeed. I'm talking about those pieces of shit who use what Roden gives them to hurt other Horigeans that no other Reaper is so keen to harvest."

I turn to stare at Proja, straight in those black, so full of themselves, eyes. "What do you do with them if they're too dirty, too sinful for a new vessel?" My chest expands, and I hold my breath for a second. "Do you recycle them for other purposes? Like that rebel on the screen?"

Amelia sighs so theatrically that Nikrah Skell and I roll our eyes simultaneously.

"Oh, don't worry, Miss Kram, I'm just twisting and turning the truth." My smile for Amelia is so fake that it hurts the corner of my mouth. "Besides, I can ask whatever I want. Roden will erase my mind like a chalkboard if I touch any topics I'm not supposed to."

My train of thought unravels faster than my mouth can keep up, and faster than the people in the room can follow, as I start pacing back and forth.

"Someone has to stop this," Tydell mutters, losing the battle with his glasses after they've slid down his sharp nose twice. Eventually, he takes them off and hangs them on the collar of his oversized shirt.

Roden clicks his tongue twice, silencing everyone. "Absolutely not. I want to hear what else Miss Crimson can come up with." His grey eyes light up with a predatory gleam.

I survey the room. All eyes are fixed on me, some begging me to shut up and let this come to an end, and some intrigued, whether by my newly found courage or recklessness, who knows.

"Fine," I say, opening my arms, addressing Popplewish and offering her an invitation to tell me the truth. "What do you have to say?" Physically and mentally exhausted, I lift my chair from where I sent it toppling moments ago and slump back on it, holding my hand up as Popplewish motions towards me. "I can clearly hear you from where you are."

She presses her lips together, pulling her silvery, ginger hair onto one shoulder. "What I'm about to say will shock you and, knowing you, probably make you angry at the people in this room…"

I pucker my lips and shake my head. "I think you've succeeded at that already."

"July—"

"I'm sorry. Go ahead."

"What we did to that man was to preserve our talents and ensure nobody would exploit the Rogues by hunting them down."

I fear what's coming. But I nod, pushing down the many questions inside me.

Miss P. moves closer, and this time I let her. "Truth is, there are no *bad* souls. Only *split* ones. Tell me, July, why do we keep answering the cries of the Horigeans even if they mainly see us as ruthless traders of souls?" She gives me time to think about it.

"This sounds like our very first lesson—"

"Answer me, please." Popplewish folds her hands in front of her.

My shoulders rise and lower with my breath. "To allow a chance at a better life to those who're willing to *sacrifice* their soul—"

"That's harsh and, what someone may say, a bit rebellious," Nikrah comments, tapping a finger on the table without looking at me.

Popplewish's face remains unreadable, her eyes steady on me. "That's one version many would agree with." Her lips twitch, and she unfolds her hands, smoothing invisible wrinkles on her gown. "It's because they were less fortunate, and it's our duty to share our gift with them, should they wish so."

Not exactly Roden's words in the screens room… I force my mind to focus.

"And because we can return a purified soul to Horigos, had its previous owner not been worthy of it," Roden singsongs, talking about souls as if pieces of mouldable clay.

Or perhaps that soul didn't want to be part of your deal from the beginning…

"Then why don't we give them a better chance to deserve that soul? You never put a limit on what they ask of you. Why don't you give them more time to repay you? Surely, you have it in abundance—" The words escape my mouth before I can stop them.

Sitting right opposite me, Amelia places her mug back on the table louder than needed, as if to mark her presence. "Remember, girl, we don't work for them. We don't owe them anything."

"The point is—" Miss P. puts both hands on the table, leaning forward as if asking for silence and no more interruptions, "It's not up to us to decide how long someone has to pay us back." A pause. "Not anymore, anyway."

Doubt and confusion must have made my face an easily readable page because Popplewish nods slightly to confirm her last words.

She exchanges a quick look with Roden, who simply opens his arms and admits, "Something—Someone, is intercepting whatever soul strikes a deal with me. And they are not making a distinction between Rogues and Nistarei. They are stealing *my* souls before their time is up, making them disappear from my radar."

"But how do they—"

"Find the Rogues without Roden's abilities?" Tydell, who's been silent for a while except for random sounds of discomfort and surprise, finishes my question. His voice has lost the gentle curve he always uses with the students.

I nod.

"Someone is selling the Nistarei. Someone from—Libera?" My lips move slowly.

"And the Rogues," Roden adds.

Am I on trial?

I push myself up, stomping my foot to appreciate the solid ground, which I fear may crumble from under me soon, "Is this why I'm here? You think I'm the person selling such information?" My hands curl into fists as I snap my head towards Popplewish.

Amelia bursts into a laugh, "Oh, girl, you're so innocent. You'd be expired if Roden ever doubted you. Sit down, and start blinking again before your eyes fall out of your skull."

I bite my tongue and go back to my chair. "What does this have to do with the man in the video?" I jab my finger at the point where the screen was.

Popplewish lets out a long breath, massaging her temples. "Roden, I think you can take it from here," she says as she sits down beside me.

Roden nods. His body seems to be carved in stone; nothing moves except for his hands, the right stroking his perfectly shaped, beard and the left holding the cane, its long fingers flexing and relaxing like tendrils.

"That man is a Rogue and holds one of the toughest souls I've ever encountered. Before *we* discovered your incredible talent, many Harvesters tried to bring his soul back to me," - his glacial look falls somewhere between Amelia and Nikrah before returning his attention to me. "But they've always miserably *failed* and only retrieved but mere pieces of it. Minuscule grains of it—useless. There was always a stubborn, last kernel missing…"

"That's impossible; by what Popplewish said, he's still very much alive and his mind is perfectly functioning," I exclaim.

Roden gives me a quick bow, placing a hand above his heart, "Apologies, my dear, let me give you some context. Rogues belong to me. I let some of them roam free and untrained past the critical age of five to see if they have enough willpower to stay alive without losing their minds. Some do and that's when your wonderful abilities become the only barriers between those *savages* and us Harvesters. But a few Rogues just become so weak and tasteless that I don't see the point of sending my most precious weapon after them. They'll eventually—be no more."

I clench my fists so furiously that my nails dig into my palms. "So, you lied. All these years… I wasted weeks crying over the fate of Rogues, which I thought you missed. I shared their pain… And you just, what? Played with them?"

"I do what I do best. I give souls a chance." He. Fucking. Smiles.

"You could save them all!" Understanding burns my tongue, as my words spit out like venom.

A wicked grin blooms on his face. "One doesn't use his best resources to cure an infected dog and I don't work with *flaws*." His eyes narrow to two cruel mirrors, reflecting the disgust spreading across my face.

My eyes widen, and something acrid and bitter sticks in my throat, stealing my breath.

"I killed every single one of them, is this what you're saying? And now you want me to do it again, to that boy?! Why can you not just leave him be, like the other Rogues. With one kernel left I'm sure he doesn't have the strength to hurt anyone." The longer I stare at Roden, the more the other faces fade into a dark fog.

Roden moves a few steady steps towards me until he stops

between Popplewish and me. He leans back against the table, crosses his ankles, and lowers the cane onto the back of his neck, letting his wrists rest on the wooden shaft.

He huffs a dark laugh, studying his nails, "Now, now, my child. No need to run to such a desperate conclusion; I'm not asking you to turn the Rogue into a pile of black powder, which is not even good enough to fertilise my flowers."

After a quick look at the Chapter behind him, Roden adds, "See, he holds a special talent, a bit like yours, and I can't allow him to use it without my supervision. The ideal solution would be to eradicate his power from the roots. But that little weed always seems to remember everything and every face he crossed path with while our Writers worked on him."

"Then, why don't you just bring him to Libera like you did for the rest of us? Train him, make him… *good.*" The word tastes awful on my tongue.

Roden slides the cane off his shoulders and rests it on the table, "Because he refuses the offer. Every. Single. Time," he says, tilting his head left and right and leaning towards me with every word until our faces are eye-level, rage and impatience burning behind his pale irises.

I hold my breath until Roden stands up, grabs his cane and walks away.

Everyone in the room follows his movements until he stops and sits beside Lily Drestall. She elegantly bows her head, and he softly kisses her cheek.

"Lily has tried her best for years, rewriting his memories, filling his mind with marvellous alternatives. Gifting him with some incredible, fictitious images of past lives. Anything her pretty, little head could think of, if only to distract that stubborn soul from his true nature." He lets out a dramatic sigh before casting a hard look at Lily, who is still staring at Roden in adoration. "Nothing worked. Nothing."

Blood rushes under Lily's porcelain face, and she lowers her eyes.

"How many times?" I ask, already fearing the answer. If nobody but me can harvest Rogues, I'm sure that didn't stop Roden from trying alternative methods to break that man's will power.

Roden counts on his right hand as if mentally writing a grocery list. "I'd say enough times to give him the opportunity to come to Libera willingly."

It's already too late to control my tears, but I don't care. "How could you?" I turn to face the rest of the Chapter, my lips trembling. "How could you let this happen to one of us?"

"He is *nothing*, by his own choice." Roden sounds distant. Cold.

"But he's only known the choices you gave him!" My voice comes from a dark place I didn't know I had in me. I shout so desperately that I don't hear the chair toppling to the floor when I stand up.

Pushing away from the table, Roden stands, seemingly strangling the neck of his cane, his knuckles turning whiter by the second, and saunters towards me. "You know, my dear, the worst way children can hurt their father is by refusing his legacy, the power he built for their future, sweating blood and tears."

He keeps walking, tracing a path on the shiny table with his index finger. "This Rogue is not only rejecting the legacy I created for all my children to enjoy when I'll be gone. But he is also stealing my souls…"

He stops and crosses his arms over his chest, waiting for my reaction.

I instinctively retreat a couple of steps, shaking my head.

Popplewish lowers her head, pushing up from her chair with such heaviness that my stomach churns.

"Roden believes he's working with a group of rebels who wish to cut ties with Harvesters and stop the Horigeans from bargaining their souls."

"Dirty, ungrateful, ignorant scum. Egoistic, little brains full of dangerous ideals—this is what they are," Roden scrunches up his nose as if a whiff of stench just hit his nostrils.

I don't remember starting fidgeting, but the skin around my nails feels raw and tender.

"Have you tried talking to them? What if these people are using him and he doesn't know how to ask for help? He's probably just confused, scared…"

"Careful, girl. You make it looks like you care for a Rogue you don't even know." Nikrah says, stretching out his arms with a big yawn.

"He is not a Rogue." I snap back.

"You're right. *He's* the reason we're all in danger… Is that a good enough reason for you?" Lily strikes her hand on the table as if the polished surface were my face. A strand of her perfect hair falls loose, framing her tense jaw.

An invisible hand slowly tights around my throat, making it hard to breathe, to think. Roden has built an intangible cage around me, word by word, and I only saw a glimpse of it when it was already too late to run away.

"What if I can't control myself and end up killing him?" My lips tremble, and I breathe out dark puffs of angry purple, reminding me how Harvesters will never seamlessly blend with Horigeans. Our eyes, our powers—the very air in our lungs; everything makes us noticeable, different. Dangerous.

Roden narrows his eyes at Lily, then turns to me and clicks his tongue, "Now, now. Kill? That's too definitive, don't you think? I only need you to harvest his soul and leave it with the Deleteri for a *special* treatment I've been working on. You get your life back with your adorable Galen, and I may even find a way to teach your unique talent to someone else if the burden is too heavy for you to carry…" He huffs a laugh, "Kill? I'd rather call it—"

"A fair exchange of goods," I echo his earlier words.

Chapter 20 - Just a Sunday Morning
July

I like Saturday mornings, but Sundays are the best. Everybody is too tired from the night before, too full of food and happy memories—mostly awkward memories they hope will remain a secret and soon forgotten.

But today is not one of those Sundays.

It was already Saturday evening when I returned to my place after the meeting with the Chapter. Miss Popplewish had escorted me outside and given me a ride back.

"I need to blindfold you, July. I'm sure you'll understand. But you can text Galen first if you wish." Those were the last words she spoke to me as she handed me back my phone.

I remember replying as if to a stranger, "I'll figure something out later. Is there anything specific I need to know, anything I should do to avoid messing up Galen's new memories?" I was exhausted and confused. And I knew that no matter what story the Chapter had concocted to convince him that he brought me home after dinner because I was pretty wasted, our friendship would never be the same—at least for one of us.

Because I made a deal with Roden. Because I accepted to be the key that will open a well of pain and who knows what else for a man whose only sin is to be powerful like me, but not squashed under Roden's will.

Yet.

But as far as Galen is concerned, I spent the entire Saturday in bed with a terrible headache and an upset stomach.

"You will receive instructions soon," Popplewish had added, her voice like nails on a board.

"In that case," I'd shrugged after fastening my belt on the passenger seat, "I think I'm ready to start living a fat, shitty lie, I guess."

And now Sunday morning is knocking at my door like an old friend, and I wish it could be Friday again so I could change it all, make different choices, and be free to enjoy breakfast by the shore with Galen.

Usually at this time, he is calling and sending silly emojis of coffee cups. Or a croissant, if I don't reply within two minutes, followed by pictures of baby owls with their beaks open. But not today.

What if they lied... What if they weren't able to play with his mind... What if. What if?

I need to feel something. Leaving my room is the first step towards a semi-normal life. My legs are tangled in my bed sheets, and it is as if I fought to fall asleep last night. My mouth is dry. I must have gone to bed leaving the window open because the night air still lingers; at least, the soft light pouring in is a welcome guest.

Outside, everything is running as usual. I hear no voices, no bikes, just the island breathing in and out, happy not to be walked on or run on, free from chirping voices gossiping, if only for a couple of hours.

When I come out of the shower, the bed invites me to nestle back into its warmth, and my muscles seem to respond, especially my back, which still hurts from all the time spent on the cold stone floor of HQ's basement. But I can't pretend it's just a normal Sunday morning and steal a few more minutes of sleep.

Today is the day I will have to lie to my best friend. This is the first of many Sundays when, if Galen doesn't call me, I won't be either. Because if I do, I'll have to pretend I'm someone else.

When I step outside my building, the crisp morning air tickles my face, and if only for a moment, I tell myself I'm fine. But when I turn the corner heading towards the little square beneath my window, I freeze in front of Roden's face, staring at me from the stone frame where it had been chiselled centuries ago. His fluffy brick-red moustache, and the fatherly expression he uses during public speaking and events—all details so familiar to me, that made me feel part of something big and good, and that are now only a constant reminder of his lies.

I lift one hand and try to scratch his eyes, but all I manage is a sore finger and a line of dirt under my nails.

"Yeah, fuck the system… You know you're too old for that, right?" Galen's voice is like an unexpected cold rain.

I'm paralysed. If I turn around now, he will read on my face that something is wrong—chipped. But when Galen comes closer, and I smell hot coffee and sugar, I choke on the stinging knot in my throat. At least if he notices the tears in my eyes, he'll think the cough has caused them.

"Hey…" I start.

"Sof, I'm sorry for the other night. Hope you're—"

"I'm fine… Great, actually." It's okay if I sound abrupt. The last thing I want is to start a conversation about what he thinks has happened, and my addiction to coffee sounds like a plausible excuse.

I snatch one cup from his hand, and I hide my face behind the swirling comforting aroma. "And where's my doughnut?"

For a little while, I want to believe we're going to be okay, and when he loops his arm with mine, I'm glad the Chapter made him forget.

The colonnade lining the perimeter of my building offers the right amount of shade, but today, I want to spend my day in sunlight—real, natural light—not some magic trick created by Roden. I shake my head to swat away his face from my mind.

Galen stares at me, frowning. "Are you okay? Is the coffee too bitter?"

"No, it's perfect. I'm just… headache leftovers, I think." I take a sip of coffee that burns my tongue, but at least saves me from saying anything else—anything inappropriate.

We walk in silence for a while, not an awkward one, but

definitely one longer than usual. I pretend to find everything around us worthy of my attention: trees, the gardeners tending to overgrown bushes, a chipped tile of the square fountain. Anything but Galen's serene face.

"So," he stops, and I almost bump against his back. He looks around, searching for a bench. "What about our usual spot? Then, you talk, and I listen."

Oh, no…

When he steps in front of the sun and I finally look at him, all I can see is his dark silhouette—not his face or expression, but he may have noticed me flinching.

Inhaling. Exhaling light purple puffs. He doesn't know…

"Listen to what?" I ask vaguely, turning my head towards our favourite bench, making sure nobody's there and distracting him from looking straight at me.

But he's not taking his eyes off me. "You know… Your inconsiderate, dangerous decision to go back to Horigos only days before our birthday? Your unbelievable desire to do something I consider life-threatening? Did I miss anything? Nothing you would say will change my mind, Sof. Too soon—*wherever* they're sending you. Just too soon."

I blink, wondering if the little argument we had in my room had distracted him so much that he forgot about some details of my next mission, like my destination, for a start. Or, perhaps Lily Drestall didn't stop at our dinner and rewrote his memory entirely.

"Oh, that, yes, right." At least no mention of our dinner. "Sorry, forgot about that." I slap the air with my free hand and walk past him, "There's not much to say, to be honest. I don't even know the name of my crop yet."

The bench is still damp from the night dew when I sit on it. I let the smell of coffee tickle my nostrils, trying to remember the sense of peace of all the mornings spent with Galen in this square.

A few moments later, he joins me. "Name or not, I still don't like the fact that you kept it from me," he says in a low voice, scanning my face.

I don't like seeing him so lost in thought. So I stomp my feet, "Where's my food? Me. Hungry." I keep my mouth open like a hatchling, pointing at my belly. Embarrassing—but I make him smile.

"Close your eyes," he says gently.

I obey, and soon after, the smell of something sweet captures my senses. "Aha, my favourite!" I exclaim, performing a little sat-down dance, shaking my fists and swinging my legs.

"You can open your eyes now," Galen whispers in my ear.

I do as asked, with a growing smile when I notice Galen dangling a jelly doughnut in front of me.

"So tell me, what would you like your Nistares to be this time? Some kind of torn artist with a passion for pain as a source of creativity, or someone who talks to vegetables and crystals and thinks we all come from dragons?" He bumps my shoulder, teasing me.

I savour his words like the grains of sugar cracking between my teeth. The closer my crossing approaches, the more I fear we will never have another conversation like this.

Comforted by the intimacy of the moment, I let my thoughts wander. "Wouldn't it be nice if we could pick our crop instead of waiting for Roden to assign us one?"

Opposite us, a man, pushing a trolley full of boxes of peaches and apples, stops and leans against a lamp post to catch his breath and wipe beads of sweat off his forehead. Our eyes meet. He's not someone I recognise, but I expect the Chapter to have ears and eyes everywhere.

Stop being paranoid. He's probably an approved courier from Horigos, delivering supplies to our restaurants.

"Would that be better, though?" Galen says before taking a sip of his coffee. "Knowing too much about the soul you'll harvest? What if you happen to *like* them?"

I turn my head slowly, keeping eye contact with the stranger for as long as I can. "That is not a thing. This is why we wear masks in their presence—to avoid accidental *contamination*."

Galen sighs, resting his back against the bench and casually extending an arm over my shoulders. "Souls are liquid and airy and in constant transformation. Nistarei, Rogues, us… We're not that different, you know. Nobody can stop us from liking or disliking another soul, no matter what *kind* we belong to. Masks protect our identities, but our minds and eyes do not answer to anyone."

The man has restarted his laboured walk; that trolley is challenging him, despite his height and strong build. My mind wanders without my permission, and I picture that man working on Horigos' southern shores, his skin tanning under the sweltering summer sun.

"Libera to July. Where did you go?"

I blink, and the image of Horigos fades away. This could be my only chance to tell Galen everything. That I know the way my next soul smiles, the look of terror in his light green eyes. And that he did not make any bargain with Roden because he is not a Nistares nor a Rogue—he's one of us, and I'm the one designated to shred his soul to pieces.

Instead, I brace my forearms on my knees, staring at the empty square. "I hope *they* won't suffer too much. Whoever they are," I shrug and put the rest of my doughnut back in its brown bag. "Galen," I take a deep breath, measuring every word I'm about to say, "Have you ever thought about leaving this place?"

His eyes widen, and the sunlight catches the little silver specks in his left iris, turning his blue right eye into a miniature lake. His cup of coffee stops halfway to his lips, and I expect to see Lily and Nikrah popping out of the bushes behind us to take him away and teach me a lesson.

Have I said too much? Did I trigger something inside him without realising it?

I peer over my shoulder and offer a smile to melt his sudden stiffness.

"What do you mean? Like a holiday?" He puts the cup down on the bench.

"Never mind." I wave one hand as if to disperse a cloud of flies. "I was just toying with the idea of an *ungifted* life, like the Nistarei's. Their souls sound so… Simple."

He cocks his head, shading his eyes from the sun rising over the horizon. "Why? You're not happy here?" His innocence will always strike me.

I play with the edge of my paper bag until it tears. "I am, but sometimes I'd like to know what it feels like to live every day not knowing what will happen next. To travel and meet new people who will remember you even when you're gone, as in gone-gone."

Galen places a hand over mine. "You mean—dead?" The atmosphere around us darkens. It's just a passing cloud, but to me, it has a different, daunting meaning.

I fall silent, searching for an answer in the pavement of clean stones with engraved little flowers.

The gentle touch of his thumb, brushing the back of my hand, and his voice, snatch me out of my reverie. "I will never forget you, Sof. Even if sometimes I wish you weren't so clingy and loud and messy and—"

"Galen Sulfridge," I spring up, nearly spilling coffee everywhere. "You should be honoured to call one of the brightest Harvesters - and the only living one who can capture Rogues - your friend…"

Friend… I recoil, but Galen is already on his feet, pretending he's offended and about to leave me here.

"Galen, wait." I pick up the pace until I'm by his side. He tries to hide a giggle, and I exhale so loudly that my breath shines bright purple in the pouring sunlight.

He mutters with his face half hidden in his hood, "You're an idiot." I spot a little puff of violet darkened by the coffee that still lingers on his tongue.

"Yes, but you taught me how to be the best idiot," I tease him as we stroll towards the shore, where we usually sit for the rest of the morning until our stomachs remind us that we need some grown-up food, and cannot just survive on sugar and caffeine.

Lost in our little microcosm, I realise we're heading for the shortcut through the wood rather than the main path with the flowery arches, and I freeze. My legs and mind recall the recent events, and I fear I cannot take another step. How do I explain to him that now I'm terrified of the trees we used to climb when we were kids?

When my phone rings, relief spreads from every single cell of my body. *Private Number* flashes on my screen, and I automatically look at Galen, who shrugs. "Maybe they have the wrong number."

Maybe. Or…

"Hello," I try to keep my voice as neutral as possible.

"2 p.m. My office."

The conversation, if I can call it that, ends with a click, which can only mean one thing: a landline. Popplewish's vintage office phone.

"Who was that?" Galen asks.

I check the time before my screen goes off. I still have a few hours before my meeting, but I need to find an excuse to skip our fancy takeaway on the beach, where we crouch between the same two massive rocks by the water, to avoid the rest of the students. And Lucretia, in Galen's case.

I'm wondering how she is. I didn't mention her name, but I'm sure the Chapter has all the right tools to track down the source of the video and whoever received it.

"Sof!" Galen waves a hand in my face, so close I can smell coffee on his skin, "Where did you go?"

"I'm sorry." I blink. "I've just remembered there are some things I must prepare before crossing. Dinner tonight? My treat…" *Shit!* I hope this doesn't trigger any lingering memories. I wait, holding my breath until my lungs no longer allow it, but he raises his finger and pokes me on the forehead.

"Your mind is such a convoluted net of thoughts. We should create a card game out of it; we could be millionaires," he laughs.

He doesn't remember.

I take a step back and get on my tiptoes to pull his hood down. "And then what? Invest in Libera shares? Buy a bench in the square and have our names on it. Maybe buy the doughnut place?" I give him a genuine smile. Galen has the special power to make me feel safe, always.

The sea lapping at the shore turns into a distant sound, calming against the rumble in my ears when Galen slowly leans towards me. He blinks a few times, confirming that time hasn't stopped.

His skin is soft, if not for a light stubble when I cup his face. We're so close the purple air escaping our lungs becomes one breath.

"If anything happens to you this time…" he murmurs against my lips before resting his forehead against mine.

"It's just another mission," I reply, breaking the whispered connection between us, setting back on my feet when my legs are too tired of standing on tiptoes to remain at Galen's eye level.

But unexpectedly, Galen wraps one arm around my waist, tugs me against him, and tilts my chin up to kiss me like he's never done before—softly, tasting the grains of sugar still stuck on my lips.

My eyes are still wide with surprise when Galen slides his hand off my face, lowers it to my waist, and pulls me closer.

Deprived of Galen's warm touch, my skin cools down, grazed by the sea breeze, blowing from the distant shore. I gently push him away, with my cheeks still stained with the idea of what that kiss could have led to. His heart thunders beneath my fingers when I rest a hand on his chest.

"Don't go." His voice gets lost in the soothing melody of the green foliage rustled by the same wind that plays with Galen's untamed curls.

I huff a laugh, "I promise I'll come back. And I will give you a haircut."

Voices that I didn't notice before begin to fill the space around us. Libera's taller bell tower begins performing its first song of the day, and from three strategically chosen spots, allowing the sound to travel all over the island, the other sister towers respond with their tolls.

"We should go back," I say, if only to fracture the tense wall between us, as I motion back to my building.

But Galen grabs my hands, "Let me speak with Popplewish—"

"No, don't." I press my lips together, forcing a smile. "There's no need. Besides… Why are you nervous about something you've seen me doing dozens of times?"

He searches my face intently. "Promise you'll come to me before your crossing."

"You're avoiding my question."

"Just say you will not return to Horigos without saying goodbye."

"Goodbye? Galen, what the fuck?" I free my hands and move a couple of steps back. "I'm not going to war."

The last word strikes something inside him. He bites his lip, hiding his hands in his pockets, and stalks past me as he sputters, "Fine, I'll come find you then. Invited or not."

I hear him stomping away, his steps growing distant.

"I didn't mean you were not… Galen, stop!" I shout, spinning on my heel and raising more than a few eyebrows from the growing crowd populating the square.

He doesn't stop but slows down enough for me to catch up.

"What was that for? Why are you being so protective?"

What do you know?

Still walking, he glances around sand picks a hidden spot under the arches leading to the square. Without a word, he jerks his chin in that direction, and I follow.

When we reach the shaded area of bricks and rows of fresh flowers looped around the metal arches, Galen leans against the wall, beckoning me closer. "Hug me."

"What?"

"Just do it. Put your head against my chest and pretend you're hugging me."

"Fine." Not that he needs to ask me twice. I lift my arms and loop them around his neck, resting my ear over his heart.

He smells clean with a hint of coffee when he whispers, "The night you harvested that woman's soul, you left me a longer message. You said something about stolen souls, but also that that woman's soul glowed red."

I tense and cling to him harder. *I didn't… My message was broken. I wrote it on a piece of paper… I didn't…*

I shake my head, faking surprise. "Why didn't you tell me earlier? Whatever it means, we need to inform…"

Who? The Chapter?

He distractedly runs his fingers up and down my stretched arms, leaning closer to whisper, "After what you told me about the Turret? I didn't want to feed your dangerous curiosity. I thought I could find something out about it, but there is no mention of such souls in any books I could put my hands on without raising suspicions."

Why did Roden decide to leave those memories intact? Is he playing with me?

This is not a coincidence. I start shaking.

"You cold?" Galen asks, tugging me closer into his warm embrace.

"I'm fine. What do we do now?" I snuggle against his body, hiding my face in the soft cotton of his hoodie.

"*We* don't do anything. You have a crossing to worry about. Don't think I forgot about it. I will keep digging around."

"Be careful, please. Especially if I'm not here to save your ass before kicking it for being reckless." I look up with a tentative smile and sigh with relief when he smiles back.

He nods. "I can't risk asking too openly about what happened to the weird red soul you captured. But I'm still a Deleteri leader; I've got some strings I can safely pull without taking the whole freaking web of security down. I'll be fine."

This is taking a dangerous turn, and I cannot even ask him to stop investigating when I'm the one who gave him the information. If I don't call the Chapter's attention to Galen by saying or doing something stupid, this will certainly do it.

A low rumble in Galen's chest snaps my attention back. "What is it?"

He cups my shoulders and gently pushes me away. "What we've just discussed, don't talk about this with anyone. Not even Popplewish."

I blink fast, shaking my head, "Not a word." *Especially* to Popplewish, if I don't want to crack the already thin line that keeps the Chapter and Roden from changing their minds about me.

"Good," he smacks a quick, innocent kiss on my forehead, and I hear a swarm of giggles behind me, followed by a rehearsed cough. "Don't turn just now," Galen adds, brushing my cheek with his thumb.

"Lucretia and her subjects?" I play with a string of his sweatshirt, wrapping and unwrapping it around my finger.

Galen lowers his face to mine, and a plume of dark purple escapes his perfect mouth as he says, "All of them, and they're walking with their heads turned towards us."

"I swear, if one of them face-plants into a wall…"

His soft laugh against my lips sends shivers down my spine. "Lucretia has tugged them along. Not without throwing daggers at your back with her eyes, though."

"Galen?"

"Hmm?" His eyes gleam with the same spark flaring within me.

"When I come back…"

"Yes… ?" His breath warms my face and my mind.

"I want to talk about this."

"Lucretia's plans to eliminate you?" He places a delicate kiss on the corner of my lips.

"Us—"

His reaction to my offer exceeds my expectations. His kiss is deep and hungry as if he's been taming it for a while. His tongue searches for mine as though he's not expecting to taste my lips for a very long time.

I melt under the weight of his urgency because the thought of what I'm about to do has never left my mind since last night, and I need the distraction. I need to feel *us*.

I bury my hands in his hair and press him against me harder, slightly tilting my head to get lost under the skilled touch of his mouth.

A deep moan in his throat tells me we should probably head somewhere more secluded.

"It's eight in the morning, for fuck's sake. Get a room!" A passerby yells from somewhere. I don't care. I want this.

But the moment has passed, and when Galen backs away, my heart sinks.

"You are addictive, July. But I like to consume my sources of pleasure *slowly*." His eyes are glazed with the storm of heat still thrumming in our veins.

And there it is—the Galen that makes so many people do silly things to spend time with him.

But I'm not many people.

I step into the sunlight, licking his taste off my lips, staring at Galen while he tries to give his tousled hair a look worthy of a Deleteri leader. "Pleasure must be deserved. I'll see you later," I wink.

We've been playing this game for so long, and yet I've never savoured the taste of that word - *us* - like I did moments ago.

I turn towards my building without looking back. It will be too difficult to separate from Galen if I do. But as I stroll down the path that led us here just over an hour ago, I can hear his laugh, deep and warm.

Except for the red soul, he doesn't remember anything.

He's going to be fine.

He doesn't know I've agreed to doom one of us to save us all.

Chapter 21 - Roofs and Chesterfield Chairs
July

I try to keep a relaxed, steady pace as I walk towards my building, but as soon as its main door closes behind me, I rest my back against it, one hand on my chest, waiting for my heart to slow down.

Us…

I could've picked any other excuse to change the subject—but, no, I had to mention that little word that makes our relationship grey and foggy.

I peel myself off the door, forcing my legs to take the stairs. I still have a few hours before my meeting with Popplewish, and I could use a change of clothes and a refreshed brain.

Perhaps, if I go to the library now, I may find it empty. I don't even know what kind of book I can pull off the shelves to while away some time. Maybe a guide on Sector 43. I've only visited once, ages ago, and I never wandered the city unless I had to deal with my Nistares. No matter how intrigued I was by the narrow alleys and dark corners, my crop was my first thought in the morning, and my last as I lay down for the night.

Besides, the air on Horigos doesn't sit well with Harvesters. Roden always warns us that spending too long away from Libera could impact our abilities.

But this time is different—my Rogue is different. Not sure I should even call him that.

I thought I'd found a way out in that room with the Chapter.

Let me speak to him. I can convince him to follow me here and join us—I'd spoken with my heart out, only to face a living wall of harsh cruelty.

Bring his soul back to me whole or *end him. I'm giving you more choices than other Harvesters ever had.* Roden's voice still rings, menacingly, in my ears.

I'm nearly out of breath when I finally reach my floor after jumping the stairs two at a time. The long, empty corridor stretches before me, lined by a row of white doors to the left and tall windows to the right, exposed to the island's south side. The sun warms my face when I peer down to ensure Galen has gone and is not lingering outside my building.

I should be relieved when all I can see are bushes in early bloom, gently waving as the wind plays with them. But a sad smile tugs at my lips when I realise Galen listened to my request and didn't follow me.

I rest my back against my door, breathing in some trace of normalcy, before stepping inside my tiny flat.

For the first time in my life, the narrow hall feels unfamiliar and cold, as if I don't belong here. The mess of dishes and glasses I left in the kitchen sink, the paintings on the walls - even the pile of shoes by the entrance - nothing screams my name. An itchy feeling creeps up on me, forcing me to hurry up as I quickly collect random pens and a notepad from the kitchen table and head out.

Once outside, I ignore Roden's face carved on the red brick wall and head straight for the back of the building. It's a longer way to the library but less crowded than the main streets, where bakeries and other shops attract people from all parts of Libera during the weekends.

I lift my hood so it swallows my head completely, keeping my eyes on the path before me and checking my surroundings to avoid colliding with bikes, trees and people.

However, my mind is still overloaded, and my attention slips even if I try my hardest. When I hear steps behind me, it's already too late.

A hand with perfectly painted nails lands on my shoulder. "Good morning, you," Lucretia chirps in my ears.

And yet, today, the prickly feeling I experience in her presence doesn't weigh like a ton of bricks on my head. It's hard to admit—but I'm glad to see her still alive and more than capable of pouting.

"Lue, hey. What… are you doing here?" I don't mean to sound rude, but being friendly now could make her suspicious. People like her may be shallow, but never gullible.

"I was looking for you, silly."

"Me? Listen, if this is about what you saw earlier—"

She presses a finger to my lips before I can finish. "I don't know what you're talking about, but if you really wish to know, I think Galen agreed to be my senior co-crosser." Her face brightens up as if soaking up all the sunlight. "I just wanted to thank you. I don't know what you did or said, but I've received a letter and an official call from Mr. Breith in person! He told me to be prepared for a big change. Tonight! That can only be it."

Her eyes gleam with excitement, and she seems genuinely happy, but I can't hold back a laugh. "He what now?"

When her smile drops to a flat line, I try to fix what I've broken, if only to make her disappear. "I'm sorry, it's just… Galen doesn't need to tell me everything, but he rarely changes his mind." I shrug.

The corners of her lips curve up as if my words were just background noise. "Will you come and see *us*? They say you will always have a special bond with the person who guides you through your first crossing… But you don't need to be jealous." She wrinkles her nose, and I have to restrain myself from laughing again.

"Sweetie," I cringe at the sound of that word, but I know she thinks it's lovely, "I have to go now, but I promise I'll save the date in my calendar, deal?"

And that's another word that will make me cringe from now on. *Deal…*

Lucretia nods so vehemently, I expect to see her head rolling off her neck.

She is still nodding when I move a couple of steps back to put some distance between us.

"Okay then, bye now…" I half smile, and only breathe when she finally spins on her heel and starts walking in the opposite direction.

I try to swat away the image of Lucretia and Galen crossing together in a pod so small you can't avoid physical contact every time you move, but it stays with me until I reach the library.

I pick a small table in a corner, the surface of which is perfectly divided in two by a column of light pouring from a round ceiling window above my head—dust dances in front of me when I set my jacket on it.

Larger desks and tall shelves loaded with books dot the space around me and offer enough privacy for those who only seek silence. Some of the books are so old I don't even dare look at them because I'm afraid their covers will turn to dust or be stained by my purple breath.

Unfortunately, the pleasant experience soon ends when the trilling voice of an exotic bird informs me that someone has messaged me, and makes me jump.

"Sorry…" I say to the empty room. I'm alone, and I think even the librarian only woke up this morning to open the building before returning to bed.

Meet me on the roof at 8 p.m. No fancy outfit. By the way, I told Lucretia I'd cross with her. Don't be jealous. I have good reasons.

Another text.

Stop laughing.

I am.

The screen lights up again.

I'm serious; stop it!

I have no idea what Galen is planning or why he wants to meet me on the roof.

If there's one thing we all know about Roden, it's that he loves a nice rooftop. Every building has one: small or large, with chairs and benches, some with many plants. They're there for people to relax, spend time with friends, and enjoy the always-clear sky of Libera.

But Galen and I have a special place, on top of one of the highest towers of the Castle—The Blind Wise. A little square with just enough space for two or three people to admire the sky while sitting on hard, uneven stones imported from Horigos. Away from the yellowish glare of lamp posts and houses, the roof offers the most enchanting view of the island and its evergreen hills that stretch towards the sea until they meet the coast in a dance of water and sand.

When I start toying with the idea that maybe Galen has organised something for our upcoming birthday, another message makes me swear under my breath. Apparently, its vibration is as aggressive as the stupid bird-ring.

Do not think the us-talk made me forget your unbelievable, reckless decision to return to Horigos so soon.

I sink into my chair and stare at the oval glass ceiling, a modern addition to the original turret. Horigos and Libera share the same sky, but everything stops moving and stands still when it enters our reality. We only have a few gulls and tiny birds, which fly so low we can touch them. Even our clouds are odd. They have dull shapes, never a dragon cloud or a floating boat cloud. Just white masses. Immobile. I can count and name them all because they have never changed since the day Popplewish brought me here.

But our sky turns dark purple at night and light blue in the morning—Horigos has not seen such a phenomenon in centuries.

I'm not a child of the Great Famine, and I don't know how Horigos' sky looked before those terrible years. But those who lived there before seeking refuge on Libera swear it was breathtaking, with a different shade of blue for each season, and pink and orange brushstrokes from dusk to dawn.

Now, Horigos' sky is just a mass of dirty grey that only gifts its people with memories of its past beauty when it rains, and rays of a sickly violet hue bleed through its thick surface.

I blink before the sunlight blinds me for good, and straighten myself up. "Time to go…" I slam my hand on the desk to scare away the nagging feeling I've had since I met the Chapter—tell Galen what happened the night before and ask him to run away with me.

But where? And who says he will follow me?

I will never forget you, Sof…

But he already has, if only a tiny part of me.

Miss P.'s door opens slowly, soundlessly under the weight of my hand when I knock. I peer inside, spotting her sitting in one of her Chesterfield armchairs, the most expensive and beautiful piece of furniture I've ever seen; a unique work of art she bought from an antique shop in Horigos when she was offered the role of Master Reaper.

"We can't talk if you linger by the threshold. Come in, please."

"You didn't need to ring me. You could have just messaged." My voice still carries that sense of betrayal that swallowed me during the meeting with the Chapter.

The atmosphere is not what I'm used to when I step inside her office. This is not the welcoming space where I spent hours looking at the hundreds of books, perfectly aligned by size and colour, on the ceiling-high bookshelves. The curtains are shut, and the yellow light that fights its way in from narrow openings is old and dusty, smelling like dried flowers and mouldy paper.

"And risk for whoever was with you to read our private conversation? You should be more careful now and limit your interactions with Galen." Her voice is raw, and her eyes weary as if she hasn't seen her bed in days.

How did she know?

"As you requested, I'm keeping my contact with him to a minimum, but I think he's planning something for our birthday tonight, and I have no intention of rejecting his invite."

I close the door behind me and move towards her like a scrawny foal still learning to walk. The Miss Popplewish sitting in front of me is not the one I've known all these years, and I don't know how to behave.

She dismisses my comment with a hasty shake of her head. The armchair's leather creaks like old bones when she stands, pressing both hands on the armrests. "Take a seat, please," she motions toward her desk, where two less comfortable chairs await us.

Her hair is elegantly plaited and pinned on the crown of her head. In a sea of ginger, greying strands turn silver in the dusty light. Her long black skirt caresses the polished floor as she glides over it.

I blink quickly, averting my eyes from her ethereal figure. "No, thanks. I'm not planning to stay long. What is it?" I would've never imagined being able to use such a tone in her presence. And yet, I cannot shake off the feeling that she's lost the privilege of being called my mentor and role model.

Popplewish inhales deeply. "As you wish. I just wanted to review our plan to ensure you're prepared. Perhaps you were too shocked that night, and some details may have gotten lost."

There is only her desk between us, which I'm glad of because I would probably start vomiting all my rage on her instead of digging my nails under the edge of the wooden furniture. Or at least try to, as I don't think Popplewish will let me scream and shout inside her office for long before restraining me.

Instead, I tap a finger to my temple, leaning over her desk, "Oh, don't worry, *all* the details are branded in my memory. As well as the faces of the Chapter. As to Galen and I—stay out of it. I'm the last, if not the only one, who doesn't want to see him harmed."

Her eyes narrow on me as she takes in my words. "That is not my wish either. Believe me, I know how important your friendship is." She pauses to open one of the drawers and hands me an envelope. "This is why I needed to see you."

I shrug dismissively and pull out the chair, ignoring the annoying sound of its legs as I drag it on the floor.

"Your new identity, address and contacts of Harvesters you might find useful should you need an extra pair of hands."

I cautiously take the envelope between my fingers because my mind doesn't stop whispering that anything offered by a Chapter member may now hurt me. Once I would've asked her what happened to the back of her hands, where short, parallel scratches gleam still fresh—but she doesn't deserve my concern.

I push away from the desk, flattening the envelope against my shirt as if to iron my nerves. "Why do we need to involve more people? I've never needed extras, and *I* certainly don't now. Ruining an innocent's life is already painful when done solo."

Something sparks behind her eyes, and she holds my stare for a second, nodding in silence. She then allows herself a too-long moment to lock the drawer and pick her words wisely. "This will still be treated as a routine mission," - a key clicks under her desk - "But we both know there is so much more at stake."

She guides her attention back to me, distractedly fidgeting with the clasp of a thin chain that has a small, brass key dangling from it.

"And?" I press on.

"There is a chance it will last longer than expected, and you won't be able to return as soon as you hoped."

I slowly slide my arms to my sides, tightening my fingers around the envelope. "I thought Roden wanted *his* soul back as soon as possible. What am I supposed to do other than harvest it and come back to base?"

Popplewish runs a finger over the edge of the desk and, using the armrest of her chair for extra support, she stands, flattening the velvety skirt and creating lighter-shaded patterns where her hand has been.

The wall behind her desk would be utterly bare if not for a square painting of a small house surrounded by a well-kept garden, a lake, and soft hills towered over by a periwinkle sky. Whoever lived there must have felt very safe and protected.

"Are you sure you still want to do this?"

I swear Popplewish was standing against that frame until a moment ago, but when I blink at the sound of her voice, I realise she's moved to one of the windows. The curtain is still shut. Her back is straight, and her posture is so serene that she would be a perfect addition to that painting.

When I move towards her, my steps echo too loudly and impolitely in the carefully designed room.

"I don't recall being given the option of rejecting the offer," I respond, more bitterly than intended.

She turns to me, and the picture of serenity bursts. Her hands are folded on her lap, and she rubs them against each other. For once, she's the one averting her eyes from mine.

Eventually, she pinches her nose, studying me from over her glasses. There is something she's holding back.

"If this is all?" I start making my way back to the door, but she holds up a hand.

"I know you've been through a lot, and everything seems forced upon you. But believe me when I say you're the best Harvester for this mission. You're brilliant, July, and I will say this just once: Do not let your feelings cloud your judgement."

As much as her words should sound hypocritical, I can't find the courage to laugh and tell her to shut up.

I nod slightly. "Can I go now?"

Please, I don't want to hear any more. Finding out about Roden being ready to sacrifice one of his precious souls only because it is different. Only because Roden wasn't able to control it. To make it obedient… That was enough to make me doubt our existence and purpose.

Her hand drops to her side. "Sometimes we have to play parts we don't resonate with. I did mean it when I said I didn't want to see Galen hurt. Or you. But sometimes breaking free may look like a long road that only leads to a precipice. You just need to remember that you're not alone."

"That does not make any sense, considering the Chapter has forced me away from the only person I can truly rely on."

"It will," she nods, toying with the chain around her neck.

She glances at the door behind me, then quickly beckons me over, sliding the necklace off and carefully lowering it onto her palm.

"I want you to take this. Take it with you to Horigos."

Without letting me say anything, she takes my hand, folds the chain, and closes my fingers over it.

Incredulous, I shake my head, "But that opens your drawer. What am I supposed to— "

"It has a twin. *If* you need to use it, you will know. But, for now, keep it safe."

"From what?"

"From the precipice."

I wiggle my hand free from hers. "A riddle? Really?"

At that, she smiles but with a hint of sadness. "A favour. I know I'm not in a position to ask for one. You can throw it away should you wish. But I hope you'll give it at least a chance."

I look down at the brass key now resting in my palm. "Surely it won't hurt me more than you and Roden have already done," I mutter with a shrug.

"He doesn't need to know. Nobody does. Please." She retreats to her desk.

I stare at her back for a long second before moving towards the door. But something is trailing behind me, the nagging thought that - maybe - I didn't get everything straight.

I glance at Popplewish over my shoulder. She's leaning over her desk, her fingers twitching as if trying to hold back her thoughts while she stares at the painting on the wall.

This is not right. With my hand already on the doorknob, I turn on my heels, slamming the door frame with frustration, "*He*'s just a person; he cannot control us—"

When she takes a deep breath, I hope—I genuinely hope…

But she proclaims as if reading a script, "We have to be grateful. We are his creatures. If it wasn't for him—"

"I would have probably still left my parents and made a better life for myself. I didn't ask to be taken away or *saved,*" I snap. "You don't know what could have happened if I hadn't let Roden train *my* gift. I mean, am I not just about to go to Horigos to kill someone who's been living a perfectly normal existence despite our *fucking* talent? Despite Roden being completely, utterly absent from his life? No frenzy, no violent episode. Has this poor bastard ever tried to steal a soul for the pure pleasure of it?"

A big sigh. "Roden explained that—"

"What? That this Rogue may be behind a group of rebels capturing his precious souls? An assumption! We are following his orders based on freaking assumptions. Where are all these enemies ready to destroy our people? Galen and I have been to Horigos hundreds of times and never felt threatened." I look at the hand I've just raised as if I could grab her shoulder from a distance and force her to look at me. My chest heaves.

"Explaining that is not my duty. I'm sorry, July." Her voice is so fucking calm.

"Explain this then—Why have I never heard of a Rogue running after Horigeans to eat their souls? Am I so fucking brilliant that I truly catch them before shit happens? Tell me, did you ever see one of these mythical creatures?"

Popplewish's shoulders drop, her fingers scratching so hard on the desk that I wouldn't be surprised to see marks on its surface. "That. Is. Not something you want to see…"

I cock my head as if she could see my reaction even with her back turned.

"I can take it."

She is shaking visibly, but her voice still demonstrates restraint when she says, "Don't ask for truths you may regret knowing."

"Why?"

She spins on her heels so fast I back against the door. Her face is pale, her lips pressed into a thin line. "Because the more you know, the more your arrangements with Roden will change." Her breath catches in her throat.

"My deal is with the Chapter—"

"Our time is over…" Her eyes pierce me, imploring me to stop. I'm dismissed.

But is it fear I read in her eyes?

I look down at my shoes, defeated. The marble floor is so shiny beneath me that I can almost see my reflection, like on my first day in Libera when Miss P. let me sit in one of her beautiful armchairs and offered me vanilla biscuits. She held my hand for so long that day while I cried until my tears ran dry. I missed my home—even my parents, a little—and had experienced the surreal journey from Horigos to Libera for the first time. I was shocked and nauseated.

My stomach is churning, like years ago, but for a different

reason. And I doubt vanilla biscuits would help.

Popplewish speaks again softly, "Promise me you'll come to me for any questions. Don't go scavenging on your own. I know you don't trust me anymore but… *please*, do not put your faith in anyone who may promise you an easy way out of this deal."

"*That* will be a problem. Misplaced faith is my speciality, apparently." I hold her gaze, forcing myself to sound final, adding, "After this mission, I want you to erase my memories. I want to start from scratch—no rebels, no deals, no Rogues…" I take a deep breath, "And if it doesn't go well—"

"Nothing will happen to you."

"You don't know that."

"You're right, but I know you."

I mumble something, maybe a stupid *thanks*, and she smiles. But I'm not ready to return the feeling.

"Stay true to yourself, July."

"Goodbye, Miss Popplewish."

Chapter 22 - Lights
July

My life on Horigos was just fine; like many others, I was a child without knowledge of life, pain, lies—or souls. That is, until my gift started to show, and my parents decided to try every creed on Horigos to purify me.

They travelled the continent from north to south, trying to find a cure for whatever was happening to their little girl, whose breath was slowly turning purple.

One day, we were roaming the streets of Brenath, and I noticed a cat resting under a fishmonger's stall. They ordered me to return when I rushed towards it, but the only thing I could focus on was the thin, smoke-like thread coming out of its fur—its soul slowly abandoning its body. Even if, at the time, I didn't know and acted by pure instinct.

They thought my sanity was irremediably gone when I began to cry, trying to push the soul back into the cat. While I was distraught to see the poor animal slowly dying before my eyes, my parents and the people around me only witnessed a child playing with something invisible over the corpse of an insignificant animal.

Everyone, that is, but a stranger with a walking cane tapping against the cobbled street.

"You're in the wrong place, my child." He'd addressed *me*. A crying little girl.

Roden trained me, made me believe I could be a protector to our people and the Horigeans.

But all he told me was just a sugarcoated version of the truth, layered with bullshit.

That's all I remember from my short life on Horigos—always being an exception, the lonely anomaly. And sometimes, I still feel like I'm walking alone—especially in my dreams. I'm a little girl, and my hand cuts through the air, searching for another hand to hold. But all I grasp is emptiness.

I had those dreams every night after relocating to Libera until I met Galen; when I told him about my mares, he gave me a pair of gloves.

"Keep them next to you when you go to sleep. They're mine, and it will be like holding my hands," he had said with such a serious face that I took his advice as scientifically proven.

I cling to that warm memory as I climb the centuries-old stone stairs of one of the five towers of the Blind Wise; the fresh air of the night welcomes me as a broad smile spreads on my face, already savouring whatever surprise awaits me.

But except for some gulls flying by, I'm alone. The square roof is empty, and Galen is nowhere to be seen.

I drop my smile, feeling foolish, and I quickly cross the distance from the arched door on top of the stairs to the parapet overlooking the Wise's inner courtyard, where, once a day, students and senior Harvesters take combat and shooting classes.

None of the castle's outdoor areas is off-limits. There is a main gate and three smaller entrances on the longer sides and at the back of the Wise, but they're never locked.

And yet, I'm surprised to hear sounds coming from the yard just below the tower, of steps and disembodied voices, distorted and carried away by the wind that blows from the north shore.

Ignoring the voice at the back of my head telling me it's none of my business, I push against the parapet and get up on my toes, craning my neck to catch a glimpse of whoever is in the garden.

"Looking for something?"

I spin around so fast that the palms of my hands scratch against the uneven stones.

"You are so inconsiderate! I could have hit you… or… or jumped… over the wall—and died. Why do you always do that? Can you not just announce yourself like a normal person?" I step away from the parapet, shivering and glaring at Galen.

"Nosy and over dramatic. I'm happy to see your mood has improved since this morning," he chortles, staring at me from under the tower's arched door, hands in his pockets, before strolling towards me.

I blow on the little grazes on my hands to soothe the sting, and the air comes out in a light violet puff. March is a month of continuous weather changes, but—when did it get so cold so suddenly?

"Look what you've done." I raise my hands, gesturing at the tiny red spots on my palms.

Galen dismisses my non-life-threatening situation with a shrug. "Blame your curiosity and the old stones, not me."

Had he not just made a subtle negative remark about my overthinking brain, I would have invited him to look down with me to find out who had decided to spend the last free hours of a fine Sunday night in the darkness of a solitary courtyard.

Instead, I mumble a pathetic excuse for my behaviour and follow his movements as he approaches the wall and looks up at the sky. "You know what? I think the last snowfall of the year is coming."

I search the sky, moving closer to Galen. He's changed his clothes since this morning, and his thick, black cashmere jumper looks so soft and warm I'd gladly snuggle inside it like a squirrel.

Resting my forehead against his arm, I whisper, "What's with the fancy outfit?" I eye his black trousers and crisp white shirt, clearly freshly ironed, peaking out from under his jumper.

Galen gives me a quick side-eye but remains silent.

I step back to take in the whole picture and pinch his biceps before pointing at his head. "Aha! And you did your hair… Are you going somewhere else later?" I narrow my eyes so much I can barely notice a smile stretching on his lips.

"Why do you always think something is going on behind your back, Sof? Always a mystery?" He tilts his head, offering me his hand. "Come on, follow me and no more questions until we are there."

"But I thought we were already there," I protest, hiding my neck in my shoulders when a gust of wind blows from behind me.

"Na-ha, no more chatting."

As I nod and take his hand, he leads me away from the parapet and back to the tower's door.

But instead of heading back down, he takes the second set of stairs towards the Wise's tallest tower, added by Roden to the original structure as a statement of his self-proclaimed ownership over the castle.

As I finally understand, I exclaim, "You tricked me!" Even if I can't see his face, I can hear him giggling.

Still holding my hand, climbing slowly so I can follow without tripping, Galen says, "Did you really think I would have let you come here before me and spoil whatever I was planning?"

"So you gave me the wrong location?"

He stops to look at me over his shoulder quickly. "Not exactly. I gave you the right location that leads to our final destination."

We remain silent for a few more steps until he asks, "How does it feel not knowing where the next step will take you?"

I open my mouth to answer, but I forget my words when a larger door appears in front of us with the dark shape of Roden's Tower rising behind it. The mist cannot conceal its thick body as its top soars sturdy and lonely against the dark blue sky.

"It feels—inevitable." I'm not sure why my answer sounds more like a question.

Galen's grip on my hand tightens before he says, "Don't lie to me. I know you need to know every single detail of your day. Even if you're going for a run. You need to know the path, obstacles, and weather forecast. I know you're dying to stop and force me to tell you what's on that tower."

My answer doesn't come as promptly as I'd like it to, and I fall silent at the irony of his words. At the monumental pile of uncertainty my life has turned into in the last forty-eight hours.

I take a deep breath, letting go of his hand to step before him and crossing my arms over my middle. "I just… like to be ready—" My voice breaks when I focus on what's waiting behind the door's metal bars.

Roden's tower's roof is only accessible on special occasions, but Galen managed to have its gate unlocked tonight. It matches the size of the room hosted inside the tower, which was converted into a vast ballroom and floored with white marble veined with real gold.

"Galen, how did you… ?" I pirouette, giggling, and find him leaning against the side wall, staring at me with a satisfied smirk.

"Someone owed me a favour, but don't get too excited; we only have access to the roof, not the ballroom," he states with a pinch, well - a spoonful - of pride.

He pushes away from the entrance without taking his eyes off me and saunters over. "Let me show you something…" He offers me his hand and, without warning, spins me in his arms, covering my eyes with his free hand. "Trust me…" he whispers, his breath warm against the shell of my ear.

I put one foot in front of the other, letting him guide me.

Until he lifts one finger at a time. "Keep your eyes closed."

For a moment, there's just me and the chilled night breeze.

"You can look now…" Galen rests a finger under my chin and gently lifts my head as I open my red Harvester eye first, then the green one.

It takes me a few seconds, but when my eyes adjust, I gasp. The stars seem to have reverted to their course. Instead of growing darker, the sky lights up with the warming tones of dawn. But I soon notice that the tower itself is igniting the sky with a myriad of white and purple fairy lights that run along and across the walls.

Joy bursts out of my mouth as I start twirling with my arms open to take in all the magical, unexpected scenery.

"Did you do this? When? How?" I chirp like an excited child.

I stop spinning only when Galen catches my hands, and I nearly stumble, stopping from bumping my head against his chest just in time. I close my eyes and take a deep breath to help my stomach settle.

When I reopen them, Galen is staring at me with a delightful smile beaming on his perfect lips.

"I'd do anything for you, Sof."

Once, he told me I was like a missing piece of his life he didn't know he'd lost.

"Sof?"

"Sorry, I was reminiscing."

"About?"

"Missing pieces." I smile and break free from his hands.

I walk to where the parapet opens onto a balcony with the best view of all the towers, and I let out a loud sigh as my attention roams over the vast park at the foot of the castle's main entrance, dotted by little pagodas with benches and tables for lunch breaks and quiet reading sessions.

The round square in the middle lies empty and tranquil, its quiet only broken by the intermittent spurts of water of the twins' green-tiled fountains at the edge of the gated perimeter surrounding the Blind Wise.

I prop my elbows on the parapet, closing my eyes to better enjoy the night breeze on my face.

"You're such a weird creature, July Crimson," Galen mutters next to me. "So tell me, were you serious when you asked me about moving somewhere else?"

I knew I shouldn't have asked. "Oh, that. Just ignore it. I was confused, you know, emotional. Stupid monthly hormones and all."

He mumbles, doubtful, so I try to manoeuvre the conversation somewhere else, "Is this all for our birthday?"

But all I get is a wicked smirk as Galen turns his back to the parapet, presses his hands on its flat top and, with an easy push, sits on the edge.

I outstretch an arm automatically. "Be careful—" But he leans towards me, catches my hand and hauls me up beside him, laughing at my terrified face.

"Chocolate?" He asks as if nothing's happened, dangling a salted caramel bar in front of me while I'm still in shock, mouth agape and eyes wide.

I slap him on the knee to release the tension. "I thought we were having dinner?" I object, testing with one hand the width of the parapet because I'm too scared to look behind me.

He shakes his head, swinging his legs like a child on a chair too high for him, "I thought we could mix things up a little and start from the dessert. I know what you are trying to do, anyway… You haven't answered my question yet," he continues, snapping a corner of the chocolate bar with his teeth, looking distractedly at the sky.

My stomach shrinks into a ball the size of a blueberry. If I don't fix this now, he will hold a grudge against me, even if only for a short time. And it will undoubtedly ruin the lovely memory of this evening.

Following his gaze, I turn my eyes to the sky and, wriggling cautiously, I get closer to him, bumping his shoulder. "How much do you know about the Harvesters that wish to continue their career elsewhere?" I ask casually to change the subject without being too obvious.

He blinks in surprise and lowers his eyes to me. "As much as anybody else, really. There are only a few placements available every year, and you need to pass an impossible number of tests before going into training. It's a too-long journey for such a boring position," he shrugs and snaps another piece of chocolate.

"Boring?" I object, "I'd rather say *thrilling*. Think about it: you get to live two identities!" I lift two fingers before stealing the chocolate from his hand. "Can you imagine how many people you can meet? All the places you can visit? I always wanted to visit Cleryce and its fried food festival. As a tourist, not a Harvester…"

I jump off the parapet, resting my back against it and searching for warmth in my pockets.

"If you want my honest opinion, you're fantasising too much about things you don't know. I've spent some time in Cleryce, and there is nothing memorable to it—" he cuts himself off as if he's now the one who wants to drop the subject.

I push away from the wall and walk across the little square to check the view on the opposite side: the inner oval training yard, divided into two asymmetrical halves by a short path crowned by brownstone arches. The wider half is used for training, whereas the other hosts a small apple and pear orchard, as well as a little pond of crystal-clear water, home to some koi carp.

And, towards the horizon, where the blue line of the sea meets the sky, only visible to the Harvester-trained eyes—the Grace Wards, Roden's fabricated wall of unique magnetised particles that divides Libera from Horigos. Should the Horigeans try to sail through it without a permit, like the one granted to Horigean food traders, they'd burst into smoke and ashes.

"Do you remember when we thought the island was part of Horigos, that the sky and the sea were just the shell of a giant marble, and we were all living inside it?" I ask Galen while fiddling with a string of fairy lights.

"Sof… ? Why do you really want to leave Libera?" His voice carries a hint of worry. When his shoulder brushes against mine, tension travels from his body to mine.

"I guess… Maybe my mind still recalls my early years, when I didn't even know I had a gift. Perhaps it's different for those like me who weren't born on the island like you."

"I know you like to feel special," he teases me, arching a brow and pushing me lightly. "But the island is full of people born on Horigos who then moved to Libera—thanks to Roden." There is a pause as he studies me in silence. "Thanks to your unique ability…"

Under the intricate web of artificial lights and the night hue, Galen's face is a puzzle of shadows and reflections, but his voice is as clear as ever, and I can't ignore how it drops when he mentions Roden.

"Hmm," I distractedly bite my thumbnail. "My ability is only good when the worst is about to happen. I'm more like Roden's personal soul-sweeper."

For some reason, I can't shake off the feeling that, lately, Galen and I have been playing a game of tug-of-war where he pulls me right back in whenever I try to break free from an uncomfortable conversation. But this is no children's game because if I pull too hard, he could end up in a treacherous pool of quicksand, and I will have to jump in, if not to save him, to share at least the destiny I've forced upon him.

My thoughts spiral—quickly.

But when I'm about to reach the bottom of my dark well, Galen taps me on the head with that open smile that works better than ten hours of sleep, "Come on, little egg. Let's go somewhere warmer before the party of thoughts in your brain cracks your shell open."

I push up on my toes to cast a last glance at the hills, now wrapped in a milky mist, while an early snowflake lands on my hand. "Galen, look," I exclaim. "I guess you were right."

"As if I'm never not," he giggles and offers me his jumper. "Promise me you'll come back." He adds with a dim light in his eyes, I can't explain. Perhaps it's just a reflection of the fairy lights.

"Only if you promise me you won't fall madly in love with Lucretia." I stick my tongue out before running away. "Whoever reaches the bottom of the stairs first decides what to eat!" I shout.

Chapter 23 - H
July

The five towers of the Wise are all equipped with two separate sets of stairs: one running along the external structure, not often used due to safety reasons but great for enjoying the panoramic view while going up and down the steps, and one built inside the towers, lined with doors that lead to the many rooms of the castle.

As I skip down the steps of the outer staircase, Galen's laughter follows me, and I wish I could bottle those notes and keep them with me forever. I brush my hands over the ancient stones until his voice and some timid snowflakes melt in the wind, which whistles behind me and through the cracks in the boulders.

Wait a minute…

Even if his voice is nothing but a fresh memory because, for some reason, Galen has decided not to run after me, the sound of something other than the wind seems to chase me not too far behind.

On an intermediate landing, I freeze halfway to check if Galen has trained so often with Popplewish that I didn't notice he was silently walking behind me.

I spin on my heel, excited to see his familiar silver and brown eyes, but I only find an empty and eerily quiet space. Pushed by instinct, I flatten against the wall as if making space for something to pass by without seeing me.

"Who's there?" My whisper comes out dark purple, and I frown at that sign of my surging distress.

The old stones are warm under my hand when I seek something to hold onto in the semi-darkness of the young night; the gleam of the fairy lights is now just a comforting memory.

"Galen, this is not funny…"

Why is the wall so warm?

I can't see much before me, and there is no other sound but the constant howling of the wind carrying the last snowflakes of the season. I slowly peel myself off the wall, taking a few steps backwards until my left heel meets the void of the next step.

"July?" Galen's scream hits me like a frozen spike to my chest, a moment before a louder noise takes over.

I don't know when the snow turned into rain, but the water hits the walls with such fury that it roars in my ears like endless thunder. I retract my hand from the wall as the icy drops roll down my skin, and the mixture of hot and cold confuses my senses.

"What's happening? Galen?" My voice is so weak compared to the rain; I struggle to hear myself.

"Sooof…"

The stones beneath my feet shake violently, and I bend my knees to keep my balance. With arms flung out, I turn my head left and right, searching for the source of my sudden fear.

Then everything stops.

I lean against the solid wall that shares one side with the indoor staircase of the tower, finding the stones too warm despite the icy, angry blades falling from the sky. I shake water and locks of hair off my face and try to slow my breath, inhaling cold droplets with a hint of something acrid.

An army of growls rolls beneath my feet, shaking my bones and the ground so violently that even the curtain of rain seems to recoil upwards until nothing but traces of its furious and brief passage remains.

When I look down, fearing the floor will split apart and swallow me, a gust of hot air lashes my cheek. I grunt, ready to fight an invisible danger, to sprint towards a safe spot—but my legs refuse to move.

"Galeeeen!" I cry. My arms go rigid at my sides as my fingers curl into fists. But I receive no answer other than the constant rumbling within the tower's body, like war drums.

Something flickers to my left, behind one of the narrow windows dotting the wall. I glimpse inside at the spiral stairs, through the iron patterns of leaves and flowers protecting the beautiful, tinted glass. Not too far, the double door that opens onto the majestic ballroom, is enveloped in coals of—

"Fire…" I mutter. Tall dancing flames lick the Blind Wise's hard skin as if savouring it before commencing the feast.

Hypnotised, I realise my fingers are latched onto the iron leaves only when their sharp edges cut through my skin. I swear in pain and jump back when a flame whips out of the ballroom, as if aiming for me.

I duck and crouch, seconds before the glass explodes, scattering shards all over. Hissing above me, the fire commands me to stay down as it tries to find new stones to destroy, pushed by the wind towards the bottom of the tower.

Safe or not, crawling back from where I came from is the only route I have left if I don't want to face the raging wall of fire growing a few levels below me. Ignoring the pieces of hot glass scratching against my wrists and hands, I draw myself forward using my elbows, keeping my head down.

I move away from the window as much as the narrow space allows, towards those spots on the floor worn out by centuries of people walking on it and where the rain has created shallow puddles of water. The sudden heat caused by the explosion has almost dried my clothes completely, so I splash my face and hair to buy myself enough time to move away from this nightmare.

"Keep moving…" I order myself to distract my mind from the slender columns of smoke spiralling up through the gaps between stones.

The Wise's old bones crack and complain. Its body shivers as stronger flames eat and erode it from the inside. This is *not* the work of someone ruthless enough to play dangerous games in the building.

What if the strangers in the courtyard… ? I splash more dirty water on my face; I'm about to climb back to the top of the burning old castle—whoever caused this nightmare is not my priority.

As far as I can see, the flames haven't yet reached the top floors and the stairs in front of me are clear of smoke. The top of the tower, where I left Galen, still rests like a placid giant among the clouds. Running to him will be easy, but the inevitable descent scares me.

When the heat becomes bearable, and I'm sure I can stand up without being scorched, I push up onto my hands and knees, ignoring the scratches and pain in my palms. The wall on my right, facing the solitary square below, still retains some of its natural coolness when I run my hand over it, searching for support.

"What the—" My voice is raw after inhaling smoke and dirt.

A hand, gloved in worn brown leather and with a grip too firm for me to break free, loops around my wrist and yanks me up.

"Going somewhere, girl?" A voice I don't recognise scratches my ear.

I wriggle hopelessly. "Let me go."

A black, shiny boot with a spiked golden spur taps impatiently on the floor as my eyes, red and burning, take in the sight of dark green trousers puffed up at the owner's thigh level.

I may not know this man, but I recognise his outfit too well.

My eyes linger on his uniform, but when I jerk my head up to look at his face - and possibly headbutt him under the chin - he swirls me around, pressing my back against his chest and blocking my arms with only one hand.

Even if my feet barely touch the floor, I try to use the momentum to kick back and get away, but the stranger is taller and stronger than I am and easily forces me down on my knees, into a choke-hold.

"Ah, ah, not so fast. We'll have time for the pleasantries later. But now I need you to stay calm and quiet."

I cough, my shoulders screaming in pain as the stranger tightens the grip around my wrists.

"Who the hell are you? What have you done to Galen?" I bite my tongue too late.

His malicious chuckle brings tears to my eyes. "Is that your little friend? Don't worry, my people are taking care of him as we speak," he spits, cold and collected, as if the thought that the Wise may collapse at any point didn't even cross his mind.

I try to look at him over my shoulder. "Is it you I saw earlier in the courtyard... How did you get in? How did you get *here?*" I sputter.

"I said quiet!" he roars, releasing my throat from his hold to lift my arms behind my back with his free hand and pull me up.

The pain blinds me. My muscles and joints strain to the point of snapping like twigs. I would scream loud enough to make myself heard from miles, but the stranger has knocked all the air out of my lungs.

My knees buckle as the man lowers my arms a little, his grip still strong on me. When he pulls me towards his chest, I retch at the smell of cigars and musk reeking from his clothes.

I hear him grunting in a language I don't understand before something cold touches my skin, and a pair of manacles snap shut around my wrists.

His breath stinks like rotten meat washed down with cheap wine when he says, "And now let's take care of your chatty mouth..." - before pressing a rough piece of cloth, wet with something sweet, against my lips.

My eyelids turn heavy, and when the stranger puts his hand against my forehead to keep my head up, terror pervades me at the sight of a thick, red *H* branded on the inside of his wrist.

"Tell me, girl", he whispers in my ear as I struggle to stay alert, "How does it feel to be in the presence of someone you thought was just a *myth?*"

Chapter 24 - A Life for a Life
July

The night before a crossing is a night of rituals.

I've heard of Reapers staining their pillows with the blood of their past crops, or spending the night in the woods between Evemerys and Anagessys, to focus their minds on the task ahead and not on the comfort of their beds.

Galen always carries with him some memorabilia, like a gemstone fallen from a bracelet, or a button ripped from a crop's jacket, after he's delivered the empty vessels to the Deleteri permanently stationed at the Fields.

"Let. Her. Go."

Although tonight, there will be no sleep. No luck-summoner gesture. Not even a morning after—by the look of it.

"You forgot *'If you hurt her, I'll rip your spine off and send it to your family'*, isn't that what the dark hero always says? And let me guess—I do what you ask, and then you let me walk away? Don't embarrass yourself, boy, and drop that gun."

As I fight to stay alert, Galen's silhouette stands out tall against the dark staircase behind him. His posture doesn't betray any uncertainty when he takes a step forward. "I said, let her go and step away. What I'll do with you after is a surprise."

"You know you won't make it far against *us*." The thick cotton of the stranger's uniform grazes my neck when he lifts me like a shield between him and Galen.

He's fast, despite his size, but also distracted enough to release the pressure on my mouth.

"Galen…" I mumble. Tears of pain and rage sting in my nose like the stranger's smell as I inhale deeply to send enough oxygen to my brain and shake my senses awake.

Despite my blurry vision, I detect a grey wall of smoke dotted by small, random explosions of orange and red rising from the top levels of the Wise. The fire breaking free from inside the building is now devouring the head of the castle as well as its foundations.

"You may want to rethink that. I offered the same choice to your friends, up there…" Galen replies, oddly calm, jerking his chin to the tower behind him. His smirk makes me shiver. His eyes darken as he shrugs and adds, "They didn't listen to me…"

There is something savage in his eyes when he raises his fist in the air, the other hand steadily aiming a gun at the stranger's head. With a husky laugh that sounds more like a feral growl of satisfaction, he opens his fingers and lets a bunch of white pebbles drop to the floor.

No. Not pebbles—

"You rotten piece of shit," the stranger barks in my ear, making the small hairs on my neck stand up, as we both stare at a bunch of teeth rolling towards us.

The man's confidence shakes and cracks like the Wise's body. His hands are busy keeping me still, one holding my cuffed wrists, the other looped around my shoulders, but his body tenses against mine as if sensing his luck is one step too close to a precipice.

Galen stalks towards us, crushing some of the teeth under his boots. In response, the stranger presses his forearm against my neck, cutting off my air supply.

Surprisingly, Galen doesn't flinch. "Did you really think you could simply cross our skies, unseen, using fire as a decoy? I thought that centuries of waiting in your filthy, shitty rabbit holes would create at least a slightly smarter generation of Herionos."

I gasp, and for a split second, Galen's eyes meet mine.

The stranger chuckles, "Perhaps not smarter, but surely better at making allies…"

As the stranger's words float and vanish in the space between us, Galen shifts his weight onto his left foot, a stance that promises nothing good. His rage is charging to a level that could force him towards a regrettable decision.

The stranger seems to notice as well, and he pushes me forward, my feet barely touching the ground, as if challenging Galen.

His lips are like sandpaper against my cheek as he lowers and hisses in my ear, "Let's see where you stand on your friend's scale of priorities."

The man loosens the grip around my wrists, his movements precise and swift.

One moment, I think I'm almost free; the next, I hear a click as something hard presses against my back. My eyes widen, and my jaw tightens when the stranger's gun bites at my spine.

"He's armed, Galen. Shoot him—" I lunge forward, but the man pulls me back by my hair.

"Ah! How observant! What were you expecting? A bunch of flowers?" he snaps, running the barrel up over my spine until it meets the small of my neck, where it rests hard and cold.

I hiss through my teeth, clenching my jaw to conceal any hint of distress my face may show. Galen hesitates, biting at his lips, his nostrils flaring. He is a great shooter and could aim blindfolded, but we both know that no bullet can fly fast enough to hit the stranger before he fires his own gun.

A fire hotter than the one raging around us burns in my veins. Images from the past days, the feeling of being thrust left and right, with no chance to make my own decisions, sparks something inside of me.

Somehow, Galen reads my intentions and shakes his head slightly.

The stranger doesn't seem to notice our silent exchange and carries on, arrogantly, "I am feeling generous today. You can either let me and your little girlfriend pass before this wreckage of a castle collapses. Or—"

Ignoring the mouth of the gun grazing at my skin with a silent promise of certain death, I tilt my head slightly to the side, faking a coughing fit to distract him while I bend my knee to brace my leg, charging my limb with anger, disgust, hate and desperation.

I have no time to study a trajectory based on our height difference, so I kick back with the sole of my shoe, hoping to hit the stranger, praying for a miracle. This is not a second-chance situation.

My heel crashes against the man's shin with a sickening sound, followed by his scream of pain. He stumbles back, letting go of my neck, and I promptly hunch down. Everything begins to move as if seconds are stretching like an elastic band about to snap. But at the violent sound of an explosion, time speeds up to normal, and I hit my cheek hard against the wet stones.

For a second, everything falls silent.

I prop myself up, groaning in pain. My hands are bleeding from a myriad of small cuts, and I taste blood on my tongue. But there is another source of discomfort I can't locate until I sit back on my heels and glance over my shoulder to check if the stranger is still there.

The top of my right sleeve is ripped between my neck and shoulder, and blood is flowing down my arm, dripping from the tip of my fingers in a pink puddle on the floor.

Realising that the wound is real makes it even more painful, but I can't help gaping, then smiling proudly, at the image of the man behind me, contorting on the floor in agony.

He is trying to sit up, without much success, stretching his arms towards his leg, bent at an odd angle, as blood gushes out from a nasty wound in his abdomen every time he moves. His mouth agape, his terrified eyes almost as wide.

I can't stop staring. I turn on my knees, wincing when I press my hands, still bound, down to keep my balance. As much as I want to believe he can't harm me anymore, I need to make sure his gun is out of reach.

I quickly scout around, searching for it until I spot it meters behind him. It must have flown away when Galen shot him.

Reality strikes.

"You. Fired…" I mutter. An odd thing to notice when I was the one who ordered Galen to kill the bastard. But thinking that I was right in the trajectory of the bullet… Had I not moved faster, I'd probably be the one bleeding to death.

"It's done. We're safe." Galen's voice is croaky when he approaches me, the familiar scent of him carried by the howling wind.

As much as I want to turn around and bury my face in his chest, as much as I need to believe his words, I keep my attention on the stranger. His fingers are battling to put pressure on the wound while life abandons him in violent spurts of blood. The subtle halo of his soul starts misting off his body like fog off warm soil.

It doesn't have any particular hue but instead just a milky tone to it. That of a soul who's never needed Roden's help. Something so rare I've never encountered before, and only ever read about.

I can't take my eyes off of him even when a wet gurgle escapes his open mouth, and the man spits blood.

I blink tears away.

Galen's bullet must have compromised more than one organ and blood vessels because the man's face is turning ashen too quickly.

Rain begins to fall again, loud and heavy, like curtains on a stage, when Galen kneels behind me and starts fidgeting with the manacles at my wrists. In seconds, they snap open, and Galen throws them away, spins me around and hugs me against his chest before I can witness the last minutes of the stranger's solo performance. Panic, anger, fear of losing my best friend—every single feeling comes to me in a rush.

I gently push away from him and cup his cheek, shaking. "He could've killed you, he…"

Raindrops run down his face, flattening his hair over his eyes. "Sof, we have to go." He brushes dirt and tears off my cheek with his thumb before casting a quick look at the dying body behind me.

He lowers his hands on my shoulders. I'm paralysed by cold and fear, but Galen's grip is the only thing that keeps me from shattering into pieces. Until he squeezes too hard, and I flinch.

"He hurt you. Where?" he lifts his hand, hissing through his teeth.

I shake my head, and a faint smile crosses my face. "I'm fine; it's just a scratch… *dark hero,*" I repeat the stranger's early words, if only to release some of the tension still building up in my guts, as I peer down at the wound, where the blood has already turned darker and thicker.

When I move my eyes back to him, Galen is staring at his hands. "I didn't have another choice…" His words tangle with the dreadful cries of the dying stranger.

I take his hands into mine and let out a deep sigh. "It is not your fault. If it wasn't for you, that could have been me." I jerk my head to the man behind me, still finding it difficult to call him what he really is.

But I can't ignore it any longer.

My heart beats fast, and my breath catches short. "Please, tell me I heard you wrong. I was panicking—the rain, the fire—" My head is heavy, and dark spots start dancing behind my eyes.

"July, listen to me. You're fainting. If we don't leave now, we will both end up trapped up here with no option but to run through the fire." Galen ignores my questions and pulls me back to my feet.

Before I can rebut, he starts leading me towards the stairs, keeping hold of my bloodied hand. I trail after him in shock, glad at least one of us still has the spirit to think straight after what just happened.

We approach the lifeless body with caution, and Galen kicks it in the ribs twice before we jump past it.

Perhaps it was all a misunderstanding.

The rain has turned into a blissful stream. In the corner of my eyes, the fire is still raging and climbing over the windows, still trying to devour the Wise from the inside, but the rain is turning the flames into wisps of harmless smoke, making our escape less frightful.

"I got another one, but I have to run... Abandon the Wise ASAP. It's not safe - I repeat - not safe." I hear Galen roaring over the commotion of water and fire as he presses a finger to his right ear. "The fire... what? That was a *decoy*... My suspicions were right—Roden knows... I'm going to the beach... pray *she's* there..."

Who is he talking to? But my brain can only process one thing at a time; I can either breathe or talk.

The way down the tower's outermost stairs is too narrow for two people to run side by side, so I let Galen lead while I throw panicked looks over my shoulder to make sure nobody is following.

We proceed as fast as we can, stopping only when a sudden burst of glass and stones fills the air with the acrid smell of smoke.

I know Galen would go faster if he weren't aware of my wound, but the way he's moving - almost limping - tells me something is not right.

Something I didn't notice before catches my attention, and I can't help but tug at his hand, forcing him to stop and look at me as I point at a stain darkening the rim of his white shirt just above his left hip.

"You're bleeding." I suck in water and smoke.

He lowers his eyes. "Just a scratch. I think he fired when you kicked him, but missed," he answers too hastily.

"It's all my fault... I shouldn't have—"

He brushes a lock of hair off my cheek, smiling. "You were being reckless, as usual, but you saved us both." Like mine, his voice is hoarse.

With a gentle pull, Galen restarts our descent to safety. "Come on."

I've always known he was a great fighter; I've witnessed it during our training sessions, and that earned him the role of a Deleteri leader. But having seen him in action put him in a different light. He didn't flinch at the Herionos - if that's what he really was - bleeding to death on the floor. That wasn't the first time he'd shot someone. We do carry weapons when in Horigos, mostly for self-defence, but I had no memory of Galen killing anyone—until now.

Until he had to take a life to save mine.

Chapter 25 - Cinders of a Wise Soul
July

The passage before us narrows as we approach the bottom of the tower, engulfed by water, flames, and smoke. Despite being slippery with blood and sweat, I hold onto Galen's hand as if my life depended on it—which it probably does.

Above us, the mouth of the Wise thunders, its stones chatter, and its head swings like that of a man about to fall under a flurry of shots.

I exhale with relief when the last steps finally come in sight, and I spot the main gate wide open, waiting for us to run to safety. I speed towards it, expecting to see people running towards us, alerted by the ominous noises and the flames, but my gaze stretches over the empty darkness of the Wise's external garden.

Galen comes to a halt beside me. "Not that way. We're going out through the back gate," he pants, pausing to approach the smaller, almost hidden wooden door on the right side of the tower's base.

"You mean crossing through the training square? If any of those who attacked us are still there or in the building, there will be nowhere for us to hide. We'll be in the open for a while."

Galen draws a big breath and closes his eyes. Something is off, but I guess the violence of the recent events has cracked his tough armour as well as mine. There are shadows under his eyes when he puts himself between me and the main gate, taking my hands in his. "Some of *us* are still fighting on the towers, buying us time."

Us?

He doesn't let me overthink it and, having shouldered the door open, jerks his chin, inviting me to follow. I rush outside, where cleaner air makes my lungs sing with joy, but where we also look like desperate ants scrambling for safety.

The wound in my shoulder shoots pain down to my fingertips every time I move my arm as I run behind Galen.

As I fight for my breath, I blurt, "Has this got to do with the Chapter?"

There is no accusation in my voice. No expectation. But we both stop at the same time. Galen's back is a trembling wall.

He slowly turns, but lowers his eyes to avoid mine. "Will you follow me if I say no?"

Right in front of me, the courtyard gleams as if ablaze. The reflection of the flames, that is, which have now reached the lower levels of the Wise and are dancing behind its windows, showering the round bushes of periwinkles and lilies adorning the perimeter in yellow and orange sparks.

The rain wasn't that powerful, after all.

I shake my head, searching for Galen's face, but he keeps his eyes on the ground. He's panting so heavily that air comes out of his mouth in dense, dark purple puffs.

I sigh. "It is true, then. Not just an uncomfortable feeling in my stomach."

"How?" he finally looks at me, wincing like the slightest movement is costing him all his strength.

"When I met the Chapter, Popplewish confessed Roden is not new to using the power of *your* Deleteri on Harvesters. I believe he did something to me. To make me forget the details of our dinner and our car ride. But—I don't know how; my subconscious retained something. And this morning, you looked so… Forcefully *unaware*. I thought my mind was playing tricks on me…"

His brows furrow. "I thought you were passed out at that point. I suggested there was no need to wipe your mind clean. That it was too dangerous…" His hand, covered in dirt and scratches, reaches for mine. His curls, damp with sweat and water, are stuck to his forehead. He seems older—stronger. Someone I've never really known.

I take a step back. "You… You're one of them," I deflate. At once, the raging fire seems friendlier than the face before me.

He drops his hand. "Evelyn asked Roden to reset only bits of that night to avoid long-term damage to your memory. *We* thought we did enough already—"

I clench my jaw to prevent my heart from leaping out of my mouth. Instead, it drops into such a dark place that I fear it is gone forever.

"How thoughtful… Then explain why, at breakfast this

morning, you pretended you didn't know my next destination. I'd already told you where they're sending me *before* our dinner." I struggle to believe that the voice I'm hearing is mine.

I don't intend to waste more time walking in the dark, putting together scraps of truth. I pretend the whole fucking thing.

I charge towards him and raise my hand, ready to slap him, but my fingers curl into a fist, nails digging into my palm. "For days, I've lived in fear, believing the fucking Chapter had completely messed up your brain as well, but you were probably just confused by all the lies you had piled up to keep me in check."

Whatever the reason for the pain on his face, either his wound or my poisonous words, I enjoy it.

Galen puts some distance between us. His boots skid on the muddy path, and he nearly loses balance. Wincing, he hunches to avoid falling on his back, a hand firmly pressed to his side.

I don't care. He deserves it. "While *I* was gambling with my life, making deals to keep you safe and away from this shitshow, you were enjoying it from the first row, pretending to be my friend—"

I stare at him; tears and raindrops run down my face while the Wise roars in despair before the atmosphere in the courtyard turns sticky and heavy as if the Blind is holding in a big breath—its very last one.

We exchange a knowing look and duck just before the castle exhales violently, showering us with a mixture of stone fragments and colourful glass shards.

The rain has lost its battle against the fire.

"That wasn't an act—" Galen struggles to speak.

We've both fallen flat on our stomachs, with our hands on our heads for protection.

"What?" I snap, slowly pushing back on my feet. I'm still wearing Galen's jumper, which is now covered in mud and falling to pieces. A dark stain is also spreading beneath my jeans on my left knee.

Galen slowly peels himself off the floor, his legs shaking under his weight. "I wasn't lying about Sector 43—I did not remember. That's why I wanted to see you tonight—" he flinches again, hissing through his teeth.

This time, I can't ignore the pain on his face, the silver specks in his eye losing their natural light, and I lunge forward to catch him should he fall. But another ominous sound and the ground shaking under our feet make us freeze. I look down at the thin cracks forming along the stone floor, one running right between my feet.

"As much as I want to kill you right now, with my own hands, I think we need to set your fucking betrayal aside and run." I glare at him sideways, but my eyes fall on the red stain on his shirt that spreads quickly, soaking the fabric.

I point a finger at his face, craning my neck to look him in the eyes, "Do not bleed out until we get away from here. I will not allow it. You *owe* me answers. Lots of them."

His voice is feeble; I hardly hear it when he says, with a grimace more than a smile, "Fine, lead the way, but I want you to have this."

He searches for something on his back, and when I hold up a

hand, flexing my fingers to hurry him, Galen produces a gun—the same he used to kill the Herionos.

"Don't wait to see someone else pointing a gun at you. If you feel threatened—use it."

"Don't give me ideas you may regret," I snatch the gun from his hand and lower it at my side. "Thanks," I add, hating the tone of my voice, which is still used to sound friendly when speaking with him.

The rain has stopped completely, and the smell of burning is nearly unbearable. Tongues of flames erupt from the Wise's head, the tops of its towers swallowed by columns of dark smoke.

We both look up.

We managed to stop them...

"I'm not waiting for the others," I snap.

"I understand."

"And you're not either."

Galen sighs and drops his shoulders. "They can take care of themselves."

I bite my lip; my feet refuse to move. "Was Popplewish there—You know what? I don't want to know."

"Sof, what do you want me to do?" Galen sounds exhausted, and the air from his mouth has turned dangerously pale.

I grunt in distress. "Just shut up, and let's get away from this place before it buries us. I hope you appreciate the fact I still have a speck of morality, unlike you, and I'm not leaving you here to die."

Conscious of his wound, I grab his hand and pull him towards the small black gate at the back of the castle.

As if to end our discussion, a couple of bricks fall a few inches from us, exploding in a cloud of dark red powder.

For once, I have to slow down to let him keep up. My run changes to a brisk walk, then weakens to a sudden stop. We've left the main building behind, its five towers only an intricate mass of black smoke and orange sparks. But we're still inside the perimeter of the Wise.

A tall enclosure of black metal bars surrounds us, topped by spiky ends in the shape of miniature towers. The main gate seems so far away, but I keep going because I know that the path running up the hill, beyond that gate, is a longer way to the shore, but it is also isolated and has a few good hiding spots.

I ask, between laboured breaths, "Why the shore?" I don't know where all my energy is coming from, but it's liberating to speak freely with Galen once again, even if not for the right reason— even if I want to stop and slap his face hard enough to leave a mark.

But he doesn't reply and only gives me a look that makes me wonder if I should knock him out and take the opposite direction.

"It is not a trap," Galen mutters as if reading my mind.

We both pant loudly, studying each other like wolves who used to belong to the same pack. I can't help but throw quick looks at his wound. It hasn't spread, but Galen's face is worryingly pale.

I nod, bracing my hands on my knees. "Right. You're lucky my only alternative is to go back to that nightmare of flames and smoke. Can you walk or—"

"Don't worry about me."

"Oh, I'm not. I don't want you to slow me down," I sound so bitter, I surprise myself.

But Galen looks at me through his dark lashes with a smirk.

I keep my expression flat but hurry to loop an arm around his, trying my best to hold him up as I start again for the gate, and to ignore the pain in my shoulder.

"I can see the path of trees that run down the hill towards the shore. We're nearly there." A pep talk for us both.

The gate swings slightly with the wind. The sea will soon appear beyond it like a dark purple line to the horizon. I can almost hear its voice—

"Stop." Galen's hand lands on my wounded shoulder like a claw as he unexpectedly steps in front of me and grabs my wrists.

"What the f—"

He pulls me into his arms, pushing my head against his chest, and turns us around so his back is to the castle. The imaginary voice of the sea turns into a whistle, growing closer by the second, until I spot a massive boulder flying towards us. I shut my eyes and bury my face against Galen moments before the stone lands inches from us and disintegrates as soon as it hits the ground.

For a moment, everything stops except for the ringing in my ears and Galen's laboured breath.

He presses his cheek against my head. "You're okay," he whispers. "You're safe…"

I push away and flinch at the state of his face. Scratches and grazes on his cheeks are barely visible under the layer of soil and dirt. Blood drips down from a cut on his forehead.

"What the hell happened on that tower?" I ask, tasting chalk on my lips.

This can't be a trap if he's just risked being flattened by a boulder to save me.

As if reading the doubt in my eyes, and perhaps the feeble hope that maybe he isn't lying and this whole freaking situation caught him by surprise as much as me, he takes my face in his hands and kisses my forehead, as I mumble, "You owe me—if we make it, you owe me big time."

His attempt at a smile puts a painful mask on his battered face.

I try to keep a straight face, "If we make it out alive, we are leaving this fucking place together," I offer him my hand. "Then I'll probably kill you."

There are no night birds in Libera. When the sun disappears behind the sea, gulls retreat inside caves by the shore, and little birds hide amongst the fat branches. Nights in Libera are utterly quiet and silent.

The day I met the Chapter, Roden spoke as if his words had no implication, "You bring me the rebel's soul, and you will be free to go as far as you want from the island. Anywhere, with whomever you want."

"And Galen won't remember?" That was my only clause in our agreement. I wanted him to forget everything about me, had he chosen to stay in Libera. Forget about my name and face—that I ever existed.

"Should he wish, Galen will be given a whole new life and purpose."

"How can I be sure?"

"Because *I'll* be watching over him as my personal responsibility," Popplewish had stepped in.

That day, I felt darkness; not because the birds had gone to sleep but because I had traded the life of a stranger for Galen's future.

Chapter 26 - Darkness
July

Only when I'm sure we've put enough space between us and the castle can I find the courage to stop, look back, and face the destruction we barely escaped.

"It's not safe yet," Galen suggests, frantically checking the same ear I saw him tapping earlier. "Shit! I lost it…" His voice is hushed by the ground rumbling beneath us and the daunting image of the solitary body of the Wise, shaking and glowing red in the distance.

The tears on my cheeks are cooler than the heat riding the violent wind blowing from the castle, and I let them dry while Galen keeps shouting something at me.

I push sticky locks of hair off my face and my eyes. My hand smells of blood and dirt when I cover my mouth in disbelief. "They have no time left… Whoever was up there with us… What have we done?"

We're standing on the hill's highest point, where fresh grass takes over the concrete path and begins its descent to the sea.

"How many?" I look briefly over my shoulder.

Galen's silence is unsettling. Once again, I'm pulled between the need to run away from a flesh-and-bone red flag and the hope of finding out that there is something he is not telling me just yet.

He takes my hand, and I let him. "Knowing won't change what happened. I told you, it was their decision." He sounds resolute despite the mask of pain on his face.

I angle my head and take a step back. The more I dig, the more Galen becomes a different person.

He sighs but keeps his eyes steady on the Wise. The silver in his left eye gleams with the orange reflection of the castle in flames when he tilts his head towards me. "They knew the cost, and the time they bought us will be wasted if we don't leave now—"

"Now..." I exhale, standing my ground. Perhaps I'm too scared to find out what else awaits.

"Sofia, we must go." An order, not an offer, even if his hand is gentle on my shoulder.

"If they were there, they knew this was coming— " I scan his face, the scratches on his forehead, his hair darkened by soot and soil.

"July!" Galen roars, and Libera echoes him, snatching me out of my reverie and throwing me against a wall of panic. Until everything around us goes unnervingly quiet.

I gape in awe, commanding my lungs to start working again.

The alarm in his eyes is enough for me. I flee, careful not to twist my ankles every time I stomp on uneven ground, following Galen when he speeds past me down the path to the shore. It falls steeper than I remember, but it all becomes insignificant in the blink of an eye—the Blind Wise bellows behind us.

A gust of hot wind thrusts me forward with such strength that I fear my spine will snap if I don't roll to the ground and down the hill. I wrap my arms around my head to shield my face from the shower of embers, hot stones, and debris that begins to rain after the apocalyptic sound.

Grass and soil, green and dark purple sky spin above me like I'm inside a wheel. When the optical illusion stops, I land face up with one arm braced over my forehead. My chest aches when I try to calm my breath down, but I'm alive.

Someone is tugging at my jumper, ripped in some places after tumbling down pebbles and rocks.

"Are you okay?" Galen coughs next to me.

"I think so—oh… Oh no…" I whimper, scrambling on my elbows to sit up. I should have stayed down, with my eyes to the sky. I should not have looked at the hill—never again.

Even from the hill's foot, I should be able to spot the majestic building towering over Libera, reddish brown and sturdy against the sky.

Not a pile of ruins and smoke.

Against the fire-lit sky, indistinct dark silhouettes run and scream, confused by what's just happened. The islanders must have woken up at the sound of the terrifying explosion and left their houses to investigate. Some head for the tall wall of dust rising from the sad remains of the castle, while others just stand in front of it, frozen by the sudden tragedy, or swinging like branches, dancing to the sound of their own lament, a constant background, a gut-wrenching, desperate melody.

I crawl away from that nightmare, shaking my head even if denying it wouldn't make it any less real. When I look at Galen, his clenched jaw and resolute expression confirm I'm not dreaming.

My thoughts race each other, and I can't control them. I try to get back on my feet, but my hands slip on the drenched soil, and I fall back on my elbows. "We need to go back—we need—" My eyes burn, but I can't stop staring at the mayhem unravelling so quickly.

"Sof, look at me," Galen kneels between my legs, obscuring for a moment that image of terror, and cups my face, "The choice is up to you. I'd follow you anywhere, even if that means marching towards certain death."

Under his damp curls, his eyes skim my face for any sign of significant wounds, like he does every time I come back from a mission, then he gently rubs a thumb on my dirt-covered jaw before lowering his hands to my shoulders.

"Has this got anything to do with that Rogue Roden so desperately wants?" I sink. Deflate.

Galen's eyes widen, but he quickly regains control. Only a nod as if saying the words will break whatever protection spell has kept us alive until now.

"Those people on the tower... the man who nearly killed us. The..." The word gets stuck in my throat.

"Herionos? It's not that simple." He nods, distractedly brushing the exposed skin of my collarbones.

Of course, it is not—especially when the closest threat comes from a myth.

The Herionos were - *are* - Harvesters who never approved of the way Roden decided to use our powers. They were the leading cause of the riots that forced the Harvesters away from Horigos. But they didn't let Roden and his followers go without leaving a trail of casualties on both sides.

Or so the books say.

The warmth I felt back at the tower, burning my skin through the stone walls and forcing me down the hill, is nothing compared to what's brewing inside me now. Pushing my hands and knees against the soft ground and digging my fingers into the soaked soil, I slowly peel myself back up.

I've spent years thinking I was alive when, in fact, I've only let others impose their purpose upon me. But now I can see clearly what I have to do and what I *want* to do.

"Ask me again? Ask me why I want to leave this place?" I look Galen straight in the eyes as he kneels at my feet.

He bows his head, and I extend my hand to help him up.

"I think I don't need to," he mutters. His eyes scan my face, reading on my scratched, sore skin the list of lies and truths thrown at me in the last couple of days.

"At least tell me," I squeeze his hand. "How did they get here? How did the Herionos evade our aerial shields and land on the Wise?" My voice breaks on the last word as if mourning a friend.

Galen's hand tightens around mine, clammy and damp with water and blood. The skin on the back of his hand is rough when I slightly brush it with my thumb.

"Someone let them in… Someone is interested in that Rogue as much as *we* are and must have gotten to the details of your mission just after Evelyn shared it with you."

As much as I enjoy the idea of someone wanting to fuck up the Chapter's plans the same way they did with my life and mind, I can't ignore the fact that many innocent Harvesters are now involved; their homes and lives irremediably endangered, like after the Great Famine.

"They should go after Roden." I dig my nails into my palm.

Galen lets go of my hand and remains silent for a moment, observing the fire in the distance as it devours what's left of the Blind Wise inch by inch.

"This won't stop Roden," he mumbles, slowly turning his attention to me. "This wasn't aimed at Roden…"

Revelation booms louder than the recent explosion. I back up, shaking my head.

"I'm the only one who can destroy that soul. They're after *me*?"

Galen sighs, "This is why I wanted to meet you on the tower. I was ordered to fly you from the island before your official crossing. The others with me on the Wise were only supposed to ensure we got away without interference. But—"

"The Herionos got there first. And the shore?"

A feline smile stretches on his lips. "*Our* people didn't survive for centuries without mastering second and third alternative escape routes."

The glaring flames shine behind Galen like a halo. I look past his shoulder. "That doesn't justify the lives lost up there."

I can't shake away the thought of me being here, close to safety, while innocents are battling not just the fire, but also against the Herionos running freely through Libera's streets.

Screams of war and cries of pain ring loudly in the air.

Galen grabs my wrist and motions towards the bottom of the hill. "People who believe in our cause are at work to save as many as possible. I know you have more questions than ever, and there will be time for explanations. But, for now, I need you to trust me."

When I hesitate and yank my arm away, he grimaces and grits his teeth, glaring at the blood stain on his shirt, which has spread a little bit more.

I step closer, meaning to lift his shirt to check the damage, but he holds a hand up, pressing the other against his abdomen.

He's fighting for breath, and it sounds like something small is rattling inside his chest. "I'm fine. Someone will fix me up, but we must now reach the shore. *She* saw me like this so many times—" He groans in pain, bending over and landing a hand heavily on my shoulder.

I stagger slightly under his weight, but I regain my balance and tilt his head up. "Are you sure this person is still there? Despite everything that's happening?"

A nod—that'll suffice for now.

Far whistles seem to follow us.

"Do you hear that?" he coughs.

"It's the rain extinguishing the fire—"

He shakes his head. "They're patrolling the area, looking for us." He grabs my hand, pulling me closer, and I can't help but gaze worriedly at his shirt splotched with blood.

The second after, we're running. My lungs burn, and my mind hurts with the thought that we're abandoning innocent people.

And I am the cause of their ruin…

The sea beckons in the darkness. The night breeze carries salty sand and the scent of the oil used to keep the torches burning at sunset. It welcomes Galen and me as we approach the beach.

There is something on the shore. Tiny lights flicker in the distance in two symmetrical lines, marking a landing path at the end of which someone waves a torch, signalling us to hurry up.

I allow myself a moment to stop and collect my thoughts while Galen, hands braced on his knees, exhales, "She made it."

The rain has stopped completely, and the sand crackles like burnt wood under my feet. Galen is a few steps in front of me, and when he turns, my heart sinks into my stomach—his face is pale, but it's not the moonlight making him look sick.

I hurry towards him. "You're going to pass out." My arms are outstretched, ready to catch his fall.

"Let's get to the platform," he groans from the back of his throat, "Tabitha will not wait any longer… I can manage."

"Tabitha? What? You can't be serious…" I blurt out,

instinctively darting my eyes towards the mysterious silhouette on the platform.

Tabitha Lorne is the second most famous name that spreads from mouth to mouth among first-year students. Second only to Roden. Well, the third most famous, if we consider the Herionos noteworthy. And I suppose now they are more than ever.

She was the head of an elite circle of Harvesters who were granted special permission to stay on Horigos and run all their business and missions from there without having to report back to Libera. They were given secret identities to live on the other side, to establish genuine relationships with the Horigeans.

But Tabitha was the only one who also married one of them, without Roden's consent, and became the reason behind the establishment of so many laws forbidding relationships between us and *them*.

She was soon labelled a traitor, condemning thousands of Harvesters who joined her vision to be stuck on Horigos. They were offered two options: to become watchdogs for Roden, compelled to obey his orders but forever forbidden from Libera, or to be stripped of their leftover rights—no more help from the island, a life of anonymity and struggle.

In a world where the shade of your breath decides if you live or die, many abandoned her, accepting to live off Roden's scraps of generosity rather than having to watch their backs from Horigeans *and* Harvesters.

I throw Galen's arm over my shoulder. "I think it's better if you stop talking and I focus on anything but rebels and traitors. I've had my fair share of that in the past few days."

A quick smile tugs at his lips but doesn't spread further. His eyes are veiled; I'm not even sure he's completely lucid. The skin of his arm is clammy and cold against mine. But I keep forcing us along the screeching wooden plank.

I squint at the towering outline of the figure in front of us. I don't care if that's Tabitha Lorne or if Galen has only imagined it. Whoever that is, they're my only hope to cross today—now.

"Please help me; I can't hold him any longer..." I yell at the stranger.

As I inch closer and the moon reaches its highest point, I finally spot a pair of coal-black eyes and thick, braided silver hair. A tall, strong woman steps towards us, carefully lowering the torch she's holding by the platform's edge to keep the flame burning.

The white of her teeth against her smooth bronze skin is like a perfect final brush stroke on a masterpiece.

Her words, however...

"Fucking bastards! Those dry, stinky pieces of shit. Look what they've done to my poor Galen."

Her Galen?

She lifts her heavily ringed fingers to her mouth. "Oh—look at the state of his little, handsome face... I'm going to rip their balls off and feed them to their mothers—raw and unseasoned!"

I witness, in silence, the graceful beauty of an ancient goddess and the mouth of a living, breathing sewer.

But there's something in her manner, the motherly way she welcomes Galen in her arms, the genuine worry in her eyes, the slight trembling of her voice, that reassures me.

"Let me see." She lifts the blood-stained hem of his shirt, and her face darkens. "That's a nasty one. Gun?" She looks at me, and I nod. "Well, not his first time, at least. The bullet didn't get in; it's a side wound, but it cut deep in the flesh."

Not expecting any more words from me, the talking mountain turns and marches towards the end of the platform.

"What are you waiting for? Chop, chop! There is no crossing without a crosser, and this one," - she looks down at Galen, passed out in her arms - "He won't be useful for hours, I'm afraid. We're lucky he's still in one piece. Have you ever done it with someone unconscious, love?"

"Excuse me?"

She raises her eyebrows. "Crossing? Have you ever travelled to Horigos with someone knocked out?"

"No," I cry out, "But can you take us to Sector 43?"

Every scratch, every little graze on my skin, every cut feels eventually real, and I fall to my knees.

Tabitha's voice strokes me gently, "Oh, love, I can do better—I am taking you to meet your freedom."

I stop sobbing and stare at her. The sound of that word feels so wrong after all I've been through. So unreal.

Tabitha snorts, "Shit, I forgot the word *freedom* is basically banned from this shithole. Ironic, isn't it?"

Galen groans, twitching in her arms, and her face immediately turns grave. She motions to the dark space behind her, "We need to hurry the fuck up! Not *gonna* lie; I've never seen him this battered. You want him to live? Forget about this stupid island and follow me."

Chapter 27 - Good Casualties
Evelyn

"That wasn't part of the plan."

"You, better than anyone else, should know that plans are feeble little creatures, Eve. What were we supposed to do? Let them take her? I saw the bird flying through the Wards, by the way. Did you think that was safe?"

From my window, the wall of flames looks like one of those bonfires young Harvesters light up on the beach to celebrate the end of Winter.

Except for the myriad of people scurrying away from it like a colony of ants fleeing their crumbling nest.

"The scratches on my hands are the only proof it was even here; don't worry about that. What's with the fire, though? Did you really need to destroy the building, risking so many lives?"

"Collateral damage… Besides, Roden played us dirty there. We had to think fast—" Nikrah's voice breaks, making his words an annoying riddle I don't have time to decipher.

"Are you sure the line is safe?" I lower my voice. Static electricity crackles in the background.

"What difference would it make now? Have a look outside again. I'm sure unwanted ears overhearing our conversation is the least of our problems now."

"They shouldn't have crossed *at all*." My voice rumbles.

"But that's not all bad news. Roden is acting erratically, Evelyn. That's scary, but also tells us he may trip and fall in one of his own traps," Lily Drestall's voice joins us from a different line.

My eyes widen, and I'm glad I'm alone in the room. I take a breath in. "We should have thought about that; we acted in a hurry and left too many doors open."

"We don't know for sure."

I stare at the phone as if speaking directly to Nik and Lily. "I hope you're wrong… Casualties?"

Nik jumps back in, "If you mean *good* casualties, oh yes. We found two of them dead on the main tower before the building collapsed, and took the bodies away before anybody could see them. Galen's artistry for sure; one was missing a few teeth."

I scoff, ignoring his tone. Luckily for Nikrah, I've known him long enough to silence my real thoughts. "Did you recognise any of them?"

"Well, we were in a bit of a hurry. You know, trying to save our lives and report to you… But—no. I've never seen them before, right, Lils?"

I sigh, not sure if I should feel relieved or reconsider my decision to bring Nik in. The echo of the bright orange light, gleaming like an early sunset, hypnotises me for a few seconds.

"Eve, are you still there?" Nik drops his voice.

"Yes," I pause to recollect my thoughts. "Any news of Galen and July?"

"No sign of them yet." Lily's smooth voice doesn't do anything for my increasing worries. "Galen didn't make it to the top, but we had a brief contact while he was abandoning the Wise. Are you sure Tabitha followed the plan? I mean, Eve, how sure are you she won't go on a tangent and decide she's done waiting?"

"She would never—"

"What? Betray her people? Betray *you*? So sentimental. Open your weary eyes, Silent End; we both know she wouldn't blink twice before aiming at Roden's head and burning the island to the ground. Despite you, or anyone else, standing in her path..."

I move the phone away enough to swear under my breath without Nik or Lily hearing it.

Then I take a big breath, pinching the bridge of my nose. "I reckon Nik hasn't shared the latest with you yet."

There is a moment of silence. Easy to imagine Lily trying to control her broken pride after discovering she's not the one moving the strings for once.

In the background, someone rushes to one of the phones, and a bottle rattles in the distance, followed by Nik's voice, "Sorry, Lily, I didn't mean to leave you out. I just didn't have time. I'll explain on our way to Horigos - if we make it, in one piece - I swear..."

"I'm good. No need. If Evelyn says Lorne is with us, I believe her."

Silence, again. This time, from my side.

"Fine. Move carefully, I'm sure the night isn't over yet. If you find them, don't look for me; take the first pod to the continent." I cut the conversation short.

"Will do," Lily confirms before her phone goes silent.

"Stay safe, Eve." Nikrah hangs up right after.

The phone drops from my hand onto my desk.

I wrap a woollen shawl around my shoulders, and I pace to the window, opening it to let in the truth of *our* miscalculation—the blast of hot air and flying stones hit me a few seconds later, and I falter, covering my eyes before dropping to my knees.

When everything seems to freeze, I reach for the windowsill with one hand and pull myself up to witness the wall of smoke and mist left by the sudden explosion. A dense orange fog turns the shade of muddy water as the rain touches it.

Beyond that, only a mass of stone, once strong and proud, and terrified voices trying to find their way out through darkness and smoke. Hundreds of them.

"It is all in your capable hands now," I say to the dark sky.

My eyes fill with tears when little blue lights appear in the sky, dropping luminous tails like falling stars, one by one, as if following a precise order.

Chapter 28 - What Hurts the Most
July

There is no other way to cross through the Grace Wards except by wearing special gear. During the journey, our bodies shrink, flex, and plump back to their original form on the other side, and regular clothes cannot survive the journey.

It's not the best feeling, and honestly, it's a bit gross to watch, but you get used to it after a while.

Also, only two Harvesters can cross in the same pod, as their chemical balance would not survive the process, and produce horrible results upon arrival. Nobody wants two heads or having to pee from an extra mouth on their forehead.

The Grace Wards dividing our Worlds are subtle and thin, but strong enough to bounce you back if you don't follow the protocol.

At least, this is what I believed in—until today.

I approach Tabitha hesitantly. "I appreciate your help, but we can't cross all together. We're one Harvester too many. Unless—" I consider the pod floating on the water behind her, pressing my lips together and arching my brows at the very old, overused, and *surely* not licensed… thing.

Tabitha raises a thick eyebrow, mirroring me. "Oh, hell no! I'm not planning to stay behind and let you kids make the crossing alone."

"That's not what I was— "

"Do you have an alternative? By all means, run back to Daddy Roden and ask if we can borrow his very own bloody pod." She waves a hand, showing me the way back to the nightmare we've just left behind.

My heart sinks at the thought of returning there, and I lower my head, burdened by thoughts of the desperation of the past few hours.

As if reading my need for someone to take the reins from me and tell me everything will be fine, Tabitha moves towards me and lays a hand on my shoulder.

"Look, I came back to save *you,* not to give Roden and his pompous acolytes the privilege of carrying my dead body around the island like a trophy. I'm not a brainless martyr." She glances behind me and adds with a smirk, "Even if I believe not much of the Chapter will remain after this glorious debacle—maybe just the ashes of their posh arses."

The need to believe her pierces my chest with sharp claws.

"Why are you helping him?" I ask, unsure if I really want an answer while helping her slide open the pod's metal door—an egg-shaped cocoon that can command the Grace Wards to open and close.

Tabitha lowers Galen like a mother tucks her child into bed for the night, and says softly, "Sometimes, you have to do what hurts the most to keep the people you love safe. Galen is a strong young man. He will make it through, or I will spank his little, back peach."

A hint of a smile crosses Galen's face, but I'm probably just imagining it.

"Okay then," Tabitha smacks her thighs, wrapped in worn, black leather trousers, "You can have a moment to curse what's left of the island with your best repertoire of insults, and then off we fuck. I swear, every time I set foot on this island, my skin blisters."

Every time?

I shake my head and step inside the pod, "I think I'm good," I mutter.

Tabitha is a chatterbox, but one who's not afraid to speak up.

"Have you done this before?" Tabitha is so tall, I feel like a puppy when I look at her. "I mean, crossing with an extra passenger?"

Tabitha smiles, her face so open and honest, then says, "I know you're terrified, who wouldn't be? But I was called here because I'm the only one who can help you now."

I nod, and my attention moves to Galen, who looks peacefully asleep now, the pain gone from his face. "Do you think Roden knows you're here?"

She looks around, distractedly chewing on a silver chain hidden beneath her black top, then exclaims, "Fuck, no! But if we spend another minute on this island, he probably will. He's got eyes everywhere, love—Roden will hunt whoever he *thinks* is a traitor.

And I'm top of his list." Tabitha's hands curl into large fists.

"But the Herionos attacked us…"

Her eyes darken, and she quickly glances at Galen.

"Yeah, well, if you want to survive out there, I'd suggest you review your *labels* and forget whatever fairy tale Roden filled your little mind with." She bites her thumbnail, concerned.

"What about the others?" I look over my shoulder at the island, at the large column of smoke rising to the sky.

"There is more to this island than you think," Tabitha says, echoing my fears. If I hadn't spent a night in a secret place covered in screens, I'd think she only wanted me to forget about the others and stop delaying our escape.

But, as easy as it would be for me to remain detached from this person, nothing about her screams danger. "Fine. Give me something to do." A plea as I pin my hair up and off my face, trying to ignore the stickiness and the rough texture of dirt and soot coating it.

"Make sure Galen keeps breathing. I can't watch over him and drive this old lady simultaneously." She pats the pod's wall. "She's enjoyed too many rides."

"What happens if he stops breathing halfway through our journey?" My chest rises as fear fills my ribcage.

Tabitha doesn't reply; she doesn't need to. She gestures for me to move further inside and reaches a hand out of the pod to pull down its heavy door, but not before scanning the sky one last time.

She lowers her eyes to the land and the hills, hesitating as if allowing herself some time to say goodbye.

"Are you waiting for someone else to join?" I ask as her gaze shoots right and left.

Her head drops, bobbing hopelessly, her silver braids wrapping her shoulders like a cloak. Her movements are fluid and light when she turns, eventually closing the door.

I sit down next to Galen's unconscious body to quiet the nervous spasms in my abdomen. The protocol requires us to fast for at least twelve hours before a crossing, but the little chocolate I shared with him over an hour ago is the least of my problems.

Someone outside the pod must constantly monitor velocity and trajectory. We travel through the Wards and in-between spaces, and the slightest miscalculation may take us to the wrong place, where nobody expects us—even worse, we can end up completely alone and missing bits of our body and mind.

Tabitha breaks the ominous silence, confirming my fears. "They're close. We don't have time to get undressed and test our equilibrium... We need to cross—now."

When water starts streaming inside the pod, I force my mind to stop spinning back to the recent events.

He knew about it, and he let it happen to me.

I can't take my eyes off of Galen, crumpled on the floor, unconscious, still finding it hard to believe that he is part of the Chapter as much as Evelyn Popplewish. My mind gallops to her. *On which side does she stand? Was she on the tower?*

Tabitha's voice is a noise in the background, a presence my

senses haven't fully recorded yet. The more I try to focus, the more the cramped space around me blurs. So do my thoughts.

"You knew…" I mouth.

I had no time to pick my side in the chaos of heat, raging flames and crumbling stones. To weigh Galen's version of the story.

Crossings are silent. They're timed by a sequence of regular breaths and the whoosh of water. While our two worlds stretch and shrink, we roll and float as the pod pushes through the Grace Wards.

But today, my breath is sticky and doesn't travel far from my mouth, warming my face with sickly purple puffs.

"July…"

Galen's face fuels fears that were only temporarily forgotten but never extinguished.

"Hello?"

What if this is what Galen wanted? To lead me far away before I could even get close to that Rogue.

"Crimson, for fuck's sake." Tabitha's slap on my cheek is a cry for help, and it hurts like hell. "Whatever is brewing in your little head, make it stop." Her voice is a mixture of authority, wisdom and maternal apprehension.

My face stings where Tabitha struck, and it is growing warmer than my toes. My shoes are barely visible under the icy cold water that has already risen to my ankles and turned Galen's trousers into a deeper shade of black.

At last, I look away from him to acknowledge Tabitha. "We're taking on water," I mumble.

"Thanks for stating the obvious." Tabitha flicks me on my forehead before grabbing me by the shoulders. Her eyes are a deep, warm shade of brown, veined with thin red lines, like molten lava, and circled by lilac rims.

She sighs. "I didn't come back to the island and risk my life only to die between Worlds. So, you keep our charming sleeping beauty alive, and I get us out of this uncomfortable situation. Understood?"

My head, hands, and whole body nod in agreement. This stranger appears to be the only one who can save us now. She seems to dislike the Chapter as much as I do and, like me, has a strong bond with Galen.

"He's got more to lose than his life…" she adds before turning to the emergency control panel, which we never use because crossings are legal and thoroughly planned. "Now, where is that little bastard… Ah-ha! Found you."

I fight the urge to check what Tabitha is doing when I hear the click of a switch. Instead, I kneel next to Galen. The water has almost reached his hips. My slippery hands and his drenched body, doubled in weight, don't make it easy for me, but I lift him up against the wall to place my ear over his heart.

"He's still alive." I let out a relieved sigh.

"Good, now keep him that way." Standing tall, legs spread like strong trees, half-submerged in water but sturdy like her desire to put as much distance between the pod and Roden, Tabitha reminds me of a captain leading her ship against a bunch of pirates. Only we are the ones facing the wrath of the so-called authorities.

Galen mumbles something unintelligible under the light touch of my fingers as I try to keep him from sliding dangerously close to the water level.

When I'm almost convinced the water pressure will crush us inside the pod before we reach Horigos' shores, Tabitha's voice booms. "Resurfacing in ten seconds, love. Hang in there, you did so good…" I'm unsure if she is talking to me or her beloved pod, but her words give me hope.

Nine… My heartbeat settles into the regular countdown in my head. *Eight.*

"Come on, Galen—" My hand slips on the wet surface of the giant egg-shaped ship when I try to touch his face. I end up on all fours, half-submerged by the water, watching Galen's body slide down the wall.

I scramble back to my feet, coughing and spitting, and hurry to adjust Galen as if he's an abandoned doll, but at least with his head out of the water.

The cold touch of my soaking-wet clothes against my skin doesn't bother me as much as the sound of someone laughing.

I can't remember when my hair became untied, pooling over my shoulders into a dark mass of waves. My mouth is stretched, or maybe it's just the salt water drying on my lips. That laugh again.

My laugh.

"Sweetheart, if you've decided to go all *rogue* on us, at least allow me to stop this wreck first. I didn't have time to upgrade to the latest version," Tabitha chuckles.

"Five…" I look up at Tabitha, giggling. I'm still shaking with euphoria; my hair is stuck on my cheeks like strings of liquorice. I must look like a wild animal who has just escaped her predator.

Tabitha nods. There is a whisper of uncertainty in her eyes, but I think she understands my behaviour when she smiles, "Hold on tight…"

I search for Galen's hands underwater and grab them the moment the pod stops for an infinite second, as if held back by a long elastic still attached to Libera. I blink. Once. Twice.

What if I open my eyes again, and someone pulls us back to the shore? My breath turns to oil in my lungs.

Tabitha is frantically striking a button on the control panel so hard that I worry the tip of her finger will snap.

Something in the water moves. Galen's fingers flutter in mine.

The elastic snaps, and I fear my heart will rip my chest open and break free.

"Oh, this is going to be fun!" Tabitha roars over the terrifying noise of cracks appearing all over the pod.

The pressure in my ears is like war drums, but not loud enough to cover the snarling water snapping at the ship.

I'm floating, as is Galen, and there is nothing I can do to stop the water's rage from throwing us against the wall like balls of flesh and bone. Meanwhile, Tabitha remains rooted to the metal shell.

"Are you alright there? Sorry, in normal circumstances, I'm a formidable driver." I hope her irony comes from a place of experience and not because she's losing her mind.

I'm still holding onto Galen, looping an arm around his shoulders to make sure he doesn't get hurt if we slam against the wall or Tabitha. But the drums in my ears have stopped, and the turmoil of water has reduced to a gentle wave that laps at Galen and me while our captain releases her hands from the panel.

"We made it." There are some dark stains on the control buttons and levers. Tabitha hasn't been reckless or without worry all this time. She was only fighting her fears off her face and voice, but they gathered elsewhere.

"Tabitha, your hands…" I gasp, letting go of Galen, now safely floating in the hug of calm waters. "You're bleeding."

Despite her best try, the inside of the pod is not big enough for Tabitha to move away from me and avoid my touch as I gingerly take her right hand in mine to examine the damage. The skin of her palm is dotted with old scars and rough to the touch. New scratches glisten red where she's pushed harder to keep the cocoon steady, to bring us safe to the other side of the Grace Wards.

"If it hurts, it means I'm still alive." Tabitha slides her hand off mine, wincing when her fist closes to hide the fresh wounds. "Besides, I'm not the one in bad shape," she says, dipping both hands in what's left of the water that almost drowned us to wash away the blood and temporarily soothe her skin. Despite her majestic frame, she looks like a child splashing water for fun.

We must have reached the shore, or been near it, because the water is receding, and I can see the bottom of the pod, covered in cracks but still in one piece.

I realise I've been staring when Tabitha looks at me over her shoulder and points at something behind me, eyebrows so high they form two perfect arches. "What? It's not like I'm stripping naked to take a bath in front of you. There's someone else who needs your attention more than me."

Maybe the adrenaline rush caused by the recent events is still pumping in my veins. Perhaps I don't want to let go of it yet because then I will need to admit that we're far away from the island, from questions I haven't received the answers to, and maybe never will. If tonight's attack was just the beginning, other people may have lost their lives after we left. So many of them have died, not even knowing why.

But then, I hear it. Galen's breath is unsteady but louder with every intake of clammy air he forces inside his nose.

"Sof… ?"

Tabitha's eyes slide to him. I can't ignore it anymore. As soon as I turn to face him, the people I thought we were back on the island will vanish.

"Hi, Sof—"

His smile is like a flash in the night. It blinds me, it hurts…

Or maybe that's just the loud swarm of sparks trying to barge inside the pod through its cracks.

"Get down!" Tabitha shouts, stretching the tips of her fingers towards my arm. But I'm already lunging to shield Galen with my body.

Both her cry and Galen's begging me to back away fade, sucked in by the rage of a chainsaw making its way through the body of the pod, melting the door seal and filling the claustrophobic space with an acrid, eye-tearing smell.

A male voice glides in - "Is anybody hurt?" - followed by a large hand that easily dislodges and tears down the heavy metal door.

"What do you think? You silly bear. Couldn't you just wait for me to unlock the port?" Tabitha yaps as if she knows who's waiting for us outside.

"Give me a hand, Jyn, and turn off that stupid light. If that was *your* idea of saving us without getting caught… You're lucky I don't have time to deal with you right now."

My head hurts, my skin hurts, my eyes burn, and I worry my legs won't carry me far once I stand up—but we're alive. Besides, I can't ignore the heated exchange of words between Tabitha and the man she called Jyn.

Something heavy pats the top of the pod twice from the outside. "… but you told me to be ready to get you out. I even destroyed little *Chella*." Jyn has the voice of an adult but sounds annoyed, like a teenager.

"I meant, be ready to get us out safe if anything comes after us. Also, I don't think *Navichella* will ever supply vegetables and meat to Libera after tonight. Honestly, man, how you made it to fifty in one piece is a fucking mystery to me."

"How I make it every day without going crazy with *you* around is the real mystery!"

Even though I'm still inside the pod, one arm around Galen's shoulder as his senses slowly return, I manage to study the two silhouettes outside.

Tabitha, sturdy as an oak, hands on her hips, and Jyn, almost as tall as Tabitha, pointing a finger at her. They stand still until something starts shaking inside Tabitha, and her entire body bursts into laughter.

The two clash into a loud hug, patting each other's backs and stopping the friendly bickering only to breathe and laugh.

"Thanks for coming on such short notice," Tabitha says as she steps away from Jyn, sliding her hands down his forearms. "It's good to see your face." Her words are warm and weary. "They're both here, by the way," she states with a relieved smile, gesturing towards us.

Jyn's face turns a cold shade of blue under the pod's spotlights when he bows his head through the melted door. The many switches of the control panel flicker and flash, illuminating his gentle expression and big eyes—the same eyes that stared at me back in the square, when I had coffee and doughnuts with Galen on our bench...

"You put yourself and them in danger—a big, deadly danger," he says to Tabitha while studying us.

"We had to rethink our plans," Tabitha states from behind him.

"Thought so. Things are escalating too fast. Can you two manage a short walk?" Jyn asks, extending a strong, bare arm to

Galen, revealing a square scar on his left wrist.

Galen shifts next to me, hissing every time an inch of his skin folds or a muscle flexes. "I guess we don't have any other options."

Hearing his voice like that hurts me, but it also brings a smile to my face, and forces me to set aside the thought that the happy stranger outside the pod was in Libera only a few days ago, watching *me*.

Tabitha mirrors my hopeful expression and pats Jyn on the back, while winking at Galen. "That's my strong boy—but better safe than sorry. Jyn, lift him up; you're carrying him."

Chapter 29 - End of Darkness
July

E ven the darkest place feels like home if it's filled with the people you love.

But it can reach a deeper shade of black when the souls of those you love act like strangers.

What if Galen faked his friendship all this time? What if… What if… But it's hard enough to run in the dark, wounded, tired and in pain, let alone with your head full of dangerous thoughts.

What was a cautious, silent walk to put enough distance between us and the destroyed Chella has rapidly turned into a race to safety, hushed only by the soft, wet forest's undergrowth. Or at least this is what I think it is because all I can hear, over Tabitha's whispered orders to keep moving and Galen repeating he doesn't need to be carried like a sack of potatoes, are the songs of night birds and the frantic scurry of animals running away from our approaching steps.

If not for the intermittent rays of moonlight slicing through the treetops, I would fall on my hands and knees every few steps.

"I thought you were taking us to Sector 43." It's the first thing I dare say, and in such a low voice that even Tabitha, leading the way inches before me and mimicking the sounds of birds, probably didn't hear me.

"She is. We're actually inside its last, natural green heart. Also—we don't call it Sector 43. Our home is not a lab." Jyn's voice hops behind me whenever he adjusts Galen on his right shoulder.

"What do you mean in the heart—" I must have misunderstood, but Tabitha cuts me off.

"Why don't we stop and start a campfire to make it easier for *them* to find us? Keep your feet moving and your mouth shut. All of you." Her steps are surprisingly light. "The glorious Sector 43, as you call it… well, you're about to see what's left of it with your own eyes. And, once we're there, please refer to it as Ventiol."

None of their statements makes sense to me, but this is all I can get given the situation.

Our steps grow slower with every leaf that crunches, with Galen's every uncomfortable moan. Each disembodied sound freezes us until everything around us is silent once again.

"We will soon be unable to lift even a finger if we don't rest and take a breather. Tabs, please," Jyn states, as Galen's pain becomes too loud and impossible to ignore.

But she replies without stopping, "Not a chance. If we stop, Merya and the others will gather our remains. We're too exposed. And we're on the wrong side of the river…"

Checking my back for the invisible threat Tabitha has been mentioning since we set foot in the forest, I pick up the pace. "Who are *they*? Are the Herionos after us?" I cover my mouth, blaming my empty stomach and fatigue for my audacity.

Tabitha comes to a sudden halt. An amused note softens her voice when she comments, "I forgot how—" but Galen starts coughing, interrupting her.

She casts him a quick glance before adding, "I forgot Galen warned me about your mouth working faster than your brain sometimes."

"I never said that," Galen objects, trying to get off Jyn's back without much success.

"Alright," Tabitha throws us a quick look, "Brilliant brain. Is that better? Now, if everyone can please stay quiet and stay low—"

Without warning, she grabs my arm and yanks me down to my knees just seconds before small dots of light start flashing in and out of the foliage before us.

"What is it?" I ask, tasting damp soil and sharp little stones under my hands.

But Tabitha presses a finger over her mouth before turning to Jyn, who crouches beside me after setting Galen against a tree.

"Am I reading it correctly?" Tabitha whispers.

Jyn remains still, staring at the odd sequence of lights for a few seconds. "Same word? How many times?" he asks.

"What are they talking about?" I turn to Galen, who's managed to prop himself up on his elbows. The lights reflect on his pale face as he looks at me silently, nodding slightly as though inviting me to do the same.

"I think it's… give me a second…" Tabitha mutters, tapping a finger on her thigh.

Twenty and something seconds, I count about one for each flash of light.

Tabitha slams a hand on the ground, with a grunt, sending shards of stone and little lumps of soil flying. "Bloody hell, you taught her well, Jyn. It says R O G U E. When did she get so fluent with the code?"

"You know, there is not much to do when you're hiding with limited access to sunlight, surrounded by the same faces every day. It is either perfecting survival skills and personal knowledge—or sex. I told them we don't have space for more hungry mouths unless those mouths can catch their food themselves."

I swallow a laugh as Galen chortles beside me, "How I missed you guys! But—sorry to ruin your little moment of pride. I don't think Merya is behind that message."

I startle. *When did he find the time to befriend these people?*

Jyn and Tabitha snap their heads towards Galen simultaneously, and with such speed, my thoughts evaporate.

"You're not saying… Jyn?" Tabitha slowly turns to him with an accusatory expression.

"He promised he would stay put." Jyn scratches his neck with a bashful smile, "But you know Mack. He's like an octopus…" He shrugs as if that helps explain everything.

Tabitha sighs deeply through her nose and slowly gets up, brushing away some dirt from her hands and trousers. "I'll have a word with him once we're back. In the meantime, don't make yourselves too comfortable. Anyone else could have spotted those lights; we still have some ground to cover."

I realise my jaw has dropped in confusion when Galen moves towards me on all fours and pats me on the back. "They may sound unconventional, but they know what they're doing."

"Do not do that to me," I point at his smile, "You've lost that power. I don't know what game you and these people are playing, but I'm still deciding if I can trust you."

"Oh." He tilts his head. "At least, help me up?" He stretches a hand towards me with a stupid smile plastered on his cracked lips.

"You have enough freaking stamina to keep secrets from me…" I slap his hand away, "You can stand up on your own."

But as I straighten my legs, which have turned numb from the time spent crouched, a firm hand grabs me by the collar of Galen's jumper and pulls me up, ignoring my objections.

"You're still alive and breathing purple, love. And talking. A lot," Tabitha hisses in my ear, forcing me around to face her. My back brushes against a tree. "What else can we do to convince you we're not the enemy here? Roden is, *and* those scumbags who support him."

I shake her hand off, arching my brows. "Well, you have to admit that if Tabitha Lorne shows up in Libera when the island falls under attack, I'm entitled to ask myself one or two questions. I'm glad I'm alive, but this doesn't kill the doubt that you have something else for me in mind—after we get to wherever you're taking me."

In the cold moonlight, her lips press to a line so thin that her mouth nearly disappears. She steps back, scanning me from head to toe, with a hand on her hips.

"Glad to hear Roden Breith still depicts me like a fucking traitor. But, remember, girl, I'm not the one who asked you to condemn a gifted soul to Roden's 'special treatment'." She jabs me in the forehead with a finger.

"Tabs!" Jyn and Galen exclaim at the same time.

"What?" Tabitha replies serenely. "I'm sure she's done two plus two a while ago. If Galen took her to me and he knew about Roden's plan…"

"And Galen has clearly kept himself busy, having fun with the Chapter *and* the rebels," I add, stepping next to Tabitha and mirroring her stance.

"Hey," Tabitha whispers.

I shrug. "Sorry, but this is how I've known you all my life. Point is, everybody seems to know a lot about this poor Rogue, except me, so…"

"Fair enough, we've been called worse. No offence taken," Jyn says, grabbing Galen by his armpits to lift him. "Can you stand on your own, boy? Yeah? Good." He brushes some locks of hair off Galen's eyes and pats him on the head.

For a moment, I study the trio's interaction: Galen smirking at Jyn pinching his cheek, Tabitha's face softening while looking at the two.

"How far do you reckon?" I ask, pointing at some lights that are flashing the same word repeatedly to break their uncomfortable bubble of familiarity.

"It's not the distance that worries me," Tabitha breaks her stare and presses her right index finger on her lips, tapping the left one to her ear as if inviting us to listen. "The right question is: can we run fast enough?"

We've all experienced, at least once, that sticky, muggy feeling that precedes a downpour. Uncomfortable, heavy. Endless—until the rain comes, bringing fresh air and freedom.

As we all fall silent, the clammy layers of an invisible threat weigh on my mind, fogging my senses. Until Jyn loops one arm around Galen's, and his boot steps on a skinny branch that cries like a massive, wounded beast.

We freeze.

Four pairs of eyes widen in unison, and we hold our breath as best as we can. Galen moans in pain and presses his face against Jyn's shoulder to muffle the sound.

The trees around us start shivering with the echo of heavy marching steps, attacking the ground with such violence I feel sorry for whatever may end up under them.

Rain finally comes in the shape of Tabitha's voice. "Shit, they've found us quicker than I thought. Fuck this! Let's make it interesting and guide them closer to our barriers. Run to the lights and do not die."

Jyn bows his head before scooping Galen onto his shoulder, ignoring his cry of pain and complaint. "Sorry, mate. We'll go faster this way."

Sprinting like an athlete, with an agility nobody could muster, while carrying the weight of another person, Jyn starts running towards the lights, looking way stronger than the man I saw pushing the fruit trolley back in Libera.

"July, what are you doing? Go!" Tabitha pushes me so hard I stumble. But eventually, my feet start moving when a bullet whistles past inches from us, burning a straight red line in the air.

It travels so fast and far, I can barely hear the explosion flaying the bark of an innocent tree. But it's enough to make me run faster than ever before. I've dodged enough bullets for one night; I don't mean to chance my luck further.

Steps rush behind me, desperate to live and see another day. Tabitha is not far. I can hear her heavy breath and random cursing against whoever is shooting at us.

"Nasty offspring of a rotten mother!"

But there are other steps, following close behind. Voices ordering us to stop and yield, hissing rounds of firearms destroying a good amount of vegetation and - by the sound of it - some of the local fauna.

The lights in front of us are the only thing I want to focus on. And the oddly shaped silhouette of Jyn, who looks like a creature with two heads and a double pair of limbs.

"You're flagging again…" Tabitha pants next to me.

"I'm running…" I sound like I'm about to throw up one of my lungs.

"Your thoughts are holding you back. Tell your brain to stop!" Tabitha doesn't wait for my answer and sprints in front of me.

She's right. Thinking about what could happen if they get to us and take us prisoners, or worse, won't help any of us. Besides, I'm the one who's now furthest behind and in danger.

"Fuck this!" I echo Tabitha. Her sturdy shape quickly melts into the dark wall of trees and undefined shadows. I don't know what I'm running away from, and I have no clue where I am heading, so I command my feet to lift from the ground as if on fire.

"Keep shooting…"

"They're not far!"

"Come on, you pathetic, useless beings. Take them down…"

The voices around me are angry and coming from every direction. The forest shakes, screams, and complains under the rain of bullets. I want to cry with it and call for Tabitha, Galen…

The ground under my feet turns from soft and unstable to hard and paved. My first step on solid, flat stones is heavy and aggressive. My right ankle twists slightly, but I save it with an awkward hop before landing on my knees and hands.

"This is a path," I whisper, touching the trail of irregular stones.

I'm not sure how and when I made it out of the forest. But mostly, I'm scared to lift my head and look up at the person standing so close to me that I can smell the leather of their black combat boots and—*sugar and lemon?*

"Tabs? Are you sure this is her? She looks like a baby bird that's fallen from its nest." A young voice asks as the boots move a step towards me. She has an inflexion I can't pinpoint but shares Tabitha's imperative yet friendly tone.

A new shower of bullets rains down in the distance, and I scramble up, turning my back to the stranger, staring at the forest we've just left behind.

"Leave her be. She's gone through a lot in the last few hours," Tabitha's familiar voice replies. Her tone is comforting before she shouts, "Walls up, Mack, now! We're all in the clear—but you're in trouble, boy." Her stomping steps grow upset and worried as she walks away from me.

"Well, baby crow…" A hand lands on my shoulder and spins me around.

She's probably my age but so much taller; the first thing I see is her chest wrapped in bullet belts and a couple of grenades attached to her waist. The young woman gives me a smirk, winks and jerks a thumb over her shoulder. "You're still on your feet and looking better than poor Galen over there. A friend of Tabs' who doesn't need me to carry her like a damsel in distress is a friend of mine. Let's go; we can save the introductions for later."

I blink, stand on my toes and tilt my head to one side to see what she's pointing at.

My nerves untangle. "We all made it," I sigh when Galen waves at me from the other side of a square that looks like a landing spot.

He's leaning heavily on Jyn's left arm, but is finally standing on his own feet, while in the background, Tabitha is waving her hands in the air and pointing at the forest behind, seemingly arguing with another person whose face is concealed by a black helmet.

I grab the girl's hands and squeeze them with no shame. "He's alive… I can still kick his butt without feeling guilty." I throw another glance behind her, ignoring her increasingly puzzled look.

Midway between us and the rest of the party, the skeleton of what once must have been a majestic gate rests on the ground. Its partially melted rusty bars still show a ghost of their original gold coating.

I circle the girl for a better look at the place. "This is familiar…"

I hear the stranger huffing behind me, "All right, Miss Obvious, if you're done describing every damn thing around you, I'd like to rejoin the others and leave."

Even though I don't object, she nudges me forward. She not only speaks like Tabitha, but she also acts like her.

Yet, I can't stop thinking I know this place. Something is missing.

"Was there a fountain there?" I ask no one in particular, pointing to a hole in the ground, when I finally reach Tabitha and the others.

But everyone seems too busy securing Galen's head and limbs with some sort of padded equipment to ignore my comment. When they're done with him, the girl and the stranger with the helmet switch their attention to me.

"What is all this?" I ask, looking from the person in black to Galen and back. He seems at ease, even if still unstable. Jyn must have gotten here quickly because someone had the time to slap a massive square patch on Galen's wound.

He smiles, nodding at the hole. "That's for the descent."

Whatever that is, it's better than running away from bullets and voices demanding our death.

I glare at him, pursing my lips. "I take it you know these people, too?" I point at the young woman and the faceless stranger.

He shrugs, mouthing a *sorry*, which I decide to ignore.

Next to Galen, Tabitha is not taking her eyes off the eerie space behind me as she nervously beckons the woman closer. There's a line between her brows as she stares at a square box in her hands, producing a low beep and flashing lights.

"Merya, can you see them? Are they still outside the perimeter? I can't hear anything…" Tabitha scans the area as if waiting for an army of wild animals to emerge from the forest and devour us.

With all the thoughts swarming in my head, I've had no time to analyse each aspect of our escape. But I finally understand the worry behind Tabitha's pressing questions. No bullets in the air, no voices in the distance. Whoever was after us has gone.

"They must have rushed to their transports when they sensed the barriers were going up. They lost a good number the last time they tried to break in. But I wouldn't spend longer on the surface." Merya rushes her words, patting Tabitha on the shoulder.

Tabitha nods, pinching her lips. "Airships?"

"Most likely. They must have sent a small group on foot after us to test their luck and take us down on the spot to make it quick." Merya replies calmly as if talking about the weather. Her profile is such a mixture of features I can't exactly give her an age. Her big eyes scout the sky like a kid in awe despite her straight nose and confident stance.

"This doesn't feel right," Tabitha mumbles, picking at the dry skin of her lips. "Why are they letting us go so easily? The barriers can kill them, but they don't stay up very long. Even they know that."

"Perhaps they didn't know exactly who they were after. Maybe they thought you were just some random rebels who ended up on the wrong side of the forest," Merya shrugs.

Tabs nods, "Yeah, perhaps you're right, but they never act erratically. If they wanted to inflict real damage, they could have. Those were scouts, and they never go back empty-handed."

Merya chews on her cheek as if testing the implication of that statement and slices her eyes from the sky to Tabitha. After a quick exchange of knowing looks, the two nod at each other.

Tabitha rushes to Galen and Jyn, imparting orders in such a low voice that I can't understand her words. She points at the forest, while Merya takes my hand and drags me to the hole's entrance.

"Mack, pass me that helmet. Quickly!" Merya orders the stranger, who is wearing all-black, and who has been witnessing the scene without interfering.

Mack—the *octopus?*

"She's got a big head. Will this fit?" The stranger's muffled voice asks as he saunters towards us, tilting his head to study me before taking off his helmet.

He's probably younger than me, but he has several scars on his face and neck—ones he shouldn't have had the time to collect at such a young age.

"Excuse me?" I snap, taken aback.

"Don't get me wrong, it's a beautiful head."

"Mack—what happened to counting down from ten before we voice what's on our minds?" Merya steps between us, stretching a gloved hand to Mack and flexing her fingers.

He looks at me in response, scrunching his lips to one side. "Right, she doesn't know." He bends over slightly, making eye contact with me and tapping a finger on his temple. "Octopus brains—sometimes one or two escape my control," he whispers.

Before I can even think how to respond, he straightens his spine, chuckles, and tosses a helmet to Merya.

Despite bearing the evidence of too many battles, it feels sturdy and strong when Merya smacks it on my head, tapping its top twice for good measure. "That'll do." She winks at me before moving her attention back to Tabitha, who's gone to Jyn's aid, helping him lower Galen down into the hole.

The diameter of the opening is so large we could all fit in at once, but Tabitha directs the operation with such confidence that I can only stand by and wait for my turn—to go where? Not sure. At this point, I don't really care.

"Hold onto that ladder for a second. Jyn will be right next to you. Once he's there, let him go first and climb down one step at a time. We haven't used this door in a while…" Tabitha orders Galen as he disappears from view.

From where I stand, I can see several ladders running down the dark hole, all shiny with watery moss but also covered in flaking rust.

"He'll be fine. I've seen him in worse conditions." Mack's voice doesn't match his face. It's deep and full of the echo of battles and losses. Despite his size, I didn't realise he'd moved up next to me. His boots don't make any noise when he steps closer to the edge and squats to look down, bracing his elbows on his knees.

I startle. "How long have you known Galen for?" I keep my tone vague, pretending I've already forgotten his first insulting words.

"Well, not long enough if I can't still predict his next appearance, apparently." He stands up and cups his hands around his mouth. "I thought you got tired of the cause, mate? You took your sweet time to come back to base."

Merya is, if possible, even more imperceptible than Mack. I could easily mistake the two of them for Popplewish's random long-lost relatives if I didn't know that it was impossible.

I jolt when she appears behind us and smacks Mack on the back of the head. "What the hell are you doing, shouting like that? Didn't you hear what I said?" She towers over him, legs apart and with her hands on her hips just over the thick belt heavy with bullets, one of its ends running down her left thigh.

Mack winces and scratches his head, looking up. "I was just saying hello."

"You were waving a massive flag with '*Hey, assholes, we're still here, come get us'* written on it."

"Don't be stupid. That's too many words to write on a single flag."

"Enough. Both of you. Down. Now." Tabitha puts an end to their argument, grabbing them by the shoulders to separate the duo, leaving me to wonder if I should really be putting my life in their hands.

Or maybe I should laugh and pretend this is normal, like Mack is doing now, trying to hide his amusement from Tabitha by pulling up his black, tight shirt's collar to cover his mouth.

"I thought I was keeping guard!" Mack bursts out. But one look from Tabitha silences him, and he nods, defeated.

"Well done, little brother. That's how you accept orders," Merya flicks his nose.

Brother? Looking at them side by side, I can see they share the same high cheekbones and fair skin. Their lips are the same, with the upper one slightly fuller. A subtle, reddish stubble shadows Mack's face, but both their nose and cheeks are peppered with freckles.

Before Mack can say anything, Merya moves agilely and fast, like a big black cat, in my peripheral vision. Without hesitation, she falls into the hole backwards, arms spread wide as if jumping off a plane—without a parachute.

Nobody around me seems to care. I rush to lean over the edge, but Tabitha calls me back, "Don't worry, she's fine. For now." She sucks on her teeth, betraying a hint of annoyance. But it's difficult to ignore the corner of her lips twitching, fighting back a smile.

"Mack, please check on your sister," Tabitha sighs.

He obliges, saluting her by raising two fingers to his forehead before jumping into the hole.

Soon after the siblings' argument starts again, fading gradually as if they're moving further inside the dark space below us.

"Any broken bones, show-off?" I hear Mack teasing his sister.

"What the fuck was that? You could have hit us and taken us down with you." The familiarity in Galen's tone surprises me. It's the one I thought he only used with me.

As the quarrel goes on and turns into a multitude of intelligible words, Tabitha nudges me gently, "Don't be scared. The ladders look rusty, but they'll hold. I'll be right behind you, and the bunch down there will catch you if—"

I hold up a hand. "I'll manage. Thanks." I really am grateful, but the additional threat of a fatal fall is not something I wish to contemplate right now.

Tabitha nods, but still offers a hand to help me with the first few steps. I try not to look down. It's so dark I can barely distinguish what lurks inches below me, and the helmet visor doesn't help. At least the voices of Galen and the siblings reassure me.

The metal ladder—there are more attached around the edge of the portal—is sturdy, but sharp flakes lift off every time I grip the next step down. As much as the visor allows, I capture glimpses of the sky, so tranquil and clear that I struggle to imagine some civil war going on. *War?* Is this what the Chapter has been hiding from us? For years?

The stench of sewage, musk and sickening dampness hits me as I leave the darkening blue sky behind. Heavy steps shake my ladder. Tabitha moves quickly, and in seconds, she's on my right, balancing on her ladder with one arm stretched up. The night sky shrinks to a timid half-moon as she slides a massive, thick metal disk across the opening.

I'm in the dark again. But no longer alone.

Chapter 30 - Walk of Knowledge
July

When I jump off the ladder and set foot on something slippery and creamy, I mentally bless the helmet Merya gave me. Loose strands of hair stick to my visor, and the air inside immediately turns clammy and stuffy, but at least I can't see what just splattered on my legs.

"All clear?" Tabitha shouts from above me as I move out of the way just moments before a hard thump lands in the darkness, and the flashlight she's holding reveals the mouth of a narrow tunnel.

Moved by curiosity, I lift my visor, look down and cringe.

"Just think about it as a pool of expensive, purifying mud," Mack says, patting me on the back. "Although—I wouldn't leave it on your skin for too long if I were you."

When Mack lifts his helmet visor, the small trail of scars on the bridge of his nose and right cheekbone lightens like lines on a map in the flashlight's yellow glow.

"I swear this shit can liquefy bones better than lye." He casts his light on the dense layer of greenish substance stagnating beneath our feet.

"Thanks for the heads up," I say, wrinkling my nose and scraping the back of my hand with the hem of Galen's jumper sleeve, hoping he's forgotten about his fancy piece of clothing.

"No need to peel your skin off." Tabitha nudges me forward with a light push. "Mack trains his flirtatiousness on the stash of books he *secretly* devours when he's not busy concocting new ways to keep us safe." She casts a motherly look at him, and Mack retreats a couple of steps back, lowering his head. "But he's not harmful, am I right, Fumo?"

"Fumo?" I ask, turning to Mack, who's fallen quiet, trying to ignore his blushing cheeks that contrast sharply with his deep blue eyes, the same eyes as Merya's.

Tabitha winks at me before signalling to the group ahead of us to make a move for the darkest core of the tunnel. "Mack's nickname. Now go. We're safer-*ish* here, but heat detectors can still spot us."

I smile beneath my helmet, remembering what Tabitha has just said about him keeping them all safe. "Well, thanks for saving my skin, Mack. I'm very fond of it, and I like keeping it on my muscles rather than melting away," I say to him with a little bow.

He stops blinking and arches one brow, then the other, crossing his arms over his chest.

I place one hand on my hip and flick his helmet with the other, feeling a rush of familiarity when his eyes brighten with an invisible smile. "I know you're smirking under that thing. Don't get too comfortable now. I haven't forgotten what you said about my head.

Come on, I don't want to be left behind."

I nudge him, pushing his elbow, and start floundering behind the head of the group.

Merya, now a human crutch to make Galen's walk quicker, leads the way. She is protected by Jyn to her right and a dark wall on her left, which she uses to stay upright and balanced. But her gait looks confident, and the slippery ground, whatever it looks like under the thick layer of gloop, doesn't seem to slow her down.

"Where are you taking us?" I ask nobody in particular. My breath is dense. I can almost touch it when I stick two fingers between my neck and the rubbery padding of the helmet, seeking some relief.

Mack chuckles behind me. Tabitha's reprimand didn't last long, and he's acting cocky again now that she's no longer close enough to hear him. I turn my head without stopping, shrugging my shoulders in a silent *What?*

My boots have disappeared under layers of mud, turning my legs into heavy trunks, but Mack quickly catches up with me despite the weight of his backpack and the little array of weapons dangling from his shoulders over his chest.

"Taking *us?*" he asks as if I am supposed to understand the reason behind his amusement. His brows arch so high that the scars on his face stretch to thin white threads.

"Am I missing something, or is this another attempt to charm me?" My voice echoes more than I thought it would, and Tabitha's shoulders - ahead of us - shake with silent laughter.

Mack huffs a laugh, "You may want to rephrase that. Taking *you*, maybe… Do you really think Galen has never walked this tunnel before or any other—"

"Enough." One word from Jyn, who's fallen into step with Tabitha in the meantime, is all it takes to silence Mack.

Even if Mack's words always seem to land heavily on me, I must admit he's not wrong. Galen has met these people before, but it strikes me that he's been here, perhaps many times, while living a second life in Libera, spending most of his days with me. How many times has the Chapter played with my memories, if I can't remember not seeing Galen for more than a day or two all these years?

Mack gives me a little nudge with his shoulder. "Ah, the gears are turning in your brain now—"

"That's enough!" Jyn and Tabitha's order booms so loudly I swear the tunnel vibrates a little. Their faces bear a prayer for me to be patient and a warning look for Mack.

He scratches the side of his neck, his eyes twinkling with an innocent smile. "Not my place?"

"No." An answer that sounds rehearsed, so perfectly synchronised. The same as their movements when they give us their back and start walking towards Merya and Galen.

"Why do they call you Fumo?" I change the subject before Mack can invite another scowl from the *adults*.

He puffs his chest up, and I prepare for a long-winded explanation. "Fumo is an ancient word that belonged to one of

Horigos' forgotten islands. That was flat, and used and abused during the Great Famine. So ruthlessly, in fact, that all its natural supplies dwindled to nothing. Its very core shrunk due to the lack of water and oxygen, and one day it simply burst into dust."

I silence a gasp and give him a puzzled look when he hops in front of me, splaying his fingers in my face. "An entire land. Gone. Forever." His eyes widen with each word.

Just simple, beautiful eyes. No purple rim, no mismatched shades like mine, not a trace of Harvester blood in his veins.

I cock my head to one side, closing my eyes with a sigh, glad the helmet is covering my mouth so he can't notice the smile I can barely contain.

Finally, someone who's willing to talk. But, as much as I itch to ask him how he ended up hiding and conspiring with Tabitha Lorne - a renegade - I decide the origin of his nickname is a more appropriate conversation to have in a tunnel.

"Thanks for the geography lesson, but I believe the land you're referring to didn't *burst into dust*. It exploded. A less romantic end, and more of a tragic one, I must say. And still, you didn't answer my question. What's a *Fumo*?"

"Ah!" He suspiciously beckons me closer, curling a finger. "It means smoke," he whispers. "And smoke is what remains of my enemies after they meet me," he adds louder, thumping a hand on his chest.

I jump back as far as the mud allows me while Mack studies my expression for a second, swirls his right hand in the air and performs a deep bow, pretending to tip an invisible hat with his left.

"I thought we agreed that smoke is the only thing left when you try to cook something." Jyn's amused laugh roars in the tunnel, causing a chain reaction that spreads to the entire group. Even Merya and Galen's silhouettes shake while trying to walk straight and contain themselves.

Only Tabitha maintains some sort of responsible behaviour, but in the narrow beams of our flashlights, her face lights up with a quick smile. "Come on, kids, don't forget that one of us is injured, and the tunnel stretches for miles."

My mind lets go of that brief spark of normalcy when Tabs turns her back to speak with Jyn, reminding me why we are here.

"Why don't you ask Merya if she needs some respite? You know she won't ask otherwise," she suggests to Jyn, who leans his head towards her with such familiarity that I, for a moment, envy.

He nods and proceeds towards the couple ahead, tapping Merya on the shoulder. But Mack's sister shakes her head. Once. Twice. Adjusts Galen's arm around her neck. Her back is slightly bent, one knee giving up under his weight.

Even though I saw him laughing and walking, I still don't know the gravity of his wound.

"We have a saying. Well, I forged it and pitched it to the rest of the group: if you can breathe, you can fight. Believe me or not, Galen can defend himself even when asleep. I've never met someone ready to fight so hard for his values and the people he loves." Mack's voice is reassuring. Perhaps this is the first time I hear his true voice. Not loaded with self-confidence or sarcasm.

"You can take that off if you want," he adds, pointing at the helmet still on my head before unlatching his and clipping it to one strap of his backpack.

His hair, damp and of a darker copper shade, falls flat on his forehead, giving him a boyish look.

Merya and Galen have also taken off their helmets at some point. I guess, despite the peculiar conversation with Mack, I was still in too much shock to have really noticed what was happening around me. Compartmentalising has always been my way of coping with accidents and events I can't control.

I fiddle with my helmet for a few seconds. When I take it off, a whiff of musty but cool air gently blows at my face.

We walk in silence for a while to save our breath as the ground beneath our feet drops a level, and we proceed deeper underground.

I swing my flashlight left and right to study my surroundings, stretching a hand out to touch the tunnel wall, which is so narrow that two people can barely flank each other without brushing shoulders.

"Ugh, nope. Slimy." I clean my hand on my trousers, adding more dirt to what is already there, casually patting something hidden in my pocket. When I slide my hand inside, I immediately pull it out as if the small, brass key I forgot about was made of fire and just burnt my fingers.

"Water?"

I startle and gasp, remembering I'm not alone, blinking at Mack, who is standing before me with a metal flask in his hand. "Wow, you were lost in some deep thoughts there." Despite his young face, a deeper level of understanding shines behind his cerulean eyes.

I pull Galen's jumper sleeves over my hands, trying to ignore all the loose threads around the cuffs. "This silence doesn't sit well with everything that's going on in my mind. It only makes my thoughts scream louder."

His face gleams with sweat and dirt, and I guess mine doesn't look any fresher. I can no longer ignore my hair stuck to my cheeks and the revolting feeling of clammy skin and dirty hands.

Mack shrugs and offers me the flask, "You're scared. I get it."

I truly am. I have been for days, but hearing someone who doesn't know me at all say it aloud makes it real. And—in a twisted way—natural.

I push my hair off my face. "How long have we been walking for?" I ask, nodding a thank you, and accepting the flask from his hand. The water is lukewarm, but I'm so thirsty I don't care as it dribbles down my chin, soaking the collar of my jumper.

"Roughly an hour. Maybe longer. Time still gets all messed up down here. And then there's you."

"Care to explain?" I rub my chin dry with the back of my hand.

I try to give him all the benefit of all the doubt before I decide whether he's a pro at choosing the wrong words at the wrong time, or just someone with a mouth faster than his brain.

Mack lifts a shoulder, then drops it. "You're slow." He pinches his chin as if rethinking it and adds, "Slow-*ish*. You don't know these tunnels. Don't worry. No need to feel guilty."

"I'm not..." *Oh my, this one is something else...*

I inhale all the sarcastic comments that cross my mind, take another sip of water, which makes my lips twitch as I press them together to keep the liquid down before swallowing. "Is this not the only tunnel?" I ask, handing him back the empty bottle.

"How do you think we move around the cities and villages without being constantly targeted by them?" Mack points at the tunnel ceiling with the flask before turning it upside down and tossing it away when no more liquid comes out.

He opens his arms, noticing my puzzled look. "There are no sources of water in the tunnels. Why should I carry the extra weight?"

The space around us is indeed dotted with small piles of old flasks and black boxes similar to the one Tabitha used to scan the perimeter.

"I see," I say before crossing my arms over my chest, grabbing at the sides of my jumper and pulling it over my head. My voice is muffled by the fabric when I comment without weighing the effect of my words. "How do you cope? Surviving in hiding, moving through dirty tunnels filled with rubbish. Is it really worth it? I mean, you're not even a Harvester..." When I toss the jumper away, my skin breathes with relief, until humidity starts coating my arms and neck.

When I think I cannot get more uncomfortable, Mack inches closer, scanning my face. "What's rubbish for you may be a treasure for someone in need. And—that was all the water I had left. You're welcome!" he states, leaving me speechless.

Until he flicks my nose. "They're leaving us behind. Come on." A laugh that sounds like he has not a worry in life, and he's off, as I battle the dense mud to lift my feet.

I follow Mack and the rest of the group, reduced to dark silhouettes in the distance, for what feels like another hour, pushing through tiredness and thirst. But when the path abruptly bends to the right, I let out a relieved whimper; the proverbial light at the end of the tunnel has never been so bright.

Tabitha, standing under a pillar of light filtering in from a small opening above us, waits for everyone to regroup around her before saying, "We're almost there. Merya, radio the others, please. We need the gate open in fifteen, not a minute later."

Mack stares at me, arms crossed. "Heart above your knees, or you'll faint."

"Is there anything you don't know?" I ask, still struggling to breathe, but slowly straightening myself up.

Despite sweat and dirt, Mack seems to nestle an everlasting ball of energy within him. But I'm glad to see I'm not the only one battling fatigue after our long walk.

Jyn's wrinkles stretch deeper as if his skin has lost all its moisture. Tabitha's warm skin tone has turned dull, and the white of her eyes is a web of bloody filaments.

Her hand shakes slightly when she detaches a radio from her belt and passes it to Merya, "I told them to be ready on channel two. Just send the message and get off the channel before they can intercept you."

Merya's face is a portrait of urgency. Her jaw clenched, her skin so stretched, when she white-knuckles the radio from Tabitha and rigidly bobs a *yes* before heading for the point where the light intensifies.

We all wait, holding our breath. Not sure what to expect, I mirror the others and remain immobile, with my eyes fixed on Merya, as she plays around with the transmitter's switches. Crackling noises fill the air like wood in the fire, but soon the noises turn into distant voices.

While Merya whispers into the radio, someone approaches me with unsteady steps. Galen clears his throat, and I turn to see his hand stretching towards me, gesturing to follow him to a spot away from the rest of the group.

Jyn intercepts us and nods as if to grant permission, "Stay where you can see us. When Merya gives the signal, we only have ten minutes to reach the gate."

"I know. It will only take a moment," Galen replies flatly.

His face has regained some of its usual colour, but it's hard to say in the weak light of the tunnel. Besides, his voice is grave, weighed down by recent events and whatever secret he is keeping from me.

He guides me towards a niche in the wall, where the dense

stream of mud has dried out to a more concrete path, and where our steps resound louder.

I fit inside the hollow without needing to bend, but Galen has to lower his head.

"Was there a door here?" I ask, running my hand over what's left of the metal hinges on one side of the niche.

He nods and stares at the phantom door as if remembering something. "This was the entrance to a secondary tunnel, but it was destroyed years ago, during an attack." His hand follows mine along the edge of the entrance, brushing it lightly.

"The people who tried to kill us above ground?" I study his face, searching for a single detail that would remind me of the Galen I used to know, but his jaw his clenched, and his eyes are full of memories he's never shared with me.

"Those were not Herionos," he mutters.

"How do you— "

He looks me straight in the eyes, and I shrink. His face is filled with knowledge—and a shadow that scares me.

His hand moves away from mine, and he traces the empty frame of the arch with his fingertips. "Another time," - he cuts me short - "I need you to promise me that whatever you see, whoever you meet once we're back above ground, you will not overreact."

"Overreact? After everything we've just been through?" I exclaim with a hint of a smile. "A bit too late for that, don't you think?" I make to move to rejoin the others, but Galen steps in front of me.

"Just promise you will keep an open mind and count to ten before saying anything."

I cock my head to one side, examining his face. "You should teach that to Mack."

"I'm serious…"

"To five?"

He allows himself a quick smirk and exhales, defeated. "Fine. Just remember, *they* don't know you—yet. We're equal here, but we've survived by codes and rules."

We. I promised an open mind starting now, despite how odd it is to listen to Galen refer to a life he could have never had while being with me in Libera.

An open mind, starting with letting go of my doubts.

An alarmed whistle breaks us apart.

"That's the signal. Go!" he prompts.

I start running towards the column of light, with Galen following right behind, and I halt right before my face can hit Tabitha's back.

Agitated footsteps scurry above us, and Galen pushes me out of the way before a shower of little stones and debris rains down from the hole. Above us, disembodied voices whisper orders.

Silence reigns again, and Tabs gives us a quick look to ensure we're all fine. "Get ready to climb," she orders with a stern nod.

Three rope ladders descend from the hole in the ceiling, thick and lined with wooden rungs.

"Jyn—you, Mack and Merya go first. Help Galen once you're up there." While Tabitha speaks, Jyn is already a couple of steps up on his rope. The siblings follow him, dangling from the other ladders at his sides.

They've done this before. They're climbing effortlessly, no matter the arsenal they're carrying on their bodies.

I look up where someone, also wearing a helmet, is leaning over the edge of the hole and pulling the ropes towards them to speed up the ascent.

Tabitha places a hand on my shoulder. "You and Galen are up next. Once in the open, follow the others. I'll meet you back at the base."

I'm not sure if she's talking to me, because I don't even know what the *base* is.

Galen responds for both of us, "Where are you going?"

Tabs sucks on her teeth, grabbing his shoulders. In the narrow space of the tunnel, she looks taller than when I met her on the shore. "Someone has to retrieve the pod. We can't leave it there. If they get to it, even if it's unable to travel, their engineers could find a way to crack the codes. They could use it to gain access to our bases. We can't risk more losses," Tabitha says.

Galen shakes himself free of her grip. "I reckon the bastards that ambushed Sof and me on the roof have already found other ways to enter the area. Pod or not, the Chapter is fucked. Someone clearly betrayed us from the inside. We lost the island—"

"I don't give a blessed fuck about the Chapter," she slaps her hands on her hips. "And when did you become so cynical?" Pain darkens Tabitha's eyes.

"It's either that or crying over those we've lost forever…"

I grab the rung at the bottom of my ladder and start climbing, focusing on its rough texture as I try to get away from the tension rising between Galen and Tabitha.

"Get on that rope." Tabs grunts through her teeth.

I look down, if only to receive permission to go myself, but I witness the scene of a fight ready to explode.

Tabs's nostrils flare slightly, and her jaw tenses as if she's fighting back her urge to argue. Galen's back is rigid, his shoulders clenched, hands in tight fists at his sides.

When I glance up, I see Merya and Mack squatting by the edge of the hole, also observing the scene, with their mouths open.

A tall black silhouette stands behind them, head concealed by a helmet. It is probably talking to the siblings because they are nodding their heads as if confirming something.

Tabitha finally seems to realise she has an audience, and she assumes a more relaxed stance, letting go of the tension on her lips and face. "I'll be back before morning. Now, please, get on the rope. I need *you* at the base."

Galen's body reacts to her promise. His hands open, fingers stretching along his thighs. I don't wait for him to turn around. It is not my place to question his attitude. I would, were this the man I knew up until two days ago. But… he is—and he is also something else.

Every muscle in my body complains as I restart my climb. The moment my skin stretches around the rope, caked in dirt and mud, all the scratches and grazes reopen, stinging like hell. Blood stains the rope, but the fast-approaching light above me keeps me going. Soft rays flicker through Merya's fingers as she leans over the opening, offering me her hand.

I give one last push, eager to see the sun again and experience what the new day may bring.

Chapter 31 - Octopus at War
July

I groan as my entire skeleton aches, imploring me to stop and give up, when I grab Merya's hand.

She easily hauls me up, but the same exhaustion that slows me down shows on her face.

I clamber out of the tunnel as if waking up from a centuries-long slumber. I squint, holding my hand to my forehead, my eyes slowly adjusting to the light, as concerned whispers fill my ears.

The light that has guided me towards the exit is nothing but a square floodlight positioned right atop the tunnel mouth. It is small, but as powerful as the restorative sunlight my body has lately been craving.

Instead—my hope deflates at the sight of a starless sky, dark and silent. The moon is hard to spot, shielded behind black clouds. The air is still, although invisible veins of cold rise from the ground and wrap around my bare arms. I brace myself, regretting the jumper I abandoned in the tunnel. My vision blurs with hunger and fatigue—

"Mind your step," Merya warns, grabbing me by the elbows.

"I'm fine; I can walk alone," I whisper.

I don't want to disturb the silence around us, and I slowly take some tentative steps on foreign, uneven ground mostly made of pebbles.

I'm not the only one who thinks staying quiet is the best choice. Merya nods and gestures me to rejoin Jyn, Mack and the other person in black, who are standing a few feet away from us in an open field of low grass—empty if not for a building that must have once been majestic and sturdy, had not a significant disaster destroyed a good part of it. Its metal skeleton is half exposed, rusty and sad, desperately clinging to what's left of the white boulders that were once its shiny skin.

I give Merya another look, tempted to wait, to ensure Galen makes it out of the tunnel, instead of going after Tabitha. But the rest of the group's impatient stance tells me I don't have time, and I'd better hurry towards the building.

Merya slowly takes my hands to stop me from picking at the skin of my thumbs. "I'm not going anywhere without him, but you need to reach the others now," she mutters. "Remember, we only have a small window before this place becomes visible on the radars."

The penumbra of the tunnel may have tricked me when I didn't see any trace of Harvester's blood in Mack's eyes, but observing Merya's - and the lack of purple in her breath - confirms that she and her brother shouldn't be risking their lives for Tabitha and her rebels.

"Why did you join them?" I ask without thinking. "You're not one of—"

"You?" she cuts me off, shifting her weight onto her right leg, arms crossed.

I shake my head, holding my hands up in front of me. "I'm sorry, I didn't mean it—" I drop my arms and sigh. "Just, if I were you, I'd stay away from the Harvesters, rebels or not, as much as I can." I shrug.

I will not blame her if she decides to leave me here to figure out how to get inside HQ for myself.

Instead, she studies me for a moment, chewing on her bottom lip, and then she clicks her tongue, "If you think Mack and I are the anomalies in this situation, just wait until you see the inside of our building. *That* is something else. But I don't want to ruin it for you. Mack won't forgive me if I do."

As if having been summoned, Mack's voice crackles on the radio clipped to Merya's hip. "We're cold and hungry. Can you two please move? Mack over and out."

Grunting, Merya snatches the radio, holding it close to her lips. She hisses, "Get off the radio. It's not a toy."

"Yes, Sir. I know, Sir. I built that not-a-toy, Sir." Mack quickly replies before going silent again.

I hold back a smile, clearing my throat, "Should I...?" I point at HQ's dark silhouette.

Pinching the bridge of her nose, Merya nods. "I'll meet you inside."

She pats me twice on the shoulder, and a timid smile similar to Mack's stretches on her lips - perhaps caused by her reckless brother - before she returns to the hole.

As I walk towards HQ, my knees remain rigid, and my teeth don't stop chattering. When I finally reach Mack, I'm happy to be in his company again rather than alone in the eerie field. I smile when I can make out the outline of his fair hair rustled by a gentle wind and his surprisingly relaxed smirk.

"Thanks for waiting for me," I say when I notice Jyn and the stranger are no longer with him.

"Everything alright down there?" he juts his chin in his sister's direction, resembling Galen when he buries his hands in his pockets.

"Nothing to worry about," I reply, trying to peer at HQ's door over his shoulder.

"Well, that'd be a first." He follows my eyes, then turns his back to me, opening his arms wide and gazing at the top of the building. "Isn't she beautiful? I personally designed her, every curve, wrinkle and charming flaw."

I move a few steps back to stand beside him, scratching my head. "You designed this…" I can't call it a ruin in front of its creator, so I settle for - "Structure?" - to sound as neutral as possible.

Mack slowly narrows his eyes at me, lips pursed, arms resting again on his chest, "What—is it that hard to believe? Is it because I'm too young and handsome, or because I can't have a creative brain *and* sexy scars *and* a willingness to kill if threatened?"

I didn't sound so neutral after all. I sigh, offering a smile. "Why do you people tend to twist everything I say? Although, in all fairness… You are *young*, and this building must have been bombed; what? Ten years ago? Look at the state of its remains!" I point at the rusty metal bars sticking out of its broken stones here and there.

His smirk returns as he leans towards me, tapping a finger to his temple. "Who said I planned *her* to look conventionally attractive?"

"Hang on—you mean, this devastation of a building—"

"Hey, don't call her that. She's my pride and joy," Mack snaps, hovering his hand over the ruin as if gently patting it.

I blink a couple of times, trying to spot hints of charm from the decrepit stones and windows - like toothless, agape mouths - that dot the leaning building, sprinkled with moss that hasn't yet fully reclaimed its reign, both inside and outside of the cracks, turning the skin of the decaying body greenish and sick.

Crouching by the base of HQ, I follow the journey of a fat, green worm that wriggles close to a chipped boulder, leaving a slimy trail in its wake, as it pauses to lift its head and decides to go the opposite way. "How come nobody ever tried to occupy this place? It's so *exposed*. I'm surprised the people who've tried to kill us haven't found you already."

Mack glances at me over one shoulder before kneeling beside me. He pats one hand on the grass as if studying the density of the soil. "When at war, your only hope of surviving is being an octopus."

I turn my head towards him, narrowing my eyes. "What's with you and this octopus?" I ask, rocking on the balls of my feet.

"Oh, here we go," Merya exclaims behind me, and I jolt sideways, throwing my right hand to the side to keep balance.

"Do I keep listening?" I ask, pushing myself up.

Merya shrugs, one of the ladders we used to climb out of the tunnel slumped over her shoulders. Her hair, loose and gleaming with sweat, runs down her back like molten copper against her black gear. She props her helmet under her arm, tilting her head while staring at her brother, who is still deeply lost in studying the grass. A hint of a smile blooms on her face as she says, "He will keep talking whether you listen or not. Your choice."

At that, she straightens her spine, assuming the strong stance and composure she had when I met her, and adds, "Mack, don't wait for Galen and get inside. We checked the ground only a few hours ago; don't stay out here longer than necessary."

In response, Mack only waves one hand at her while crouch-walking along the perimeter of the building, patting the grass and sniffing random handfuls of soil.

"I convinced Galen to come back and let Tabitha go. I'll see you inside," Merya sighs, takes a left turn and *vanishes* behind a corner of the building.

I stare. Agape. Pointing at the spot that has just swallowed Merya, where there now remains nothing but exposed metal scaffolding and thin air.

"I told you. An octopus." Mack taps at my shoulder, his hand carrying the scent of wet grass. "Alteration is key."

The sound of an opening door catches his attention, and I cannot be more glad the awkward conversation is over.

Jyn's head pops out between a wall covered in moss and the void that once formed the left side of the building. Startled and without thinking, I push Mack aside to inspect it more closely. One rushed step after the other; I aim for that trickery. My right arm stretches out, my fingers ready to touch the incoherent structure.

"I don't think that's a good idea." Amusement, but also a warning, in Mack's words.

"July, wait—" Sheer urgency in Jyn's voice.

"Oh, fuck. Merya didn't tell her…" Mack's voice pops like a soap bubble.

The rush of electricity shocks me as soon as my fingertips scrape against the *non-void*, leaving me only enough seconds to register my heart speeding, before the inevitable blackout hits me.

Chapter 32 - One of Us
July

"What were you thinking?"

"Oh, well—I'm sorry if, after the mayhem of risking my life to save yours, and being chased and forced to spend hours in a tunnel, I forgot to mention a little, *well-known* detail too—has she always been so nosy?"

"Shut up, Mack, she could be—"

"Mind your tone. All of you…"

The voices shouting in my head pause, but soon an annoying ringing noise takes their place.

"She could have died, for fuck's sake. And don't play the hero card with me. You probably begged Merya to take you along."

Nope. Ringing and voices can apparently coexist inside my poor head.

"What the hell are you two doing?"

"Can you please just stay quiet?" At last, my voice joins the others, husky and weak, even if all I want to do is shout at whoever is around me, despite black being all I can see.

A gentle touch on my hand makes my body tangible again after the sudden awakening. My mind floats for a few seconds before rediscovering the existence of my limbs.

"I can't see anything," I mutter, struggling to form the words, gaining a giggle to my left and a disappointed growl to the right.

"Come on, Galen, she's alive; drop the *Who did this to you*-look."

The same fingertips that have woken my skin run up my arm, tracing a path from my wrist to my shoulder, pinching here and there. "Can you feel this?"

"Merya?" I think I'm smiling when I call her name, but I can't say if it's all in my head. "Yes, yes, I can."

"Well, the good news is, your nervous system and hearing are not damaged."

"What about the bad news?" I mumble, my lips peeling off my teeth in a wince of pain when I try to move my head.

"Just stand still."

A shorter explanation than I hoped for. This cannot be a good sign.

Steps approach me. "Let me do it, please."

Galen…

A sigh. "Sure, but it will hurt the same, whether I do it or—okay, okay. Suit yourself."

I'm resting on something rough, slightly bent to accommodate my weight. My hands search for something familiar and find a stretch of plastic looped over metal bars—some sort of camping cot.

My breath stops when a warm, soft hand caresses my forehead, followed by Galen's reassuring voice, "Sof, I need you to trust me. Try not to move, please." Not that I could manage much movement right now, with this stupid headache and a half-senseless body.

"High-voltage barriers protect HQ. You barely touched it, and you're lucky your brain is still functioning." Galen's touch travels down towards my eyes, one fingertip at a time.

"I planned it to perfection—"

"Shut up, Fumo." Merya hisses, very close to me. I think she's tried to keep her voice low, but my head perceives it like an army of stomping elephants.

My neck is one of the last parts of my body to have regained sensation. "Why can't I feel my eyes?" I curl my fingers to contain the sudden shock of pain. My mouth is dry, and when I try to swallow, my throat stings.

"That's what I like to call the gem of my creation—"

"Get out, Mack, now!" Galen's snarl hurts every fibre of my brain.

"I'm sorry, Sof, I didn't mean…" I must have winced in pain because his voice drops suddenly, but I can't be sure because I have no perception of the space where my eyes and eyebrows should be.

"Get on with it. We need her up as soon as possible," Merya whispers. "July, hold my hand and squeeze if you need to."

Galen's fingers move further down my forehead. And then—they've gone.

The scream is not comparable to anything else I've experienced so far. It rips my heart from the inside, clawing at my nerves and skin, lacerating every cell in my body, and setting my head on fire. Even my hand, holding onto Merya's, is in pain. Or is it because I'm clenching too hard? Am I crushing her hand, and is it Merya's scream I'm hearing?

I try to sit up, but someone pins me down on the cot, and my back arches so much I fear my spine will snap.

"Focus on your pain and use it to breathe. Breathe the pain in and out."

"We should have waited a bit longer; she's too weak."

A door quickly opens and slams shut. "What on Horigos is going on? We heard her scream two levels below."

"What the fuck are you doing here?" Galen barks, his fingers twitching against my skin.

I clench my jaw, preparing for another wave of pain. But, the same way they started - unexpected and unannounced - the spasms stop; I jolt upright, touching my face to check my eyes haven't fallen out.

"Easy, Sof." Galen is by my side, holding an empty syringe. "Open your eyes slowly. Your sight may be blurred, but it's just a temporary side effect." He averts his eyes only for a second, to discard the used needle in a plastic bag on the floor.

I do as he suggests. My neck is so stiff I have to throw my legs over the cot and turn my whole body to face the rest of the people in the room.

"What happ—" I wince at the sensation of needles in my throat.

Someone rushes to the cot and gingerly brings something to my lips. "Here, drink some of this. It will soothe the pain, but try not to speak too much for the next hour or so."

"Thanks," I'm not sure if I'm smiling—but I *really* hope so. "Coffee?" I ask dubiously, as if expecting a magic potion instead.

"You're favourite—I was told."

By the sound of his voice, the person kneeling in front of me is a man. Perhaps the stranger I saw with Jyn outside HQ. But it's just a canvas of smeared greens and browns and whites.

"We haven't been officially introduced."

"Because we have more important matters to discuss." Galen's voice draws my attention away from the stranger.

Heavy boots approach, followed by a resolute remark. "Ahem."

"Yes, Mack?" both Galen and the stranger ask curtly.

A short, nervous laugh, then, "Sorry, knights in shining armour, I just wanted to say, well… Not that my barrier is something to be sorry for, but…"

I know what he's trying to say, and turning my head toward the tall blur standing behind the stranger, I utter hoarsely, "It's all right, Fumo. Apologies accepted."

The hazy figure claps once, or so I believe, his movements are too quick and too energetic. "Amazing, she called me by my war name—she's officially one of us. Welcome to New Hera, July Sofia Crimson!"

For a split second, everything and everyone seems to freeze.

"Aaaand—that's my cue. I'm just. Going. Yes. I'll be downstairs if you need me… Gone." The Mack-mass seems to retreat towards what I think is the door.

"Good idea," the stranger replies, huffing a laugh. So natural and so real it squeezes something inside my chest.

There are other people in the background, including Merya.

Galen, however, ignores them and sits next to me. "You need some rest. I'll kick them out."

I begin to smile, but a sudden, soft kiss on my cheek shuts down all my thoughts, but one. The memory of Roden's hand on my cheek, back in the monitors room, flashes behind my eyes, unstable as if not receiving enough signal. *How about I show you the truth?*

Maybe it's the lack of sight, maybe my body is completely drained, or perhaps my senses are all messed up.

Galen's demonstration of affection makes my heart hammer in my chest, as if he's never kissed me before.

And hearts only beat this fast in excitement—or fear.

Chapter 33 - The Pang of Life
July

"That pang you feel in your chest is not your heart failing. It is the life of a Harvester or Horigean running out of time," Popplewish said while we sat at my mother's living room table, the good one, made of crystal and white oak that she only used when we had guests.

"But I don't want it. It hurts." I was just a little girl who didn't know anything about death. Only that it comes and takes away people and animals forever. But I was the one suffering every time and having nightmares after it'd happened, sometimes for weeks.

"It's okay, dear. I will teach you how to turn that pain into strength and about the beauty of your gift."

That was the moment my parents left the room without a word. I saw them again when they handed me my luggage and waved goodbye from their front door.

"You have a special heart, like mine, and many other people like you." Popplewish had a book with her that day, and she opened it before me. "Have a look at this. Tell me, can you read, Sofia?"

I never liked that name; it didn't feel like *mine*.

"Yes." I lied. I was scared the nice lady would leave without me if she thought I wasn't good enough.

My little fingers run across the lines, back and forth, tapping on the words. "We… ar… are… pr… pro-te… protrep…"

"Protectors. We are protectors of souls. Do you know what a *protector* is?"

I kept my eyes on the page, hoping to find the meaning there. But it wasn't the word 'protector' that bothered me.

"What's a soul?" I asked instead.

That was the first time I experienced a hug, a real one, not a cold pat on the head. Popplewish held me tight and only let go when I was ready to walk on my own, with her by my side.

I crack open my right eye, happy with the almost total absence of light because even the weakest ray of sunshine would split my head wide open. There's a pounding discomfort behind my eyes, and my mouth is so dry I could drink water until I drown.

The idea of water brings an image to my mind: a stranger offering me something to drink after Mack's barriers had knocked me unconscious.

I sit up so quickly that I immediately regret it. My stomach churns and spins, and I cover my mouth with my hand, fearing the worst. But as I give myself some time to inhale and exhale normally again, a sweet aroma tickles my nose.

I have to gingerly turn my head left and right to scan the space, until in the dim light filtering through the only window in the room, I discover the source of the inviting smell on a bedside table, where someone has left a teapot and some cake.

Following the recent events, food has dropped to the bottom of my priorities, but it's also the one thing that could help my brain work better and understand what's happening. So I fling my legs over the edge of the cot and pluck a small bite of cake, washing it down with some lemon tea to make it easier on my throat.

"Oh, this is so good," I mumble, chewing the perfect mixture of sugar and orange.

But when I lift the plate for more cake, muffled voices from the room beside mine catch my attention.

Barefoot, I cross the floor and press one ear against the wall I share with the adjacent room.

The voices are so hushed I can barely catch a few words. But one thing is sure—Galen is in there.

I toy with the idea of leaving my room and standing behind his door, but when I push away from the wall, my head starts spinning, and black dots appear behind my eyes.

"… you what?!" Galen yells from the other room, and I silence a gasp, covering my mouth before it can betray me.

When nobody comes knocking at my door, I flatten my ear again against the wall. Someone is pacing up and down, and words get lost in the background noise, but I'm sure Mack is the second person in that room.

They're arguing - well, Galen is, while Mack sounds otherwise amused - until a door slams, followed by a thump as if something has dropped on the floor or someone has sat down heavily on something.

For a few seconds, I listen to my heart thumping in my ears, as it relaxes into its natural rhythm after the excitement of behaving like a naughty child. But soon it starts to gallop when Galen begins to speak again.

But it is not Mack, talking back at him…

I never thought a minute could last a lifetime, and mark your existence as if you had fought a thousand wars—and lost them all.

I force myself to push away from that damn wall as if waiting for someone to tell me that all I've heard was a joke.

"This can't be real…" I repeat a few times as I walk back to the bed-cot and sit on its edge, facing the window. My fingers ruffle the blanket, opening and closing, tensing and releasing. But my usual trick, the one I taught myself as a child, to relax my nerves and thoughts, doesn't seem to work.

I stand and open the curtains, letting the light in. It hurts, but for a split second, it silences the echo of what I shouldn't have heard.

I rest my forehead against the window, breathing a purple puff that stains the glass momentarily before disappearing. Despite the sunshine, the glass is cold to the touch, numbing my skin enough to trick my brain into thinking that that is the issue I must focus on—not the conversation I've accidentally just listened to. I close my eyes to savour the pleasant sensation when I hear a laugh coming from the little garden below the window.

I peer outside, looking for that sudden source of normalcy and happiness. "Who would want a child to live here?"

So far, I've seen the half-destroyed carcass of what Tabs called HQ and this room. But now, trees and green grass surprise me, populating a pretty little orchard with low bushes of pink and white flowers here and there.

Not so different from the orchard we had back in Libera. Except for the lack of a training square—and a burning castle.

The last few days' events come back in a violent wave that crushes me.

I fiddle with the latch to open the window and let fresh air in, but I stop when footsteps shuffle and stop outside my door.

Something rustles outside. I hold my breath to avoid making any noise, but nobody knocks or comes in.

I take a deep breath as if I have forgotten how to use my lungs. My heart starts racing, warming up my chest.

"Who's there?" I ask timidly, unsure my voice is strong enough to pierce through the door.

When I receive no answer, I move away from the window and slowly walk over. One step at a time. Stopping halfway. Another noise, like a scratch, as though whoever is outside is running a hand up and down the thick wood.

I'm only a few steps away when a sigh confirms my doubts.

"Galen, is that you?" Even if he's the last person I wish to see after what I've just heard.

But, if that's not Galen…

I cut across the space between *us* as quickly as possible, fearing my heart would stop if I didn't.

He was the person who was talking to Galen just a few moments ago. I'm sure of it.

I nearly slam against the door, my right hand stroking the hard surface at my eye level. "Is it *you?*" I whisper, ignoring the tingling feeling in my fingertips, like that of Nistarei's kernels wrapping around my hand before dripping inside my vials.

A gasp.

Someone else walks out of the room adjacent to mine.

Heated whispers follow.

I bust the door open—but I've waited too long. Only an empty corridor welcomes me.

All I want to do is cry and fill the void left inside me by the invisible presence with tears.

The wooden door is warm beneath my hand, and the pang in my heart is the same one I tried to explain to Popplewish when she showed up at my childhood house.

The whisper of a life that's about to end.

Loud steps make me jump, snatching me out of my reverie, and I rush back to the cot. I sit down, pretending the window is the most interesting part of the room, when all I want to do is to run after the soul who's just left a hole in my chest.

Chapter 34 - Growth
Galen

"**I**'m sure you were glad to find your room exactly like you left it. I took pictures before moving in—"

"Mack, you what?"

"Chill, mate." He remains by the threshold while I inspect every inch of my room. "I needed a quiet place to work on my latest invention. Merya was getting on my nerves, and it was either blowing up our room—accidentally, with Merya inside—or, well, your bed is still here, so…" Mack gives me a thumb-up and rushes away, slamming the door behind him.

I would chase him downstairs, but the recent events occupy my mind entirely. Mainly because Kristyon showed up in July's room as if it were the most normal thing to do. And that Tabitha forgot to mention the *minor* detail that he is here, mere meters away from July, where the smell of his soul can easily attract Reds, like bees to a fucking field of sunflowers.

"This is a mess…" I let out a breath, closing the curtains of my window.

I need to send word to Eve before she freaks out, convinced

that July and I have died in the explosion. Or have been taken hostage.

"Unless Nik and Lily have already filled her in regarding the little mishap we encountered on the roof, " I mumble, combing my hair back with one hand.

They're here already. That can only mean Libera is no longer safe.

"I'll leave that to Tabitha to sort out," I sigh.

I turn my back to the window so I can take in the state of my room without Mack hovering, like a fly high on sugar.

And—he was right. My room seems pristine. Even cleaner than the last time I was here.

Even the bed sheets look crisp and fresh, so inviting after hours spent running from a fire and bullets. But a knock on the door saves me from wasting time napping.

"Too soon, Mack. I'm not ready to forgive you. Or to admire your latest contraptions."

I slump on my bed, waiting for one of Mack's usual grand entrances despite my request to leave me alone. But the face looking at me through the threshold makes my spine stiffen and my jaw tense.

"Now I know why Eve and I couldn't reach you on the usual channel. But I'd love to know why Tabitha has allowed you to go rogue - no pun intended - and make your own stupid choices without checking with us first." I can't stem my anger seeping through my voice.

"Galen, look. I know what you think, but this time is different. You've seen it in there. She didn't even flinch when I spoke to her."

"She was temporarily blind, you reckless idiot." I almost hope someone's heard me because I will knock him out if nobody comes to stop me.

His voice may sound more profound than the last time we spoke, and his hair longer. However, not even the short beard could trick the eyes, especially after Eve told me Roden had decided to show his video report to July. I bet she's memorised every line of his face, the colour of his eyes, the curve of his lips.

I slap my bed to avoid aiming my frustration directly at him.

"Kris, you'd better close that door and lock it," I say in the flattest voice possible, leaving my bed and beckoning him in. "There's something you need to know, and you won't like it."

He looks at me, doubtful; there's still a shadow of a smile on his face, but he does as asked.

"Are you talking about your last-minute trip to Horigos without Roden's blessing?" he leans with his back against the door, hands buried in the pockets of his cargo trousers.

I shake my head. "Not exactly. It's more to do with a deal July accepted. This time, there is a strong chance she'll take you to Roden. He didn't leave her much of a choice."

I let the words sink.

"And you call that news?"

"She has a reason this time," I lower my voice.

Kris tilts his head, such an innocent gesture that it makes my blood boil.

How can he not flinch? Not fucking once.

"She's always had one, and look at me," - he flexes one arm - "I'm standing in front of you, living and breathing, and talking."

I huff a laugh, "That's hard to prevent, I'm afraid." I rub my face, studying him through my fingers. "How long have you been here? You've started to sound like Mack. This is serious. Her memories haven't come back yet—"

Kris arches a brow in disbelief, "But?"

"But she knows I am part of the Chapter."

"Interesting." Kris pinches his chin, staring at me. "So, you're not her favourite anymore. How are *you* still alive, then?"

Exasperation bubbles in my belly. "Tabitha explained the situation better than I could on our way here. But that's not the point... Too many variables have changed, and I can't really say how July will react. This time."

He shrugs; not a trace of fear crosses his face.

I stand up from my bed and start pacing in silence.

"Oh, oh. You're chewing the collar of your t-shirt. That must be bad."

I stop and turn on my heel. "What's wrong with you?" I say with frustration more than anger.

I regret it as soon as he hums with a sad smile, lowering his eyes to the floor. "Have you ever thought that perhaps I'm tired of this? All I want is to end this *thing,* that is. Once and for all, so I can finally stop hiding and settle somewhere. Anywhere. Or just stop being?"

The months we've been apart creep up on him, revealing the man he's become—the person I wanted him to be since we discovered his power and curse.

"So you're just giving up?" I open my arms to keep them busy, as otherwise, I will slap him—or worse. "And what about the sacrifices I had to make? What about Tabitha, Jyn and the others?"

He pushes away from the door, stepping into the narrow path of light pouring in from the curtains. Lit by the sunlight, the emerald in his eyes transforms into molten gold, an ability that used to frighten me when I began spending a bunch of forbidden, dangerous hours with him, supervised by Evelyn.

"Don't play the victim with me. Tabitha and her people were deeply involved in their war before they knew I even existed. I'm just a useful addition to their arsenal. As to you—you don't really have a choice," he smirks, mirroring my stance and crossing his arms over his chest.

And he is so right; I wish I could lock him in this room and throw away the key. But he's not a little boy anymore.

I throw my hands in the air, defeated and more worried than I was a few moments ago. "July is first in line to be the death of me; but you are a worthy contender. At least promise you won't go looking for her, talk to her, or even spy on her from afar."

Kristyon opens his mouth, but I stop him. "I was being rhetorical. You will *not* seek any contacts unless I say it's safe." I mark every word with a step towards him. I only stop when we're so close I can see the gold recoiling inside his pupils and his eyes returning to emerald.

"Fine," he mumbles, disappointed. "I've waited longer than ever this time. I can spend a few minutes without seeing her."

"Days," I snap.

He cuts me a mischievous look. "Hours is the best I can do."

We both stumble towards the door at Kris' back when I grab him by his white shirt's collar, growling, "We're not bargaining the fish price at Brenath's market, for fuck's sake. This is your life I'm trying to keep safe."

His gaze doesn't falter or roam away from mine. He stands his ground, gritting his teeth but keeping his frustration in.

"As you order," Kris hisses. "One emotional, temperamental brother in the building is more than enough. If we're done here, I'll go and hide somewhere in the dark. But don't blame me if she senses my insubordinate, charming presence and goes looking for me."

I let go of his shirt, dropping my head. "Get out—before I knock you out to make it easier for everyone." I dismiss him, pointing at the door and keeping my eyes on the ground to avoid his contagious, unbreakable smile.

"It's good to have you back, brother," he says, opening the door behind him but still looking at me. "I promise to remain alive so you can argue with me a little longer."

The door slams shut, and I stare at it as if Kris is still there. "Good to see you too," I mumble. Seconds later, my stomach rumbles when the smell of something delicious finds me, travelling from the kitchen through the vents.

But before I can tend to my hunger, I need to ensure July has recovered and is strong enough to face what's coming—but not fatally strong to kill Kris by harvesting whatever soul that reckless man has left after having cured too many Reds, against mine and Evelyn's opinion.

I hear no sound when I crack the door open and peer inside. Although more light than when I left is bouncing against the walls, turning them whiter than they are, and casting an ethereal hue over July's silhouette.

"Sof, how long have you been awake for?" I ask quietly, so as not to scare her.

She's sitting on the edge of the cot, facing the window. Her hair has become untied in her sleep, wrapping around her shoulders like a dark halo.

If she's heard me, she doesn't show it. So I walk in, closing the door behind me. "Can we talk?"

The room smells of lavender and sugar. On the bedside table rests a tray with a half-eaten slice of cake and a steaming teapot.

"Are you not hungry?" *Please, talk to me.*

Her shoulders shudder. I grab a blanket from the chest of drawers by the door and rush to her. But when the soft fabric grazes her naked arms, she stands up and backs away from me.

"Don't… I'm fine, but still shaken." Her voice is so weak, so distant.

"Of course. Last night wasn't easy for anyone." I move slowly, giving her enough time to feel comfortable around me.

But she moves to the window, facing Mack's artificial orchard, and distractedly runs a finger up and down the glass. "What happened to Sector 43? This is not how I remembered it."

I wait to see if she's willing to look at me, but she remains immobile.

"Last time you were here, this part of Horigos was still free land. They, the people who attacked us, were still confined beyond Cleryce's mountains in the northernmost part of The Mother. But that was… a while ago."

Shooting me a glare over her shoulder, she finally turns. "Why do you all keep calling them *they?* With or without Roden's involvement, Herionos attacked us in Libera. You've mentioned them. What's the point of pretending they don't exist?"

I know her words are meant to hurt me, but her voice is so cold she doesn't sound like *my* July.

I drop my head, moving a few more tentative steps towards her. "It's not that easy. Not all the Herionos are despicable like Roden likes to depict them."

"Nothing is easy. It looks like nobody appreciates simplicity anymore…" She sighs, curling her fingers into fists at her side.

I'm expecting her to burst into anything: laughing, crying, shouting… For her to run away even. But she just stands by the oval window, staring at me as if my words never actually reached her.

"How much do you know about this man that Roden wants so desperately gone for good?" She asks, tilting her head.

At this point, I have no reason to pretend. I can only try to contain the damage.

I approach the window, and she doesn't move away this time.

"It is—"

"*He*," she retorts.

"He has a singular soul. One that Roden and the Chapter members loyal to him have tried many times to confine in its current existence, but a soul that always managed - one way or another - to remember its previous lives. The good and the bad parts, including the people he met. Those who tried to destroy him. Those who loved him."

She leans against the window, hands braced on the sill, tapping one nervous finger on the white stone. "You forgot to mention that he is also closer than we thought. But you knew that already." She purses her lips, her eyes piercing mine. "You *know* him…"

I flinch, lost for words because I've rarely seen her like this, restless, running her hands through her hair to keep them busy.

"You weren't supposed to find out—" Wrong choice. Too late.

Her arms fall heavy at her side. "And I agreed to destroy his life. Even if I start to think that probably extinguishing his soul forever will be a blessing, given the alternative is to deliver him to Roden…"

I fear her whole body would crumple to the floor, deflated. I know what she's about to say, and I can't stop it. "And I said yes for us. For a chance at that freedom that I believe we were never destined to have. And probably never deserved." She stabs her chest with her finger like a knife to carve out her guilt.

"I'm sorry I didn't tell you earlier. I couldn't..." I glance at the window and then at July, asking for permission to get closer. Only when she nods do I take a step forward.

Our shoulders brush, and my heart jumps, but she doesn't flinch or recoil.

"So, what side are you on?" she asks, folding one hand over the other.

The orchard is greener than the last time I was here. Mack must have found a way to purify the lake.

I let out a relaxed laugh, the first in days, leaving a faint purple halo on the window. "Tabs would have never let me in if I wasn't on the right side—her side," I admit, obtaining a puzzled, sideways look from July.

I mirror her stance, bracing my hands on the windowsill. "We'll have an urgent, last-minute debrief later today. Tabitha would like you to attend so she can explain everything. And answer all your questions." I nudge her with my left shoulder, "I know you may have one or two."

I offer a tentative smile that she doesn't echo. But she doesn't run away or slap me either.

"Why can't Roden just leave him be?" Her eyes roam around the room as if imprinting every detail on her mind.

Without waiting for my answer - I'm not even sure if she's

talking to me or herself - she steps away from the window, lost in thought, and approaches the table with the slice of cake, lifting a tiny piece to her mouth. A shadow crosses her face, but she quickly blinks it away.

When she remembers I'm here with her, she slowly turns to me, "Roden told me he stripped part of that man's soul many times, trying to break him," - she swallows what I'm sure is rage and tears she doesn't want to see me - "But even Roden cannot do what I do to Rogues, and I've never seen this man before. Then—who helped Roden and the Chapter *before* we joined the Harvesters?"

Is there judgement in her tone?

Her attention shoots to the wall separating our rooms…

Oh, shit…

I shake my head. "I wish I knew. It must have been someone with your gift."

"Someone horrible if they agreed to make that poor soul suffer repeatedly. I wonder if there is something Roden didn't tell me."

Her eyes flick to me, her hands balling into fists, the only movement confirming she hasn't turned into a marble statue.

I need to get out of here before she asks the right question, and I give her the one answer she shouldn't hear from me.

I turn to the window and freeze. Jyn is leaving HQ with Nikrah and Lily, followed by Kris, who snaps his head up and meets my eyes. I quickly shut the blinds, fearing they will come off their loops.

"Why is he so important? Why has Roden tried so hard to keep him alive but he's now dropped the final decision on me? Why me?"

Even if I can't see her, her voice is like a sword slowly piercing my back.

I search my brain for anything safe to reveal without her growing sceptical. Again.

"His soul is the only one that has the power to reject Roden's orders. And that can only mean one thing."

I master a regular breath - and find the courage - to face her again. Recognition blooms on her face. Her fingers relax. "He doesn't *belong* to Roden, then. He's nothing like us. And yet, he shares our talents?"

I nod. "Partially, yes." I can't blame myself if she digs up some truth on her own.

"How do we know he's the only one?"

"We don't."

She dashes towards me in a rush of doubts but stops by the cot, using it like a barrier between us. "And all the lives he's been through, every time Roden had someone like me harvesting a kernel of his soul—why can we not just let him be until his natural death? Why— "

"July," I push away from the window. "You've had a rough day—we all have. Let's pause for a second and wait for Tabitha's meeting."

She hums in response, and I take it as an invitation to leave her room, give her some time to get ready, prepare her list of questions, and breathe.

I make for the door, but her voice calls me back.

"Galen?"

"Yes, Sof," I smile, searching her face over my shoulder.

"Was there someone here with me while I was asleep?"

I don't like the sound of this. "I checked on you once or twice. Mack, as well. I think you've carved a soft spot in his heart."

She pinches her lower lip. "Hmm, no, that's not it. I remember a face and a voice, but I can't quite place them in my memories. It was pleasantly familiar, and it makes me sad at the same time."

I swear I'm going to kill him myself this time.

"You probably had a dream. You've met so many new people lately…" I look away, conscious that my expression will betray me.

But she rushes to my side, her eyes reduced to two suspicious slits, like when we were children, and I told her she could grow fins if she stayed in the water long enough.

"Okay," she grins, a smile too broad and too rigid, and dismisses me by waving her hands. "You're right; shower and food before the big talk."

I linger by the door while she rocks back and forth on the balls of her feet.

"As you wish," I bow.

When I open the door, the floor seems quiet, except for high-pitched laughter and quick little steps coming up the stairs.

I turn back just one more time, "You sure you don't need anything?"

"A million percent."

"Great. Will you meet me downstairs when you're ready?"

She clasps her hands behind her, "I don't need a bodyguard. Please go."

That sounds more like *Leave me the fuck alone…* but I'll take it as an alternative to not speaking to me at all.

I step one foot out of the door when her voice strikes. "Who were you calling an idiot earlier in the other room?"

My knuckles turn white around the doorframe, and my arm becomes so rigid that it could snap like a twig.

"That was him. You brought me to the only place you shouldn't have…"

"I didn't know he was already here," I drop my head.

"Does he know who I am?"

I nod slowly.

"What will happen to him if I decide to hold up my end of the bargain?" She approaches me slowly, steps as measured as the tone of her voice.

She brushes my back and gently turns me around. "I heard you before. It sounded like you two knew each other very well. How many times did you witness his suffering while pretending to be on the Chapter's side?"

Her hand feels too warm when she slides it up my arm; my skin tingles when I lift mine to cover hers.

"It wasn't easy." I turn her hand in mine to place a kiss on her soft palm.

"Would you have kept the truth from me had our last night in Libera gone differently?"

I sigh into her hand, breathing in the light smell of cake lingering on her skin.

"I see," she whispers, tilting my chin and cupping my cheek. "And I think I understand."

When our eyes meet, the little girl Popplewish brought to Libera years ago is gone. July's gaze is fierce.

Ready for the truth.

Chapter 35 - Cakes and Traps
Tabitha

I never understood the meaning of the word family, and I've never considered myself fit for it. Though the one that chose me is the only one I'd ever dreamed of—the one I would die for.

Walking down to the kitchen - occasionally the emergency room - Merya is the first one I cross paths with when she moves away from the open oven, carrying a tray of something sweet-smelling and zesty. "Tabs, just in time. Want some?"

Sitting at the long dining table, the others lift their heads only to honour me with quick nods of acknowledgement before returning to their freshly baked slices of cake.

Mack is about to attack a second slice, but gives me one of his innocent smiles before saying, "Sorry we started without you, but *Sable* was throwing a tantrum."

"Hey!" A small, objecting voice comes from under the table, and my heart flutters with joy.

"Thanks for looking after her while I filled in Nik and Lily with the latest. I was surprised they made it here before us. But, given the exchange of news we've just had, I understand why they rushed.

I'll brief you as soon as I can, but first…" I proceed inside the kitchen and stop to ruffle Mack's hair before squatting beside him to have a word with the person sitting against one of the table's legs.

"What did I tell you about eating like a civilised person?"

The most beautiful pair of dark purple eyes I've ever seen looks back at me with what is supposed to be the attitude of an upset grown-up. But the overall image of the child sitting on the floor makes me forget why I should be reprimanding her instead of laughing.

"She said she's working on a plan to defeat the bad people once and for all. That's her secret lab," Merya states solemnly while setting her latest, delicious work of art by a window to cool down. "I tried very hard to lure her out with an extra slice and hot chocolate, but she's more stubborn than her mum."

She nudges me with her bare foot and points her chin at the kitchen door with a silent question.

"I think she's still asleep. I let Galen stay with her," I reply.

"Galen asked if I could take Kris with me. And, by the rush in his voice, I bet he needs to explain a thing or two," Jyn says, gulping down a tall glass of milk, then slamming a hand on the table, prompting a little cry from Sable. "I need to go. Lily and Nik asked me if they could get some supplies from my orchard, and some dried meat. Apparently, the numbers in The Mother are growing, but so is their appetite," he adds, pushing his chair back and brushing cake crumbs from his trousers.

Jyn is the spitting image of a gentle giant. Strong, calloused hands, kind eyes, the strength of ten fighters and a sweet tooth worse than my little Sable.

"Thanks for today, Jyn." We have our disagreements, but he knows I love him like a brother.

He pats my shoulder on his way out, his fingers tightening as he says, "Don't mention it, Lorne. Let's hope she makes the right choice. If she decides to go back to Libera—"

"She won't," I reply too quickly, but I need to believe a bit of luck will sprinkle upon us this time.

Years of battles flash behind his eyes when he gently bumps his forehead against mine. "I pray you're right."

He waves us goodbye, and I turn my attention to Mack, who's helping himself to another piece of cake, eating it straight from the tray by the window and blowing on his burnt fingers.

"Fumo, we need to check the perimeter around the woods. Make sure the barriers didn't suffer any damage after last night. And—you need a shower. Look at the state of your face. Did you remember to get some sleep last night?"

Sitting on the kitchen counter, Mack's face is a canvas painted with black smears of dirt and sticky spots of syrup.

He rubs his cheek, smiles and gives me a thumbs up while chomping on food, "Yes, Sir. I've actually checked the perimeter, the lake and the outskirts while you were all comfortably snoring. Hence, my rough, but still attractive, appearance."

"You what?" I blink, ignoring the *sir*.

"Couldn't sleep last night," - he shrugs - "I thought I might as well make myself useful."

I run a hand over my face, "Where do you find the energy—never mind. What about the armoury?"

Mack jumps off the counter, balancing a mug of coffee so well that not even a drop spills. "That, I can do. I've received some *explosive* supplies I'd like to play with before using them on the field. Nik *kindly* offered some of his blood after I told him Lily would surely appreciate his extra help to the cause." He winks. "Well, I'm sure she'd say something like that if she knew."

Any conversation with Mack could go on for ages, especially if he's passionate about the subject, but likely for me, a small hand pulls at my trousers. "Can I go with Fumo, mummy, please?"

Sable's eyes are the only weapon that could seriously damage my heart. She's built lean and petite despite sharing my blood. But her determination sometimes prevails against me.

Merya steps in, kneeling and pinning back a strand of black hair that's escaped Sable's braid, "Why don't I teach you how to make a trap instead?"

My little earthquake starts jumping up and down, clapping her hands, "Like one of those that makes you dangle from a tree and then… and then… Fumo's barrier comes up, and you go *Bzzz!* and then you're like *Ghh!*"

When she's exhausted her repertoire of sounds to explain the picture in her mind, Sable sticks her tongue out, pretending to be electrocuted.

"All right, enough." I must pretend I still have a say in the matter. I lift Sable in my arms. Her cheeks are flushed with excitement, and her face is covered in cake crumbs when she presses it against mine.

She smacks a sticky kiss on my forehead, "Thanks, mummy. I promise I'll shower *and* brush my teeth - all of them - when we're back."

In the background, Mack is scraping dirt off his fingernails and giggling at my evident defeat.

"I didn't agree to anything yet."

"No worries, Tabs. We'll prepare just a couple of small ones, big enough for rabbits. And," Merya holds up a hand before I can speak, "I won't let her go near the lake."

I sigh, putting my child down, and bend to flick her nose. "Sable Elpis Lorne, you put one tiny toe in the water, and I take away all your books for a week." I'd never, but she believes my mother-glare.

She looks at me, squinting her eyes. Something is brewing in her sophisticated brain. She purses her lips, enunciating with the tone of an experienced negotiator, "Will you get me a new book if I don't touch the water?"

I suck on my teeth and hold her stare. Merya coughs twice as if to gain Sable's attention, and out of the corner of my eye, I see her shaking her head as if to say *You're pushing it now.*

Sable puffs her cheeks, moves back a step, blows me a raspberry and rushes for the door with a trail of giggles.

"Where did I go wrong?" I ask nobody in particular.

To my surprise, Mack approaches, extending a slice of cake towards me. "If I could choose a new mother for myself, that'd be you. I would hug you, you know, but I smell like one of our tunnels. A beautiful, but nevertheless smelly, genius," he adds, leaving both me and his sister lost for words.

Mack's innocence is his brand. He can say anything, even the most inappropriate thing, and still come out forgivable and likeable. If we survive this shitty situation Roden forced us into, I will tell him I'd be honoured to have a son like him.

"He's not wrong, you know," Merya says, checking her brother over her shoulder before pulling out a chair and gesturing for me to sit. "You've checked on us, made sure we're all fine and well fed; now, please take your time and let us worry about the rest."

She makes to leave but then stops by the door. "I was meant to ask you, but Sable and Mack captured the audience. Do you think it's safe to have July and Kris in the same room so soon? I know they met briefly because Mr. Reckless couldn't be bothered to listen to orders, like always, and she was still recovering from the shock. This is why she hasn't gone looking for him just yet. But things have changed dramatically. As far as we know, her gift may have grown into a dangerous weapon. She could strike, and we wouldn't even notice until Kris lies soulless on the floor."

I dissect my slice of cake with a fork as if searching for the best solution in its crumbs. "Don't you think I know that? The thought has been tearing me apart since I decided to risk a trip to Libera.

But we don't have many options, or much time. Galen told me July had been scratching the surface a lot this time. There are some truths she already knows that we can't ignore."

Merya places her hands on her hips, resembling a taller, ginger version of me. "Galen should have handled the situation more carefully. Let me know if you need me to beat him up a little. I could say it's just a training session."

Her offer rings with a slightly amused tone, and I know she won't even pull a hair on his head. But that doesn't shake off the feeling that we're running out of time and must act quickly, risking everything, like we never have before.

Her steps fade quickly as she leaves me alone in the kitchen.

She's grown so much from the day I found her and Mack roaming the streets of Ventiol. I still don't know how she's turned into this beautiful, strong, excellent at baking woman without any guidance, if not mine. And I'm definitely not good with sugar and flour, nor with expressing my opinions in a less blunt way.

Sometimes, I struggle to remember that enjoying the sunshine - even if weak and never as warm as it was before the Famine - and the smell of new flowers growing outside the barriers is potentially lethal because we could be intercepted in less than thirty minutes.

At least the little orchard Mack manages to keep in bloom all year round gives us the illusion of a normal life. And I don't have to force Sable inside like a kitten in a cage.

I'm sitting on one of the stone benches when Galen comes out to meet me before our official meeting. He's showered, and in his light blue jeans and white shirt, he could easily pass for a Horigean, if it wasn't for those bright silver flecks in his iris.

"Your eye looks better. How's the wound?" I ask him, shifting along the bench to let him sit beside me.

"Merya stitched me up pretty well, but it will leave another scar. Thanks for coming to the rescue, Tabs; I know it was on short notice."

I turn to meet his gaze. His face is more tanned and freckled compared to those who chose or were forced to stay on Horigos.

I study his face. "A question has been nagging at me since we left Libera. Why the rush? Evelyn told me we still have a few days left—"

"I thought the same. But Roden has been acting erratically since discovering where Kris was hiding. He pushed for July to cross as soon as possible. As to the people who attacked us, I strongly believe they did not arrive in Libera that night. They were already on the island…"

I nod. "Do you think that was a decoy to cover what was happening here? We've never seen so many red souls travelling so fast and in such numbers. The armed forces Roden sent our way scared the shit out of me. We managed to save some, but Roden's dogs took the rest."

Galen runs a hand through his damp hair. "That is no

coincidence. Roden sent July to harvest a red soul not far from here. I'm sure he thought Kris wasn't far, and July could have led the Chapter to him. Evelyn thinks Roden is working on a plan B we didn't see coming." He looks away, contemplating the orchards. "Now, I have a question for you."

He stretches a hand to the tree beside him and picks a peach, juggling it before biting into its juicy flesh. "What is Kris doing here? I thought we were going to wait for July to steadily get back on her feet before dumping everything on her. Again."

That's it. Here's why he didn't join the others for breakfast, and why he's been so distant with me. I mirror him and grab a ripe fruit for myself. Mack did a great job; it tastes exactly like the original ones.

"This was the plan from the beginning, and Kris gave it an extra push by curing all the Reds he could get hold of. He's hiding it well, but his mind and body are growing weaker by the day. I assumed, at this point, there is no need to keep them apart—"

"You do realise that's a bomb ready to explode?"

At my puzzled look, Galen smirks, shaking his head, "So, Eve had time to call you but didn't think it crucial to tell you about one little detail."

He bites into the fruit, bracing an elbow on his knee.

"What are you talking about?"

His low laugh is anything but happy. "July made a deal with Roden. He promised her freedom. From her duties. From Libera. She only needs to deliver Kris' soul to him. Not his body—just his *whole* soul. He must have sensed Kris' energy drop to a dangerous level. And thanks to you - and your decision to bring him to HQ - we may have just given her the chance to do that before she could even learn the whole truth."

My half-eaten peach drops on the floor with a squelching sound. "She did what? Why? Hang on, hang on. You left her alone for hours, risking her walking around and ending up face-to-face with him?"

Galen allows me a couple of seconds to gain back my breath, munching on the peach before saying, "Well, excuse me, but apparently I wasn't the one shoving them under the same roof and—"

"And *apparently*, I am the one still not aware of many things. That seems to be the leitmotif of my fucking life lately. Care to explain?"

We both turn our heads at the sound of July's voice to find her staring at us from the kitchen's back door, as another ripe peach hits the ground, falling from Galen's open hand.

Chapter 36 - The Face in My Dream
July

Galen and Tabitha leap to their feet like the bench is on fire, and they stare at me as if I have ignited the flame.

I shift my weight onto my left foot, staring back. "Lost for words all of a sudden?"

Galen attempts a timid step in my direction, and all I want to do is to smack that guilty smile off his face.

"Oh, no. You stay where you are. And you…" I concentrate on Tabitha, pointing a shaking finger at her face. My whole body is trembling. "I bet even those trees know more about me than—fucking me!"

"July, why don't we all sit and discuss this—civilly?"

I sense the fury in my eyes when the colour abandons Tabitha's face.

I lower my finger and force myself to ignore Galen standing in my peripheral vision. It seems he's decided another step would be too much, and he halts as soon as I curl my fingers into fists at my side.

Tabitha clears her throat, holding her hands up. "Tell you what, if you don't like it, you can punch him."

"What?" Galen exclaims.

I admire her quick thinking and how she's just come up with a way to channel my distress and divert it away from Galen. I pretend I don't notice, but it works because all I can think of right now is that one name, a blurred face and a gentle voice offering me a drink to soothe my pain.

Tabitha's eyes quickly dart from me to Galen to ensure he gets the warning and doesn't move a muscle.

I step away from the kitchen door, marching straight for Tabitha and ignoring Galen, who throws his hands in the air, points at Tabitha, then at himself in a silent monologue.

"Where. Is. He?" I control every word. They don't need to know about the thunderstorm happening inside me.

Tabitha steps to one side, gesturing to the bench behind her as if offering a safe space to sit and talk.

Except for the limited view offered by the window in my room, this is the first time I can admire the odd beauty of HQ. Everything behind its walls seems luxuriant and alive compared to its wrecked, dangerous façade. Its grass is green, as if the Great Famine never touched this place, its trees heavy with fruit I only tasted in Libera, and the air is so pure that only a shy purple tinges my breath.

I blink away the distracting wonders of this place.

"The building, its garden—everything you see is special and unique. And we try to protect it the best way possible." Tabitha breaks the silence.

"By killing whoever comes too close, even if by accident?" I can't control the bitterness in my voice.

Sitting on the bench, Tabitha gives me a motherly smile and pats the empty spot beside her. "Wouldn't you like to know more *before* going after him?"

I consider my options, then trudge to the bench, dropping beside her with a loud sigh. "I wouldn't mind knowing what the hell this connection is. Especially because I'm supposed to have it with someone I've never met before."

"Ah, she heard that too," Galen mumbles, and I fire him a look that lands like an invisible slap.

I study him for a second, then click my tongue and slide my attention back to Tabitha, ignoring him completely. "I'm not sure Galen is still worthy of my trust. But you seem nicer—and I'm not stupid. Clearly, there is something else going on. Going after this soul feels like the tip of a far more dangerous iceberg."

"Hmm," Tabitha nods. "I didn't want to believe what Galen told me about your deal with Roden." She exchanges a quick look with him that I can only interpret as an invitation to let her speak without interruptions.

But Galen rushes towards us. "He tricked her," he says, "Roden tricked you."

"That, I've assumed on my own; thanks for stating the obvious," I snap without looking at him.

"What Galen is trying to say," Tabitha chimes in, cutting him a glacial side-eye, "Is that Roden put you in a truly challenging situation that's left you with no other choices but to accept. So, don't feel guilty for what you've agreed to do to Kris."

His name being spoken so openly caresses me like a gentle breeze, making the hair on my arms stand as if I've been too long under the scorching sun.

Galen coughs, and Tabitha makes an annoyed sound, throwing her hands in the air.

"I was getting there—"

"I call it procrastinating," he retorts.

Tabitha slaps her hands on her thighs with a grunt. "Well, I call it follow my ways or get out."

"I'm already outside." Galen rocks back and forth on his heels with his hands in his pockets.

"Oh, for the love of souls, Galen! I forgot how similar you two can be." Tabitha pinches the bridge of her nose, closing her eyes and inhaling deeply.

"You've only known me for two seconds—and we're nothing alike," I exclaim.

"Wasn't talking about you, dear."

Before I can add anything else, Tabitha places her hand over mine. "What Galen was *trying* to say is that Roden never intended to hold up his end of the deal because this has never worked before, and he believes you will fail. *Again.*"

"He did everything to convince you this choice was yours only." Galen's voice sounds distant.

A soft breeze sweeps over us from a place I cannot locate. It rustles the trees nearby, carrying the scent of seawater and tender grass. I should enjoy it and feel at peace, but my body is frozen, and all I can hear is the echo of Tabitha's last word.

Again.

My chest rises and falls, air fills my lungs, my blood pumps—but I can't move.

Everything around me is alive. Galen's hair has dried a little, fluttering in the gentle wind; Tabitha's lips stretch in a tentative, reassuring smile.

Life continues before my eyes—but I forgot how to use my freaking mouth.

A warm hand presses over mine, and Galen appears in my field of vision. "Remember when I asked you to keep an open mind?"

I nod, and a stinging feeling rushes down my spine, like when I was a child and used to clench my teeth to stop myself from crying.

"Can I?" Galen motions to the space next to me.

Another wordless nod while my vision blurs because I've been holding my breath for too long.

Again.

I exhale, and time restarts its natural cycle. Spinning. Rushing, as if Nature itself knows there isn't much left.

"How much do you remember of your childhood?" Tabitha's voice is like the first gentle wave after a storm at sea.

My mind runs back to the only picture I have of my parents, locked in a drawer I rarely open, hidden in a box so I don't have to look at it unintentionally.

I shrug, lowering my eyes to the space between me and Tabitha as if my memories may be carved on the white marble bench. "I was born with the gift, but it started manifesting when I was about two. I couldn't stay out for too long, or my nose would start bleeding, my lungs shrinking. And I would start screaming in pain when someone close to death walked past me. It felt like I was dying with them."

Galen shifts closer to me, close enough to brush my shoulder with his.

"That is the pain all Rogues experience when they grow up not properly trained," he mutters.

"And why they could become a danger to others. And themselves," Tabitha adds.

But above all the words she's speaking to me, one screams louder in the back of my mind—*again.*

I shrink, removing my hand from under hers and folding my fingers on my lap.

"What else?" Galen asks, but there is no urgency in his tone.

"I began to isolate myself, and my parents never objected because not having me around people was a relief. Until—Roden sensed me and sent Popplewish to take me away from Horigos to start my new life in Libera."

I study Tabitha's face for reassurance that my answer is exhaustive enough, and that I don't need to dig deeper, but she struggles to hold my gaze until she averts her eyes completely, searching for Galen's instead.

Realisation whacks me.

I whip my head towards him. "What does it mean? Again…"

His eyes dart across my face, then to a point behind me. To Tabitha. And back to me.

"I need you to think deeper, Sof. Do you remember ever seeing pictures of you as a baby? Do you remember at least one of your childhood friends?" he asks, pivoting a little on the spot to face me better.

He's so close I can smell lemon and soap permeating his freshly cleaned shirt. I close my eyes, trying to dig deeper—to find that door I locked and forgot about—to barge inside my past.

But there is only a quiet, motionless ocean of emptiness, and the more I try to remember, the more my stomach twists into a knot.

"A birthday?" Tabitha presses on.

I bite my lips, and my eyes fling open, resting on Galen's familiar gaze. His bruises and cuts have been cleaned and stitched, and his skin has regained some of its natural, healthy tone.

"Do you remember your room? The colour of the walls…"

I know he's trying to help, but any attempt to recall a past that I'm not even sure belongs to me feels like heavy rain hammering my head.

"No…"

"Your favourite toy?"

"No, I don't…" I dig my nails into my palms to silence the soaring nausea.

I don't even know who's asking what anymore.

Galen gently cups my cheek, and I lean into his reassuring scent.

"Roden took all my memories," I say in one breath.

Galen nods, letting go of my face and leaving a sudden cold patch on my skin, where his hands were until a second ago.

For a moment, I forgot Tabitha was still sitting next to me.

Again. I slowly turn to face her, this stranger who seems to know me more than I do.

"How many times has Roden asked me to bring him back, to make *him* suffer—Kris? *How* did I fail?" A sudden rush of sadness and longing burns inside me when his name touches my lips.

She doesn't answer, but waits as if knowing I'm not done with my question.

How many times? I'm about to turn twenty-two. It's not like I've completed so many missions that I forgot one or two.

My eyes widen, and Tabitha lowers her head.

My chest aches.

"How old am I?"

Galen's hand reaches over my back, closing over my shoulder as if something terrible is about to happen, and he's preparing to stop me if I decide to run away.

Tabitha slowly peels herself off the bench as if in the presence of a wild, scared animal ready to attack her.

"Where do you think you're going?" Galen asks without moving an inch away from me.

She smiles, pinning her silver mass of braids on top of her head and fanning the back of her neck. "It's getting too hot for me out here." She addresses Galen, and they exchange some silent understanding for a moment.

Galen drops his hand from my shoulder, conceding to whatever unspoken request he read on Tabitha's face. "I guess you're right. It is better if this comes from me." There is gravity in his voice.

"I'll leave you two alone." She hesitates a moment. I can feel her eyes on me.

I lift my head, shading my eyes from the sun rising behind her. She looks like a marble statue, solemn and imposing.

"Relax, I won't punch him," I shrug. "He still has a lot to answer for. But I need you to promise me something…"

Curiosity and the hint of a smile bloom on Tabitha's face. "We can negotiate."

"I am free to leave this place. Whatever the truth about me, whatever the consequences if I don't follow Roden's order. I want to pick my next path. Even if it turns out to be short—and my very last one."

I'm not even sure what I'm referring to, but Tabitha seems to understand.

"Very well." She stretches her hand out.

I lean forward and take it. "Forgive me if I don't call it a deal. That word leaves a bitter taste in my mouth every time I say it."

"Then, it's a promise." She winks and, having let go of my hand, spins on her heel, slides her pale blue shawl off her shoulders and heads towards the building.

The grass doesn't make a sound when she walks away, swinging her strong arms as if she's marching towards a battlefield. Having met her and her people at night, covered up head to toe in fighting gear, I'd not had the chance to take in the human faces hidden under the black helmets and tons of firearms. But all I see now is a middle-aged woman, barefoot, in bright yellow trousers and a white top. And deep inside my heart, I'm jealous of how carefree she looks.

I wait for Tabitha to disappear inside the kitchen, then stand, crossing my arms over my chest and distractedly brushing my shoulders.

"Would you like to go somewhere else? Somewhere more… private?" Galen asks.

I ignore his question. Let's start by cementing the foundations. "Kris is the soul that Roden - so desperately - desires to control."

The tentative smile on his face drops. "I thought you wanted to start from *your* truth."

I impatiently tap my foot on the grass. "Given what I've been through lately - been lied to, drugged, shocked by an invisible barrier, deprived of my memories multiple times - I'm entitled to decide where to start, what to ask and when you fucking speak." My voice rises with every word now that Tabitha's stabilising presence is no longer with us.

As if we never left Libera, I feel free to argue with Galen again, like in the old times.

"How old *are* you? What are you? Wait, are we vampires?" I blurt out, sticking one arm under direct sunlight, but drop it when my skin doesn't start to blister and burn.

Galen tilts his head to the side. "One question at a time, perhaps?"

I nod. "Fine."

"No, we are not creatures of the night, despite your hate for garlic," he rubs his hands on his thighs, "And, yes… Kris is *definitely* your soul."

"How many times has he been a 'Kris'?" I urge, drumming my fingers on my arm.

"Every time. He's never wanted to change his name. He thinks it will help you remember."

I flinch but continue, "And… he knows I'm here. The person he should be avoiding at all costs. And, still, he wants me to remember all the times I failed to harvest his soul? That's stupid and sadistic and…"

Something on Galen's face, a sudden melancholic smile, silences me.

"All the times you *willingly* failed to harvest his soul entirely and to deliver it to Roden."

I let his words sink in. Every single one. Counting them. One by one, they push down my need to run and make a memory of all this. One Roden cannot take from me.

Galen tortures his bottom lip as if fighting to hold something back, while studying me, trying to read the next question in my eyes.

I stretch my hands towards him. A peace offering. But he shifts back on the bench.

I drop them back by my side, lowering my voice. "I heard you two speaking in your room. Why did you ask him to stay away from me if you know I've never hurt him before?"

When he doesn't answer and keeps chewing at his lips, I rush to him, kneeling before him and searching for his hands. "Please stop doing that. Just answer me. What made you think I'll act differently this time?"

But I'm left with nothing but my doubts when Galen stands up and puts some distance between us.

He runs both hands through his hair, letting his fingers rest in his curls, his eyes wide as he stares at me in disbelief. "I could explain that to you a hundred times in every language we know. That Roden tricked you, forced your hand over and over. And nothing will change. It has never changed," - he throws his hands in the air - "For fuck's sake, Sof, you've just discovered that he stole your memories, throwing you into this spiral of chasing and failing, and all you can think of is Kris and his life?"

"I... I..."

Galen's hands lower into fists at his side as his face slowly softens with sadness. "Exactly that. That's what you should focus on—*you*. And yet, all I hear is his name. I've been hearing you saying it for ages in your sleep. Dreaming about the many times you let him go and cried in pain while Roden was sending your mind back to oblivion."

Galen moves so quickly that I don't have time to back away. He grabs my shoulders and lowers his eyes onto mine.

"Please tell me who I am," I whisper.

His double-coloured eyes soften, and he pulls me into his arms, holding me so tight that I don't think he will ever let me go again.

Every second I spend in his arms strips away heavy layers of lies, doubts, and pain. I press my face against his chest, inhaling the fresh scent of his clean cotton shirt.

His chest rises once before his hold on me loosens a bit, allowing me to lift my chin and look up.

"You're Roden's daughter. The only one sharing his blood *and* part of his soul."

Something cracks inside me, but before every single sharp piece drops and makes me lash out, Galen cups my cheeks and forces time to stand still by bringing our faces close together.

I can almost feel the softness of his lips over mine, lips that I only remember kissing me with fierce and desperate need. Lips I sought to wash away the bitter taste of days spent harvesting souls whose only fault had been seeking Roden's help in their most desperate times.

I'm unsure how long my heart has been hammering, and I cannot say if it was because of sudden exhilaration or fear.

My eyes dart from Galen's face to his mouth and back. I'm lost in such a daze that I can't even find the words to reject his unexpected revelation.

"So, I'm just another one of his secrets. One, he decided to use against an innocent soul. And he made me suffer over and over, despite my failures, only to wipe my mind clean and start again... Why?" I throw my hands out.

Galen's fingers on my cheek twitch, his eyes narrow for a second before softening with a smile. "Because you are the only Harvester who can hold *and* destroy souls with your hands. Completely. Any soul. Rogues, Nistarei. *Harvesters...*" A pause that feels like aeons before he adds, "Without anyone's aid. Just your simple, raw power. Roden trained you to do it, but never to your full potential. He never taught you *control...*"

Galen's mouth purses with a note of disgust. I'd probably feel the same had I been so close to someone capable of such utter destruction.

He lowers his hands onto my neck, stroking his thumbs against my exposed collarbones and the chain Popplewish gave me. Someone must have found it on me after I got knocked out by Mack's genius and put it around my neck while I was unconscious.

My heart tries to escape from my rib cage. The way Galen is touching me—his hands in the perfect position to snap my neck. *Me...* Not his friend, but someone with the power to claim his life forever.

"And you stayed at my side all these years knowing this..." My throat bobs with my next thought. Something far flashes behind his eyes, then quickly disappears.

I wriggle, trying to get away from his unsettling touch. "Roden made you his eyes and ears, didn't he? He wanted to be sure I wasn't going around annihilating random Harvesters. Why would I even do that? How?"

He smirks. Galen looks me straight in the eyes, registers the confusion, doubt, and fear slowly devouring me, and grins.

Then he sighs and, for a split second, I swear he focuses on the brass key at my neck before his fingers and shoulders relax, and his wicked expression softens into a sweet smile.

"I hoped seeing me interacting with Tabs and the others would convince you I'm not on Roden's side. Tabitha wouldn't even let me set eyes on HQ if I were a threat." He drops his hand, and my heart returns to its normal rhythm.

I unintentionally touch my fingers to my warm - I'm pretty sure - blushing cheek. But blaming the heat doesn't make me feel less awkward. Or guilty.

"As far as Roden knows, you're still his big secret. The Chapter's members are aware that your gift is a bit different from the other Harvesters. They know you can harvest Rogues. But a *few* found out about the extent of your abilities and who you are to Roden."

"Like you—" I cut him off.

He tilts his head, shows me his hands and curls down a finger. "And Evelyn." Another finger folds. "Tabitha, of course," he crosses his arms over his chest, jerking his chin to the building behind me. "Everyone in there, really. Thanks to Mack. He... he studied your blood cells."

"For the love of souls, please do not say another word, this is…" I shiver, sticking my tongue out, and brush my arms as if covered in spiders. "So, why am I still—"

"Alive?"

I arch an eyebrow, shifting my weight onto my left foot. "I meant—here."

Galen's gaze darkens quickly, and I can't help noticing it before he turns to face the walls surrounding HQ, stretching for miles tall and thick. "It is not your nature. Nobody, not even Roden, can manipulate your talent to make it lethal. But you did make a deal and promised to bring Kris back to him, despite knowing the truth about him—well, part of it. You've never done anything like that, so Tabitha decided to keep you closer."

My heart feels heavy, like his voice.

I should stop digging. The more I do, the more the image I have of myself rots into something disgusting and cruel. "But I wouldn't even know where to begin. Even if I harvest his soul entirely, I wouldn't know how not to turn him into dust. I'm useless anyway..." my voice breaks.

In the bright morning light, the locks of hair dancing on Galen's forehead catch the sunshine, turning copper and golden brown.

When he finally looks at me, the sadness in his eyes makes me want to disappear.

"You've never known how because I always asked you to stop before you could find the way."

I gasp. For all the times I accepted this mission, Galen risked his life to sabotage Roden's will.

I run a hand over his arm, inviting him to face me - the real me, not the Harvester who could harm him - the one he knows best.

"Was it because you knew I might regret it?"

A nod. "Yes, that and," - he scratches his neck - "Kris is the living proof that the idea of Rogues that Roden has been feeding us for years is not completely true. And the Herionos…"

"Herionos? What do the Herionos have to do with Kris? And you. And the people in there?" I point at the building behind me, my hand shaking.

Galen's silent response, the spark in his eyes. Everything about him screams something I'm not ready to hear—not after learning that I don't simply *belong* to Roden—I'm his fucking *child*!

My legs start shaking, and I slam my hand on a tree to hold myself upright.

Galen rushes to my aid, but I shake my head.

"Remember the man who attacked you on the roof?"

"How could I not? You told me *he* was one of the bad people."

"And I also said it wasn't as easy as it seemed." His lips quirk with a bashful smile.

The fresh scent of the leaves wafts over me when a gentle wind plays with the tree I'm leaning against. My head starts clearing. I raise an eyebrow, "Bad-Herionos?"

The sound of Galen's laugh, something I forgot I used to love so much, fills the air. "Sort of."

"And is what Mack called New Hera… good-Herionos?" I hate that my vocabulary seems to have shrunk to that of a three-year-old child.

He approaches me, leaning against the same tree and giving me an amused side-eye. "Just the type who's trying to make things better for everyone—Harvesters and not."

I lay my back against the trunk, my head resting against the young, smooth bark. I turn my head to the side, studying Galen's serene and relaxed face as if a boulder has been lifted off his chest.

"Tabitha and the twins?"

Galen pushes away from the tree, stepping in front of me. "We all share the same ideal. Our mutual cause put us on each other's path."

"And Kris is with the good-Herionos as well." Not a question, as otherwise he wouldn't be allowed on HQ's ground.

A carousel of feelings spins across Galen's face—but guilt is not one of them when he grabs my shoulders and says, "Correct—and he's the only family I have left."

Chapter 37 - Home
July

I was told I was special.

I was told my power was my strength.

And that was all a lie.

When I joined the Harvesters, I thought my talent was common, and I didn't care because I was finally an anonymous grain in a sea of ears of wheat. I was happy to be a Reaper.

Popplewish told me only a few had the stamina to be trained into higher ranks. Like the Donatori, who can gently guide souls into their new vessels, or the Writers, who are masters in reshaping memories so that souls will only treasure the good they did, carrying it from their past lives into their new.

When she explained the role of the Deleteri, I promised myself I would never befriend one of them.

When a soul is too tainted, hopeless, they wipe it clean. Despicable memories, dark feelings, rotten passions—the Deleteri scrape souls to their very core, destroying even the little good they may have done in their past (and last) life, returning only dry crops. Their empty vessels are so sterile that they will never host a new soul and can only be abandoned in The Fields.

I broke that promise when she introduced me to a boy, too tall for his age, and with the sweetest smile.

A swarm of lies and secrets rings in my ears.

… Roden's daughter.

… I always asked you to stop before you could find the way…

Galen's mouth moves, then stops. He stares intently at me before talking again—words with no sounds.

"Shut up," I blurt out, overwhelmed. "I don't want to hear any more. Please!" I beg him, pressing my palms to my temples, looking down to blink away my tears, without Galen noticing, but achieving the opposite result.

He steps closer and gently brushes my wet cheek with his knuckles. "Sof, I wanted to tell you. But they wouldn't let me. I…"

"Don't call me that…" I can't hold back a sob.

I can't even remember why I hate that name.

With one swift motion, he hugs me so tight that the world remains trapped outside our embrace. The swarm in my head melts into a soft hum that tastes like Libera's meadows—sweet and reassuring.

"Why did you stay? Why didn't you flee Libera and remain with Kris to protect him from… people like me?"

Sometimes we have to play parts we don't resonate with, Popplewish's voice echoes in my mind.

Pressed against his chest, I can barely breathe, and I cling to his shirt like my sanity depends on it.

He props his chin onto my head and chuckles softly, "Believe me, my brother doesn't need protection. Besides," he releases me just enough to take my face in his hands, "When I accepted to be part of all this, I wasn't aware of how addictive you are."

I wince and open my mouth to say something. But when I reopen it, for once, I'm left without words.

Something in Galen's eyes makes me believe I could ask a million questions and still be miles from the truth.

"How many times have I tried ending your—hang on?" I wriggle my head free from his hands. "Kris? Is your brother?"

Galen's eyes narrow. "Non-identical twin. But I'm the good-looking one. Did I not mention he's *family*?"

I feel stupid the moment he says it.

"I thought you meant 'family', as in a close friend or a long-lost cousin. A..." I study him, chewing on the inside of my cheek. "Your brother? If you two share the same blood, why does his power—Oh, my head hurts."

Galen throws his head back, laughing and throwing me into an unexpected pool of embarrassment.

"Not even Roden knows, but that's why he decided to separate us," he says, catching his breath and holding his side.

There isn't any sense of pride or relief in admitting that; it's just a simple statement. "Our father's only sin was not sharing the same idea of the future Roden had, but our mother didn't care when she fell in love with him," - he flicks my forehead when he notices my lips dropping with sadness - "Kris is just a lucky bastard, the one that got to live for years without Roden's cold breath on his neck."

I study the palms of my hands, tracing the lines of one with my index finger as if recalling past events. When nothing magically appears on my skin to help me understand my messy situation, I start pacing back and forth until I find my words again.

I look at Galen as he patiently waits for my doubts to subside. "When I met the Chapter, Roden told me that this dangerous Rogue," I wince as the word rolls off my tongue like a drop of venom, "I mean Kris—Roden told me that Kris was just a rebel that didn't want to join *his* people—us."

Galen nods. "Roden wasn't *technically* lying. But that's because of the words our mother left for him before she died. The truth about his father, me and his *other* people. I think Roden wants him gone for good because he's finally realised he will never be able to tame him."

The more I look at Galen, the more his features seem to change, blurring into a face that both belongs to him and to a stranger—a stranger who is teasing me with tantalising secrets but also holding back crucial details.

"But he can't be the only one. There must be others like him. Why does Roden want me to go only after him? I mean, how many Herionos and Harvesters have fallen in love and had children before he forbade that kind of relationship?"

I start fanning my face when a rivulet of sweat drips down my neck. *How long have we been out here?* When I scan the sky, the sun is so bright that it doesn't feel real. There is not a cloud in the sky. Not even a bird.

Galen is also starting to feel the rising temperature, and he suddenly gestures toward a canopy of trees that offers enough shade for both of us.

We walk in silence for a bit, side by side, until Galen decides to answer my question. "Hundreds. Thousands, maybe, but Roden put an end to them before their souls had the chance to grow stronger inside their mothers. We were lucky, in a sense, because our mother gave birth to us in Libera. Yet, Roden sensed something within Kristyon, something different, and gave her a choice. He *asked* her to pick one of us, and doom the other to spend whatever shitty years he had left on Horigos." He gives me a moment to think and put the pieces together.

He's never shared much about his family, and I stopped asking years ago when I realised his voice would always drop and his eyes darken while reliving the past.

He always told me, repeating the details as if it was a story branded in his mind, that he was born in Libera the day his mother died. She was on a mission with his father - an easy one they were promised - because she was pregnant then. But Galen's father never came back, and his mother was brought back to the island by the rest of their team—bleeding. Gunshot. Something had gone dramatically wrong. She refused to let go of the soul she'd been sent to harvest and had used what was left of her vital energy to save it. And to preserve her unborn child.

That day, a soul was offered a new chance in life while Galen's mother was closing her eyes forever, staring for the first and last time at her newborn son, carried away in Evelyn Popplewish's loving arms.

"The child in your story," I hold my tears, "That was Kris. Evelyn took him away. That was your mother's last wish…"

He doesn't answer me straight away. When we reach the cooling shadow of the trees, Galen stops a few steps before me with his head hanging heavy between his shoulders as he mumbles, "Yes… My mother drew her last breath holding in her arms only one of her children." The first straight answer in a while.

The trees protecting us from the heat have large trunks, but the bark looks young and tender when Galen easily scratches it off from one of them. His shoulders tense as he leans against the tree, one hand bearing his weight against the trunk.

The grass complains under my rushed steps as I shorten the distance between us.

I run a hand over my face. "What is so wrong about his talent that Roden didn't even try to raise him in Libera? Why not give him a chance like you had—"

I startle, muffling a gasp behind my hand at the sound of Galen's fist hitting the tree. His shoulders tremble with every shaky breath.

I approach him, intentionally making my steps heard. When he doesn't react, I brush his back with my fingertips, hoping to distract him from my next question with a friendly touch.

I don't want him to suffer, but I need to know. "What happened after Popplewish took him to Horigos?" I drop my hand, giving him time.

Galen bows his head against the tree, shaking slightly. His voice is a low rasp when he says, "Evelyn told Roden that the baby had died during the crossing. She knew Roden gave my mother a choice only to maintain the image of the forgiving, loving saviour in the eyes of his people. He was already planning to send someone to find my brother and put an end to him in secret, without staining his precious Libera. The little taste Roden had of Kris' abilities the day we were born was enough to make him a threat."

I fight the urge to hug him tight. "Instead, she asked Tabitha for help?" I mumble to myself, to turn the supposition into a hopeful truth.

Galen nods. His fingers have never stopped torturing the bark despite his knuckles being visibly raw and scratched.

"Galen, please, look at me." Once again, I stretch a hand towards him, but he turns on his heels so quickly that I move a step back.

His eyes scan my face, begging me to understand. To stop. But I can't. Not yet.

"How long have you known about this? How long have you been playing both sides?" I ask, bracing myself when a gentle breeze coming from somewhere beyond the trees brushes my bare arms.

The smile on his face is beautiful and sad, and I'd kiss him if only to wipe it off. But I remain still.

"Evelyn had my memories erased. She thought it was best to cancel Kristyon from my life, for my own good and my brother's—and I forgave her a long time ago. She told me everything after my first mission when I accidentally ended up on the *wrong* side of Horigos and met Kris for the first time. Evelyn never confirmed it, but I believe she'd sent me there on purpose…"

I narrow my eyes, taking his rediscovered will to talk like an invitation. "What happened?"

Galen sighs loudly, pressing his lips together, "You're not letting this drop, are you?"

"Nope." Something warm sparks in my chest when his voice regains some of his natural confidence. His laugh is more like a low rumble in his chest that makes my heart flutter.

"Fine. Ventiol was still called Sector 43, and I was sent here for a quick reconnaissance operation. There were rumours about some Rogues roaming around the gentrified areas and causing turmoil. I only had to locate them and report back to my superior."

"And..?" I invite him to continue, waving a hand in his face when he pauses too long.

"And I never found them because Tabitha captured me."

My jaw drops.

He shakes a lock of hair off his face, lowering his eyes. "Funny, eh?"

"Shocking that you're still alive."

"Well, she didn't find me by accident. Evelyn told her exactly where I'd be. Tabs had fun polishing knives in front of me for a few hours while I was tied to a chair in the kitchen. But then she introduced me to Kris, and my memories unlocked the moment he started talking nonsense about feeling connected to me, as if we were mated souls, destined to be together and save the world." His gaze softens. "Until I threatened him to punch him once I had the chance, and Tabitha had to step between us, amused but also running out of her already thin patience. That's when Kris told me he was my brother—the good-looking one."

An uncertain smile tugs at my lips. There he is again, my Galen, a perfect knot of rules and compliance, that switches into someone too passionate to control himself when people he truly cares about are in danger.

"Do I want to know if this is now the right side of Horigos?" I step closer.

Galen tilts his head, looking at me sideways, hiding his hands in his pockets. "Have I overestimated your little brain, Crimson?"

I drop my smile and slap his arm, but he doesn't flinch or move. Instead, he leans his back against the tree. Waiting.

"It's not that easy," I begin. "How am I supposed to pick a side when everything around me seems to change every time I blink? I was a nobody until a moment ago, and now you're telling me that my birth-father is someone I'd gladly throw off a cliff, and that your brother is very much alive and very much in danger because of me *and* my lunatic father. And let's not forget the little detail that I've been living the same pathetic attempt to destroy part of your family for who knows how many times— "

"About ten times," Galen states, counting on his fingers.

"Ten? Are you sure?"

"Pretty sure," he bobs his chin twice. "I was there every single painful time."

His last words snap something between us. The last thread that so desperately tried to connect us—broken.

His eyes linger on my face, searching for a reaction. They're the only moving part of his body, confirming that he is still alive and is not slowly merging with the tree.

As Tabitha did with me earlier, I feel like he's treating me like I'm some feral animal ready to jump at the slightest sign of threat. But he's feeding me minuscule pieces of truth one at a time—the more I chew, the hungrier I get.

"So, where's the rest of you? It can't only be you, Tabitha, and the others fighting this war. Fighting Roden…" I point at the building that gleams in the sunlight.

A flash of pride sparks in his eyes, and he smirks. "I did teach you well. I could probably stay here, just looking at you, until you get to the bottom of the story on your own."

"No digressions," I warn him.

He throws his arms out before crossing them over his chest. "Fine—The Horigos you know it's only a small part of a bigger continent. The *approved* section. Let's think about it as a vast training ground."

"Approved by Roden and the Chapter?"

"Chapters." Galen's features are carved in stone; only his eyes betray the relentless tempest of thoughts in his mind. "We are not the first risking our lives to stop Roden's insane plan. We were only lucky to keep our heads down enough for him to trust us all these years."

"And by we, you mean Evelyn as well?"

"Amongst others, yes. Look, July, I know deep inside you're still deciding if I'm trustworthy, but Kris is only the tip of the iceberg. We were always told that the Herionos stayed behind to work against Roden, but the power they seek today is no less dangerous than Roden's. And he knows."

Finally, that opening I'd been wanting for days. I start to feel at ease again, even if there is a side of Galen I've never been part of. The questions pile up. But I force myself to stay focused, pacing up and down, pinching my lips to keep them shut.

"What is it? Spit it out?" Galen sighs and lowers to the ground, sitting cross-legged.

"Roden showed me the screens-room, or whatever it's called. Well…" A bitter laugh escapes at the memory, "*Daddy* kept me hostage there. What do you really know of the Horigeans he sent me to harvest all these years?"

I look down at Galen and then towards the walls surrounding the building. The sun is at its peak, and in the distance, it glistens over what seems to be a lake.

Galen seems to ponder his answer. He plucks a blade of grass and lifts it to his eyes, bending it between his fingers. "Some of them are real debtors, as wrong as that sounds now that you know the truth. As for the Rogues…" he drops the piece of grass and jumps back onto his feet. "Those are Roden's failures. His forever stain. Some of them will crave souls if not stopped. But only because of what Roden is trying to do with them."

"Which is?" I get closer, almost pinning him between me and the tree at his back.

"Creating indestructible souls that solely obey his orders. Nothing like us. They have no conscience, no feelings. And the more they live, the more their soul changes colour—and becomes *red*." Straight to the point.

I cover my mouth, shaking my head in denial. "Like that young woman, I harvested before this shitshow fell upon us. Well. Upon *me*. You were kind of already drowning in it." I smirk.

But Galen remains serious, rubbing at his chin, pondering something until his eyes dart to mine. "We've never seen so many all at the same time. Roden is powerful, but he can't be everywhere. We believe he decides to find allegiance in those he used to hate and that wanted to destroy him—us."

I move closer. "The Herionos we feared as children are still out there then. The man who tried to kill us on the Blind was one of them. You didn't lie…"

Galen's eyes close with the weight of that night's image. "I never lied to you. I was trying to protect you—and stay alive in the meantime." When he reopens his eyes, the brown one shines bright with hundreds of silver specks.

"That man was sent *not* to kill you - we believe - but to *kidnap* you. If his plan was successful, Roden probably wanted to use that to explain your sudden disappearance and blame it on Tabitha and her rebels. But Evelyn had a suspicion. Mostly caused by the amount of red souls we spotted lately. Roden knows they're marching towards Kris because they sense his power…"

"Oh…" I nod. Then, I shake my head. "Is he like me? Can he—"

For a moment, Galen stares at the top of the tree, lost in thought. "He's so many things, but nothing like you. You can harvest our souls; you can destroy them - well, a good thing you've never learnt how, or I could be dead by now," he allows himself a quick shrug and a smile, "Kristyon can't harvest, but can cure them and put them back wherever he pleases. That's why Reds are attracted to him. They seek revenge for what's been done to them, and his soul smells like a miraculous elixir."

The words of the woman in the alley punch me in the face. I kneel before him, taking his hands in mine. "Because they were *stolen…*"

He looks at me, his eyes heavy with guilt. "We lost so many. They only have a small window of autonomy after Roden starts playing with them. But those who made it are safe within The Mother's territory."

I brush my thumb over his fingers. "How does he do it? How

does Kris help these souls if he can't harvest them?"

Galen's chest deflates in a way that makes my heart ache. "He sacrifices a small part of his soul. It's the only way. He can willingly let go of a tendril of his soul to purify a red one. But he can't do it forever without…"

I don't want him to say it. I take his face into my hands. "I can help him. That's why Roden wants him, because we can complement each other with our abilities. Is this why you stopped me from learning my true power?"

Something sparks behind his eyes. He touches my forehead with his, running his hands over my arms. "The meeting will start soon. But if you wish to stay out here for a bit longer…"

"I get it." I get up and put some space between us. "You don't want to spoil the surprise." A light sense of freedom warms my chest as I can finally look at Galen like I used to.

"I missed you," he mumbles, pushing himself up as well.

"Missed you too." I slap his arm. "Thanks for keeping me alive."

He shakes his head, and his gaze roams towards the high walls protecting this place.

I follow suit. "That's definitely a lake!" I blurt out when I capture a faint shimmering in the distance.

Galen lets out a surprised sound. His profile waves and changes in the sunlight every time I blink. Another Galen is trying to break through the face I know so well.

"That's not possible." I hear him saying under his breath.

He places himself between me and the supposed lake, frowning.

"July, did you *guess*, or do you *actually* remember the lake?"

"I… I don't know, but I have a strong feeling that there is water down there and that nobody should ever get too close." My voice drops, heavy with uncertainty.

I should be scared and confused, but the more I let the blurry image of a lake sink inside me, the more I feel—at home.

Tears start running down my cheeks. "The room I woke up in this morning—"

Galen tilts his head as if struggling to understand what I'm saying.

"Is that *my* room?"

I take in every detail of Galen's face, the sweetest smile slowly blooming on his lips and the spark in his eyes, and my heart starts beating wildly.

He lets his arms rest by his sides, but he's fidgeting as if to stop his hands from doing something else.

"I'm telling you everything I know, Sof." He opens his arms, defenceless, "Like I never could before because we need you to be ready this time. *I* need you to be prepared."

"Why this time?"

Every inch of his face calls to me: the sudden melancholy in his eye when he lowers his lashes, the slight drop of one corner of his lips, his gentle gaze on my cheeks.

"Because the one thing Roden never lied about is that the souls he touched *belong* to him, and sooner or later, they will bend to his will. We don't know where his power comes from, but Roden is growing tired of *educating* his children. And if taming Kris to his will doesn't work, he may try something drastic." He distractedly plays with my necklace while his words come out like a river held by a dam for too long, fed by tempests and secrets.

I know Galen's every smile—when he closes his eyes and allows his whole face to show true happiness, the smirks that lift only a corner of his lips and make even strangers blush and their knees weaken.

But the one stretching now on his face makes my heart ache. It speaks of longing and regrets.

My hand has a mind of its own. As if watching from outside my body, I see it slowly lifting and stopping inches from Galen's face. My fingers tremble. My chest rises and falls fast, betraying my desperate need to eliminate the distance between us.

"Sof…"

For the first time, the name that's never spoken for me sounds like the perfect representation of who I really am.

I let my hand linger in mid-air. I don't care what's happening around me—us. There is no breeze to distract me, no distant image of a forbidden lake. The sun is just a bright sphere in a fabricated sky. Its heat is not real.

What am I thinking?

I close my eyes. They say your senses enhance when you can't see.

"Sof…" His voice is like a caress on my skin that soon makes space for his lips, gently kissing the palm of my hand.

"Can we just hide here? Forever?"

"I wish…" His voice tickles my skin.

I force my eyes to stay shut, calling for darkness.

Faces dance behind my eyes, and the hand I think is Galen's turns out to be mine. A kernel burns in its centre. Purple. Then red. Hot and cold. A dancing flame, alive and happy, growing larger. It is bigger than my hand, but so light it will fly away if I don't curl my fingers around it.

A sudden wind blows my way, and the kernel bursts into white ashes.

"Where did you go?" Galen whispers.

I open my eyes and step away from him, gulping air until I can feel the tendons in my neck tensing.

"I don't want to crush it." I don't make sense, but nothing that happened lately does.

Galen approaches me, but something disturbs the leaves above us, breaking the spell. My hand is still in midair, reaching for something.

"Sorry to interrupt…" A voice calls from the top of the tree.

"Oh, here we go." Galen's voice sounds different, lighter, unbothered.

"Oh, you are boring." The hidden voice replies.

As soon as I look up in its direction, the voice takes the shape of a man who gracefully jumps off the tree despite his build. He lands on the grass between Galen and me, on one knee, his head of light brown hair bowing, like a knight out of place and uninvited.

"Let me guess?" I ask, standing above him, akimbo.

"July, meet Kris." Galen cuts in, bending to grab his brother by the collar. "Again." He adds while pulling him back onto his feet.

Chapter 38 - Page Two
Kristyon

When you spend ten of your lives running from the gruesome possibility of being annihilated, you have two choices.

One: you keep running.

Or two (my favourite): treat every life like a chapter from an exquisite book. The first page tells pretty much the same story with more or less seasoning, depending on the author's mood. Sometimes, you have to scrap a page and start redrafting because some characters may need a push, or be stopped before their adventure becomes a tragedy.

But what happens on page two makes the story worth reading to the end.

Again.

"It pains me to admit that I may have underestimated the distance from you two and my first-row seat up there." I wave a finger at the treetop while my brooding brother pulls me up.

The hand I slammed on the ground when I landed hurts, but I keep a perfectly stoic, straight face.

"What happened to stay hidden until I say so?" Galen hisses in my ear before letting me go to theatrically massage his temples. "The death of me…" he mumbles.

I flash him a smile, poking his arm. "I was, *brotherling*. And—if it weren't for my athletic entrance, you two would probably still be trying to resolve the mystery of the Century." I bow and graciously tip my invisible hat at them. "*Moi.*"

"I wouldn't call that athletic. Your hand is bleeding, and your hair is a mess."

Her voice strikes me like a perfectly shaped thunder, turning my performance into a rough piece of glass.

"Ouch, your words slash my ego worse than the stones in my skin." I press a hand to my heart, wincing when the debris *indeed* hurts my palm.

After our brief meeting last night, when she was nearly blind due to Mack's mad genius, I can finally look in the eyes of my beautiful, dangerous destiny.

"I couldn't be asking for a more perfect end." I extend my clean hand.

"Are you sure you two are brothers?" July ignores my offer and turns to Galen with such a familiarity I'd throw my brother in Mack's artificial lake if we were standing closer to it.

"I'm afraid so."

"And I'm still here trying to salvage what's left of my reputation." I wriggle my finger in the air.

"You've never had one. Stop being a clown and be grateful you still have enough breath to annoy me." Galen smacks me on the head.

But my attention is already somewhere else.

July approaches me with her hands behind her back, and I don't dare move a muscle. Not even when her face is inches from mine.

Her eyes narrow. "I understand we *could* help each other. But your *bloodline* hasn't struck me as worthy of my trust recently."

I swallow and take two steps back, cutting Galen a glare. "About that… What happened to 'let's wait until July is ready'? You've nearly told her everything while I was pretending to be a fat duckling waiting for his mother to come back, and left nothing for me to say in a more *captivating* way."

"Ducks don't nest in trees," Galen states, crossing his arms.

"And metaphors don't yield to the mundane rules of logic," I retort.

He sighs, pinching his nose like I've seen him doing every time he's stressed. Or uncomfortable. But I can't help but smirk contentedly when July hides a note of amusement, biting her lower lip.

"Let's just say that our planned arrangements encountered some obstacles." Galen sounds unbothered, but the quick, meaningful look he shares with July tells me that's not even a quarter of the story.

"What are you not saying? Spit it out."

A pair of bare feet appears under my eyes as I brush off soil and grass from my trousers. Her toes wiggle as she clears her throat as if trying to get my attention. *As if that's even necessary…*

When I look up, July stands before me, hands on her hips. "Galen loves keeping secrets lately. So, get in the queue, Kris. Although I'm glad to see I'm not the only one fighting to pull threads of truth from his mouth."

"You say it so perfectly," I smile like an idiot—and proudly so.

"Pardon me?" She tilts her head.

My name.

I scratch my head, plastering a silly smile on my face. "I mean, describing Galen's idiotic way of believing cryptic is a synonym for enchanting."

She pouts, studying me in a way that makes me feel naked. "Right… a bit like those people who use big words to mask their real thoughts."

I open my mouth. Close it. Reopen it, letting out a sound between a gasp and a yelp.

"Enough, you two," Galen snaps, coming closer and ignoring me as he halts between July and me.

"Sof, can I have a word with my brother, please?"

She gets on her tiptoes and surveys me from over Galen's shoulder with her mouth slightly pinched and her hands still on her hips.

My silly smile doesn't falter, and I double down with a click of my tongue and by mimicking a gun with two of my fingers, "I'll make sure he doesn't kill me before you can have your chance."

Galen's eyes widen, and he opens his mouth, but July pushes

him out of the way. "Fine. But if I suspect that you two are out here discussing more secrets…"

She spins on her heel and stalks away, then stops. Her hair shines like dark vinyl under the sun as she tosses it to one side and adds without turning, "What Roden asked of me is cruel and wrong."

She pauses as if to find the right words, peering over her shoulder. "But I don't know you. When mine and Galen's happiness is at stake, everyone can become *my* enemy…"

I clench at the fabric of my shirt, as if struck by an invisible bullet, and she fights back a smile before scoffing and walking away, in time to miss the true pain caused by that bullet as it spreads across my face.

"What were you thinking?" Galen snaps the moment July disappears inside the building.

"I could ask you the same, *brotherling*. What's up with the charming voice and the sideways looks? Don't you think I didn't notice it?" I stab the space above me with a finger.

Galen shakes his head, grunting. "You don't understand. And stop calling me that! I'm older than you."

"Seconds older. But *I've* dodged death more often. That makes me more *experienced*. Besides…"

He studies my face, his gaze serious, as if sensing the tone of what I'm about to say.

"She's starting to remember without Tabitha's help. I've heard what she said about the lake. That can only mean *our* souls have already recognised each other." My voice softens

We're so close I can see the silver specks in Galen's eye shimmering, his pupils dilating.

His nostrils flare when he says through his teeth, "And you thought it was okay to force her memories to the surface by making a grand appearance?"

A shiver runs down my spine. We've been apart before, but this is the first time I have to remember he's not a stranger. My fingers itch, imploring me to slap that unfamiliar expression off his face. "You're overstepping," I warn him.

"You should thank me— " His voice is so low I can barely hear him.

Galen's muscles twitch when I stab his chest with my finger. "Don't pretend you were doing it for me. You told her *you* begged her to let me live. For fuck's sake, Galen. Why did you *lie*?" The words are out before I can think.

His jaw clenches so tight I fear it may break as he growls, "You don't have the right to tell me what to do. Besides, there is a chance she may not listen to anyone this time but herself…"

I can't hold back a bitter laugh. "Well, her last words surely weren't what I wanted to hear. Worst case scenario, she'd run away, leaving us all in a giant pile of *Oops* and *Oh, shit!* And, if she decides not to help me cure the Reds, I will keep doing it my way. Until my soul runs *out*… and fuck Roden!"

Galen shakes his head. His hair, falling over his eyes, cannot hide the regret spreading across his face. "Roden promised her *freedom*. Our freedom. And, in exchange, he will wipe her mind clean of all we've been through together. I didn't ask for this. I didn't ask for things to change. It—happened."

As if wanting to miss my reaction, he pulls his hair back, turns away from me and stares at the sky. "She will forget me—and I don't think I'm okay with that…"

The breeze is like a gentle observer. It cradles a smell that belongs to the sea, not an artificial lake, and the sounds of distant seagulls.

"You love her…" My words join the choir of gulls.

Galen's head drops, and the echo of my words showers over me like an unexpected ice-cold rain on a sizzling day. I don't need to search for the truth on his face. His body is screaming it. The twitch of his fingers, the slight shaking of his shoulders.

"I should've listened to Eve and let the Chapter erase every memory July had of me. They could have picked someone else to train her, to guide her. I could have left that damn island and stayed here with all of you. Working on a plan, fighting with you. Maybe things would have gone differently."

For how long did he hide this pain? I grab his left shoulder and force him to look at me. His eyes, so different from mine yet equally determined, are full of desperation and rage.

"And then what? Let her become Roden's perfect cub. Breathing only to fight against us, the *bad* people, with the sole purpose of cutting open our chests and crushing our souls?"

My words bounce off him. I study his face, the shadow of an old bruise under one eye and a light stubble on his chin. But nothing moves.

"You've said it yourself. Things change, and you can only keep living and make the best of what's to come." I ruffle his curls.

His lips quirk and he sighs. "I didn't mean to… But we spent so much time together, and she is so…"

"Addictive?" I smirk. "Yeah, I heard that too and cringed on your behalf."

"I'm sorry."

One moment, I'm talking to my brother, the man he's become. And the next, I see him running in the field, chasing after me, during one of his secret visits to Horigos, with Eve always by his side.

And a man who's just stabbed my heart and made a poultice of it. But, as much as I'd love to stuff that poultice down his throat, I can't blame him and pretend this is just about two brothers sharing the same refined taste for intelligent, dangerously powerful women.

"Look, you did nothing wrong. But stop manipulating her mind like you've done earlier on. Sof's past is a pool of faces floating underwater, and if any of us forces them up… We could lose her for good."

His eyes narrow, and something flashes behind them - distant - and for a second, I feel like I'm just a filthy Herionos standing with no chance against a righteous Harvester.

"For your information, she hates that name now. I'm the only one using it without being slapped or punched." He huffs a laugh.

I drop my hand, straightening my spine. "The July I know would never use violence for such a silly reason."

"If there's something good the Chapter taught me, it is that souls are like water. They are fluid and adapt easily to challenging circumstances. She said she may help you—but she's still Roden's offspring. And she hates that more than she may love me—or anyone else."

I open my mouth to reply, but he holds up his hand. "I can no longer tell her true nature. Neither can you. July… Sofia… she could be holding something inside her soul that she cannot even remember yet."

The wind whistles, carrying the noise of a door opening, a child's laugh and indistinct voices.

I take a big breath, weighing my words carefully. "I've never lost sight of my role. I suggest you do the same. I fear you've spent too much time with Roden Breith recently; if I didn't know it differently, I'd think you're starting to sound like him…" I blow harshly on his face.

His cheek brushes mine when he whispers in my ear, "And look where you are now. Trapped in a loop because of our mother's sweet promise. She might have led you to believe you're the chosen soul destined to end this war. But she's gone. Dead. Rotting somewhere in the deep waters between Horigos and Libera…"

I grit my teeth, tilting my head. "Where is this hatred coming from?"

In my peripheral vision, I see him closing his eyes, biting his lip—fighting back whatever is bubbling up from his darkest core. "Do you really think you're the one who suffered the most because of her choice? You had a carefree childhood thanks to Tabitha. But I needed to grow sharper teeth and poisonous nails to stay afloat, breathing Roden's same air, knowing what he did to our family."

The blood in my head thrums hot. I grab the back of his neck, pulling him against my chest. "You're speaking of mother almost as if she deserved it…"

"She had a choice and decided it was better for me to live among lies. I could only fit in or end up like you—a nobody. A vessel with a *cursed* soul," he barks.

"Her sacrifice saved both our lives!" I can feel my face turning red, the air burning in my lungs.

I let go of his neck and shove him away. His face is contorted with rage, his hair a messy drape over his forehead, those eyes I always envied when I was little scowling at me.

"Roden has poisoned your blood. Is Evelyn even aware of the person you've become? This game has been going on for too long for you. You're confused, and your feelings for July—"

The impact of his fist in my stomach is power and rage and pain and sorrow. So strong, I stumble backwards, losing my footing as a metallic taste fills my mouth.

I wipe off the corner of my mouth with the back of my hand. "If you wish to tame your confusion with a fight, you've picked the wrong person, brother. That'd be too easy."

"Stop pretending you know who I am. We're not the same," Galen pants as if we indeed just fought.

I sneer. "Maybe not. But we both enjoy her laugh and can't stand her absence."

I wait for another punch to hit me right in the face, but Galen remains still, if not for a quivering muscle in his jaw.

I limp forward, massaging my stomach, and with the most friendly smile I can manage, I say, "We have more pressing priorities to worry about. A war, for example? Since the last time you were here, things have gotten more… explosive. The Reds have grown in numbers, and we're struggling to keep them away from our borders. People in the southern villages are terrified. They're seeking refuge in Brenath by the hundreds each week, because Cleryce is registering too many episodes of wild souls acting feral. They're losing hope in our ability to keep them safe; we don't know how long it would take for Roden to turn them against us."

A crack starts showing in Galen's brooding glare as he quickly blinks twice. And *I* thought I was the most dramatic of the two.

"The southern villages? I thought we managed to confine the Reds north of Cleryce?" he presses. Every bitter accusation against our mother quickly forgotten. Or momentarily set aside.

"Someone from Horigos is helping Roden—conservative Herionos, fed with their ancestors' hate for Harvesters. They despise Roden, but he's also the source of the same power that could turn their voice of discontent into a legalised and approved creed. One that could break our legs in a matter of days."

He shakes his head. "How can you be sure?"

"Lily and Nik captured a couple of them. They pretended to be on our side, joined the New Hera and even took down some bad seeds. But a few weeks ago, they crossed The Mother's mountain range, heading to Corlea. Lily and Nik followed them and discovered a nest of hot-headed, old-school Herionos camping on the borders, waiting for *someone* to give them safe passage across the bridge to head south without being intercepted by Tabitha." I pause, studying his reaction.

He starts torturing the neck of his shirt with his teeth, and his eyes dart to me. "And we know this because…?"

I scratch my neck, looking past his face to the building. "Merya was there and had some *fun* with them. They're still alive - if you were wondering - sent back to The Mother, where they started—but a few levels below their old rooms."

When his shirt becomes useless to his thinking process, Galen starts chewing on his lower lip. "Why Corlea? There is nothing on that island worth their energy. It's only a port to—" His gears click and fall into the right - worrying - places.

"Brenath and our base." I steal the words from him to ease his increasing nervousness and to stop him from drawing blood from his lip. "They had a ship ready on the other side of the island, carrying unstable Reds. Like the one who caused the accident in Brenath a month ago—"

And—goodbye to the attempt at saving his lip. "You… didn't

know," I state, already confident in his answer, when his eyes widen and his jaw locks.

He looks at the sky, struggling to hide the exasperation caused by my revelation. "Nobody cared to keep me updated."

"You had other matters to be worried about. Me. July. The Chapter. Surely your hair wasn't one of them…"

"Just be serious for once." His fingers curl into fists before he plunges them into his pockets.

"Sorry, I… *Apparently*, Roden has decided to make good use of the more unstable Reds he can find. A man in his forties reached Brenath's shores on a raft and asked to be fed and to rest. He also said he had some urgent news to deliver to Tabitha Lorne, but didn't know how to find her."

Galen nods, quickly putting all the pieces of the puzzle together. "Roden knows Brenath recently opened its gate and showed interest towards the New Hera. But his citizens may also betray our location if he plays his cards well before they're completely sold to our cause." He starts pacing left and right, chewing again at his shirt. Some things never change.

I step before him, holding my hands up to stop him. "That's not all. Forget about Roden for a second. The man I told you about—he never made it to Ventiol because his blood was so poisoned, overloaded by tons of scrapped souls that he exploded in the local Town Hall."

There is no softer way to deliver the news, but Galen's eyes bulge as if I've punched him in the stomach.

"Casualties?"

"The poor bastard, of course, and some villagers who brought him warm clothes and food. They were killed almost immediately. His blood melted them like acid. But from the inside, as if they had inhaled toxic fumes. I was there with Jyn when it happened." I shiver, trying to chase away the memory of their screams.

I fall silent, lost for words—I don't want to find those words again in my head.

Galen's hand lands heavily on my shoulder.

"That explains a lot. Do the others know?"

I replay his words in my head quickly. "Explains *what*?"

"Kris, just answer me. Do the others know?" He grabs me by the collar of my faded green shirt.

I wriggle free, giving him a puzzled look. "I told Tabitha, and she shared with the others a summary but left the more gruesome details out of it."

Galen ponders my words, lost in thought for a moment. "That must be him," he mumbles.

"Him?"

"The man in the video that Lucretia and her friends were watching in the library. July thinks that was you during one of the many times Roden tried to erase your memories."

"Who's Lucretia? Galen, remember, you hit me. I didn't touch you, but you are the one talking nonsense." I flick his forehead.

"I need to speak with everyone. Whether Tabitha is willing or not, this can't wait."

He pats twice on my shoulder and runs away towards the building, leaving me agape and with a massive bruise blooming on my otherwise perfect stomach.

Chapter 39 - Chasing Monsters
July

Why are my stupid legs shaking? And why have all my thoughts gone quiet, but my mind keeps playing *his* voice in a loop?

The distance between me and the building stretches like an elastic band without a breaking point until the kitchen's back door appears from nowhere in front of me.

I cling onto its pommel, fearing I won't be able to stand upright on my own for much longer. I breathe in, shake my head to clear it and step inside.

Kris' smiling face lingers behind my eyes. The same sweet expression that I've crushed so many times in my nightmares. During those nights full of images of me causing pain to someone I'd never met, and yet—someone whose pain would become mine the moment I opened my eyes, accompanying me the whole day, no matter Galen's attempts to cheer me up and distract me from what that really was…

Just a dream.

And now those pale green eyes, with a hint of pulsating sun in their centre, have a voice. They are so different from Galen's, yet they share the same spark for life. A spark I could easily snuff out.

My hands rush to my hammering heart to make sure it will not jump out of my chest.

"Are you running from a monster or chasing one?" Mack welcomes me, standing by the wall next to the door.

"What if I am the monster?" I reply without thinking, distracted by the kitchen space.

On the opposite side of the large dining table, Merya is busy entertaining a young girl who strikes me as a miniature copy of Tabitha, if not for her jet-black hair and petite build. They're both busy conversing while a bird squawks, flaps and scampers on the table as if trying to get their attention.

I make eye contact with mini-Tab, and a wide, partially toothless smile lights up her face.

"You're the pretty lady," she squeals, pointing at me.

Merya finally lifts her head, losing interest in what seems like a first aid box. Bandages, some still new, some stained with blood, plasters, and a pair of scissors are scattered on the table before her.

"Happy to see you up and *running*," she says before turning to the little girl. "Sable, what have we learned about good manners?"

Staring at me with large, dark purple eyes, Sable pouts. "That we don't point at people, we don't point at things, we don't point at anything." She lowers her small hands onto the table, interlaces her fingers and bows her head as if ashamed of her burst of excitement.

The bird stops its attention-seeking dance and hops to her,

snuggling its white, feathered head in the space between her fingers.

My heart shrinks as I approach the table, smiling. "It's okay; I used to point at everything when I was about your age. Even the clouds in the sky and my reflection in the mirror. Sable, is it?" I ask, keeping an eye on the odd bird.

As if sensing me, the animal rotates its head and glares at me, making me wonder if our Donatori accidentally gifted it a soul.

Sable nods, and I relax, seeing the smile back on her heart-shaped face.

"She's the most fearless member of our group." Mack lands a hand on my shoulder with the confidence of someone who's known me for ages. But then he immediately drops it, realising we probably shared the same thought.

"You've all become very good at this." I drop the bomb to taste their reactions.

"I'm not following," Mack replies, stepping away from me and sitting on the edge of the table with his ankles resting one on top of the other and arms crossed. A shaft of light pouring in from the door's glass panel ignites the copper in his hair, giving him a boyish look.

"You've never been known for being the smartest between us," Merya comments, not looking directly at us and pretending the chipped surface of the table is more interesting.

I saunter along the table, running a finger over its rough surface. "I mean—pretending you've never met me before." I slowly walk up to the kitchen sink to wash the heat off my face as well as the uncomfortable stickiness of all the information Kris and Galen have just thrown at me.

Behind me, the silence is dense with whispers and the noise of a chair being pulled from under the table. When I turn, water dripping over my top and with some fine strands of hair stuck onto my face, I find Mack and Merya sitting next to each other, both agape, looking at me as if I've just caught them stealing from a biscuit tin.

"You can stop acting now. The charming brothers out there told me everything. Well, most of it." I lean back against the grey stone kitchen top, studying my fingernails one by one.

Mack raises a finger, opens his mouth, sucks in some air and puffs up his cheeks, only to eventually push the air out with a loud sigh. His hand drops on the table as if too heavy to control.

Merya cuts him a glare and shakes her head. "My brother is trying to say that we're sorry we lied to you, but that's how it's always been since this all started. The way it was before we even joined Tabitha and her fight."

"I understand you were just following orders—" I start.

"Nobody is forcing me to make sure you don't kill Kristyon," Mack blurts out.

"Mack, shut up." Merya jabs him in the ribs and rolls her eyes towards Sable, who doesn't seem interested in our conversation. She's quietly talking to the kestrel as if they're sharing secrets. But, having been her age, I'm sure she has eyes and ears everywhere.

"If you'd let me finish…" Mack squints at his sister before

moving his attention back to me. "That's true. Merya and I met you before, but only a few times when we're not stationed in The Mother, and it's hard to avoid slips and mistakes when we interact with you. As per Kris, I would stand by him against my sister if I had to." He shrugs as if talking about the weather. "You know, should she go berserk and move to the wrong side," he then adds with an innocent smile.

My heart shrinks when Merya keeps her eyes on me, but stretches a hand to brush Mack's briefly.

"Horigeans are dying," - Mack continues - "and their souls are stolen every day, even if they never made a deal with Roden Breith. And all because that fuck—" he quickly looks at Sable, "That soul-sucking parasite wants to create a new generation of perfected Harvesters."

His voice dims while my eyebrows arch higher and higher, "… and you didn't know about that. Great!" He makes to stand up, but the back door bursts open, flapping angrily on its hinges and hitting the wall a couple of times.

The weird bird tries to fly away while Sable stretches her little body over the table to catch him. "You'll hurt yourself again, Zephyr. Stop," she cries out while Mack pushes away from the table, sending the chair toppling to the floor.

I understand the presence of the aid box when I notice one of the animal's wings hanging down, seemingly broken.

Merya is the only person in the room not bothered by the sudden turmoil. Her eyes roam from one side of the room to the other, then she drops her chin on her interlaced fingers.

Galen also doesn't seem to care about the havoc he's just caused by barging in like a tornado. "As far as I'm curious to know why Mack looks so guilty, there is something we need to talk about. Where are Tabs and Jyn?"

"Sable, why don't you go find your mama? You can take Zephyr and show her what a good doctor you've been." Merya pats Sable's head gently without breaking eye contact with Galen and the rest of us.

"And I can feed him more worms," Sable squeaks with excitement, bouncing off the chair like a spring.

"All the worms." Merya nods with a smile.

"They're very squishy, you know; he loves them. But mama says *I* can't eat them even if they taste better than her soups!" Sable exclaims, jumping up and down, while Zephyr fights to remain perched on her left arm.

We all wait in silence for Sable to hop out of the kitchen, singing a song about a fat bird and a fat worm becoming friends and going fishing together.

"Where is Kris?" I ask when I'm sure Sable is gone and not eavesdropping.

Galen pants, leaning against the doorframe, his hair tousled and his cheeks flushed, when he eventually looks at me.

"Mending his broken ego somewhere." He dismisses our still unvoiced questions. "This is about *the* video."

I give him a questioning look. "Has this anything to do with

Roden's using Horigos like his personal souls marketplace instead of waiting for desperate people to ask for his help?"

"Do I want to know who told her?" He scans the room for the culprit.

In the corner of my eyes, Mack shrinks a little. "What is she talking about?" he asks, trying his luck.

"Read the room, Mack," Merya mutters, gathering plasters and bandages still scattered over the table.

"Everybody shut up," Galen bellows, turning to the siblings. "Kris just told me what happened in Brenath. Whatever you think happened there, think again—it's twice as dangerous. Evelyn had a theory that Roden was collaborating with conservative Herionos to relocate nearly empty, dilapidated vessels from The Fields to a secret location. He needs fresh bodies to create stable Reds, but couldn't make too many disappear without raising suspicions among the Writers."

"Where do you think he hides them?" Merya urges him.

Galen shrugs. "Corlea seems a good starting point if the Herionos Lily and Nik captured told you the truth. What I'm sure of is that Roden knows what a destructive weapon those unstable souls are and will use them against us. He just needs to *find* us..."

"Wait a second." Merya stands up, head shaking. "What stops him from using the Herionos who are helping him? Surely they're expendable, in-good-health-pawns. And they're not stupid..."

Galen approaches the table slowly, finally unfreezing the atmosphere around us. "If Roden promised them freedom in his new kingdom—the chance is too high to ignore… And he still needs their trust and for them to do his dirty work on Horigos while he holds Libera together."

"That must be wrong," Mack complains, with a powerful voice I didn't think he had in him. "We blamed it *all* on the Herionos. Fuck—we sent squads after them. Merya tortured them!" A moment of silence. Of cruel realisation. His eyes widen with horror.

"I'm sorry, Mack, but we know how expert Roden is at turning bullshit into a credible, alternative truth. Especially if that plays to his favour." Galen pinches his chin, pacing back and forth almost on the spot.

"Brenath is the latest province that has agreed to join our cause," Merya mumbles.

Galen nods, pensively. "Roden is trying to turn them against us before it's too late, while their minds are still processing the reality of the danger. Our side-battles with the Herionos were the perfect alibi at the right moment. When was the last time you had contact with Brenath's Mayor?"

"The day that man's body burst into a corrosive killing machine and liquefied some of the citizens in the Town Hall. The Mayor asked us for some days to mourn their loved ones," Mack replies.

"Thanks for the delightful, vivid reminder," Merya replies in a low voice, bracing her elbows on the table and massaging her temples.

I've been listening to them talking, understanding only half of their conversation. I move closer to the table, addressing everyone. "That would have given Roden time to send messages to the Mayor and convince him that the blood of his people is on Tabitha's hands."

I shift and turn to speak directly to Galen, "Please tell me something, now that we're all so ready to speak the truth. The man in Lucretia's video wasn't Kris. And it wasn't the Herionos torturing him. That was Roden creating a Red. That's why some Chapter members were so on edge the night he *kindly* summoned me. A few knew about it and thought their position was at risk…"

Galen's face pales with my every heated accusation. "Roden couldn't do everything on his own. The Deleteri are very good at that, as are the Writers," I add, playing with the key at my neck.

"Oh, nice to see you're wearing that," Mack comments unexpectedly. "Galen, where's yours? I thought—"

Distractedly, my eyes fall on his neck, but his voice calls me back to attention.

"If you're accusing me or my Deleteri, you're very wrong," Galen snaps, shutting down Mack, whose cheeks flash red before he hides it by lowering his head.

"I wasn't, but you trained them, and you clearly know that something horrible like hybrid souls is doable, so…" I shrug.

"Not fair," Mack mumbles, still affected by Galen's abrupt reaction. "Please don't blame it all on him. We've all been investing our lives to find a way to stop Roden, and Galen is the one who risked more than everyone else. But war is never a clean business.

It's a nasty rat that nibbles at your bones and infects you even if it wasn't you starting it."

I opened my mouth, unsure whether to reprimand Galen or praise Mack's undeniable loyalty, but a familiar voice interrupts me.

"I hope this Lucretia is worth our attention because she only sounds like a troublemaker so far."

With the sun at its peak, turning the shiny surfaces of the kitchen bright white and silver, Kris silhouette strikes me like a portrait I've seen somewhere before—an image that I tucked in the back of my mind. His features are in the shade, but the way his hair touches his shoulders, waving at the ends and framing his face with light tones of brown, captures my attention completely.

I blink and push the thought back when Galen steps between us.

Foxily, Merya stretches her arms and upper body across the table, resting her right cheek in her hand, as if preparing for a good show.

"Please, don't mind me." Clearing his voice, Kris walks inside the kitchen and leans against the wall behind Merya, crossing his arms and patiently waiting, like her, for his brother to speak.

I try not to follow his every move, but all my cells, nerves, and thoughts pull towards him. And for a split second, I swear I can feel his gaze on me.

Galen's nostrils flare slightly as he takes a deep breath, mirroring his brother's posture.

"What killed those people… it's not acid," he starts.

"It's blood," Kris confirms.

"Fascinating, but—we already know that," Mack mumbles.

Merya and I cast him a questioning look, but Mack's too busy taking notes on a scrap of baking paper.

"Despicable," Galen reclaims everyone's focus. "But I can see why you find it interesting. If used well, it could be an almost undetectable weapon."

"How did Roden manage to create such a *thing*?" I sound on the verge of breaking, but that's what anger does to me.

Galen closes his eyes, massaging his forehead as if recalling what he knows.

"He didn't. It happened years ago. By accident."

Nobody comments or moves. Even Mack is lost for words as he grabs a chair and sits down, gnawing at the flat end of a pencil.

Galen nods as if to allow himself to tell the story.

"Eve and I were sent to harvest and erase a soul from Cleryce. Roden told us he'd detected weird notes vibrating through this specific vessel, as if memories of its past life had, somehow, managed to reemerge. The subject was acting erratically and had already scared a few random people met on the streets, asking them to dig a hole in his skull to extract the voices in his head."

I can't help but gasp, but I'm not the only one finding it hard to hide their emotions.

Kris shifts against the wall, then pushes away and walks towards the table. Our eyes meet, and he doesn't drop his stare until he sits next to Mack. When he does, I start breathing again.

"Shit," Merya swears under her breath, raking her fingers

through her hair and messing her already loose braid. "We heard of rebirths gone wrong, of Horigeans waking up with flashes of their past lives but quickly discarding them as nightmares—"

"Yes, but those episodes usually last a few days—weeks maximum. Until the soul adjusts inside the new vessel. What does the Chapter like to call them?" Mack claps and waves a hand towards Galen, asking for help remembering what he can't.

"Regressions—" Galen mumbles, following Merya as she stands, stretches her neck and approaches her brother.

"How original! I call it *we-fucked-up-but-we're-proud-pieces-of-shit*." Mack tilts his head at every word, making a note of the name on his piece of baking paper. Shorter locks of hair dance across his eyes.

"Here, use this." Merya pulls out a small notepad from a side pocket of her wide maroon trousers. "That piece of paper is oily; your scribbles will disappear in minutes, and I don't want to hear your tantrums later on," she grunts, snatching the scrap of paper away and pressing the notepad in her brother's hands. But she ruffles his hair in such a motherly way that I feel jealous of a family I never had.

"You need to find a better insult if you want to use it next time we meet the big bad Chapter," Kris playfully elbows Mack in the ribs.

"Big C… as in big Cu—Ouch!" There is no trace of playfulness in Merya's hand smacking his head.

Kris and I scoff simultaneously, and his light green eyes find mine again. They're so vivid, unlike those I've met in my dreams.

When he looks away, I linger a little longer on him, trying to recall more details that could help me remember.

Until Galen clears his throat.

He's pacing the room again, the sound of his steps a steady, almost hypnotic rhythm.

"Regressions, or whatever you want to call them. The soul from Cleryce was experiencing something completely different. Those weren't just voices from his past life. They never belonged to him to start with."

"The poisonous blood. Acid. Whatever that is. Was that the natural reaction of his body trying to cleanse him from unfamiliar souls?" Kris' voice carries sad notes that pinch something inside me. When I look over, his eyes are fixed on the table as if hiding his true emotions.

"And everyone let this event be swept under the carpet without raising questions—why?" I ask, attracting all the eyes on me.

"Unfortunately, that's a collateral effect we've only witnessed once—until now. We thought Cleryce was done and dusted and a once-in-a-million-years event." Tabitha materialises by the kitchen's main door, silent like a cat. Her voice follows the trail of my question, capturing - with my immense relief - everyone's attention.

"But we were wrong."

Chapter 40 - Water Graves
Kristyon

"You knew as well?" Two voices merge into one, the same astonished look matched in Merya and Mack's blue eyes.

Merya lunges for the table, the only object separating her from Tabitha, and slams her fist on it, sending cutlery and mugs jangling and rattling across its hard surface.

"And, *still*, you sent us out there to fight what we thought were just Herionos—bastards with no powers… like *us*." She throws a hand behind her, pointing at Mack, who seems glued to his chair and lost for words.

Tabitha sighs but smiles at her. "You knew from day one that this wasn't an easy job. Besides," she holds her hand up when Merya opens her mouth again, "*Their* blood is like water to *us*. Otherwise, Roden would have used it against the rebels since the accident in Cleryce. *We* have been studying it ever since that day to try to find a cure. But you were never in danger, believe me—"

In the corner of my eye, a chair topples to the floor, and a sound like an animal in pain makes me shiver.

"What about our nature? As much as I like to think of you as a mother, our freaking blood doesn't protect us from *shit...*" Mack gasps for air, holding one hand to his chest while erratically fidgeting with the other and scratching the skin around his nails.

I intercept July's puzzled look while I stand up and reach out for Mack's arm. She starts to move towards us, but I shake my head slightly.

"I've always kept you and your sister under strict surveillance. I'd never endanger your lives, but I didn't want you to be left out because you would hate me for that. You're invaluable fighters in this war, just like the others..." Tabitha brings her palms together in front of her chest, but Mack ignores her plea.

He slaps my hand away. "But we're also expendable," he hisses, his voice resounding like one I haven't heard in years.

I jump between him and Tabitha before he decides to act irrationally and, pressing a hand onto his chest, I invite him to sit back. "Mack, please, listen to her before saying something you may regret later."

A large cloud crosses the sky, dimming the light inside the kitchen and turning Mack's eyes a darker shade of blue. Blood stops pumping violently beneath his cheeks, and he retreats against the wall, clutching the notepad as if wanting to strangle it.

Tabitha's wince lasts a heartbeat, but I can clearly read the shadow of pain in her eyes when she forces a straight face and moves further inside the kitchen, pointing at the doors.

"Galen, please close the back door. Kris, the main one as well, before Sable decides this clamour is worthy of her invisible attention." She sounds tired.

Her face is so tense I don't even dare answer. I just nod and ensure Sable's little eyes and busy ears are not hiding in the corridor before closing the door.

In sullen silence, we all take a seat at the table.

Except for Merya, who, for everyone's sake, has decided to brood by the kitchen sink with her hands in her pockets—away from knives, forks, and anything she may throw.

"I can see the dislike for scissors and haircuts runs in the family," July welcomes me, leaning sideways when I drop into the chair beside her, bobbing her chin towards my brother first, then me.

I rest my chin in my hand, narrowing my eyes at Galen when his head pops up from behind July, giggling.

"Wipe that smirk off your face. I bet you let her style your locks because that's the only way to have her hands on you—"

Galen freezes and rolls his eyes, mouthing something I can't understand.

July's face enters my view. Her unmistakable Harvester eyes study me, one eyebrow arched with unspoken questions.

"That came out wrong, I'm sorry, I…" I mumble.

It doesn't matter how long Roden keeps us apart. Every time she comes back, it's hard to stay still and pretend that I don't know what makes her laugh with tears, how being by the water makes her feel at peace, or the feeling of her fingers through my hair. I will always know—but she will always forget the way my eyes smile when she does all these things.

But I'm still a stranger to her, and I've just acted like a total idiot, probably embarrassing her in front of the others. *Please, just slap me,* I pray, hoping she reads my mind and takes me out of my misery instead of staring at me.

"Skilled hands that will do their best to stay away from you. Unless I decide to use them otherwise." Turns out, words can hurt more than a slap.

"At my full potential—" she continues, drawing her attention to her fingernails. "On your soul."

My jaw drops.

Deigning me a quick smirk, she leans back in her chair, letting Galen fully back into my view. His profile is the perfect picture of indifference, even if I know he's gloating inside.

The opposite of Merya, who, still standing by the sink, tries to swallow down laughter with water.

A knock on the door is a welcome distraction. Mack exhales loudly from his spot, and I throw a quick nod in his direction to make sure he's calmed down. But also to stop thinking about how close I am to July when her left thigh brushes against my restless leg.

"Come in," Tabs says hastily. But her features relax when Jyn's head appears through the door.

"Can someone give me a hand, please?" he asks, gingerly shouldering the door open wider, a pile of rolled papers stuck in his arms, swinging dangerously.

Mack and July rush to help him, racing to grab as many rolls as possible.

"Thanks, kids," Jyn laughs, holding his belly with one hand and blotting the sweat off his forehead with the hem of his brown linen shirt.

"What's all this?" Merya asks, stretching her arms up like a cat that's just woken up, sauntering towards Mack and July, her initial discontent seemingly forgotten.

"Have a look for yourself," Tabitha gestures to July to hand her over the scrolls.

Having picked the longest, she undoes the piece of string tied around the paper, unfolds it and invites us to gather closer.

A partial yet well-detailed map of Horigos appears beneath our eyes.

"Hey!" Merya complains as her brother forces his way between her and Tabitha.

"I don't remember drawing this one." Mack leans forward and scratches his head, tapping a finger on a white square in the lower-left corner of the map. "Our base is too small. And where is my lake?"

The version of a hurt and disappointed Mack, already tucked away in the past.

"Your lake? You *created* that?" July comments over Mack's shoulders, balancing on her tiptoes and using his right arm as a support while they bend over the map to exchange quick words with a rediscovered familiarity I cannot ignore.

Merya and I lock eyes, sharing a brief smile. She plops her right thigh on the only spot on the table not occupied by the huge map and, dangling her leg, crosses her arms over her chest.

"You can spend hours asking whether Mack is behind this or that contraption. He has built ninety percent of this building. Here's the quickest answer," Merya says, encompassing the whole map with a swipe of her hand.

"And the tunnels," Mack interrupts, looking at July to his right and puffing his chest with a boyish grin. "And drew all the maps, of course." But his chest deflates and bright pink warms his cheeks when he realises July is still holding onto his arm.

"Impressive," July comments, stepping away and pretending she didn't notice Mack's reaction. I've witnessed many versions of July, but her natural gift to read people has never changed.

"Well, not all of them." Jyn decides to join the conversation, squeezing his way between Tabitha and Galen. "*This* is a map from before your time." He taps a finger on the image of the building, tracing its walls and the green patch of wild land surrounding it. "This was how Ventiol and its outskirts used to look years ago. Centuries ago—we think."

An intricate net of thin black lines branches out from the base of the building and runs across the four sides of the map, gathering here and there into larger dots.

"What are the names inside the dots? I don't recognise any of them." Merya asks, wedging beside me to better observe the other side of the map.

"Let me show you." Tabitha steps away from the table to open a drawer under the sink and comes back, holding a marker.

She uncaps it and starts crossing the dots. "You don't recognise the names because these villages and towns no longer exist," she says, without lifting her head, striking names off the map as if listing casualties.

When only a few places remain untouched, Jyn steps behind her, placing a hand on her back—an invitation to stop staring at the map, which now looks like a graveyard.

We've been listening as if stuck inside a bubble of silence, but the sob that escapes Tabitha bursts it. A tear, stronger than her will to look unmoved, rolls down her cheek and drops on the map, darkening a little spot on the paper. Her fingers, splaying over the map, threaten to claw at the extent of lands and flat versions of long-gone town squares and to shred the miniature reproduction of Horigos into pieces.

Jyn scans our faces while stroking Tabitha's back, meeting the same sadness that's now shadowing her eyes.

"I found similar maps hidden in one of the tunnels. The same we used to take you here," he addresses July.

Another loud sob shakes Tabs' shoulders, but she eventually straightens her spine and rubs one finger under her nose, sniffling.

This is the first time I've seen this fragile side of her, and I'm sure it's the first for many in this room.

"I'm sorry," she says, squaring her shoulders and patting her cheeks with the back of her hands.

"At least now we know you're not some perfect killing machine. Unless what's wetting your eyes is the lubricant of your engines." Merya shrugs and, surprising all of us, smiles, melting the remnants of their earlier disagreement off her face.

In response, Tabitha gives her a glare from under her dark lashes while rolling up the map and setting it aside on the floor. But we all notice a quick smile tugging at her lips.

Jyn slides a chair from under the table, gesturing for Tabs to sit, and only mirrors her when she seems comfortable, her elbows propped on the table and her chin resting on her interlaced fingers.

We follow their lead, trying to be as quiet as possible, and take our seats while the atmosphere, still tense and gloomy following Tabitha's early revelation, softens. Next to me, even July seems to fit perfectly in the scene, as she offers shy smiles to Merya and Mack. She reserves a quick, sad look for Tabitha, but only when nobody seems to be paying her attention.

Nobody but me—and Galen, whose glare lands on me like a boulder when I shift my chair to the left to make room for him.

"You're unconventionally quiet, brother. Something tickling in your mind?" I smirk, patting the empty seat.

He gives me a wicked look. "Yes, actually. Something I can't seem to scratch away for good."

As if sharing the same uncomfortable feeling, July pretends to ignore our quick exchange, tracing the pattern of the table's amber veins trapped under a thin layer of glassy resin.

Our fingers brush briefly, and I retract mine immediately, as if pricked by a needle of energy, causing her puzzled look. Every part of my body is drawn to her. Even the hair on my arms stands up, trying to get closer.

Galen's feral expression glues me onto my chair. I smile nervously, looking away and hoping the heat in my chest will not turn into smoke coming out of my every orifice.

"You two need therapy." July's voice breaks the dark spell, and I finally forget about my unbalanced sibling and focus on the matter ahead.

In her newfound, confident voice, Tabitha says, "We believe that's Roden's doing. He used those souls for his experiments, and when there was nothing left, he tore those villages into ruins. He's probably done it for a very long time… Other - older - maps show islands that are not even depicted on that one," she points at the paper on the floor.

July shifts on her seat as if to ask permission to talk without really interrupting. Tabs nods slightly.

"But how did he manage to empty entire towns without being noticed? I mean, traders and visitors must have realised that something was not right, especially when a whole population vanished into thin air." July stops to take a breath and to search for an answer on our faces.

For once, her knowledge equals ours. In turns, we all look at each other, mirroring shrugs and clueless expressions.

Jyn covers 'Tabs' hand with his and gently squeezes it, his gaze falling on July. "He did it right in front of them. That's how. His most loyal Harvesters surely helped conceal the vessels and any remaining traces. Roden is powerful, but he needs the assistance of his people. We believe he used a well-crafted lie to charm the village he was targeting, and to gain free access to its inhabitants." Jyn closes his eyes as if to visualise his following words, but Tabitha stands up, cutting him short.

She paces the length of the kitchen, from the table to the sink and back, stroking her shoulders as though seeking comfort from the cold despite the warm day.

"We do not know if Roden was the first Harvester to use our gift when the Great Famine began. But we believe that something weakened him after the Famine, and he started to surround himself with exquisite pieces of shit willing to do everything he asked for a slice of power. The fact that he's now seeking aid from the Herionos is only proof that he's running out of time and resources—*his* people are opening their eyes."

Tabitha heavily leans over the sink, facing the window above it, her back to us as if allowing herself a few moments before dealing with the shower of questions she knows is coming.

"Some Reds are willing Horigeans, tired of fighting poverty and hunger. But once a Red explodes, like the man in Brenath, that soul is gone forever. Not even Roden can save them, and the Herionos are the fastest way to gather more subjects without raising suspicions. Roden is clever; I'm sure going over the possible side effects of his offer is never part of their discussion."

Nobody seems to find the right way to voice what's on our

minds, except for Merya. "Who would abandon their family to follow a stranger? Especially if that stranger is Roden?"

"Why did you go with Tabitha?" Jyn asks instead.

"Because of me," Mack replies. His eye fixed on Tabitha. "Because we had nothing left to lose, not even ourselves. And Tabitha was the best option."

At last, Tabs turns around to face us all. "Roden may think himself a saviour, but he also knows that miracles are what turn a mass of flesh and bones into gods. And he had years to learn how to walk and talk like one."

"But if the Harvester's blood is diluted and hard to find on Horigos, how does he fuel mixed souls with such skills?" Mack sets his fists on the table, slowly joining them together, mimicking the fusion of two souls.

"He's feeding them his blood." My voice comes from a dark place in my throat.

The ticking of a large, old, square-shaped clock Mack found somewhere during his reconnaissance trips adds to the already heavy atmosphere.

My attention is drawn to the female face painted on the right side of it: black hair, red lips and the smile of someone who was born before Roden's time.

"Initially. Yes." Jyn confirms my fear. "Roden believed the easiest way to make them *new* Harvesters was to mix their blood with his several times until their Horigean essence was utterly replaced. Only those who accepted to undergo the painful procedure were granted access to Libera."

The happy female face fades out of focus at the sound of Jyn's words, and I remember to blink. In the corner of my eye, July is studying me.

I slowly return the look, wanting to say something, but Tabitha comes back to the table and gently places a hand on my shoulder, nodding at the room.

"And for a while, they did feel *different*. Their minds began to work more quickly and effectively as if a veil had dropped between their reality and the truth beyond. They experienced our *gift*; they could sense the souls of others and how much time they had left to live. The beating of hearts they've never met. Probably never would."

"What went wrong?" July asks in a whisper, shivering.

"Everything," Jyn presses his fingertips together, resting his lips against them. "Their bodies couldn't handle it. Their blood began to reject the new cells. It didn't take long for Roden to notice. And yet, he let them live in Libera's most remote villages by the water. Until it became clear they were a threat, he shipped them back to Horigos and exiled them to the outskirts of Cleryce. Roden-made abominations with *infected* blood, neither Harvesters nor Horigeans."

The sound comes out muffled, as if even recalling past events is a sin to be kept untold.

"To keep the Harvesters safe?" Merya doesn't sound sure of her theory.

Tabitha shakes her head and makes to approach the back door, hands wrapping her elbows. "Not only that. Cleryce was a secluded area at the time, perfect for discarding damaged vessels, doomed to turn to dust. This is why, for a long time, nobody was aware of his real experiments."

July clears her throat to hide her discomfort. "What about the souls? Did he go back to collect them?"

Tabitha suddenly stops in the middle of the kitchen. Surprise and gravity mark her voice when she admits, "A soul cannot survive for long without a new body. The majority simply were no more after a few days." She looks over one shoulder, and her eyes quickly find mine. "But we believe that some found their way to a new life—treasuring memories of what Roden had done to them."

A nod, then she walks up to the back door, tracing a scratch in the glass panel overlooking the orchard before pressing her forehead against it.

"Imagine being so greedy as to risk your own life, and still be able to make it even after Roden's discarded you like rubbish, while full-bloodied Harvesters lost their lives to a water burial only to save a mixed-blood soul..." Galen's comment comes unexpectedly.

My head snaps towards him, and I'm not the only one. July is staring at him, as well as everyone else, even if she probably doesn't understand what he's talking about—our mother and the despicable end Roden offered in exchange for her loyalty.

In exchange for her sacrifice to save the children of a man Roden despised. *Our* father—a mixed soul who survived Roden's playtime…

Galen's words sting. I can see it on Jyn's lips, pressed tight to keep his disappointment at bay, on Merya's hand hovering over the table in search of Mack's to stop him from peeling the skin off his thumb.

Tabitha's nails scrape on the glass, a painful cry which, I'm sure, matches her feelings, followed by a bitter laugh.

"Don't you see? He's still doing it." She turns and faces us with a sad smile, her hands now resting in her pockets. She cocks her head to one side.

"Roden still has the power to infiltrate our minds, even from a distance. We could take down hundreds of his soldiers. Those who want Horigeans to believe we are the real threat. He will always be moving our strings, whether we realise it or not. But this ends now."

Tabs slaps a hand on her thigh, making Mack jump.

"We've been fighting a years-long battle - never a war - trying to contain Roden and those who are happy to follow his cruel dream of superiority. To make their actions just a fraction less disruptive for Horigos and for what remains of its people. At what cost and with what results?" Tabs seems to ask everyone, but nobody speaks.

"Exactly," she continues, "We've done nothing but delay the worst from happening."

Merya bolts upright, confusion and a hint of panic in her eyes, making her brother jump again. "But what about the people we kept safe? All those villages and towns we rebuilt from scratch? They must count for something."

"What about stopping scaring Mack to death?" he pleads, raising his hands, palms up.

"Dramatic," Merya snaps.

"Boring soul," Mack mumbles.

"Stating the truth is not really an insult, brother. You'd better work on that," Merya comments, taking a step back to give him a judgemental look.

"How do you do that?" July asks, and when six heads turn to her at the same time, she looks down at the table. "I mean, since I've been here, I've witnessed all of you jumping from tales of terrible events to arguing, in the middle of a serious conversation, about ridiculous matters. How do you not crush under the weight of what's happening?"

"Because we don't have the privilege to have our memories reset like yours."

"Mack!" Merya, Galen, Jyn and Tabitha shout at once.

For the third time, Mack jumps, but this time, he pushes his chair, sending it toppling to the floor against the wall. "Enough. Give me a script next time."

"No, please. It's… okay. Mack is right." July's voice carries a sense of want, a desire for answers so intense I want to take her hand and tell her that everything is going to be okay.

But Galen gets there before me. His fingers are already closed around hers.

"I know it must be hard pretending. You don't need to and I hate this feeling of having something right in front of me, but that I can't grasp." Her words linger between *us* even if her eyes are trained on my brother.

"This is why I wanted all of us to have this conversation," Tabitha finally speaks again, her leader's voice and stubborn gaze slowly making a comeback.

"Are you sure about this?" Jyn asks.

Tabitha nods, gently squeezing Jyn's arm. "I received news from Libera that I can no longer ignore."

"How? When?" Galen asks without letting go of July. He silently reads Tabitha's face, slowly tilting his head. "Evelyn?"

Tabitha hums in response, bracing her hands on the table. "She used one of Mack's kestrels. Those grumpy birds know the way here, so Evelyn could send a quick message, even if ignoring our coordinates. But it was enough to explain the extent of Roden's madness. His plan this time was never to give July another chance to succeed at what he had tried for years. He doesn't care about Kris anymore because that beautiful, special soul Roden desired for so long is now but a weak flame. Kris helped us save many souls that were about to turn red, but that came at a cost... and Roden figured it out."

"*... there was always a stubborn, last kernel missing...* That's what Roden said to me." July's hand slips from under Galen's. She sighs, looking at me with watery eyes. "Roden always used me like a tracker. He would have ended this if he had the power to find Kris on his own otherwise. But he needed me to bring him to Libera, where he is at his full potential. Before that last spark of soul…"

"And Roden can't leave Libera; he's tethered to the island. With Roden gone, Libera will implode." Mack completes July's words, pinching his lips and seeking confirmation from Tabitha, with growing panic in his eyes.

Her shoulders rise and fall. "That's true, but Roden has apparently grown tired of his exile and decided that it is time to father a new generation of Harvesters."

"Tabitha?" Merya backs against the kitchen counter, bracing a hand on its edge. "What else did Evelyn's message say?"

We all hold our breaths. Tabitha runs her hand over her face, inhaling deeply, her chest expanding.

"Libera is on fire."

Chapter 41 - Nobody's Child
July

The faces of all the people I met in Libera flip before my eyes like the pages of a book I'll never finish reading.

I push my chair back, getting slowly on my feet because my stomach threatens to jump out of my mouth if I move too quickly. "That doesn't make any sense." I hear myself mumbling, ignoring the background voices asking me to sit down.

"I know, my child, but Roden is not seeking sense. He desires a rebirth, a clean cut. He was only waiting for the right time to come and for his patience to run out."

"I'm nobody's child." I snap at Jyn, my hair slapping my face as I turn to point a finger at him. "A tool, this is what I am. A weapon—"

A hand lands on my shoulder and slides down my arm, gently inviting me to lower it.

"You're July Sofia Crimson," Kristyon's voice brushes my cheek like a sweet spring breeze. "You love the feeling of ladybirds crawling on your fingers and the sound of thunder when you're about to fall asleep."

He lets his hand rest on my arm, waiting for me to decide if I want to break the physical contact.

I lower my eyes to the floor. "I am his daughter. His blood runs in my veins. How could you ignore that and remain so close to me?"

"Because we—"

The bubble of quiet bursts, pricked by a groan that quickly turns into a muffled scream. I spin around, but the source of the sound remains invisible to me, shielded behind Kristyon's body. Nothing good, judging by how quickly Merya reaches for her brother to drag him away from the table while he fights to break free and run to—Galen.

"*He's* trying to get to him. Let me go!" Mack twists his upper body, trying to escape Merya's grip. "He's not wearing the key. Where the fuck is the key?"

"Get him out of here. Now!" Tabitha shouts over Mack's words.

"The key?" I bring my fingers to the silver chain around my neck. "It has a twin…"

Shutting off Tabitha and Merya's alarmed voices, I push Kris out of my way, lunging for Galen, who's now bent over the kitchen sink, pressing his palms against his temples and groaning like a wounded beast.

"Is this what Mack means? Is this what you need?" I make to slide the chain over my head, but Galen throws his arm back, stopping me from getting any closer.

"No…" he growls in a voice that I almost do not recognise.

"Roden is on Horigos, and he's trying to get inside my head to find *you.*"

The sudden silence rolls down my spine like a drop of liquid ice. I let the chain fall back on my neck. "But that means—"

A hand rips the veil separating me and Galen from the others and lands heavily on my shoulder.

"That our time here is up, and we have to move. Fuck—this is worse than I thought." Tabitha doesn't sugarcoat her worry and pulls me away from Galen, who's, in the meantime, fallen on his knees. "Whatever happens, you do not take that necklace off, understood?"

She spins me around, pointing a finger in my face and not moving until I nod. "Good girl. Now—you go with Kris and Mack. Merya and I will take care of Galen. If we're lucky, we probably have until sunrise tomorrow to understand what the fuck is going on, and come up with a last-minute plan."

Merya steps towards us, with Mack in tow, followed by Kris, who seems ready to catch him should he decide to act wild again.

"He's strong," Merya states, nodding at Galen, who's curled up against the kitchen counter. "But do you really think he will be able to hold out until tomorrow morning? Tabitha, we need to give him the key—"

"NO!" Kris and Galen shout at once, the first stepping before me, towering over his brother.

"I'll take July and Mack to The Mother. That will buy us some time," Kris says, earning a subtle nod from Tabitha but also managing to relight Mack's fire.

"Absolutely-fucking-no! I'm not leaving Galen like this. I'm probably the only one who can help him."

"You don't have time to create another key. Stop being so sentimental." Merya hits the counter with a fist, searching the room for Jyn, who has not yet expressed his opinion.

"Stop punching things," Mack yells before shrinking and turning away when Jyn stomps towards him.

"Come on, boy, time to go, either on your own legs or on my shoulders. Your choice." Jyn puts himself between Galen and Mack, fists on his hips.

"Mack, please." Galen's voice reaches us, weak as if coming from a dimension far away. "I'll be fine. The tunnels will give us some cover, and Roden won't be able to detect me. At least until we are all ready to go."

It pains me to see him like this, struggling to get back on his feet as if he's just been hit by hundreds of bullets. But it mostly hurts me to see Galen forcing a reassuring smile when his own face is so ashen and his eyes red.

As I try to make sense of everything, I start playing with the key at my neck. "Why are you not wearing yours?" I ask, even if I still don't know how such a small piece of metal can be a barrier between Roden and our minds. Not that I ever thought something like this was even possible.

Kris clears his throat to call my attention and the others. "Because he gave it to me." He digs two fingers beneath the collar of his shirt, fishing out a leather lace with a key identical to mine in shape and colour.

We all turn to face Galen.

Me: mostly curious to understand why he did such a stupid thing, knowing now what the key protects us from; Mack, on the other hand, openly showing defeat on his young, freckled face.

"You gave up. That's the only explanation. Stupid, if you ask me, and—nope, just stupid. I'm—fine," - he quickly waves Jyn away - "I'm not going to lash out again."

"Yes." Galen snaps. "I was going to drop everything and leave July, my brother and everyone I love at Roden's mercy. Think again, you silly genius! Why do you think Evelyn gave *her* key to July?"

I gasp. *Her key…* but the others ignore me. Except for Kris, who brushes the back of his hand against mine.

Mack's eyes widen.

"You get it now, right?" Galen bites his last words as if they're struggling to come out. He grunts, seeking the edge of the sink with his left hand. "We weren't hundred percent sure, but Evelyn noticed something had changed in Roden's behaviour. Lately, he was more secretive, even with the Chapter. And then—he let July make that stupid deal with him as if he'd ever set her free. We've never seen Roden acting so erratically. He was just covering all the bases—" He spins around, coughing in the sink.

When he faces us again, fresh blood gleams on the corner of his lips, stretched in a wicked smirk, his eyes - those beautiful explosions of silver and rich browns - veiled as if trapped under a thick layer of ice.

"Hello, my children. It is not polite to start a family gathering without your *father.*" His voice coated in century-old, almighty smugness.

"Nobody move…" Tabitha opens her arms, a human barrier between us and Galen. "Hello, Roden, you decrepit piece of shit. I was wondering when I would hear your voice again. Such a shame you're not here *yet*; my hands are thirsty for your blood…" She tries to force a stern tone, but the tips of her fingers are shaking.

Galen's head cocks to one side, a lock of hair falling over his Harvester eye as he studies Tabitha head to toe, clicking his tongue. "You've aged, my dear. Tell me, is that little lamb of yours still around? Or did you eventually give her away? I'd understand if you did—after all, she's half-bastard with no powers—"

With an explosion of strong muscles and a mass of loose silver braids, Tabitha lunges for him. But Merya's response is quicker than our surprise. The young woman shoves me out of the way and pounces to grab Tabitha by her waist, followed by Mack, who dashes behind her before Jyn snatches him back towards the secondary door.

"You stay here, or I knock you out, boy." Jyn rumbles in his chest, never losing eye contact with Galen. When Mack opens his mouth to voice his complaint, a final glare from Jyn shuts him up.

"Don't get down to his level. This is what he wants," Merya implores Tabitha, holding her with one hand while the other is slowly caressing the holster looped around her thigh.

Kris' fingers flutter against mine, and I remember to breathe.

Unmoved by Merya and Tabs' reaction, Roden chuckles through Galen's mouth, "He's fighting, you know? He's actually telling me to *fuck off*—"

For a split second the Roden-Galen creature flinches, and I see my chance.

"Galen, I know you can hear me. Tell me what to do, tell me—" I step towards him, but Kris catches my hand.

The familiar green eyes that I saw almost every night stare into mine, not letting me think about the nightmare that has just barged into our reality.

"July? It's going to be fine. Don't look at anyone but me, and keep hold of that key."

This must be a dream.

Blood thrums loudly in my ears, but I can't get hurt.

This is a dream.

"Ah, how romantic. But not even Mack's mind can create something so powerful to break the bond between a father and his *precious* daughter." Roden's voice, coming out of Galen's mouth, congeals the blood in my veins; Galen is gone once again.

"What more do you want from me?" I spit the words out with the same poisonous tone the woman in the green dress had used for me. "Make another deal? Serve you Kris' soul on a silver plate? Join you on the throne to help you turn every soul alive red—puppets you can play with when you feel you're no longer needed?"

Galen's eyes widen, and something - pride - flickers on his grin, but I cannot say if that belongs to my lifetime friend or to Roden.

"You're too ahead of yourself, my child. I created you, but do not think you're special. If I haven't toyed around with another Nistares to repeat my first success, it was only because I found it more entertaining to watch you and this," - he waves a hand at Kris - "*Mistake*—falling in love every time I sent you back to him. Seeing him voluntarily donating part of his soul to you, suffering every time while you harvested a single kernel thinking that that was the very first time while you were - indeed - draining him to death… Ah, that was delightful." Roden forces Galen's hand to his mouth and sucks on a finger as if coated in chocolate.

He stares at me, flashing his sickening smirk between Tabitha and Merya's heads as the two women try to create a wall before me.

The vortex of panic spinning in my head halts. I open my mouth to gasp, but air and words get stuck in my throat.

Click.

"Put that gun back, Horigean. You're so insignificant, I wouldn't even touch you with someone else's hands," Roden snaps at Merya, dragging my attention to the source of that noise. Galen's eyes are so white I can no longer detect any trace of their natural shades. "I'm only here for *her.*"

Roden confidently starts to move towards me, ignoring Tabitha and Merya, curling a finger towards me. "It's time to come back home, my dear."

His words strike something sharp and hot inside me as

revelation sparks. "If you're in Horigos, that means there is no home to go back to." Tears sting in my eyes.

Roden grins. "Clever, little July. It's such a shame your spark of independence and the love for this filthy being carved indents in your otherwise perfect soul. But I can fix that. Now, this was fun, but my time is precious, and yours is… up."

All of a sudden, Roden raises Galen's hands, palms out, in front of his face, and Tabitha and Merya fall to their knees, screaming and covering their ears.

In the corner of my eyes, Jyn and Mack sprint towards us, but Roden slides one hand to his right. "You stay there, I'm not planning to waste time killing you. But I can always spare a minute."

Jyn and Mack are petrified, frozen with only their eyes darting left to right, terror filling them and their nostrils flaring as if struggling to let air in and out.

"And you…" Galen's head turns to an odd angle as if he's trying to stop Roden from moving. The tendons in his neck tense like violin strings when *he* finally looks at Kris and hisses, "Step away, and she will be removed from this place with all her lovely limbs still attached. But remember, I don't need her legs or both arms; her power will be the same even with a bit or two missing."

Kris swears under his breath but doesn't let go of my hand.

In the background, Tabs and Merya's weeping is impossible to ignore. Their shoulders shiver as they try to fight Roden's oppressive weight, keeping them crouched on the floor.

My chest shrinks to a size too small for my hammering heart.

Galen's hand, hovering above Merya and Tabs, closes into a fist. He - no, Roden - smirks a second before the women collapse to the ground—and stop moving.

I charge, ignoring the sense of void when I break contact with Kris. The only thing I can see is Roden's face hiding behind Galen's familiar features. But instead of dodging me, Roden opens Galen's arms wide, exposing his chest and laughing.

The impact with Galen's hard muscles gives me back lucidity, but when it's already too late to rethink my actions.

One moment Kris' loving hand is protecting me; the following, I'm in Galen's arms, Roden spinning me around to press my back against his chest, his heart - Galen's - galloping with fear. Or excitement.

"Please don't hurt them," I whisper, searching the room to check on the others.

Despite Roden having his hands busy with me, Jyn and Mack remain still like statues, still like Tabs and Merya even if their backs slowly rise and fall.

Galen's stubbly jaw tickles my face when Roden lowers it to my ear and grumbles, "I don't take orders from my rebel daughter." He brushes Galen's lips against my cheek before pressing a kiss that makes my stomach roil.

With a silent call, Kris beckons my eyes onto his. He hasn't reacted at all, but his fists are white-knuckled by his side.

"Let us go," I mumble, every word piercing my chest like a hot needle. All I want to do is to close my eyes and pretend nothing is really happening.

But if I block it all out, I will have to say goodbye to those green eyes. The only presence that matters. *The eyes I cannot remember falling in love with...*

Tabitha groans, interrupting my thought.

Roden jerks, flinging an arm towards the sound, causing Kris' low, satisfied growl. "You're not so close as you wanted us to believe, after all. Your power is flickering."

Galen's body twitches against mine. Kris' words must have struck the right point. But his blow is short-lived.

Roden loops an arm around my neck and forces Galen's weight onto my back, pushing forward, past Tabitha and Merya. Something gleams in his hand.

"What? Have you lost your voice?" he taunts Kris, slightly pressing a pocket knife, the one I gifted Galen for his eighteenth birthday, against my neck. It stings and draws blood, but Kris' eyes, turning darker and hopeless, hurt more than anything.

This is how we say goodbye for the very last time.

Chapter 42 - Family Portrait
Kristyon

Everything around me turns black as if thick paint drips from the ceiling, coating everything and everyone in the room but Galen and July. Their silhouettes are neat and defined as my brother holds her against his chest, slowly walking away from me, Roden grinning behind Galen's eyes.

"Good dog, stay, and she will see thousands more days, oblivious of who you were," Roden speaks through my brother's lips, ignoring July's tears rolling down his hand. "But if you try anything stupid…" The same hand moves closer to her neck, the knife grazing the spot he's already scratched.

He doesn't avert his eyes from mine, and his smirk grows larger as if challenging me.

"Where are you taking her?" Tabitha's voice reaches from behind me, hoarse and muffled, but I can't find the courage to check on her and lose sight of July, even if only for a few seconds.

"Nowhere, my dear. I just need to see with Galen's eyes where you rabbits are hiding so I can finally honour you with my *true* presence. Besides, what I do with my daughter is none of your business, but I thought having her with me would make you think twice should you wish to try your luck. I've let you believe you had a say in what's inevitable for too long, but it is now time you learn your place."

"You're a coward," Merya comments hatefully. She's gotten back on her feet but is still suffering from whatever Roden did to her; she clings to my arm unsteadily. "Why don't you tell us where to find you, and *we'll* come to you? One last battle on even ground."

"Don't tease him," I whisper, keeping my eyes on July, her face emotionless if not for the quick shake of her head when Merya tries to push me out of the way and move towards Galen.

"Mummy?"

The frightened voice coming from the main door seems to surprise Roden. For a split second, Galen's eyes shine brown and silver again, but the hope is gone after one blink.

Five short fingers with little orange painted nails curl around the door frame, followed by Sable's sleepy face.

Merya's fingers dig into my arm, and Tabitha hisses to my left while Galen spins around, never letting go of July, giving us a clear view of Sable's terrified face.

"Mum? Why is the pretty lady bleeding?" she asks as tears fill her eyes.

"Sable…" Tabitha mumbles and shoves me away, dashing for her little girl, as if Roden is no longer in the room with us.

She kneels, beckoning Sable inside her protective motherly embrace. "It's okay, little bird. We were just playing *soldiers* like you sometimes do with Mack."

Sable nods but snuffles loudly, hiding her face, now streaked with fat tears, in the space between Tabs' neck and shoulder.

Not far from me, Mack gasps. The unexpected event must have set Roden's focus off balance and broken his hold on Jyn and Mack. But we all know him too well to let our guards down, including July, who remains still and quiet in his dangerous embrace.

Huffing like an increasingly irritated beast, he shuffles towards his left, pivoting enough to regain full control of the room.

"Where has that giant of a man gone? He didn't strike me as the sharpest tool in the room, but I was at least expecting the same idiotic sense of loyalty you other sheep have towards the *great* Tabitha Lorne. Ah well," Roden makes Galen shrug, "One less problem to think about."

Tabitha turns cautiously, protecting Sable's innocent eyes from Roden, even if he's wearing Galen's features. Rage gleams on her face, but also a satisfied smile, which I understand when I look in the mirror above her head. The spot by the backdoor where Jyn had frozen under Roden's power is empty; Jyn? Gone.

"You're letting your emotions have the best of you, *daddy*—" July starts before a sudden jerk of Galen's arms knocks the air out of her lungs and makes my blood boil.

"Mummy, daddy… What a perfect family we would make if you'd only understand what a waste of time your dreams and hopes are. But, *no*… you had to play the part of the misunderstood children…" Roden sighs, lowering his gaze to Tabs and clicking his tongue in annoyance. "And look what your choices brought you—friends with defective blood and a child who will soon blame you for her mediocre existence."

His words would break everyone's last string of patience. But Tabs is made of a substance stronger than steel because she's a mother.

"Let *him* go," she orders with a stern voice, even though I'm sure her whole essence is crumbling, her strength wavering when she raises her eyes to mine. "I'm sorry, but I cannot let him hurt Sable…"

My mouth goes dry when I read the lack of hope in Tabitha's eyes. The choice that, like a claw, tightens around her heart and mind as she slowly gets back on her feet with Sable in her arms, caressing her head and dotting her cheek with quick, soothing kisses.

I follow her eyes when she eventually looks at July, mouthing a voiceless *Sorry* and stepping away from the kitchen door.

"Tabs, no! There is nothing - nobody - protecting her out there. This will only give him the opportunity and the time to land on Horigos in his own time and gather the entire continent against us," Merya cries out, automatically searching for Mack.

Galen's dark laugh, so alien and distant, makes me shiver. "After everything you saw, you still think I need a *continent* to tear you down? My dear, dear, silly child. Come to find me later, and I'll teach you a lesson about humility. Here's a little taste: We'll all experience the unfairness of life at some point. You'd better kick it in the teeth before it bites too deep. Now, if you'll excuse me..."

In the moment that follows, all I can think of is July. Her eyes, lost in mine, glinted with rage and disgust, but also something else. An increasing look of annoyance mixed with exasperation.

The plan she concocted while we were all too busy arguing with Roden becomes clear when it's already too late for me to try and stop her.

"I think that's a valid lesson, *father*." She straightens her spine against Galen's chest. "And the only one I would ever thank you for."

With a single move, fluid and precise, she bends her knees, dropping like a dead weight, sliding off Galen's cruel embrace and sinking her teeth into his bare forearm, ignoring the knife too close to her face.

I leap forward, but chaos explodes around me with a mixture of frenzied, overlapping voices that only stop when a firearm goes off.

Something hard hits the floor, followed by Mack's muffled swearing as he drops next to me, on his belly and with his hands over his head. "Women are reckless! This is why I'll always prefer an octopus over a girlfriend."

Chapter 43 - Game of Secrets
July

Biting someone with rage is undoubtedly painful for the person you want to hurt. But an arm full of muscles and tendons is not like attacking the tender meat of some grilled chicken.

Galen groans in pain when I lock my jaw, and my teeth lacerate his flesh. But my gums also scream in agony, as if my teeth were pushed back inside my skull.

Blood spurts in my mouth, and I retch, letting go of his arm as my eyes tear up, concealing for a second the chaos happening all around me.

I slump on the floor, hitting my knees on the hard tiles and spitting red saliva. My ears ring with the sound of Galen's pain like the aftermath of an explosion.

"She's bleeding—"

"She's alive and, *clearly*, capable of defending herself. Don't overreact. Mack? Shut that door, and—*you*—stop blinking like a fool in love and drop that ridiculous knife. July managed to break the connection with Roden, but we don't know for how long."

"Fuck!" Looking at the knife as if holding a ball of fire, Galen drops it and scrambles away from it - and from me - shaking his head. "You don't know the half of it. Roden was in my head... But I was in his as well." He winces, his voice weakening with every word.

"We don't need to," Kris laughs bitterly but with a hint of worry. "If half of his plan was to threaten the life of his own daughter, I don't even want to hear the rest of it. Besides, nothing simmering inside Roden's mind will ever make any sense."

For a moment, the only noise in the room is that of nervous breaths, like wind rolling over a soon-to-be battleground.

I try to push myself up slowly, but fall back down when Galen swears in pain, ignoring Sable's presence.

"What the fuck have you done?" he yells, staring at someone behind me before throwing his head back, hissing in pain as his hands stretch for his right leg, a pool of blood quickly spreading from under it. "I would have never allowed him to hurt her... I cannot... This fucking hurts, Merya!"

I jerk my head to the right, wincing when the thin cut on my neck reopens, and look up at Merya, still holding a smoking gun in her hand.

A sudden wind bursts from the window over the kitchen sink, carrying the scent of distant rain and surprising everyone, including Tabitha, who must have flattened herself against the wall when Merya fired to protect Sable, now howling in her mum's arms.

"For soul's sake, Merya, two inches to the left, and that would've been me," she shouts, her naturally rosy cheeks flushing with a darker shade of panic.

"But it wasn't… Hey! You stay down, or I swear, next time, I'll put a hole in your chest. Roden is clever, and I still need to decide if you're *you* again."

I struggle to tear my eyes away from Merya when a hand gently cups one side of my face.

"You're okay," Kris' voice soothes my senses, his gaze as soft as his touch.

… falling in love every time I sent you back to him. Roden's words come back to me, and for a moment, I let myself dive into Kris' eyes, setting aside the image of Galen bleeding. But it's hard to ignore Merya and Tabs bickering over Merya's reckless decision to use a gun in such a small space, Galen's increasing demand for help and Sable crying her eyes out.

I gently take Kris' hand and lower it before getting back on my feet and filling my lungs with air. "Enough!" I shout with all the despair I've so far nested inside.

Everyone stops talking, even Sable, who hides her face against Tabs' neck, whimpering. I feel a bit guilty, but if she's half as strong as her mother, she will get over it.

"Do you want to keep talking about something we can't go back to and stop and let Galen bleed to death? Or would you like to hear what *I* felt while Roden was acting like a megalomaniac father of the year?"

"Wow, I like this new July even more." Mack sits on the floor cross-legged and elbows Kris in the ribs.

I cautiously approach Galen, who's managed to rest his back against the wall but whose face is increasingly turning pale and tired. Our eyes find each other, and his gaze drops to the thin red line on my neck, darkening with sorrow.

"I'd like a few minutes alone with Galen," I ask, trying to keep at bay the memory of Roden spitting hate from Galen's mouth. Trying to ignore the thin, milky veil slowly disappearing from my best friend's eyes.

I'm glad nobody can hear my heart, or they will know how stupidly scared I am to be left alone with him.

"Are you sure?" Tabitha asks, moving away from the wall but keeping a hand on Sable's head. The little girl is now breathing slowly, relaxed, and probably asleep after all the turmoil she had to go through.

I nod, feeling Kris' presence behind me, not invasive, but surely worried. "I'll be fine, and I don't think Roden will be back soon if what I *saw* is true. I promise I'll give you all the details, but there is something I need to discuss with Galen."

Merya walks past me, stopping next to Tabitha. She silently scrutinises me, then Galen, before offering me her gun. "If he tries anything—"

"That won't be necessary," I interrupt her, mainly to rush everyone out of the kitchen, conscious of the blood Galen has already lost.

" I—I'll go check on Jyn. Who knows what that cuddly bear was thinking of doing when he left?!" Mack begins to ease the tension pressing heavily on us with his relentless, friendly ways.

Tabitha nods, directing her words more to Galen than to anyone else. "I need to find somewhere safe to leave Sable, but I'll be back, and Merya will be waiting just outside…"

Having holstered her gun, Merya crosses her arms, scrubbing the floor with the point of her boot and chewing on her cheek. "I meant what I said; if I have the slightest doubt that Roden is still in there, lurking - friends or not—"

"Okay, okay, we get it. You wipe me off the face of Horigos. Got the message; please come back to stitch me up, though." Galen waves a hand before wiping the sweat off his forehead with his sleeve.

His chest rises and falls with a rhythm that speaks more than his eyelids, heavier with every second that passes.

I turn to Kris, fighting the urge to take his hands in mine because if I do, I will never find the strength to let him go. "Ten minutes. Then Merya can fix his leg… Then we *will* talk."

Understanding beats behind his green, crystalline eyes, and a hint of gold starts spreading from his pupils. He bends over, his brow nearly touching mine as he whispers, "Waiting for you is the most exciting part of my life. Until we meet again…" Gentle, shy lips brush my brow, firing the spot on my skin and stealing one of my heartbeats.

I close my eyes to capture that feeling, but when I reopen them, Kris is already by the door, guiding Merya out as she turns her head to give Galen a final threatening look.

Only silence remains once everyone's gone, pressing on me like one of the falling boulders that Galen and I miraculously escaped during our last night in Libera.

"I am sorry," Galen mutters weakly, resting his head against the wall. He tries to stretch a hand towards me, but only lifts it halfway before dropping it with a grunt.

"That wasn't you," I snap, still trying to erase Roden's shadow off Galen's face. "But Merya was right. I *saw* him, Galen. He's moments from Brenath. And he's bringing an army."

His wounded leg twitches, and he bashes his fist on the floor, biting his lip to suffocate the pain.

"Don't move." I dash for the kitchen counter, opening all the drawers and checking all the cupboards. "These will do for now."

I kneel before him, gingerly sliding a clean kitchen cloth under his leg.

When he tries to speak again, I wave a wooden spatula in his face. "I can talk and save your leg at the same time. So, shut up and listen. I know where Roden stashed all the empty Nistarei and Rogues he sent me to harvest all these years. I often wondered how he could dispose of so many bodies, and now I have my answers. Caves! Thousands of them, underground, hidden between The Mother and Corlea."

Galen's throat bobs, either because of my words or the pain as I start tightening the cloth around his leg using the spatula as a home-made tourniquet.

"Yeah, that makes sense—and that's Merya's favourite baking spoon," he hisses, biting his lip.

"You can buy her a whole new set, once we've finished with Roden. In the meantime, tell me what you know of these caves." I lift my hands from the spatula, contemplating for a second the wood slowly turning red with the blood soaking through the cloth.

Galen reaches for my hand, and I let him. "I've only been there once, years ago. There were other Deleteri with me, but after a few months of visiting the caves, they disappeared from Libera. I assume that was a test because that's when Roden gave me a seat in the Chapter. But he'd stopped even mentioning that place years ago. This is why Tabitha decided to station some of her people there; close to the Caves, but not enough to spark Roden's suspicions, in case he was still using them."

I sigh and sit beside him, mirroring his pose and leaning against the wall. "The irony of this fucking shitshow! I was helping Roden create his army while he let me think I was doing something good…" I drag my nails on the terracotta floor to soothe the increasing guilt boiling inside me.

Something rattles inside Galen's chest when he tries to speak, but when I snap my head towards him, he lifts a shaky hand, silently asking me to listen. "This is why I hoped you wouldn't ask for your memories back this time."

"I knew…" I state flatly.

"How?"

"Roden's primary desire wasn't to find this location. Surely, being inside your mind helped him, but he was here for *me*. He wanted to show me the *real me*, at least the version of me he wants me to become, because he knows I hid something in those caves and he wants it back. This is why he's acting so erratically. If he loses me, he loses the war for good. I'm not his weapon, I'm his last chance at survival."

Galen's genuine look of surprise melts my heart. I caress his cheek, softly, scared of hurting him by only breathing near him. "You're not the only one who's good at keeping secrets. I need to speak with Kris and Tabitha urgently. Before Roden reaches Brenath. I'll get Merya. You - well - stay here."

I get on my feet, feeling light as if I've just discarded a bunch of stones rattling inside my heart, slowly grinding it into dust.

I'm not surprised when, popping my head outside the door, I notice Merya waiting at the end of the long corridor, leaning against the wall with her arms crossed.

"Did you hear enough, or do you need me to repeat everything?"

She pushes away from the wall, flipping her copper hair over one shoulder. "Enough to know that my favourite baking spoon has served a higher purpose. And that, *you*, Crimson, have a lot of talking to do."

Chapter 44 - Us
July

The night swept over us, silent and shy, settling our souls and helping our minds regain some lucidity after Roden's unexpected appearance.

Once I'm sure Galen will not lose his leg, thanks to Merya's mending skills, I end my watch with a soft kiss on my friend's forehead. My mind has been such a cauldron of memories lately that whatever Galen and I had in Libera feels like a story belonging to strangers.

I brush away a lock of hair from his eyes, and he stirs in his bed, mumbling something that only makes sense in his dreams.

When I exit his room, the corridor's soft and warm penumbra welcomes me, accompanying me as I descend the stairs to the ground level.

There is only one place that may stop my thoughts from stirring wildly, and forget about Roden for a little while. When I open the kitchen's back door, it shimmers in the distance, calling me, and I can't run fast enough to reach its shore.

When I'm finally by the lake, its surface is so still it's hard not to confuse it for a solid slab of glass. Mack warned me against breathing too close to it, but what if I dipped an inch of my finger to ensure this is real water?

I only need to lean forward a bit more…

"Having your memories fully back will stop you from even looking at this thing."

I curl my hands against my chest and inhale so deeply that something acrid burns my nostrils. I immediately step away, lingering before slowly turning towards Kris.

His face carries the signs of what we all had to endure lately; there are shadows under his eyes, and his hair is tousled, but nothing seems to have cracked his smile. The same I met when he jumped off the tree, the same I glimpsed in my dreams.

"How is he?" He runs his hand through his hair and crouches over the grass that turns yellow the closer to the lake. "Let me guess—yapping, pretending he doesn't need to be kept under constant supervision?" Kris rolls a pebble between his fingers before throwing it into the lake. It skips a couple of times, causing a trail of smoke, until the acidic waters consume it to a bunch of dust.

I step behind him. "He was asleep when I left. Mack is with him now."

Kris scoffs, "Tabitha toyed with the idea of locking him up for an hour or two, just to be safe. But I convinced her not to…"

The sound of the grass changes beneath my feet as I step on the leaves whose life has been destroyed by the poisonous waters, and I sit next to Kris. "I saw the key around his neck—thank you."

He shrugs, dismissing his gesture as the most normal thing to do, and lifts his gaze to the wall beyond the lake. "If Roden is really getting close, the range of protection of those keys will soon be nothing but a pleasant shock tickling his mind. It won't stop him…"

"What about you?" I mumble, mostly to keep the Roden subject away from our conversation for a little while.

"Still here," he stretches his legs before him, throwing his head back to study the cloudless night sky.

I copy him, testing the ground to find a soft spot. "Have you ever thought about disappearing, from everyone, from all of this?"

I regret asking when he stops staring at the sky to focus on me.

"From you?" he exhales, letting go of something he's been holding in for almost a lifetime.

I take in his expression, unable to say anything for what feels like an eternity. His lips are slightly apart, as if the weight of his answer is still affecting him. His imperfect haircut casts a shadow over his face, yet some of his traits still manage to shine through: the straight profile of his nose, similar to Galen's but slightly raised at the tip, his long lashes, a tone lighter than his brother's, the smirk growing at one side of his mouth…

He huffs a laugh and bumps his shoulder to mine. "Some may say staring is rude, but you can keep going if you want. Although we have some pressing matters to discuss."

I blink. Blink again. "Oh, my… I wasn't—I was, wasn't I?"

"You certainly *are* many things, July Crimson, but rude is none of them." His subtle smile turns quickly into a roaring laugh that spreads over the lake and echoes around us.

My body responds before I can stop it, and I find myself laughing with him, shaking with the need to let go for once and feel normal again.

When the moment has passed, all that's left is silence and *us*.

"Roden found me, every single time. When all this started, I tried running away, creating a new identity, and hiding in the most remote part of Horigos. He could sense me wherever I went, but somehow he was only able to hurt me for a while, to send his power straight into my soul like a sword until I'd bled for days from this wound in my chest. But he never managed to kill me."

"That must have been daunting; waking up every day not knowing if Roden would try again or leave you be." I study his profile, the slight twitch of his eyebrows.

He nods, leaning back on his hands, swaying left and right. "For some time, I managed to build a normal life in the northernmost part of The Mother, among the rebels. And Roden did stay away from me for a while; I thought he had given up. I knew who he was, my adoptive father told me, but I didn't know why he loved to make me suffer so much. That was probably the question I kept asking myself: what did I do wrong to deserve this?"

As he tells me his story, probably one I've heard many times and forgotten about, I can't stop thinking about how at ease he seems around me despite our many pasts.

He gathers one leg to his chest, resting his chin on his knee and smiling at me sideways. "I lived a boring, unflavoured life for a while. Until, one day, this *wonderful* woman showed up in my life, trying to end it and failing—every time. The worst part was that she would always come back, and repeat the same action without remembering my face, the sound of my voice, or the addictive effect her smile had on me..."

A wince, my lips twitching. As if all my thoughts have suddenly appeared in capital letters on my face, he tilts his head, narrowing his eyes.

"Am I sharing too much? I thought that might help with your memories," he says as he reaches out with his right hand and stops mere inches from my fingertips.

"I know that's not true," I blurt out to cut the awkward silence.

"Oh..." He averts his gaze. The moonlight, bumping off the lake, casts a silver sheen over his face.

I crawl closer to him, fearing my confession will travel too far should I speak too loudly. "I know what's in the caves. I know what *we* have done and kept a secret from the others. The only thing I still don't understand is *why?* If we share it with Tabitha, she may help us find a way out. Because I don't want to take any more of your soul... I can't."

His hand finally finds mine, and I forget how to breathe when his eyes bore into mine.

"What about all those souls we could save together? Do we abandon them to find *our* happiness?" His voice drops, echoing in his chest and melting mine.

"What? No, I didn't mean to abandon everyone and forget about what Roden did to us…"

He arches a brow, pivoting to face me fully. "What do you want to do with your life, July Sofia Crimson? With your power?"

"Oh…" It's all I can say. I really want to tell him I hate that name, even if I don't know why, but it sounds right when he says it.

A little smile blooms on his lips, and I hope it's not because of my puzzled expression.

Realising I've been on all fours for too long, staring at Kris like an idiot, I sit back. "I want to make it count, but I don't want to hurt you again." I swing my focus from the dark waters before me to the tall walls running around the building.

In the corner of my eye, Kris moves closer to me, his breath warm on my cheek as he whispers, "What hurts me the most is knowing that Roden made you forget about *us*—"

I gasp, and the grass to my left swishes. A solitary frog jumps at my feet, dangerously close to the lake. I instinctively lunge forward to grab it, but Kris' hand is on mine before I can save the little creature.

"What are you doing? I'm not really keen to see a living creature bursting into dust like that pebble earlier." I glare at him, surprised by his lack of compassion.

He is smiling. He's about to let that frog die, and he's freaking smiling while the little red creature leaps towards the water trap.

"Just wait. Before you go chasing it, how many red, furry frogs have you seen before?" His hand gently pinning mine down.

"None but that's not the point. Would you let me save it if it were bright yellow?" I frown.

He purses his lips, averting his eyes to look everywhere but at me.

"And you are about to laugh at me because…?" I cock my head.

With a single, high croak as if to catch our attention, the frog inflates its throat, swipes its webbed feet across its eyes, and jumps, spreading its limbs in the air, gliding over the lake.

I blink and rub my eyes like a giant, human frog.

"Forget about red frogs, have you ever seen one doing *that*?" Kris slowly releases my hand when he's sure I will not run after the animal.

I quickly stand up to follow the creature's journey as it lifts higher, no longer gliding but flying, until it is so far that I can barely distinguish its little feet flapping like wings.

Slowly, I turn to Kris. "That's a Mack Frog."

Kris's eyes grow teary as he tries his best not to laugh in my face. "Sure, we can call it that from now on. That's a scout. They're handy when we don't want to venture outside. Mack has his own little army of frogs, birds - you want to stay away from those entitled beasts by the way - mice… worms, even, but they're only good for overgrown bushes."

I secretly thank the dark for masking my blushing face. I probably wouldn't be in this situation if I had my memories. But I don't need to remember everything to know what a scout on a mission means.

As though reading my thoughts, Kris studies the lake's surface with worry. "If that frog is flying outside the perimeter, Mack must have spotted something on the cameras. It may be nothing, perhaps a random *real* animal approaching too close to the fences. It's happened before."

He pulls back his hair, staring at the wall, and holds up a finger, kindly asking me to stay quiet for a moment.

"We should go back inside," he mutters, beckoning me closer.

I do as he asks, also following my gut feeling, which is shouting to run back to the building. "I thought the fences were strong enough to stop anything from breaching the walls.

"They have been because Roden has never managed to locate this place. We don't know the range of his power… your power. What he did to my brother, without being physically close to him… he could do the same to everyone in here that has Harvester blood. He can't control Horigeans—but we are his product."

To my ears, his explanation is almost perfect, except for one small missing detail.

"That means… I could do the same to him. Hurt him like he did to you. To us. Without being near him."

His face lights up, and he stops running his fingers nervously through his hair to stare at me instead.

Without notice, he devours the space between us and grabs my hands. "I forgot how good it feels when you say it…"

"What?" I squeak, forgetting I can speak like an adult.

"… us."

"Oh…"

His skin against mine is more than I can take, more than my mind can endure without coming undone. My hands in his find the perfect fit as an image slowly pushes to the surface. We've been here before, many times, by this lake—just the two of us.

A net of light flows from my palms up to my arms and all around us, but Kris doesn't seem to be scared. It's warm and comforting, and it speaks to me.

It's telling me to go ahead and that this is the right thing to do. For me, Kris and the rest of Horigos. I wriggle my fingers until I'm the one holding his hands. Tight. Tighter. And when his eyes widen, staring at me with a hint of dread, I realise I'm harvesting *his* light.

His soul.

I drop his hands, inhaling sharply, and pulling back, hiding my face in my hands. "No, I don't want this…" I shake my head, turning my back to him.

A firm but gentle touch weighs down on my shoulders.

"What was that?" I ask, my voice so weak, I struggle to hear myself.

Kris gently spins me around, tilting his head, with a soft smile. "You've just relived our last night together. Somehow, you remembered."

"I was harvesting your soul…" I blink, agape. I was willingly stealing his life, without my vials, no tools—only my bare hands.

I fight the urge to push him away. What if I touch him and take what's left of his soul by accident? I try to withdraw from his grip, but he remains unfazed.

"July, stop."

My body responds. I close my eyes, hoping my guilt won't show anywhere else.

"Look at me." He brushes my cheek with his knuckles.

"I made you suffer like Roden. Worse than Roden did to you. I…"

My face collides with his chest. His smell reminds me of Galen, but there is something else beneath, something feral that everybody should be frightened of—but me. His arms are strong around me, but his hand is protective when it dives through my hair, keeping me safe and hidden from the rest of the world.

"I gave it to you. And I would do it again if that's the only way for you to return to me, a hundred times again."

I blink furiously, tears running down my face, wetting his shirt. I sob like a child, unable to speak but half words, undefined sounds of pain, joy, relief and fear.

He keeps stroking my hand in silence, letting me take everything in—the deepest meaning of his confession, the worrying realisation of it.

"It's still in the caves… I've never given it back," I mumble against him, pressing my right cheek against his chest, staring at the lake.

I look up; his sweet, resigned smile breaks my heart instantly. "It was the only way to convince Roden that you tried, obeyed his orders, and kept yourself safe. This is why you hid my soul in those caves. The idea that you made me suffer was enough for him. And when he found out the shards of soul you brought back to him weren't mine, he let you continue because he gloated at seeing us trying to work against him."

I bite my lower lip, closing my eyes at the image of it.

"But you didn't." He pinches my chin lightly, and I find the courage to look at him again. "You could never hurt me. I'm happy for you to take what's left of my soul because, even when I'm no more, part of me will always breathe, laugh, and love. In here…"

His right hand lowers to my heart, hovering above it, but I pull it against me as he falls silent, studying my movements.

Warm vibrations hum and thrum, flowing inside me from where our bodies connect.

"How have I forgotten about you?" I mumble.

"You didn't. Not completely. Roden doesn't have the power to control you like he thinks. I know you could see me. Feel me." Kris bows his head, a lock of his hair tickling my brow.

"Only when I was sleeping, when my mind wasn't fighting to keep your memory away. Because if I remembered while in Libera…"

"Roden would have seen it too," he finishes my sentence.

An uncontrollable feeling of loss spreads through me, and I snap my head up. "How much have you got left?" I break the contact to move back and take his beautiful face in fully.

"Enough to be here with you one last time. To hold you one last time."

He follows every word with one small step towards me.

"To kiss you one last time." His lips graze my cheek. His smell overpowers me, sending my mind spiralling into lovely darkness.

"To tell you one last time that I—"

"No, don't—" I stand on my tiptoes to press a finger on his mouth. "I'm not taking whatever's left of your soul, even if only to keep it safe. This is madness. There must be another way."

"Don't you think we've never tried before?"

"We can try again."

Kris sighs through his nose, gathering my hands and kissing one, then the other. "July, things are happening faster, and I believe Roden has a plan to strike harder this time. We don't know how much time we have left, but I don't want to waste even a minute of our last life together talking about what-ifs."

My brain goes blank. Then starts working again. Fast. Spinning.

In the darkness surrounding us, his eyes almost glow, light green and gold, alive, hungry, when he tilts his head, closing the distance between our faces.

And my brain finally finds some peace.

"I'm sorry to interrupt... *this*, but there's something you need to see. Someone, *actually*. She's outside the fences, shouting for Tabs to come out, and I'm afraid she'll remain there until her lungs can hold. Also—she holds one of my frogs hostage."

I wiggle free from Kris' arms and, patting my face with the back of my hands, I smirk at Mack. In the cold moonlight, the scar above his lip twitches as he looks down at his hands and the grass beneath his feet.

"It's okay, Mack." I pat his shoulder. "Do we know what this stranger wants from Tabs? Does she look in danger—or threatening?"

Mack shakes his head, his friendly smile back where it legitimately belongs. "She looks *rough*, but I swear those orange eyes pierced through the cameras. She scares me and Rary."

"Rary?"

"My frog."

"Right," Kris jumps in, looping his arm around Mack's shoulders. "Let's go save Rary from the scary lady."

Chapter 45 - For Rary
July

The atmosphere inside the house is worse than expected. Internal alarms must have gone off simultaneously when the stranger approached the barriers, their deafening echo whistling louder the closer we get to a door with no handle or lock.

But when Mack presses his thumb on a spot on the sleek metal, at his heart level, the door *purrs* like a kitten happy to see its owner back, and slides open inside the wall.

"Where is Tabitha? Why didn't you go straight to her?" Kris pants as we rush down the stairs towards a subterranean wing of the building.

"I couldn't find her anywhere, you silly," Mack argues, waving a hand in the air, marching a few steps ahead of us. "Maybe she just needed some time away from all of us after the awful trick Roden played on her. I still can't believe…"

"Mack, one thing at a time. Don't let your mind go after every single thought you have in there." Kris stops him, landing a hand on his shoulder.

We come to a halt in front of another locked door.

Mack speaks to us without turning, "She's gone after Merya told her Galen would survive. What if Roden broke her? What if she couldn't take it anymore and decided to leave us for good?"

"Mack?" I step in front of him, searching for his eyes. "Would you like to show me how this wonderful door works? I bet this is one of your creations as well."

His face lights up with a large smile. "I know what you're trying to do. Distracting me to put me back on the right track."

"Is it working?" I smirk.

"Of course it is, *I* taught you what to do when my mind goes on a trip of its own."

Kris clears his throat, but I don't have time to investigate his reaction because I'm suddenly trapped inside Mack's hug. My feet lift a few inches off the floor, and something sparks in my mind.

Mack and I are sitting next to each other in a tunnel, his arm covering my head. He whispers that everything is going to be fine. A whistle grows louder in the background before turning into the roaring sound of an explosion.

I gulp in some air, and Mack puts me down gingerly.

He stumbles back while Kris' face fills in the space where Mack was until a second ago.

"Another memory?" he asks, leaning in to brush my cheekbone as if it's the most natural thing.

I nod, still catching my breath. "I… I think so. An explosion outside a tunnel similar to the one we used to come here." I slide my eyes to Mack, who's staring at me agape. "You were there with me."

"Mack, what is happening? That memory doesn't even belong to her." There is urgency and worry in Kris' voice.

"It's your soul, Kris. What's left of it," Mack replies after a moment. "I've been thinking about this since your last visit." He glances at the metal door, then tilts his head to address me. "July's mind had to adapt to bits of your soul being hosted inside her, to make space. We don't know what memories the Deleteri took from her, and we don't even know if they could distinguish between what belonged to her and what were, instead, traces of your own life."

I pinch my lower lip, nodding as everything begins to make sense. "Perhaps, some of my memories simply went to sleep, and the Deleteri couldn't take them because they weren't even available for me."

"Correct!" Mack snaps his fingers. "But that means that your mind is probably nearly over maximum capacity and is pushing out all the memories you unconsciously laid to sleep. Tabitha probably knew as well, and that's why she wanted you to retrieve your past lives as soon as possible, to avoid some sort of mental explosion." Mack mimics the image of a bomb going off, clenching his fists above his head, then spreading his fingers wide in the air.

Kris starts pacing back and forth, nodding at some internal mind-dialogue. Then he comes to a halt, snaps his head at Mack and marches towards him. "My friend, you're a genius!" he exclaims, smacking a kiss on Mack's forehead before moving his attention to me.

"Let's see what that trespasser wants from Tabitha first, before they attract too much attention." He's next to me in one step, so close, yet not enough. "Then, we *will* discuss our next move. And if Tabs is half as clever as I think she is, I probably know where she's gone. If I'm right, you won't need to harvest the last of my soul, but you will need to retrieve what's in those caves." He smiles, losing his gaze into mine.

"Ah, the caves—" Mack blinks like a child who's just discovered his voice.

Before he can add anything else, I open my arms, scrunching my face to hide the guilt of - most likely - the biggest elephant in the room. "I may have hidden bits of Kris' soul in the caves under The Mother…"

I wait for Mack to snap, to tell me I acted irresponsibly, abandoning his friend's soul so close to enemy territory.

Instead, he studies me, tapping his finger to his nose. "If you would let me finish… We came up with that *majestic* plan together, Missy *Forgetty*." Mack slams a hand on the door, making us jump, then braces himself, reminding me of a pangolin. "Sorry, Kris, I couldn't tell anyone else. I didn't know if and when Roden might burst into our minds, and I didn't have enough protection keys. But—yeah, we need to retrieve your soul as soon as possible."

Something gurgles in my stomach. "Mack? What happens if we leave it there for too long?"

When Mack's face goes dark, I regret asking.

"A soul, even if powerful like yours and Kris', needs a vessel.

And if it doesn't have one, it will do whatever it takes to find one. The idea was to infuse Reds with a drop of Kris' soul because he's the only one who can purify them—"

"But?" I urge him.

"But you refused even to try because you didn't want to lose him… So you locked part of his soul in the caves and then - well - you forgot where exactly. And because you didn't show anyone, that's a memory hard to unlock—even for me!" Mack lowers his eyes, tousling his hair in distress.

Kris brushes my back with his fingertips, but I instinctively shy away. "I'm selfish as much as the monster that created me," I mumble, but the shape of the staircase carries my voice away.

"That monster made me shoot my best friend. Not you!" Merya booms from the top of the stairs, with Galen beside her, a bit pale and holding himself against the wall, but alive.

"I'm not sure you noticed, but there is a woman out there, in what looks like very expensive silk pyjamas, shouting for Tabitha. She also keeps yelling that she left all her nice clothes on fucking Libera!" Merya stomps down the stairs, followed by Galen, his expression changing rapidly from worried to shocked, like mine, when Merya mentioned the island.

"That's not possible," Galen and I say at once.

"Unless… If Roden is on his way to Horigos, Libera is just a pile of dust sinking to the bottom of the sea, but that doesn't mean Roden is travelling alone. He's probably sent scouts all over Horigos to find us. His brief visit in my head may have given him a hint of our location," Galen adds, pausing midway to rest his wounded leg.

"Quick, Mack, open that door," Merya jumps off the last two steps, waving at her brother, who doesn't wait for her to ask again.

He quickly turns around, facing the door as a ray of red light shoots out from a minuscule hole in the metal surface, straight into Mack's right eye.

While Mack steps away, the door starts sliding to the left. Cold blue light pours out of a dusty room, lined with giant monitors transmitting images from the building's outside perimeter and, kneeling on the ground, only mere inches from the fences that nearly killed me—Lucretia.

"Can I speak to her? How do I—is this a speaker..." My eyes dart over the complex control panel in the middle of the room.

"I wouldn't touch that, unless she is someone you really hate," Mack gently nudges me away before I can push a black button.

"Do something, please. Tell her to stay there until *you* pick her up," I implore him, and almost forget that it's Lucretia's life I'm begging for.

"I do what?" Mack shakes his head, confused.

"Right, you know that woman." Merya saunters between Mack and me, studying me first, then Galen, who's stalling by the entrance. "But we don't. Why should we let her in?"

"Because I will vouch for her," Galen mumbles. "Lucretia can be frustrating and a tad selfish, but she's not a spy, if that's what you're afraid of. Mack, please open the comms channel before she attracts unwanted eyes."

Mack's finger brushes a red switch but lingers while he scans Galen from head to toes. "I'm only doing it for Rary," he snaps, flipping a switch and lowering over a small, round black speaker. "Hey, you, do as I say if you want to live."

Mack's voice sounds normal to our ears, but the speakers' volume must be louder because Lue stops shouting and springs back on her feet, holding something in her cupped hands.

"Yes—what? Tabitha? I'm looking for Tabitha Lorne." She moves dangerously close to the fence.

"No, stay there," I can't control myself and shout into the speaker.

Lucretia snaps her head back, looking up at the building's skeleton, her eyes darting left to right searching for the source of my voice.

"July?" she mumbles, pulling her hands to her heart. "Is that you?"

I glance at Mack, silently asking permission to use the control panel, and he nods, offering me some space.

"Lue, you need to listen to me. Stop yelling and don't touch anything. Someone is coming for you. They will bring you inside, but you must swear you're alone."

Her tiny image on the monitor shrugs. She nods a few times,

looks behind her and drops her head. "I am now. Miss Popplewish was with me, but…" By coincidence, she makes eye contact with one of the hidden cameras; her eyes are red, tired, and her face is covered in scratches. "I think she betrayed us."

Everything becomes silent. Not a heartbeat, not a breath.

My finger is stuck on the switch, my neck so rigid it hurts when I look behind me, at the line of stunned faces that, like me, are fighting back the weight of Lucretia's words.

Chapter 46 - The Deserving Ones
Lucretia

I stop screaming, not because someone who sounds precisely like July has told me to, but because I don't want to ruin my voice.

I distractedly caress the weird frog's little head, its soft fur oddly soothing against the cuts and scratches on my fingers, while I wait for someone to pay me attention.

Eventually, another voice speaks to me. "Do not touch the building, do not get any closer. To be clear, whatever you're thinking of doing, just don't. And, please, let Rary go."

The sound comes from everywhere as if this disgrace of a building is talking to me. "Fine, and, for the record, I wouldn't even brush a finger against this *thing* covered in moss and surely infested by every sort of insect." I look at the frog in my hands. "Rary?"

A confident bark comes through my fingers, and a skinny webbed foot pops out between my thumb and forefinger. As much as I like the effect of the frog's skin on my wounds, I kneel and gingerly open my hands to let it go. The frog hops away, trilling and chirping.

"Done," I push myself up, patting my knees and wincing when my raw skin scrapes against my silk trousers. My legs also ache, and my left knee has been throbbing since I fell badly on it while running away from the people who tried to capture me, after Popplewish and I got separated in Brenath, after having fled a burning Libera… My eyes sting at the memory of it.

I press a finger on my swollen knee and hiss, clenching my jaw.

"Are you—nope, clearly you're not okay."

That voice again, only closer, younger and… *friendly?*

I look up to find someone who wasn't there a moment ago, standing only inches from me. "How did you?" I tilt my head to the side, searching for a door, some sort of entrance to the destroyed building.

With the moon setting at his back, the young man's silhouette radiates an impossible shade of copper and silver, from his hair to the freckles on his smiley face to his silly orange shirt.

"You're not Tabitha Lorne." *And who sounds silly now?*

"I hope not," he quickly assesses his statement by touching his face and chest before rushing to offer me his hand.

I swat his hand away, cursing silently as pain explodes in my body with every slightest movement. "Don't touch me, I can manage."

His face drops, "I'm sorry, I thought you needed—Thanks for letting Rary go, by the way."

I look him straight in his boyish, cerulean eyes. "I don't need anything *and*… You're Horigean, what are you doing with Tabitha

Lorne?" I move closer to better study him and make him blush.

"Was that July Crimson I heard?"

He nods, seemingly happy for me to change the subject. "She asked me to come and save…"

I narrow my eyes.

"Show you the entrance."

"Well then?" I raise my arm to jab him in the shoulder, but stop when I notice something bulging on my wrist.

He promptly steps back, pointing at my hand. "That needs my sister's knowledge, and I'd like to know *how* you and July are friends," he comments, ignoring my insulted face and giving me his back.

"I'm Mack, by the way."

"We're not friends," I snap. "And I'm not interested in hearing another word from you." I trudge behind him.

"Are you sure this is the way?" I observe my surroundings, unsure whether to turn around and run in the opposite direction.

My head starts pounding.

"If this is another trap…" I blurt after Mack.

He glances at me from over his shoulder, bringing two fingers to his lips and turning an invisible key at the corner of his mouth before theatrically tossing it away.

"Fantastic," I grumble, picking up my pace, surpassing him by a few steps, but before I can get any closer to the decrepit building, he nudges me away, waving his hands in my face.

"This is ridiculous. Speak, you weird Horigean, before I pluck your soul from your body," I command, puffing light purple breath in his face.

He releases a loud sigh, hands on his hips, scrunching his lips. "You don't look like the type of person surrounded by friends, but for some reason July thinks we should listen to you… Interesting."

His words strike something inside me I don't even want to contemplate. Dealing with betrayal from my own people is one thing. Arguing with a simple Horigean, so openly rude, is something I can only discuss after a shower, food and my beauty sleep.

Despite him still staring at me, immobile, the skeleton of rust and stones at his back starts creaking and hissing.

"Follow me, but don't touch me. I don't want a *molecule* of my soul to end up in your hands."

His voice sounds like that of a child mimicking an adult.

"You know I'm a Harvester, right? You know what *I* could do to you?"

But as I rant after him, louder with every word, he takes a step back and disappears in thin air, leaving me agape.

"Just keep walking, Harvester. The fences won't be down for long. Your choice. Follow me and live to keep listing the bad things you could do to me, or…" His disembodied voice fades away. "Stay there, friendless, hurt and smelling awful!"

"Take them off me!" I frantically pat every inch of my body, shaking my head upside down as hundreds of invisible little legs crawl over me and under my clothes.

"Those are not creepy crawlies, you squeamish Harvester. Only millions of highly trained, thinking particles of electricity." Mack chortles, standing crossed-arms in the centre of a vast hall with three doors. "After a while, you'll get used to it. It's actually *pleasant* if you learn to enjoy it. It makes you feel alive."

His tone is relaxed, despite our earlier altercation.

"What is this sorcery?" I pant, brushing my hair off my face.

"Says the one who threatened to suck my soul a moment ago. No magic, Harvester, just genius."

He's mocking me. He's irritating me. So much so that I briefly forgot why I had even come here in the first place.

In the dim light of the atrium, warming up the naked walls and the simple terracotta floor, Mack no longer resembles the young, annoying boy I met outside. He owns the space, as he marches from one door to the other, making sure they're all locked.

When he gets to the third one, at the end of a short corridor dividing the hall into two hemispheres, the door *purrs?* under his touch and slides open. "This way, Harvest—"

"Lucretia, for fuck's sake. My name is Lucretia. Stop calling me that."

He cuts a smirk from over his shoulder. "Oh, don't worry. I know your name."

"Mack, stop teasing her and come down now."

A female voice I don't recognise resounds from a hidden speaker above us.

"Boring soul," he mumbles, taking the stairs behind the door and slowly descending, disappearing from my view.

I hurry after him as much as my sore feet allow me. The staircase is well lit and, to my great relief, has only ten or twelve steps before it ends in another door, which Mack holds ajar, waiting for me at the bottom of the stairs. A slice of light flows from under it, disturbed by someone moving behind it.

"After you, Lucretia."

I hold Mack's mocking stare until the imposing female voice speaks again. "We don't have the whole day."

Mack pushes the door completely open, and my eyes widen.

Galen and July are standing with their backs against a flashing, beeping control panel. Next to Galen, a stranger, is another woman who shares Mack's colours and annoying smirk.

"Finally," she exhales, "Mack, restrain her."

My jaw drops, and - it can be a trick of the light - but Galen and July seem to share my reaction.

But Mack nudges me gently to one side, stepping before me. "Excuse my dramatic sister," he sighs with a hand to his heart. "Merya, you can't be serious. She's one against all of us, her wrist is probably broken and - I mean - look at the state of her!"

I scoff, averting my eyes from the back of his shirt, clinging to his lean but broad shoulders.

The woman he's just called Merya studies him, then her ice blue eyes fall on me. "She's a Harvester." She bares her teeth, disgusted, before addressing Galen and July, "No offence."

"None taken," they answer in unison.

"And her wrist is *simply* torn," she adds after looking at my hand.

"Broken or not, she's wounded and clearly in pain. Shouldn't we let her talk and understand how she knows Tabitha is here and why she's looking for her?" Mack asks.

I give him a nod and guide my eyes across the room, silently asking everyone for permission to talk.

Moving slowly, as if close to a wild animal, Mack pushes a chair towards me, and I fall onto it, exhausted.

"I'm not a threat," I tell them, uncertain whether they'll believe me when I'm the first to doubt myself.

I feel July's eyes on me—another person I cannot yet place on my already extremely shrunken list of amicable acquaintances.

Leaning against the panel, arms folded and with a bandaged leg, Galen breaks the wall of awkwardness that divides me from these people. "How did you get here?"

"Miss Popplewish told me the way before we got separated…"

"Evelyn knows this place?" July's confusion matches mine as I'm still trying to understand how Miss Popplewish could be involved with the rebels we've often heard about.

I nod and let it all out. "We took a pod and abandoned Libera because it was on fire, and we got chased by bad people… And they followed us to Brenath… I watched a video… I think it's my fault… and then—Popplewish stayed with them…"

Nobody dares say anything. Even Merya offers me some respite by averting her judgemental eyes to focus on the screens behind her, while Galen approaches my chair, limping.

"Are you sure? Perhaps you were just—in shock?"

I twist my fingers nervously. "I saw what I saw. She helped a man get away from the shore, and there were no firearms pointed at her…"

Galen turns towards the others, opening and closing his fingers.

"This was all *his* plan. The attack in Libera, the Wise… But Evelyn…" July exclaims, moving closer and looking at me with apprehension.

Galen picks at the stubble on his chin. "I refuse to believe she's been on his side all this time. There must be another explanation."

For a split second, I watch the shadow of a doubt crossing July's face before she slides a hand up Galen's back. "If she told Lucretia to come here, it was to keep her safe. She knew she could trust Tabitha. But if Roden is with her now, he will force her to lead him to us. It's only a matter of time."

"All very true and very *wrong*." Merya towers above my chair. "How the hell does she know where we are?" Her voice cuts through the room like a hard ice shard, straight towards Galen.

"It wasn't me, if that's what you're thinking."

"We had a deal," Merya replies as if everyone except her and Galen has left. "Tabitha took you in with the promise that Evelyn would never know where to find her. I knew I should've aimed higher. You may have already revealed our location to *Roden*!"

Galen consumes the space between them with only two steps despite his wounded leg, making the floor shake under his rage.

"You don't know what you're talking about." He stops inches from her face, panting dark purple puffs, one hand stretched towards her heart.

His entire body quivers as he grunts, "Pathetic… Horigean… Always ready to judge, ignoring how insignificant your life is…"

A faint yellow glow starts pulsating from beneath Merya's black tank top. She glances at her top and then back at Galen. Her face betrays no emotions, but her eyes gleam with unwanted tears.

"I know what I'm seeing," she hisses, her face beading with sweat.

A man I haven't been introduced to yet, but who has been silently checking on July all this time, jumps between them, facing Galen and pushing him away towards a wall lined with bookshelves, while Merya, despite her stoic reaction, drops to the floor panting and coughing.

"Galen, stop. Are you crazy?"

Shocked by the impact, Galen blinks, gaping as if out of breath, nostrils flaring, before taking his attention back on Merya, ignoring the man who's just hit him.

"What just happened?" I hear myself asking, gripping the armrests so tightly that the skin of my knuckles and my injured wrist hurts.

July mouths me to remain still as she slowly begins to move towards Galen.

"July…" the stranger calls after her.

She stretches a hand behind her, inviting everyone to wait, "I've got this, Kris."

Backed against the wall like a feral animal, Galen's eyes dart around the room, his breath changing to a lighter shade of purple as he slowly calms down. But when July is close enough to touch him, he shakes his head and shimmies along the wall, away from her.

"He's closer," he mumbles. "It was just a flash, but I saw him and he has Evelyn." Galen takes his head in his hands, pulling his hair and sliding down the wall onto the grey stone floor.

July kneels in front of him, gently brushing his leg. "Did he speak to you again?"

My gasp matches Mack's as Galen raises his head, shaking, staring at July through slightly veiled eyes. "He showed me Libera as it imploded, taking with her those who didn't want to follow him. He told me it is time for the deserving Harvesters to end their exile and finally enjoy their promised kingdom."

In the room's opposite corner, Mack stops tending to Merya at the sudden noise of a beeping alarm coming from the largest monitor.

"What is it?" Kris asks, voicing everyone's thoughts.

July extends a hand to Galen, helping him up, and I mirror them.

In the room's blue light, I know something is wrong when Mack grasps the edge of the panel with both hands, leaning forward, his spine rigid, knuckles white.

"Roden's here."

Chapter 47 - Reunion
Mack

If I could, I'd switch off all the screens, pretending what we're witnessing is not happening. It's all a bad dream.

But I can't ignore the loud stares on my back, anxiously waiting for me to confirm their fears aren't real, and the cameras I strategically placed outside the building are simply malfunctioning.

My sister's hand threatens to push me to my knees when she rushes beside me, climbing on my right shoulder while screaming and crying for us both because I'm too shocked even to shed a tear.

A small group of people, led by Roden Breith, advances towards the main entrance, ignoring the popping sounds and sparks released by the barriers.

Roden's face is the same as Tabitha showed us many times, so that we wouldn't forget it. The top of his walking cane twinkles like a small beam of light; his dark, long coat lined with dense fur clashes with the overall aspect of the strangers behind him, all battered and tired, some of them helping others to stay upright.

Next to him walks a woman, tall and slender but visibly curved as if crushed under guilt and hopelessness.

"Miss Popplewish," Lucretia whispers behind me, but her voice soon dies under Merya's bellows as Galen and Kris try to pull her away, as far from the screen as possible.

One of Roden's arms is stretched to his side, his fingers curled around Jyn's neck. He's tilting Jyn's head left and right as if playing with a human-size doll, keeping his body lifted a few inches off the ground.

"Let me go!" Merya roars as someone grunts behind me.

I have just enough time to check what's causing the turmoil, Kris bending over, bracing his middle, before Merya shoves me away and whacks the speaker button with her fist.

"You coward piece of shit! Stop hiding behind innocent people."

Roden's miniature reproduction snaps his head towards one of the cameras and grins. At the same time, Evelyn Popplewish addresses the group behind her, intimating one of them in particular to stay where they are, with her fingers splayed in the air.

"That's Tydell," July exclaims, too close to Merya, who is still operating the speaker, waking the curiosity of the man who, like Roden, brings his attention to one of the cameras, performing a clumsy bow.

"Ah, there she is, my beloved daughter." He raises his cane towards the camera, tipping its top as if saluting us; the hand holding Jyn steady in the air. "The challenges a father has to accept for his offspring, and be the better person—even when his child partners up with Horigean scum." Roden's voice roars in the room, taking us all by surprise.

"But—our family is reunited at last. Me, you… and our little pet—dearest Kristyon. Why don't you come out to meet me? There is no point in delaying what is inevitably going to happen. Or making me waste more of this succulent soul."

Roden's teeth flash white and sharp as he grins and opens his hand. Jyn's body hits the ground with a thump so loud it echoes through the speakers.

Petrified, I watch my sister collapse to the floor, her mouth opening and closing with no sound as though she's already screamed all her pain.

"Mack," someone shouts in my ear and shakes me until the sudden fog that's blurring my vision lifts. A pair of concerned burnt orange eyes with bright purple rims stare into mine, turning the dirt on their owner's face, the light honey locks of hair grazing her cheeks, into a focal point I can concentrate on to claim back my lucidity.

"You need to take your sister out of here," Lucretia orders me, her eyes blinking like a countdown at the end of which I'm sure she won't think twice before slapping me.

"We all need to leave," Galen echoes her, hissing and crouching by Merya to pick her up.

"Why don't we make a deal?" Roden's voice thunders, and we all look at each other. "July and Kris, in exchange for your stupid talking bear—Libera won't need his peaches and pears anymore anyway… Then my Harvesters and I will go away seeking a new start somewhere else. You can even keep Galen—although I can't promise he'll still be able even to *think* once I've stripped his soul of all his powers. I'm done playing with that sentimental puppet, even though I found it so entertaining shaping his *love* for July. Such a malleable soul." Roden sighs dramatically.

"Liar!" The sound of a wounded animal escapes Galen's mouth as he momentarily loses his balance and uses one hand to stay upright.

"Do not trust him." Feeble but fighting its way to us, Jyn's voice makes Merya's head shoot up.

We all dash to the screens. The wave of relief caused by Jyn's voice soon fades away when I zoom in on the screen.

He wriggles on the ground, scrambling on his hands and feet as far as possible from Roden, who is sauntering after him, spinning his cane.

Taking advantage of our distraction, Merya sprints for the door. "I'm taking him away from there—"

But Tabitha is waiting behind it, fully geared up in her combat black suit. She is flanked by two special soldiers wearing helmets. They're usually stationed beyond the Fields, and recognisable only by the red letter *H* sewn on their right shoulders.

"Nobody," she says, her eyes sweeping the room and stopping on Merya, "goes out there without my permission."

"You're just going to let him die? After all he's done for you, for the cause?" I can't see my sister's face, but her voice speaks more than hundreds of her brooding looks.

Confident like the leader that had trained us, not the sweet female presence that had many times lulled me to sleep, Tabitha blocks the entrance. "Jyn knew the risk and agreed to be responsible for all of you in my short absence."

"He's your *friend*," Merya snaps, turning towards us as if seeking backup.

"And my second in command." Without hesitation, Tabitha pushes the door wide open, forcing Merya out of the way and marches towards the control panel.

Her fingers don't falter when she switches the speaker on, and with the other hand, adjusts the camera on Evelyn Popplewish.

"Roden Breith, you're not welcome here. Abandon this ground immediately, or we will use our firepower against you and your people, no matter their true intentions."

Her last words linger in the air, her gaze on Evelyn, who is seemingly arguing with Roden, but too quietly for my devices to capture the sound.

I mentally note the technical defect, if only to quiet my mind and my heart, which have been hammering for too long.

Roden's roaring laugh resounds so violently that Tabitha stumbles away with a grunt.

"*Clearly*, you've missed the updates on my late achievements. Let me give you a small taste. It's not perfect yet, but see for yourself."

We all remain in silence, not knowing what to look for, including Merya, supervised by the two soldiers.

Until Galen takes his head into his hands and dashes for the exit. "Let me out, now! He's trying to take control of me—again."

Without flinching, Tabitha raises one hand towards one of the soldiers, who nods, stomps towards Galen in his heavy boots, and knocks him out with a single blow to his jaw.

Then sighs with relief, "That was like punching Roden in the face. I wanted to do that for such a long time." The soldier chortles inside the helmet.

"Professor Skell?" Lucretia and July exclaim at the same time, both rushing for Galen, unconscious on the floor.

"Nice to see you both alive and breathing," Nikrah replies with his usual unbothered tone, taking off the helmet and placing it under his arm.

If Nikrah Skell is in the room with us, the other person behind him can only be Lily Drestall. And that explains where Tabitha has been this past few hours, guiding the *happy* couple safely inside.

"Did you really need to do that? Removing him from the room would have worked just as well," Lily pushes past Nikrah, eventually revealing her face.

Her hair is in disarray, and her face is pale, tired despite her poised gait when she approaches the centre of the room. She studies our faces one by one, pausing on those who are most surprised by her presence.

"Nice to see you two are no longer bickering over sexy Galen," she addresses July and Lucretia with one of her rare smiles, but her face drops. "I'm sorry, I heard what Roden said about him. That was a low blow."

"Yeah, well, we will make time to give him back what he

deserves." Tabitha opens the door wider.

Timid light pours in from the top of the stairs, casting a deep shadow on one side of her face as she flattens against the wall, averting her eyes from us as she adds, "Nik and Lily agreed to take you to The Mother."

"Wait—what?" Merya snaps. "That's insane. It'll take us days to get there via tunnels."

Tabitha glances at my sister sideways, still avoiding the rest of us. "You are not going. Only July, Galen and the young Harvester." She nods at Lucretia.

"No…" July and Kris' voices melt as they both lunge towards Tabs.

Peeling her back from the door, Tabitha raises a hand, but July ignores it.

"You can't separate us now. I've only begun to understand what happened to us. I won't let you—" Her head turns towards Galen, still unconscious on the floor after Nik's right hook, as if her words could hurt him even now he can't hear her.

"What then?" Tabitha barks, fully turning to face her. "Roden will magically stop going after you two and let you live happily ever after? Do you think he will drop his plan of turning every single Horigean into a perfect soulless puppet for the love of his daughter? Open your eyes, dear, the longer you and Kris are together the more fucked up our future looks like. Horigeans and Harvesters alike, we're all doomed if what you've taken from Kris ends up in Roden's hands."

Her words hurt. Not only July. They struck all of us for different reasons. I can see it in Lucretia's orange eyes, even if she's only understanding half of it, in Kris' hands curling into fists.

Merya notices as well. She sighs bitterly and laughs, "But you'd rather send the Harvesters away and let us deal with Roden…"

Her lips twitch as she glances at the monitor over her back. "I get it now. When did you decide it was safe to reveal our coordinates to Evelyn Popplewish? She was supposed only to be an intermediary between us and Galen."

I'm about to open my mouth to convince my sister that her theory is rubbish when I notice Tabitha's shoulders drop as she exhales.

"When things started turning for the worst, that was the only way to make sure she could help us." Her voice remains strong despite her body seemingly shrinking under Merya's judgemental glare.

"You figured out that I only have a kernel left," Kristyon addresses Tabs, helping her with the words she can't seem to voice.

"We don't know what would happen if July completes the harvest, what Roden can achieve if he manages to take full control of her mind—and your soul. You've seen what he's done to Galen," Tabitha quickly points at him. "Imagine the power he will hold if he succeeds at merging your souls in one vessel…"

In response to Tabitha's revelation, July steps closer to Kris, taking his hand in hers, when a sudden pop from the control panel takes us all by surprise. We all dash for it, gingerly avoiding Galen's body, but I don't need to see what caused it.

"Someone's touched my fences," I state.

"No," Lucretia replies, bent over the main monitor, "Roden is forcing his people against them to take down the barrier."

Chapter 48 - The Love that Was
Kristyon

"I'm tired of waiting. You! Come here."

I cannot avert my eyes from the screen as Roden points his finger at one of the many Harvesters, beckoning towards him.

My hand is in July's. Her fingers tighten around mine while we all watch in silence the poor bastard tottering towards the barrier, while Evelyn tries to pull him back, only to be thrown to the side by a single, swift swipe of Roden's hand.

Tabitha whimpers, towering behind me.

"He's going to die," Mack voices our fears. "I could lower the voltage; he will probably pass out for a few hours."

"Do that and you'll doom us all."

"But, Lily, he won't stop until the fences are down, and I promise you, it will take twice the number of Harvesters out there to slightly damage the barrier."

"She's right, this is what Roden wants. He's counting on us not letting people get hurt. What he doesn't understand is that he's buying us time." Tabitha takes a big breath, splaying her fingers over the control panel while, on the monitor, the Harvester nods at

Roden and hurls himself against the invisible fence.

The impact releases so much electricity that all the monitors go black for a few seconds, leaving us in complete darkness if not for the light still pouring in from the door.

I blink to adjust my view and pull July into my arms without thinking. The idea of being separated from her once again hurts more than ever. She won't forget me this time, but I can't ignore what Tabitha said about the danger of having our souls - in their entirety - under the same roof. July's delicate hands desperately cling onto my shirt, and she presses her cheek against my chest. I dip my fingers in her hair, brushing her head with my lips and inhaling her scent. A moment stolen from the darkness. A memory we'll both carry and protect as if our last.

"What happened?" Lucretia whispers.

"Give me some space," Mack demands.

I've never heard him so alarmed, as he shoves us away and starts fidgeting with the panel's many switches and buttons.

We break our embrace, but don't stop holding each other's hands.

"The impact was so harsh that it has activated my second-level defence protocol."

"Meaning?" Lily asks, surprisingly calm.

Mack turns to face us all, his head dipped, eyes fixed on his fingers as he nervously twists them. "That either we abandon the building within the next hour, or remain stuck here for days. I've programmed a stronger security response, but I thought we would never have to use it."

"Well, that wasn't our plan anyway." Nik intervenes, approaching Mack and landing a hand on his shoulder. "Can you turn the screens back up? Before venturing out there, we need to know what the rest of the perimeter looks like."

"It'll probably take me a few minutes. This has never happened before—"

"Great! I'll gather *all* the weapons I can find and gear up," Merya exclaims, already on her way to the door.

"You are not going anywhere," Tabitha grabs her by her right arm. "I need you to visit Brenath and all the villages still on our side. Our resources in The Mother won't be enough if what we've witnessed today is only a small part of Roden's army. He's been preparing for a very long time… And I need you to keep Sable safe. She's in the tunnels now…"

Merya shakes her arm free, curling her hands into fists at her sides. "You can't be serious. I'm one of your best fighters."

"Exactly, and one I can trust to be my voice and my eyes while I try to delay Roden for as long as possible."

"I'm not a diplomat," Merya's voice quivers.

Tabitha crosses her arms, nodding towards me, then Mack. "That's why you're taking them with you."

July lets go of my hand to move closer to Tabs and Merya as my fingers close around a dreadful void that chills my blood.

"I can take care of myself. Send Lucretia and Galen to The Mother. But, please, don't take him away from me again—" She bites her words, her eyes widen when she glances at Galen, who's come back to his senses and is slowly pushing himself up using a wall.

Her plea pierces my heart. But it hurts even more seeing my brother pretending his heart is not shattered into pieces, as he averts his gaze to look at his bloody bandage.

"I'm sorry, July. Sometimes, we need to do what's best for the many. Your soul will heal..." Tabitha mutters.

"You don't understand. I need—" July lunges forward, her voice breaking.

Tabitha moves aside to avoid July's desperation. The room freezes, full of her cry as her hands grab only air, and she drops onto her knees, her back shaking with each violent sob.

I survey the room, locking eyes with Galen. He immediately reads my worry, then nods at Nik. They move in unison and gingerly help July up, holding her still should she try again to hit Tabs again.

My heart aches with the need to run to her and hold her in my arms, but if I get close enough to her dark hair, to smell her skin, I will never be able to let her go again.

"Tell them this is not right. We'll find another way..." July starts kicking and jerking her head back, searching for me.

A hand hooks my right shoulder, trying to turn me away, but I swat it away. If she's in pain, I want to feel the same. If I do not see her again, I don't want to waste our last moments together looking the other way. She needs to know I'm suffering because...

"I—" My words burst into nothing as Galen and Nik move towards the door. My legs burn with the need to go after them while July sobs, imploring me to hold her again, to hide her from everyone. My eyes sting like the palms of my hands, where my nails are digging, drawing blood.

"Kris, please…" She steals one last look at me. "I can't lose you again… please."

I will never lose you again. She can't remember this yet, but those were the words she screamed last time we had to say goodbye.

The same hand reaches for me again.

"You know that's for the best…" Mack warns me.

It is, but there is no reasoning when I'm around her, and I don't want her to treasure this memory as our last.

I shove Mack out of the way, ignoring his and Merya's curse as someone - probably Mack - collides with the control panel, and I charge towards the door.

"Oh, for soul's sake, do not complicate things." I hear Lily complaining as I rush past her.

Alerted by Lily, Nikrah momentarily abandons July's side and stomps towards me. I can feel the blood pumping beneath my skin when I skid to a halt inches from him.

"Let me pass," I growl.

"You practically begged us to take her away," he opens his arms, with an idiotic smile on his face.

"And now I *command* you to step aside—"

"It's okay, Nik. He only needs a few moments," Tabitha sighs, surprisingly understanding.

"We don't have a few—alright, fine. Fine!" Nik stumbles back, raising his hands, when I shove him out of the way.

With two steps, I'm behind July, unable to speak, to breathe, while Galen carefully loosens his grip on her arm and walks away. He gives me a look that chills the blood in my veins, before putting the metal door between us, a barrier dividing him from me and the woman Roden *forced* him to love.

She slowly turns around.

I don't care if everyone's watching. Roden can teleport into the room, and I would still not give a fuck about anyone but her.

"I remembered… earlier on, by the lake," she says softly, inhaling deeply to push the tears back, as I gently take her face in my hands. "All those times they took me away from you, I never had the chance to tell you…"

I dip my head and steal her words from her mouth with mine so they can only linger between us.

"I *loved* you. Every time we met, I couldn't help it…" she whispers onto my lips before looping her arms around my neck, making the whole world disappear.

As if resonating with each other, our souls thrum in unison, trying to free themselves from our bodies and melt into one. I've kissed her many times, yet today is like our first. I can't have enough of her hair through my fingers, her teeth gently playing with my lips, my tongue hungry to rediscover every inch of her mouth.

Unexpectedly, she breaks the spell, gently pushing me away,

pressing her hands against my chest. "I *loved* you…" Her eyes narrow moments before the ground starts shaking.

Chapter 49 - Goodbyes
Merya

A thin shower of cement pours over us from tiny gaps in the ceiling as light flows through old fractures in the walls and floor.

We all exchange worried looks, and our chests don't stop nervously rising and falling even when the sudden shaking stops.

"What was that?" Mack asks seconds before a disembodied, raging scream fills the room, like a shock wave.

It throws me off my feet, knocking the breath out of my lungs when I hit the wall. White dots appear behind my eyelids, streaming down like shiny snowflakes every time I blink, trying to regain full view of the room.

Beneath the ringing in my ears, a voice calls for me.

"There's a fracture—the barrier will not hold for much longer…" My brother offers me his hand as I cough up dust, and my legs try to remember how to hold me upright.

Inhaling rough air, I grab a glass of water from a trolley to my right and splash my face. Surprisingly, the room is intact despite the debris on my mouth and hands.

In the fading mist of cement, Mack's features take shape. Except for some scratches on his forehead, he seems unarmed. Other figures are rising behind him like ghosts on a battlefield.

He brushes off more dust from my shoulders, takes my face in his hands, and slowly turns my neck left and right. "No visible trauma," he nods, satisfied, but as if delaying the answer to my question.

"Mack?" I urge him.

He drops his head, avoiding my scrutiny. "Roden thought it was a good idea to send all his people against the fence—at once."

In the corner of my eye, some monitors cast flickering images of the outside perimeter. They are unstable, but crisp enough to show the devastation caused by Roden.

As the voices of the others reach me increasingly defined and louder, I dash for the wider screen. Bodies lie on the ground, some twitching in silent pain, some charred, their clothes fused to their skin: my hand moves and zooms in despite the horror uncoiling before my eyes.

"Where is he? Where is Roden?" I pant. I'd do everything to distract my mind from the idea that Jyn may be among those corpses.

"He's looking for a way in." Tabitha's strong, reassuring hand turns me around, blood running down her cheek from a cut to her temple.

Mack steps beside her, guilt on his face. "And it won't take him long to find it. With the fence malfunctioning, every access to HQ, disguised by my building in ruins illusion, will soon be visible to the naked eye."

"What about the tunnels?" Nikrah approaches, limping and using Lily like a living crutch.

"Their defence system is not connected to the fences. Roden shouldn't be able to find them. However—"

"He can sense *us.*" Galen's face is pale with traces of white dust that make him look drained and on the verge of giving up. But the way he's protecting Lucretia under his arm, the young Harvester curling her shaking fingers against her chest, forces me away from the monitors, from a scene of death I can no longer control.

We're still alive.

Behind them, July looks at me, nodding as if understanding my increasing fear. The last image I can recall is of her kissing Kris, just moments before the explosion of light. They're still holding hands when July steps forward. "Roden's connection with Galen's mind is something he must have trained for years, but it was the only mind he could access from afar. Until now. We don't know what he can do with me now that there is nothing between us…" She eyes the key at her neck. "Not even Mack's genius will stop him now that only mere meters divide us."

She glances at her fingers, interlaced with Kris', sadness veiling her eyes as she gifts him a smile, unspoken words they can only hear.

Their hands separate.

"Ms Drestall? Take us to The Mother," she calls to Lily, but keeps her eyes on her hands as if directing the order to a *July*, who would rather forget about everyone and remain with Kris.

Lily pats some dust off the embroidered H of her long-sleeved, black shirt, after having lowered Nikrah on a chair, who stretches his right leg and tries to mask a grimace of pain with one of his usual proud smiles.

"Do you think you can keep up with us with that leg?" She slices a feline glance at him, a corner of her still perfectly rouged lips twitches with amusement.

"I bet she still hasn't forgiven him for what happened with Amelia," Mack whispers in my ear, gaining a puzzled look from Lucretia, who is finally standing alone without Galen's help.

Grunting like a wounded bear, Nikrah pushes himself up, the chair groaning under his weight. "I can travel through those tunnels carrying you and little Sable on my back."

At that, Tabitha clears her throat. She's been observing us, probably wondering - like me - when and if we will see Jyn again and if we can even leave this room before Roden finds us. Unless it's already too late.

She steps between us, hands folded on her front, her voice rough with dust and fear, "Sable is safe in one of the secret rooms in the north-west tunnel. I thought Brenath may be safe, but The Mother is where our stronger firepower is. It's been hard convincing her that I will follow up soon. *Please*, protect her at any cost…" Tears shine in her eyes, tears she tries to hide, rubbing her face. "It's time to go. There are supplies upstairs. Take what you can carry."

We heedfully climb the stairs to the upper levels in silence, like a mountain of sharp rocks and shards of glass. Tabitha leads the group with Galen, followed by Nik, and Lily just behind him to catch him should his leg give up.

Mack mumbles behind me about possible improvements to the building and new animal scouts like his Rary. Nobody interrupts his train of thought because we all know that's his way to relax and think straight.

The young Harvester climbs beside him, listening to his monologue, enthralled.

July and Kris close the line. They're quiet, not even a whisper escapes their mouths. I've seen them like this before. Every time they had to say goodbye, before Kris would confine himself to his room for days, conscious that July had probably already forgotten him.

A new wave of Roden's power nearly swipes us off our feet on the landing between the first and the second floor.

"He's getting stronger *and* closer. Galen? Any hint of his mind trying to infiltrate yours—" Another, angrier blow rattles the building from its foundations. Books and picture frames fall off the shelves, carved inside the walls, and the tubular lights oscillate above us, threatening to come off their hinges.

We regroup on the landing, around Tabitha, who rolls up her sleeves and pulls up her silver hair in a tight bun, the dancing lights catching at the metal rings decorating her thin braids.

"This is where we go our separate ways," she whispers the dreadful words between her teeth, biting them as if to make them less painful. "Say your goodbyes now." Her eyes linger on July and Kris before considering the rest of us.

Mack walks up to me, but his attention is on someone else. "I don't need much, only a change of clothes, better boots, my maps and notes. I can help *others* gather their essentials."

I'm about to open my mouth. I know how distracted he can get if he is overwhelmed by too many tasks, especially if he is on his own and in a rush.

But Lucretia precedes me. "I don't know the building; I don't mind having a guide. Besides, I can't go anywhere in this." She runs her hands up and down her body, on her poor choice of clothes.

"You've never been anywhere but Libera, have you, Harvester?" I comment, causing, to my surprise, not her reaction, but Mack's.

"We don't call them that anymore, sis. Remember?" He nudges me with his elbow.

I scoff, intercepting Tabitha's stern look. "Fine, do what you must, but meet us by the lake in thirty. You as well," - I point at Mack - "I'm not making exceptions. If you're late, you're on your own. Hesitation doesn't rhyme with war."

But *family* does, and he's all that I have left.

"Yes, sir!" he asserts, bringing his fist to his heart before holding out his hand to Lucretia, causing a brief moment of amusement among the rest of us.

But as soon as they disappear up the stairs to the bedrooms and the attic, where we store spare clothes and backpacks, the atmosphere becomes oppressive again.

Tabitha starts pacing across the small square space, her boots smudging the white marble floor with mud and dry soil.

"Are you sure going separate ways is the best option?" Galen asks.

"Unless you want to serve us all to Roden in one meal." Tabs retorts with a sharpness that doesn't belong to her. But I understand that the thought of my only child being alone and in danger would turn me into a snapping snake all the same.

"I'm sure Galen didn't mean to sound rude. Or selfish. Or ungrateful. Or…"

"We get it, Nik. Now shut up and get our stuff ready. We need extra backpacks for July, Galen and Lucretia." Lily chimes in, annoyed, before focusing her eyes on July, like little diamonds in a sea of black lava. "You can ask your million questions, I'm sure you have, later. And, please, if you need to give Kris a *special* goodbye, do it quickly and away from us."

Moved by the increasing tension, or just needing a quick reminder that I'm still alive, I snort a laugh. A loud one that sounds more like a bark.

"I'm so—I'm sorry."

"Thank. You." Kris drops his elbow on my shoulder, resting his head on it. "We're not dead yet. We've been here before…" In the corner of my eye, I see him staring at July as if she's the only one in the room.

"We will make it to the other side *again*." He proclaims with such hope, I'd kiss him if he had no stubble and softer breasts. He spins towards me, grabbing me by the shoulders and gently bumping my forehead with his. "I couldn't ask for a better soldier to go on an adventure with. Let this battle be the last so we can celebrate properly with some of that mind-blowing blue concoction Mack brewed by accident."

He then turns to Tabitha. "I'll miss your attempts at cooking soups. I promise I'll show you all the spots in the garden where Sable and I poured our portions since she's been able to walk and conspire like an adult."

The loud echo of Tabitha's steps fills the space as she marches towards him, hugging and lifting him off the floor.

"Okay, you can put me down now. I won't tell Mack I'm your favourite."

As she lowers him down, Tabitha gently pats his face. "You stay alive." She touches a finger to his nose, sniffing the same way Sable does, scrunching her nose like a giant bunny. "Move at night and stay underground as much as possible," she orders, quickly glancing at me.

I nod a silent *Don't worry*.

On the opposite side of the landing, Galen has been observing us in silence, leaning against the wall with his hands behind his back. What he did to July only a few hours ago still burns in my mind. Even knowing that Roden was behind his odd behaviour, stitching up his leg, without anaesthetic, was cathartic enough.

"Are you not going to say 'see you soon'?" I mumble.

He scratches his neck, considering, before pushing away from the wall to stomp towards me. But I meet him halfway, throwing my arms around him.

"Keep an eye on those two ladies," I say against his neck.

He pats my back, breaking our embrace. "If anything, I'll come back alive thanks to them." His gaze flutters towards July for a second. I can't begin to imagine how heavy his heart feels.

Forcing a smile, I ruffle his hair. "Don't miss me too much…"

Because I will.

In response, Galen flicks my nose and bows. "I'll never deprive you of my wonderful presence."

Someone behind us clears his throat. "I know I can trust you…" Kris approaches us, his eyes struggling to settle on his brother's face, but speaking volumes of what's in his mind. *Keep her safe.*

July. The last person he has to say goodbye to. The hardest goodbye. The one we don't have the right to witness.

"I'll be by the lake," I quickly inform everyone. I can't hug Tabitha; that'll destroy every last particle of stability I have in me. We have too many things to say to each other.

She knows, as she briefly nods at me.

And as I scurry away, I hear Lily, Nik and Galen bidding Tabitha and Kris farewell, followed by Tabitha's hushed last words to July and Kris, as she struggles to find the most delicate way to expedite their separation. "I'll give you ten minutes. There are too many lives on the line…"

Chapter 50 - Awake
July

I loved him.

The echo of what we could have been sings in my mind, leaving space for nothing else as I run up the stairs with the others.

In the minutes following another invisible blow from Roden, we steal painful hugs and goodbyes, tears and promises.

Galen is the last to go, his face a carousel of masks: pain, disbelief and longing for something he was forced to believe true.

Until there's just *us*.

Reality washes over me like a winter's first, timid snowfall that grows confident by the second, slicing my heart with its cruel, sharp flakes.

I inhale through my teeth, blinking away a veil of confusion and denial.

"If Roden takes me back, I don't think he'll let me return to you this time." I hate the weakness in my voice.

Kris gently tilts my chin up, imploring me to look at him.

"This time, *I* will find you. I'm not going anywhere, July…" His voice is soft like his lips on my forehead. "And we will make him pay."

I search for a speck of doubt in his bright green eyes and find none.

I take his hand in mine, studying the thin lines on his palm and running a finger across his skin as he observes me in silence. His breath is warm on my cheek when he lowers his head to follow my moves.

I sigh, kissing his fingertips one by one before pressing his hand over my heart. "I will harvest Roden's rotten soul with my bare hands to take back the happiness he denied us all these years. I will do it one kernel at a time while he watches his daughter slowly taking his life. I want him to witness the monster he created…"

My heart races beneath his hand. When our eyes meet again, a fire is burning behind Kris', his chest expanding with his every deep breath.

"If vengeance is what you seek, I'll stand by you. Always. We can be Roden's downfall, until it's time to reclaim our peace." He bites his lips, pushing back the same need I struggle to ignore.

My hands travel up his forearms, and I grab him by the shoulders, gently pushing him against the wall but leaving him no room to protest.

Before someone sees us, before Roden breaks us apart again. Before we remember that there is a war out there. Before any dark thoughts can stop me—our mouths crush.

I forget to breathe, treasuring every second I have left to learn the shape of his strong back— again; his muscles twitching and tensing every time my nails dig in. My lips slowly remember how to move best to savour his, until my body shivers with pleasure when he decides to abandon my mouth and gift my neck with light touches of his lips.

When his teeth find the more sensitive spot below my ear, I squeak, gaining a guttural laugh from his end.

"You used to like that…" he breathes against my tender skin, tracing the outer shape of my ear with his lips.

"I'm sure she loved a lot of things you two did. But you won't be able to show her without a limb. Or without your life." Nikrah's voice ripples down the upper level, making us jump. "Now—move up here, you romantic idiot!"

Flushed-face and short of breath, I silence a giggle by nuzzling Kris' shirt, my hands lingering over the hardness of his chest. When I look up, his eyes are glazed as they rove over my face, pausing on my mouth, surely swollen like his.

"Come back to me. With all your limbs attached," I mumble, straightening his shirt that has crumpled under my fingers as they rediscover familiar skin and muscles.

"I have to." He leans forward to place a chaste kiss on my cheek, making my heart flutter with the blurred memory of someone I've known for a long time. "You've hidden my soul and I *can't* live for too long without it… especially with what's left of it inside me."

My jaw drops. My heart sinks, and the floor starts shaking violently. But the dread it causes is nothing compared to the paralysing voice whispering in my head.

Hello, my child.

A kernel. This is all Kris has left. I nearly harvested it all and, no matter what I hid in the caves, if I take the last bit—he will die.

You see it now. Roden's voice is so strong that I search everywhere for him.

"July, what's wrong?"

"Roden has made it through the fence…"

All I ask you is to harvest that little kernel for me. And everyone else will be free. Even Jyn. He's still breathing, but… for how long— that's up to you. Oh, and *sweet Sable—*

"No!" I shout at the ceiling, shutting my eyes, nearly dropping to my knees if it wasn't for a pair of strong hands keeping me up.

"Push him out, July." Kristyon slowly caresses my temple with his knuckles, giving me the strength to reopen my eyes.

Every breath I take burns my chest as if I'm fighting Roden's presence like an infection. I nod frantically, losing myself in Kris' eyes, until my mind is clear again.

He smiles—one last loving smile before I have to accept the truth.

"I *have* to go." My words are so broken, I struggle to hear myself. Tears run warm on my cheeks as I interlace my fingers with his. Only for a second. Enough to carve the feeling of his touch in my mind. The shade of his eyes, always brighter when he looks at me.

I let him go, dropping my gaze to my hands, now holding only memories. I force my eyes down as he remains quiet for a moment.

His boots start moving, turning away from me before he stops on his way to the stairs. "When you're far away, remember I loved you from the first time you threatened to harvest my soul with a teaspoon…"

You disappoint me, Roden creeps inside my mind once again as I cling to the key at my neck. But a smile slowly comes to my lips. His voice quivers with something coating his usual tone of command: doubt. Distress.

Hello, Father. I send my thoughts as deep as possible, hoping the invisible channel between us works both ways.

I'm coming for you. My mind explodes—a bright purple light bursts behind my eyes before turning red. I jerk my head up, gulping air, my arms wide at my sides, my back arched.

Like scorching rain, images from the past drip inside my mind. Hands, hundreds of them, reach out for me. Trembling, scarred, bleeding. I can't see their faces, but I know they're calling my name while I'm running away.

Save us…

Darkness is all around me, but warm, loving light bursts from my hands. This is what those hands want and what I cannot give away.

Save us…

I didn't choose them. I didn't listen to them. I let Roden turn them *red* while I hid my monstrous, selfish soul in a cave.

I'm not the one you would have to forgive—you are. And I'm worried you won't be able to...

Acknowledgements

Writing a book in your second language is like going on a mission for Roden. You have a vague idea of what that soul of words and images should look like, but the risk of mistaking it for something else is always breathing… purple… down your neck.

When I started The Souls Harvest, none of the characters you met today existed. Their names were completely different, and July was just a confused, scrawny, little creature with floppy limbs.

I am proud to say that she's grown into a strong, at times snappy, woman.

And that woman wouldn't have gone anywhere without the help of my little army of support soldiers.

To my friends and beta readers. Iulia and Lola—thanks for cheering for all my characters, even when all you wanted to do was to snap their necks or tell them to go the other way!

Thanks for pointing out odd typos. Yes, Iulia, I'm talking about birds sitting for brunch.

Lola, thanks for the octopus sketch and for praising Roden's attire. But—Go, go Tabitha!

To Jenna, Meg and Mailyn, my squad. Ladies, thanks for keeping me sane with our serial dinners.

Jenna—I'm sure you'll appreciate that there are no clowns in my book.

I cannot forget Paisley, my editor. I couldn't have found your account at a better time. Thank you for your lovely words and for shining such an appreciative, and professional light on my work.

A massive thank you to the real woman behind Popplewish, who shared her love of words and literature with hundreds of students. Mum, you're the best.

To the readers. Whether you stumbled upon these pages by accident, or consciously made the choice to hold hands with July, Galen and Kris—thank you. You are what makes me an Author.

Last, but absolutely not least, to Marco—my husband. The incredible mind behind my book's cover, maps and design. The man who can make me laugh and drive me crazy at the same time. My past, present and future.

The man who holds my kernels in his heart.

I love you.

Can we please get a Cocker Spaniel now?

ABOUT THE AUTHOR

ADE L. SARDO grew up in Italy, surrounded by books, folklore and the betime stories her mum used to invent on demand.

The switch from writing in her first language to English came naturally after she moved to the UK, to follow her very own Harvester.

When she's not writing or reading, she's probably eating dark chocolate, or pestering Marco to get a puppy.

You can find more about Ade on TikTok @adelsardo and Instagram @ade.l.sardo.author